THE RADICALS

ALSO BY RYAN McILVAIN

Elders

THE RADICALS

RYAN McILVAIN

HOGARTH
New York

Copyright © 2018 by Ryan McIlvain

Published in the United States by Hogarth, an imprint of the Crown
Publishing Group, a division of Penguin Random House LLC,
New York.
crownpublishing.com

HOGARTH is a trademark of the Random House Group Limited, and
the H colophon is a trademark of Penguin Random House LLC.

Library of Congress Cataloging-in-Publication Data
Names: McIlvain, Ryan, author.
Title: The radicals : a novel / Ryan McIlvain.
Description: First United States Edition. | New York : Hogarth, [2018]
Identifiers: LCCN 2017032393 | ISBN 9780553417883 (hardback) |
    ISBN 9780553417890 (ebook)
Subjects: | BISAC: FICTION / Coming of Age. | FICTION /
    Literary. | FICTION / Cultural Heritage.
Classification: LCC PS3613.C535 R33 2018 | DDC 813/.6—dc23
    LC record available at https://lccn.loc.gov/2017032393

ISBN 978-0-553-41788-3
eBook ISBN 978-0-553-41789-0

Printed in the United States of America

Jacket design: Rachel Willey
Jacket photograph: Glenn Glasser/Gallery Stock

10 9 8 7 6 5 4 3 2 1

First Edition

FOR SHARON

THE RADICALS

It didn't feel quite right that Sam should be there in the first place—Sam Westergard, clearly fish out of water in our graduate course in Marxist theory. He didn't look the part, anyway. He wore stretched-out polo shirts to class, or old road-race T-shirts, an almost constant smile. He intrigued me. On the night Sam showed up in an oversize Roger Federer shirt, I rustled enough to pay him my compliments on it. I was a fan myself. "Hey, really? Hey, *cool*," he said, with startling enthusiasm.

Pretty soon Sam and I were playing tennis together most Friday mornings and whenever else we could get away from the city and classes, the teaching, underpaid, the life, underpaid. Tennis was a balm and a crucible all at once. We each wanted to win, obviously, very badly, but we also wanted to maintain the illusion that our "practice sets" were only that—a little practice, a lark, a pair of pale intellectuals disgracing the game with our play . . . It wasn't an easy false premise to keep up: The sweat started pouring off me usually in the first game, or else I'd notice Sam's jaw, strangely squarish for his face, jutting out like an old cash drawer after he sent a ball into the net or sailing long. I started calling him Lockjaw. Or Little Lockjaw—a reference to his tall, lordly stature. I probably didn't know Sam well enough to joke with him like this, not at first, but what else could I say? I couldn't have known I was standing across the net from a murderer, and neither could he.

"M or W?" I said one morning in April, the cruelest month, apparently. I had my Wilson Pro pinned, head down, to the grainy green of the court, the frame making its thin crackling music as I rotated the handle between thumb and forefingers, ready to spin it loose.

"No, no, no," Sam said, smiling at me. "Do the thing." He saw my face and said again, "Do the thing. From last time? The one about the revolution—right, comrade?"

In the last few outings he'd started calling me *comrade*. I didn't know how to read it, or what he wanted from me now. His face was simple and expectant, eyes gray—neutral eyes. A little curl still hung around his light brown hair at the sides and bottom, but at the top, all wispy like smoke, all you saw was the sun on his broad forehead.

" 'Up with the revolution, down with capitalism'?" he said. "Wasn't it something like that?"

"Oh, yeah. Well, so you know it already."

The racket spun and clattered to rest, the white *W* of the Wilson logo pointing up. "Up with the revolution it is," I said.

"I forgot to call it," Sam said, looking guilty.

I let him serve first, suddenly impatient to be back at the baseline. Was I a performer to him, a bearded lady? I couldn't read his smile. We played to four–all in the first, all my slices coming back with interest. I'd noticed Sam was weak coming over his two-handed backhand, so I swallowed my pride and kept it high and to the ad side, looping the balls high over the net, Nadal-like, the yellow orbs rising and falling like suns. At the zenith of a shot you could see the ball freeze-framed against the Hoboken trees, tall beeches, and the power lines beyond, the rich brownstones with the wrought-iron balconies and the zigzag of fire escapes—the playground of the gentry, and we were crashing it. Anyway, we were graduate students, de facto experts in our contradictions: squeamish adjuncts, fake-casual athletes, complicated atheists. Sam was once a Mormon, he'd told me, and come to think of it he still looked the part—blond, looming. For my part I looked like my Russian Jewish father—dark hair, easy five o'clock shadow, a certain basset hound wariness about the eyes. And the old man's paunch, too. Tennis was supposed to be my exercise.

By the second deuce of the four–all game, our play had devolved into clay-court bullshitting, lob after yawning lob, a game of chicken more than tennis. A pair of seniors warmed up on the next court over, looking askance at us in their golf shirts, high shorts, stinging white socks, their rally balls ticking back and forth metronomically, and low over the net, like grown-up shots. The next ball to land at all short I took early, ginning myself up for a crosscourt screamer. Good knee bend, snapping the racket up and over, the ball buzzing the net cord—I was in my prime again. I followed the shot to net, split step, lunge, and fuck if the ball wasn't by me. The passing shot landed an inch from both lines; I stared dumbly, panting, my racket puddled at my feet.

On the next point, advantage Westergard, I sent a flat serve halfway to the back fence. The second serve came off my racket like a badminton birdie, floating to the middle of the service box, sitting up a foot above the net for Sam to angle easily away.

"Fuck," I said, loud enough for Sam to hear me across the net—his sudden chagrined downcast look, the disapproving stares of the men on the next court.

Sam held to love in the next game to take the set. When he started his lope toward the water bottles sentineling the net post, I intercepted his path with my outstretched hand. I was done for the day. Tapped out.

"You're sure, comrade?" he said, and that same gnomic smile again. He held my handshake a beat too long, my hands wet and red at the extremities. A crescent of sweat glued my shirt to my upper chest, a spidery network of perspiration lines ran down my forehead and into my eyes. Yes, I was sure. And why did he keep calling me *comrade*? What was that about?

"You okay?" Sam said.

I was staring at him.

"'Comrade'?" I said. "Am I a comrade to you?"

Sam's face changed so suddenly, eyes wide and adrenal, I knew I'd let in my Trotskyist street voice, my meanness. I hadn't meant to.

"I wasn't trying to offend," Sam said. "I was just kidding."

"I'm not offended."

"Oh . . . good . . . I just—"

"It's okay," I said. "I just wasn't sure what you meant by it."

I went over to my racket bag, arranging my gear just so: spare balls, grip tape, shock absorber, keys, phone, wallet. Tinkering, really. Sam stared at his feet as he fingered loose the laces of his tennis shoes, taking out of his bag the faded brown loafers he usually shuffled into class in, like moccasins he'd worn them so thin. Tall guy, tiny shoes—at least in that he followed the uniform of the day.

"I mean," Sam finally said, his voice upcurling in a gesture of détente, an olive branch, "I guess I thought I was using the word like you use it when you talk about your friends, your 'comrades' in the East Village? Not much of a proletariat around NYU, I wouldn't think."

"You'd be surprised. You can have a trust fund and still care about social justice," I said. "And most of my comrades live on the Jersey side or in Queens."

"You're serious, then? You're a believer?"

I bristled at Sam's choice of words—it wasn't the first time, it wouldn't be the last—but yes, I said, I was a socialist. You couldn't sit through hours-long ISO meetings without a certain conviction to gird you, and you sure as hell couldn't stomach five years of reading in abstruse Marxist polemics. It did matter to me. It mattered a lot. It took up a lot of my time, but I gave it gladly.

Sam Westergard blinked at me. He looked chastened and sensitive, his pale face rounding into some kind of recognition, but I wasn't sure of what, and I don't think he was either. He looked like he wanted to ask me something but stopped short, tentative now.

"Take last month," I said. "Some of my ISO comrades at NYU—that's the International Socialist Organization, by the way—do you know it? Well, they were organizing a sit-in to put pressure on the university administration. The university wouldn't disclose their real estate holdings, didn't want to admit to the embarrassingly large swath of lower Manhattan they either own or have investments in. Classic sign of corporate excess: Shut the blinds, turn the lights off. The monopolist doesn't take kindly to people asking about his monopoly—cramps his style. The sit-ins were entirely peaceful, laid-back, no destruction of precious NYU property, nothing like that, but they weren't going to move until their demands were met.

Finally the campus security got called in, people got dragged out of the building by their hair in the middle of the night. It got ugly. The administration showed their true colors, and it was all on TV. Anyway, those were some of my comrades."

"Did it work?" Sam asked.

"Did what work?"

"Did the university disclose its holdings?"

"Not yet," I said.

We passed out of the park on the west side, where Sam's tan spreading Buick sat in the canyon shade of more apartment buildings, more wrought-iron balconies, dappled shadow high up on the dun-rose brick—it was a beautiful spring morning. I didn't like the thought of going into the city that afternoon, descending into the close fetid caverns of the PATH, rising up into the noise and hurry of Sixth Avenue. Is it heresy to say that I sometimes tired of New York? That the streets and crowds and great vanity of the place could jump-start the blood as well as sap it? Not to mention the ungraded papers that waited for me in my office, the endless papers . . . It was still early—too early to think about the city, the papers; I supposed I could grade them over the weekend if I needed to, or early Monday. In the clear morning light you could see why the earliest base-ballers took their city game across the Hudson, crossing over to the relative green and space of Hoboken, getting away for a few hours. Somewhere nearby was the home plate they'd laid for that genesis game. A monument now. I'd never seen it.

In the car I rode on a towel, over Sam's objections. He really didn't care, he said. What did he care? His upholstery dated to the Reagan administration. I'd heard these protestations before, kind, gentlemanly ones—Sam was often a gentleman around me—but I suppose I knew enough not to take them at face value. Sam had a new pine-tree air freshener twirling from the rearview mirror, for one. And I think I'd begun to notice other cross-hatchings, the little complications that shaded Sam's gentlemanliness. He drove aggressively this morning, as he always did, riding the bumper of a tall black Range Rover, rushing a pair of yellow lights. Warehouses, gas stations, abandoned grassy lots shot by my window. When another car inched out from a side street, Sam hit the brakes to let a woman in a hijab pull slowly, slowly out into the opposite lane—a little selective in his doing unto others, but I did note it. It was one of the few things he'd held fast to when he jettisoned the faith of his fathers, he'd told me. I'd noted the phrase: *hold fast*. Something antique about it, touching. He was quoting Paul. Myself, I've always preferred Hillel's negative version of the Golden Rule: "What is hateful to you, do not do to your neighbor." More realistic, more manageable. More humane. It's never been clearer to me that the lessons of history and economy combine to shout: *Modest, be modest! Baby steps, baby steps!* All we can hope for, really. The human stuff is too fragile, too fallible.

"These *lights*," Sam said under his breath, stopping short at a clear red. A sudden jolt threw us forward, the whole car, with the dull staccato crunch of broken glass coming from behind us. Behind us, a dark-haired wide-eyed boy, late teens at most, stared openmouthed through the broad scuffed windshield of a brown Jeep Cherokee. The car couldn't have been more than a few years newer than the ancient Buick we rattled in. Sam asked if I was okay. He put his right blinker on, pointing largely and elaborately for the teenager's benefit to a garden center's parking lot to the right of us, nosing the Buick right.

"The fucker's making a run for it!" I said.

The Jeep whirred in reverse and pinched high on its back tires, pivoting and peeling out into the left-turning traffic of the opposite lane. I tried to get the license plate but a gray sedan, honking and braking, blocked the back of the Jeep as it sped away.

"That little *fucker*," I said.

"Did you get the plates?"

"I was about to but—"

Sam whiplashed the car around into the oncoming lane. Another horn was blaring, a quick, bending Doppler howl as a car ran up behind us and just managed to swerve around. Sam spurted away after the teenager, separated now by the gray sedan and the other car, a low-slung black sports job that didn't appreciate Sam's jockeying and tailgating. The car flashed its brake lights in warning when we came up too close on a turn, the brown Jeep hinging visible three cars ahead like a boxcar that segments and breaks from a turning train. When Sam got to a little turnoff in the lane, he threw the car left and floored the gas, the big beleaguered engine responding like a crazed bathroom fan, slingshotting us forward. We split the two lanes for several hundred feet—corridor of cars, horn fanfare—then jerked back into the right lane, cutting off the black sports car and its mutely shrieking driver. I realized from the mounting pressure in my forearms that I was squeezing either side of the worn leather seat, my veins rippling and cording, corrugating. Up ahead was one of the lights Sam had rushed a few minutes before, and now as the gray sedan braked at the end of another yellow, Sam threw us left and right again, button-hooking the sedan and shooting the intersection just ahead of crossing traffic.

"Jesus!" I said, almost laughing for fear.

Sam was silent, his gray serious eyes straight ahead, his sickle jaw slicing the air, pointing *avant, avant!* With the fan of the engine whirring crazily, factories gas stations abandoned grassy lots blurring by, we managed to get within tailing distance of the Jeep. I kept one hand anchored to the leather seat and with the other snapped a cell-phone picture of the license plate, blurry but discernible.

"I got it," I said. "Got it."

"You got it?" Sam said.

Up ahead another traffic light loomed, stubborn red, with a line of three or four cars brooking no escape. When we pulled to within rear-ending distance of the Jeep, I took another picture of the license plate for good measure. We sat there idling, watching the teenager's dark motionless head through the glass.

"Well, this is awkward, isn't it?" I said.

Sam put on his right blinker again. He rolled down the window and hooked his pointing hand over the roof. He honked the horn once, a restrained, staccato beep, almost polite, continuing to gesture with his other hand.

"I can only assume he's hard of hearing and seeing," I said. "Wait, what are you doing? I got the license plate!"

Sam was up and out of the car, striding up to the driver-side window of the rusted brown Jeep. My breath caught in the sudden dinging, in the wan overhead dome light of the Buick. Sam, in reed-thin loafers and baggy shorts, a pair of stork-like pasty legs stretching in between, Sam in his sweat-grayed tennis shirt, the incipient tonsure of his bald spot catching the light—Sam knocked slowly and deliberately on the teenager's window. He spoke in a loud, slow voice. "Excuse me, but you hit my car back there. Will you please pull over to the side of the road so we can talk?" Then he stepped back a pace, held both hands up, palms out, at shoulder height, as if to show the young man that he wasn't armed, or maybe to baptize him into the proper repentance. In any case, it worked: The Jeep's right blinker lit up, ticking audibly, and the car rolled over to the shoulder of the road.

Sam trotted back to the Buick's open door, slid into the seat and into gear. Somehow the light had stayed red—no angry honks pierced the air, no sounds at all, really. The air inside the car felt close and gauzy as we pulled up behind the Jeep, and Sam's sly voice sounded distant as it said, "Good, right?"

Good. Right. A man of action, apparently. A complicated man of action. I stood at the right front corner of the Buick's spreading hood as Sam again approached the driver's side of the Jeep. The teenager stayed inside his car, rolling down the window and speaking softly, apologetically from the sound of it. Sam's voice carried back to me—variations on I understand, I understand but damage has been done. He'd heard the crack of glass himself. At one point he called out to me ("Comrade? Damage report?") and I went around back to inspect Sam's car: a rubbery stain on the bumper, black streaks like frozen current, and a good-size jagged hole, vaguely New Jersey–shaped, punched out of the left brake light. I took a few more pictures with my phone. By the time I got back to the front of the car the teenager's hand was holding what looked to be twenties out the window. Sam slowly shook his head. He stretched his long crane-like arm onto the roof of the Jeep and patted it twice in benediction.

"Go and sin no more," he said to me, showing a wry little smile as the Jeep pulled away behind him.

In the car Sam said, "Probably on his phone—saw him try to hide it when I came up to the car."

I stared at him, waiting.

"Which isn't actually his car. It's his older brother's—so he said. Anyway, he did apologize to me."

When we came to the scene of the accident a few minutes later, another red light stopped us. The giant Legoland of the turnpike and Route 9 tilted up to the right of us, the ramps rising and curving away. In the shadow of the freeway was the garden center Sam had tried to turn into, its white wooden trellis hanging rows of round flowering plants, pinks and yellows, like pixie wigs. Closer by, I thought I saw red brake-light glass scattered in the road, glinting.

Finally I said, "Speaking of confrontational politics . . ."

Sam laughed a little, blushing. "Yeah," he said. "Sorry about all that."

I held up a clement hand. "Can I ask you a question, though? I've been meaning to ask it for a while. Deeply invasive, deeply personal . . ."

"Do your worst," Sam said.

"Why are you in a Marxist theory class? Not that you don't belong there. This isn't a purge. It's just that, well, I'm curious. I'd always heard you guys were above theory, or you thought you were."

"You mean poets?"

"All you MFA types."

Sam nodded his head in time to the road's vibrations. We were moving again, crossing the great highway plaza. "You first," said Sam.

"Why am I in the class?"

"You're ABD. You already know the stuff cold. Why go into campus when you don't have to?"

"Boredom," I said. "You get really bored. Do a doctorate, you'll see—boredom, isolation. Alienation. The dissertation cuts you off from your 'species being.' You remember that one—comrade?"

Sam smiled, shook his head.

"Well, it's an embarrassment of jargon, isn't it? Especially in Hahn's class. I sometimes think she should have a translator."

"She should," he said. "You."

I laughed.

"Why not? You TA one of her classes, don't you?"

"An undergraduate class. A general ed class."

"A general education is what I need. It's decided. You shall intercede with the Mother," Sam said, turning onto my street, the caged pin oaks and ivied fences, the painted garages and porches and stoops. When we pulled up to the clapboard row house I rented a room in, Sam held out his hand. "You were soundly beaten today, sir. Until soon?"

"It's your turn," I said. "Why are you in the class?"

"Ah, yes." Sam repeated the question to the windshield, smiling. His gaze slid down to the empty air around the old slotted tape deck, the grimy knobs and buttons going soft at the edges like rounds of cheese. "Same reason as you, I guess. Boredom. Or I don't know. I went to a few Occupy marches when all that was going on. Were you involved with any of that?"

"When there wasn't real activism to do, sure. It was a good party."

"Can of worms?"

"Not really. That's the extent of it for me."

"I guess for me, with the class, I was just tired of poetry workshops, and maybe a little curious. It's been a good vocabulary builder if nothing else."

"Here," I said, "hold on a second."

I ran upstairs to my room, four walls, three of them covered with jerry-built bookshelves, pine planks and cinder blocks, books on labor history, civil rights, the Marxist canon, the smattering of poetry and prose that I'd kept from my undergraduate days, Continental philosophy, science fiction, a little fantasy, architecture, art, a clutch of Audubon guides, my swollen backlog of *The Nation*, a long, low, wall-hugging shrine to literature, books like wainscoting, a cluttered riot of books—better that than IKEA shelves. I plucked a narrow reed from the bulrushes, took the stairs two at a time back down to Sam.

"What's this?" he said when I handed the slim volume through the window, his voice mock scandalous.

"Oh it's dangerous all right. Few things more dangerous than a lucid Marxist."

Sam was holding the book up to the light, turning it sideways, squinting. "Looks a little thin—I don't know. Not much chance of the kind of Stockholm syndrome *Capital* gives you. This won't hold me captive for more than the weekend."

"Read it slowly," I said. "And don't worry about *Capital* for a while. Hahn never makes good on her threats of reading quizzes—and socialism has evolved. Callinicos is good, up-to-date, a proper introduction. I'll be curious to hear what you think."

"Okay," Sam said, "I'll read it. And tell you what I think."

One other thing I remember from that morning—not a particularly proximate start to my story, but somehow it feels like the start: a tennis match, a car accident, a car *chase*, a loaned book in the aftermath.

I waved Sam goodbye telling him I was sorry about the fresh damage to his car. He stuck his face out the window, as if he could crane around to see the punctured brake light, and gave a full-faced shrug. "The things of this world, right?"

That was typical of Sam—always signing off with some cryptic biblicalism, as if we'd all spent our formative years in a seminary. We were worldly-wiser now, of course, wry and unillusioned and yet still beatific enough to believe in causes. Or something like that. I've since had plenty of occasion, urgent occasion, to think of what that particular quip might have meant to Sam—something about the transience of all earthly things, wasn't it, but what did that transience mean to *him*? Was it a good thing? An enabling thing? The more I think about the phrase in Sam's mouth the less it sounds like a quip at all. Maybe more like a prophecy, or a threat.

Anyway, I shouldn't get ahead of myself, or not more than two or three days at this point—skipping ahead to an elevator ride up to Dr. Hahn's office, late Monday afternoon, and where the hell had the weekend gone anyway? What to say to the good *Frau Doktor*? Hahn and I were relaxed enough around each other, and I was certainly seasoned enough in the academic game, that I felt I could dispense with the tepid, transparent excuses for why the batch of twenty essays still lay on my office desk, inevitably, ungraded. Not a family emergency, no—my folks sat quietly in suburban Massachusetts like little Matryoshka dolls, tidy and neat: Take off their shells, they'd keep surprising you, but the calm lacquered exterior was calm indeed. And no mononucleosis either—no one to give it to me. No crippling depression (no chemical depression, anyway), no psychotherapeutic Rolodex to flip through and pluck from. I was a hale, hearty, well-adjusted child of loving, educated parents—one of the lucky ones. I just couldn't bring myself to give a shit anymore. Was that an admissible excuse? Dear Dr. Hahn, I feel my veins fill with lead at the prospect of reading another paper about checks and balances, or the shameful Three-Fifths Compromise. My limbs like salami, heavy and dead. It's the same with my own work. It's a sort of soul-soddenness, the weight of waste. What did it really matter *what* thirties-era radicals did to try to disrupt the New Deal? Why history? Why yesterday? Wasn't Time's winged chariot assembling now, and now, and now? Randolph's famously open curriculum, a doctorate in Politics, simply, had given me so much rope to hang myself with that I'd now collapsed under the weight of it, crushed under the coiling coils of it, the pile rising on top of me like toxic soft serve, or a funeral cairn, like the brainy abstract involutions I'd once plunged into headfirst. Theory! Ideas! The dialectic! It was Alex who'd cut to the quick of it all a year ago—had it already been a year?—when she dropped out of her fancier program at Columbia, ABD. *I could jerk off to Deleuze and Guattari for two hundred pages . . . or I could actually do something.* We were lying in bed when she said it, in a Florence *pensione*, no covers, no cover at all. She'd made the lazy masturbatory hand gesture, the wet raspberry sound to punctuate the pause. I looked down at my bare flaccid penis, father to none. Alex and I broke up a month later.

Did I miss her? Of course I did. But what I also missed was some dimly remembered sense of purpose, the orientation toward *doing* that Alex had apparently reclaimed. Dear Dr. Hahn, is it too much to ask that my life be more than the sum of its little routines? Dear Doktor, what should I do about the sense of hollowness that overtakes me, spreading inside out until my skin feels like a mold?

The elevator dinged and in walked a pretty girl.

A redhead.

Short. Shortish. Not tall, in any case.

Small freckles on her face, light brown, massing at her cheekbones and nose bridge like the drips in a Pollock painting.

She pressed her lips together in a thin smile, acknowledging me. I gave the same look back. Her red-brown hair was long and thick, loosely ponytailed, piled into the hood of a navy blue Randolph sweatshirt, her skin that much whiter by contrast, a little waxen in the pallid chrome elevator light. She hit the Lobby button and swung a leather knapsack around to her front, rummaging around in it—scent of vanilla on the tiny breeze, and what else? She'd installed herself in the right front corner of the spacious elevator, weirdly empty, I realized, though it was late in the day. The twin rows of descending silver buttons were partly covered by her body, and as the doors drew shut she turned her head and asked was I going to street level? Did I need something else? Her thin auburn eyebrows stretched in the most modest solicitude, and I couldn't contain a wider smile. A slight quirk in her look, brown crescent eyes pulling narrower as if by drawstrings, little lines, the faint parentheses appearing at the corners of her face. I was staring, obviously.

"Was that eleven?" I said.

The floor began to move underneath us.

"Yes," she said.

"Ah."

"You needed eleven?"

"I needed eleven."

"I'm sorry."

"What for?" I said.

She was half facing me now, one hand on her bag strap, the other burrowing into the sweatshirt's hand warmer. The eyes were narrow, lightly brown. She had light brown freckles like a pale constellation across her narrow, smooth, slightly waxen face. She could have been ten years my junior, and she was beautiful, the kind of beauty that stands just around the corner from typical, traditional beauty, the kind of beauty that forgets itself on a tired Monday afternoon and is all the more striking for it. These impossibilities free you up to be yourself. I complimented her sweatshirt. Very germane, I said. The sartorial laws typically frowned on the wearing of a Randolph sweatshirt, say, on the Randolph campus, but she was obviously above all that.

She looked up and down my outfit, slowly. "Sartorial laws, huh?"

Tan canvas shoes, black jeans, a T-shirt, French style, white with gray horizontal stripes—I eyed my reflection in the dull mirror of the elevator doors. A passable build, ignoring the slight swell of my stomach. My flop of late-period John Lennon hair, a little raggedier than usual today.

"Well . . ." I said.

The floor kept falling beneath us, lifting us back down to earth and the bright Formica expanse of the lobby that looked out on Twelfth Street, the trees outside giving off a greenish glow. When the elevator slowed and dinged again, the doors opened onto this scene, prearranged, and the beautiful girl stepped out into it.

"Better luck this time," she said, smiling the same curt smile over her shoulder.

I saw that the button for eleven was already lit.

When I got upstairs I knocked a brief apology, a lilting little knuckle tap at Dr. Hahn's office door. It was ajar. I was told to come in, sit down. I was asked how I was. It was a rhetorical question.

Hahn sat with her arms crossed in front of her on the table, holding court at the small, Arthurian slab in the near corner of her office, a sort of breakfast nook, really, one of the petit bourgeois touches that belied her fierceness and endeared her to me. Around the table sat the two other graduate students I shared the TA-ship with, Greg Baxter and Tiffany Wong. Our work together amounted to a batch of sixty papers split three ways three times a semester. The study sessions we led didn't hurt much; office hours were barren, paid reading time, really—but the papers hurt, the papers cost. Greg with his round fleshy face and staunch eyebrows, from the Sociology Department, known to wear bow ties, like today, liked to dock his students for split infinitives, prepositions at the end of sentences, all that Strunk and White bullshit. Tiffany was more sensible. A casual friend from the Politics Department, she studied race theory and Asian American solidarity movements and had picked up the extra course, I assumed, for the same reasons I had: money first, money second, money third. She was watchful and precise, always soft-spoken, the skin of her face smoothed back as if by a permanent gust of wind. She once referred to a movie that had "chinked out" white actors in Asian roles, a trick of makeup and lighting that she described through gentle scoffs. A sharp, unsentimental mind. I suppose I was a little cautious around her.

And then there was Hahn—grumpy, graceful, small-toothed, bob-cut, lithe, bespectacled Hahn. In her office she wore the white blouse and gray sleek pants, matching coat draping the chairback, that a lesbian friend of mine had once apostrophized: "Oh how I love you, Professor Hahn's pantsuits!" But she was fierce, a Stalinist, unrepentant, known to challenge her students, as she'd once challenged me, if they recited the well-known crimes of the Maoists. *Look, famines do happen, don't they?* She didn't hesitate to criticize her former employers, either, the bosses at Princeton who'd accused her of goading her students to riot in the protests around the U.S.–Contra collusion. She left Princeton before they could force her out, drifted for several years, organized, wrote. Among the talented misfits and castoffs at Randolph College she found safe harbor. Twenty years later I drew on her work on Ralph Ellison in my senior thesis, the cream of which I submitted to graduate schools. It couldn't have been my undergraduate GPA that got me into the program Hahn more or less ran now. It might have been pure luck.

"Did you get a chance to average out your papers?" Hahn said, looking sidewise at me.

"You mean the grades?" I said.

"Do you have an aggregate? Greg's hard to please, Tiffany's on the cusp I'd expected for a second paper—B, B minus. How did your students do?"

Idiotically, I reached into my backpack, shuffling around for the papers that weren't there. I must have left them in my office, I announced. I stepped across the hall to the windowless room with the gray felt walls and the quartet of thick metal desks, each of them shared by two graduate students—the Animal Cubicle Farm, we called it. There was the untouched manila folder, thick with papers, lying brazen on the far desk.

I tried to keep the folder close to my body as I settled back down next to Hahn, the papers like a losing hand at her table. When the manila cover bent and kinked open against me, Hahn eyed the first essay as I pushed the cover shut. Traitorous reflex! With a curdled expression she removed my hand and the first essay from the folder, flipping through the unmarked pages. "You need to make more marginal comments than this," she said. She flipped to the last page, also bare—no marginal comments, no terminal comments, no grade, nothing. Greg and Tiffany tipped their eyes down in concert, suddenly very interested in the grain of the table wood. Hahn took me in with her lips turned inward, a faint white pressure line where the mouth used to be. Her eyes were flat and dull under the slanting bangs.

"Can an atheist make confession?" I said.

Hahn took out another paper, lifted the pages, let them drop. She took out another.

"I was in bed all weekend," I said. "I'm sorry."

"You were sick?" she said.

"I wasn't feeling well at all."

Hahn sighed into the silence of the room. She reached into the stack of ungraded papers, adding two more to the pile in front of her. She dealt them all together, rapped them smartly on the table. "I can do these five," she said. "Anyone else feeling charitable?"

"I'll do five," offered Tiffany, faithful Tiffany. Blessings on the hand that received the stack across the table, blessings on the eyes that smiled at me, a little mischievously.

"Greg?" Hahn said.

"Sure," he said, though he mirrored Hahn in the turn of his lips, his fat fusilli eyebrows rising—a curse on those eyebrows.

"Which leaves five for ailing Eli," Hahn said. "Do you think you can handle that?"

"Of course," I said. "Thank you. I am sorry, guys."

"We need to have these back to the students by tomorrow's class," Hahn said. "Greg, if your papers are that bad, they're that bad, but take another look and consider curving up. Like I said, B, B minus is more or less where I'd expect the second paper to be. Thanks everybody. See you tomorrow."

I thanked Greg and Tiffany again on their way out, keeping my seat. When Hahn and I were alone, her mouth reappeared and drew lopsided, winching up into a head-shaking almost-smile. She nodded at the plusher seat across from her desk and I dropped into it heavily. The office window brightened with a sudden swell of sun through the clouds, the white fine horizontal slats of the blinds glowing orangely at their bottom tips. Hahn's curt blond bob was backlit too—there couldn't have been ten windows on the entire street that got light at this hour, but she was blessed. I would have to make my intercession.

"Well?" she said.

"I don't know. I don't know what's wrong with me. I'm sorry."

"Why do I think you really were in bed all weekend," Hahn said.

"I was."

"But you weren't sick."

"Not strictly speaking, no."

"Am I going to have to find a replacement TA in the middle of the semester?" Hahn looked at me levelly through her glasses, reflecting the room at me. "I'll withdraw the question for now. But you need to carve some time out of your standing existential crisis to get your papers done, understand? Either that or I'll have to start quoting Mao to you on work and solidarity."

"God no," I said.

"Or I'll have to replace you. Clear enough?"

With her fingertips, absently, Hahn slid a photocopied flyer back and forth across her desk, and suddenly there she was again, smiling out at me: the same round pretty face, slight eyes, the constellation of freckles in the mounting cheeks, the long hair done up into a sleek chignon to match the sleek sleeveless dress she wore, a formal photograph. In black-and-white the auburn hair looked charcoal-dark, the skin of her arms lightest gray. Below the photograph in a large fine font were the words *Jennifer Daugherty, Senior Piano Recital, April 9, 7:30 p.m., Church of St. Joseph.*

"Ah, yes," Hahn said, "that was the other thing I meant to tell you. Our friend"—she turned the flyer toward her—"our friend Jennifer Daugherty came to see me just before the meeting you were late to."

"Daugherty?" I said.

"She came to complain about the grade on her first paper, which she said she just got back. A C plus."

"I remember the name, but I didn't know who she was. Why didn't she come to me?"

"I told her that. I held the line," Hahn said. "I looked through her paper and more or less echoed what you'd said—descriptive, not argumentative. Not that you'd said much. You really do need to mark up these papers more, Eli."

I tried to picture where she could have sat in the sunken amphitheater hall. If I'd seen her coming into class or leaving it, I'd forgotten. Which seemed unlikely. She must have sat near the front, or it could have been the middle, or anywhere on the left side of the room, really. I tended to slip in late, perch at the right back corner of the room, and slip out early. I supposed the remarkable thing would have been if I *had* seen her. A senior. Jennifer Daugherty . . .

"I might go a bit easier on her in the future," Hahn said. "The prose was good, good organization. If an argument shows up, she's a top-of-the-stack writer."

I remembered the papers under my hands and flipped through the five remaining to me. Jennifer Daugherty's wasn't there. Probably for the best.

"Her senior recital?" I said, nodding at the flyer. "What's a senior doing in Poli Sci 110? She's a music major?"

"It happens now and then," Hahn said. "You leave the required courses you're dreading for last. That way they don't impact your GPA as much. You never tried that? She told me it was writing-heavy classes she dreaded. I told her she didn't need to, her grade on the first, late-returned paper notwithstanding."

"I know," I said, "I know." I was penitential now, Christian, bowing my head all the way to the wood-warm desk. I was generally unworthy.

Hahn stood up, pulled the coat from her chairback, and slung it rakishly over her shoulder. With the other hand she closed down her computer, replaced a pair of pens in a garish red coffee mug that asked, in loud white capitals, TWO PARTIES FOR THE BOSSES, BUT WHO'S FOR US?

"Where's your next stop?" Hahn asked me at the door.

She'd added my ungraded papers to her shoulder bag, and Jennifer Daugherty's flyer too.

"Home, I guess."

"Your undervalued student here is playing Mahler tonight. I told her I might just stop by. Have you eaten?"

Outside on Twelfth Street the trees moved gently in the wind, the wind turning the leaves matte-side, then shine-side, shimmering them light against the dark-shaded backdrop of the brownstones. The wind made no sound, or only the sound of the cars and trucks and taxis motoring past, the horn peals, sirens, the great windy rustle of pedestrians, crosswalk signals, music floating down from upper stories—nature's lip-synch. Turning onto Fifth Avenue, Hahn and I passed the bus stop just beyond the college's main entrance where a group of mostly students, I assumed, waited. Bohemian in dress, concerned in their unconcern, they talked a little, flirted, tipped their faces down for sly glances at their glowing phones—the politer ones were sly, anyway. I'd half expected to see Jennifer Daugherty waiting there in her Randolph sweatshirt, casual and pretty, though by now she was probably at home getting ready for her recital.

Which meant what exactly? Doing warm-up scales? Meditating? Doing her hair? O brave new world that has such music majors in it! Or maybe she was brooding on the overhasty C plus I'd given her first paper. I remembered her curt smile in the elevator. Did she know who I was? But she must have known. I felt the urge like a stinging cattle prod to ask Hahn if I could see the flyer again—and for this reason I resisted it.

We'd decided on a Moroccan restaurant. Hahn knew a great place right on her street, with a great wine list. She deserved some alcohol, she said. Apparently Mondays were her new Fridays.

"I just need to stop off at home for a few minutes to check in on things," she said. "You don't mind?"

I said I didn't mind at all.

Hahn continued down the sidewalk at pace, leading just slightly, leaning into her steps, a toe walker.

Suddenly she slowed. I watched her face cloud over.

"Or if you'd rather wait for me at the restaurant . . ." Hahn said. "You could get us a table. It shouldn't be too busy at this hour, but you never know."

The sun-split Arc d'Washington Square grew large at the end of the avenue, and we were in NYU territory. We turned left onto Eighth as a pair of students swung by us on swan-necked rent-a-bikes, the Citibank logo running down the blue center tubes. This was Soc territory to our Greaser, though of course we all swam in the same money, most of us. I knew Hahn certainly did, and she knew I knew. Why was she suddenly so shy of her apartment? Or was it her husband?

I'd actually visited Hahn's apartment once before, and met her husband, though maybe she'd forgotten. It was in my second year of the program, an end-of-semester party for her Labor History seminar, and I can tell you that Hahn's sixth-floor penthouse was nothing, but nothing to be ashamed of: It was huge, bright, high-ceilinged, with a view of the Tompkins Square trees at the end of the street, though you saw them through a warren of scaffolding on the next building over. There were fine paintings on the apartment's white plaster walls, fine rugs on the hardwood floors, recessed lighting, a fireplace, you name it. During the party Hahn's husband, Stephen, had come out of his study to tell us hello and to make ourselves at home. He was a tall, frail, stately man, a retired ophthalmologist, with a shock of white hair and a genial wave as he stepped back behind the whitewashed door. I'd heard about the minor tremor that put an end to his career as a sought-after surgeon, but I understood he still consulted, and that the condition was manageable. I retained in my mind the image of George Plimpton, a slender, sad-eyed, harmlessly patrician old man.

At First Avenue we stopped for a traffic light, cars and buses sliding by in the fading day, a little drained of their color, a little depleted.

"My place is just on this next block," Hahn said. "The restaurant's a few doors down from it on the left. Cafe Mogador. Why don't you go ahead and get us a table. I'll just be a few minutes."

"Whatever you prefer," I said.

"It'll just be a few minutes. Tell them Linda will be joining you if there's any trouble getting a table. I've practically moved in there in the evenings—I'm like Sartre at the Café de Flore. Well, a little better than Sartre. Sartre used to take up a table for the entire day, and he'd only order a single cup of tea. That's how he wrote *Being and Nothingness*, did you know? That massive doorstop?"

"There's your brief against the existentialists," I said. "Table hogs. Hogs at life's table."

"I'm sure I tip better than Sartre did too."

I added, apropos of too little, probably, "Did they ever get rid of that scaffolding on the building next to yours? I remember it was bugging you and Stephen when I visited with the Labor History seminar. Do you remember that party?"

Hahn said, "We're on the ground floor now."

The traffic light changed. The little white man of the crosswalk signal bade us come, chirping. Over the chirping came a car-horn beep, and another, high, polite. A dark-haired woman in a gray sculpted minivan was waving at us, nosing slowly onto St. Mark's Place from First Avenue, smiling and waving.

"Do you know that woman?" I said to Hahn.

"Oh," she said. "Oh." She lifted her hand in a wooden wave. "Well."

"Neighbor of yours?"

"Nurse," Hahn said. "That's Renilde. That's Steve's nurse."

When we got to the red-brick building where Hahn and her husband lived, the van was already unfolding itself onto the sidewalk, the large black metal tray lowering itself down, coming to rest with a long hydraulic hiss. Hahn stopped just short of where Renilde operated the controls at the side of the van. Renilde, olive, plump in a blue windbreaker, her brown hair in a loose bun, turned to Hahn in greeting. I was introduced as a young colleague from the college, a gross overstatement of my position, though later, thinking of it, it made my heart swell a little. They'd gone up to the West Side marina,

Renilde said. To take the boat out a little. Did Hahn still need her tonight?

The ramp ground down into the sidewalk pavement with a low dull scrape, anchoring itself.

"All ready, Steve," Renilde said.

Out of the shadowy maw of the van came Hahn's husband, pivoting, in a motorized cart, cresting the top of the ramp. The thin whine of the motor preceded him down into the last light of day. He moved slowly and steadily down the ramp, not nodding, not smiling at us, but acknowledging us with his eyes. He was horribly changed. The eyes slewed in our direction, and in them I saw the same look I had seen before, steady, a little sad, but now the sockets that contained them were hollowed out and dark, the skin of the face too, the head motionless and slumped against the chair's padded headrest. The eyes were like living things fallen into amber, the truest things remaining to a false and mutinous body. The skin of the neck, too, was changed, shrink-wrapped around the muscles and bones of the upper shoulders. It was the same with the forearms, exposed from the shirtsleeves down. Stephen's left hand gripped the cart's controls in an ungainly, fisted way. The forearms and the thighs looked dropped into position haphazardly, the top half of the body skewing left compared to the bottom, as if the body were being seen half in water, half out. I looked down at the gray particulate sidewalk to reset my view and looked up again, smiling.

Hahn made the introductions. She told her husband he'd met me once before, briefly. He said he recognized me. He'd heard a lot about me. The voice was slow, slurred, atonal—the word *mongoloid* stole into my mind before I could banish it. The sentences issued from Stephen's mouth with great difficulty.

Yes, he'd heard a lot about me from Linda. His mouth hitched up into a wayward, curtailed, plasticine grin.

"Almost all of it good," he said.

I laughed at the quip—too loudly, perhaps. I suddenly had no idea what to do with my hands. Stephen's lay at the end of the armrests, soft and inert; I didn't dare reach out to shake one of them. I found myself clasping my hands in front of me in a bizarre, vaguely Asian gesture of respect—strange gesture for a dying man.

And he was clearly dying—memento mori in the hollow cheeks, memento mori in the eyes.

At dinner Hahn confirmed it: amyotrophic lateral sclerosis, ALS, or Lou Gehrig's disease—degenerative, terminal. Three years earlier when I'd met Stephen for the first time the first symptoms were there—they knew this now, in retrospect—but they'd tracked any number of other symptoms of other maladies, lesser maladies. It could have simply been the tremor doubling down a bit, intensifying. Old and gray and full of sleep, and a little trembly, right? That's what we were all born to. Hahn mustered a smile, her lips inturned. At the time Steve still spoke normally, he moved normally, he was normal. Until he wasn't anymore.

"I'm just so glad we never had children," Hahn said. "It's bad enough for me to see him change like this."

"I had no idea," I said. "I'm so sorry. I didn't know the extent of it."

"A month ago he was walking on his own power. He could walk up the stairs and into the apartment on his own—it was slow, but he could do it. Now he needs the wheelchair for everything. He's in a wheelchair. It's accelerating. This thing—it's breaking into a run."

"And what comes next?" I said. "I mean about treatment options. Forgive me. I meant in terms of treatment."

"You mean in terms of management," Hahn said. "That's all that's left. The doctors are masters of evasion, false optimism, statements that sound substantive until you think them through—every one of them could run for office—but even they don't give him more than two years. It could be two months, two weeks. We're living like children, in the horrible present."

Hahn laughed suddenly, bitterly, wagging her head at the filigreed teakettle at the center of the table. "Do you know where they went today?" Hahn said. "Renilde and Steve? It wasn't to the marina, I can tell you that. Renilde isn't licensed to captain the boat and Steve's not able anymore—and he knows I know that. He's not even trying with his cover stories anymore. No, they went up to Woodlawn Cemetery. How they made that wheelchair-accessible I don't know, but they went there to visit the grave of Herman Melville, at Steve's insistence. In his retirement he's started reading more, and the heavy stuff, too, Melville, Beckett, all the godless metaphysicians, and so today he goes and leaves a pen at Melville's tomb. That's what he does now. He reads books about endless water, and visits cemeteries."

"God . . ." I said.

"Yup. Yup."

Hahn forked through her plate of chicken tagine, half eaten in a rubble of couscous. What pinot noir remained in her glass looked purplish, the color of a dark bruise, almost black in the dim lighting of the restaurant. We sat at a smooth simple lacquered table near the bar. Wineglasses hung upside down above the bar and caught the light going down in a perspective row, glinting like Christmas ornaments. I watched the bartender, thirtysomething in an old Brooklyn Dodgers jersey, bearded, head shorn, light a row of tea candles along the bar top with sacramental care. The little fires warmed the underside of his face and the faces of the few people hunched forward against the bar at the outset of dinner rush. A few more showed up in the time I watched. The restaurant began to glow orangely, cocoon-like against the darkness outside. The couples through the sunk-in picture window and the metal scrollwork of the patio sat fading in the gloom, disappearing. Beyond them, across St. Mark's Place, squares of warm yellow light began to climb up the apartment houses.

When we parted company that night, I told Hahn I'd probably just head home too. She was bloody exhausted—those were her words—and she had homework to do because of me. A little water lit up her small eyes behind the glasses. Neither of us said anything. She did give me the music flyer, just in case. I hadn't asked for it. I folded the paper and put it in my pocket, left Hahn with an uncharacteristic hug, and didn't take the paper out again, and didn't unfold it and behold its round serious pretty face again, until the spot-lit glowing arch of Washington Square loomed up out of the darkness at my left.

St. Joseph's Church was a white Grecian temple in the middle of Greenwich Village. Dramatically lit, its thick fluted columns stood to either side of bright red double doors, an incurved arch for the prayerful Lord just above them—the building could have been a stylish stock exchange, or a town hall. The gold stubby cross at the apex of the roof appeared to be something of an afterthought. I was ten minutes late.

A side door, also red, stood ajar, leaking thick muddy chords, fierce attacks, out into the cool dark air where I stood hesitating, checking the time on my cell phone, gripping the door handle, ungripping it. I had turned toward the flight of granite steps when the last chords of the piece rang out, unmistakably tonic. I stepped into the hall under cover of thin applause. The U-shaped whitewashed balcony, a line of blazing crystal chandeliers, a high flat blue-and-white pie-latticed ceiling stretched above me, and I was one of ten, maybe fifteen people in the room. Jennifer Daugherty, her thin white arms pressed flat against her sides, bowed stiffly from the waist at the front of this bright-lit expanse. She stood close to the black piano bench beside the hulking black of the concert grand, its lid uptilted like a massive wing, as if the instrument might take flight at any moment, spiraling up to the ceiling and lifting its nervous conductor up with it. Thirty meters separated me from Jennifer, but in the stillness and emptiness of the crowd—a bevy of gray heads in the front pews, a few friends, presumably, in young dresses and jackets, a goateed priest in his Oreo habit—in this sparseness I could easily see the stress lines on Jennifer's face, and she could see them on mine. Her eyes widened a little as they took me in, then seemed to settle back. I couldn't have left now if I'd wanted to.

In her simple black pants and vest, a blue blouse, long earrings dangling down beside the red-brown wavy forelocks broken free of the chignon, Jennifer Daugherty resumed her seat at the piano. I scurried up to the third row, behind the goateed priest, who turned to me and nodded a smile and handed me a program. I gathered it was Liszt we'd just heard. A delicate Bach partita followed, sprightly, precise, the voices twining and untwining. The interpretation was obviously indebted to Glenn

Gould, not one of my favorites, but the playing was good, very good. The playing was exceptional—who was I kidding? All I'd ever done was dabble in the piano, achieving proficiency at most, learning just enough to know how little I knew compared to a real player like Jennifer, a real musician. Sing, O Muse, and tell of the long-necked, round-faced, auburn-haired girl who nodded her head in time to the allegro section! Her body began to relax into its intricate tasks, first with the Bach piece, then a Schoenberg, no less intricate for its loss of melody. A piece by Scriabin followed the Schoenberg, then a long, minimalist piece by John Adams, "The Radicals," with its chords like chants, with eerie passages coming to abrupt, silent halts. (The piece was "a musical record and a critique," according to the program, of the medieval Christian attempts to impose God's kingdom on earth: "Thy kingdom come, thy will be done / On earth as it is in heaven.") The tempos were slowing now, the pieces getting longer, more contemplative, as if the concert had run from the shore into the foam and the breakers and waded out into deep, dark water, drifting, slowly swelling—the endless sea.

Out of these depths came the songs I remember best from that night, the songs Hahn had mentioned to me and the ones Jen would later play for me again and again at my request, even teaching me certain sections of them—the Rückert-Lieder by Gustav Mahler. One of the finely dressed young women in the front row had gotten up beside the piano and now began to sing a series of searching, dreamy arias to Jennifer's deft accompaniment: "I Breathed a Gentle Fragrance," "Look Not on My Songs," "At Midnight," and finally "I Am Lost to the World." This last song began deep in the bass clef, the same muddy depths where the concert itself had begun. Slowly the music climbed up to ground level, a starting place, and then back down, and back up again. Into this unsteady progress came the mezzo-soprano's long, sober, beautiful lines, reprising the bass part.

> *I am lost to the world,*
> *with which I've wasted so much time.*
> *It hasn't heard from me in so long*
> *it might as well think I'm dead.*

Slowly, slowly, a lento march—each word, each phrase an age. The singer's thin face strained visibly, her throat tight and striated, to sustain the effortless-seeming notes. This was Mallory, one of Jen's closest friends, though at the time she was only her voice, the vehicle for that low-flying sound that Jen had provided for us, ceding the stage to this voice and these songs because she loved them so much, she felt grateful just to participate in them, and also, she later admitted to me, because she was struggling to get to an hour of memorized music for her program, as her department required, and needed something repetitive, something verse-based and simple. And lovely, and true. *I have died to the world's turmoil*, sang the soprano, *and I rest in a silent realm* ("*stillen Gebiet*"), the note stilling on "*stillen*," low and perfect.

It was the kind of music that could make you fall in love.

Quickly, then—to the summer months. Thirty days had June, thirty-one July and August. I spent most of them with Jen, in her bed or mine, no covers, no cover at all from that *forno* heat. I couldn't help but think of Florence from the summer before, my trip with Alex. The thoughts came to me in the languorous times before and after with Jen, every *after* a *before* if we waited long enough. Suddenly Alex in her pink frayed hoodie would materialize, and sometimes she wore nothing at all. She was the last woman I'd been with, the woman I'd loved casually, by which I mean easily, effortlessly, like water, and in those moments a certain undercurrent of loss would pull on what was newly found. Jen. Jen with her lithe piano-player fingers, with her stack of music books in a wicker basket by the piano, an electric model, which she played with headphones on as often as not, conscientious of her neighbors through the thin plaster walls. Jen with her HGTV shows—*House Hunters International, Property Virgins, Love It or List It.* Jen with her Agatha Christie novels, Dorothy Sayers, P. D. James, and also George Eliot, the Brontës, Thomas Hardy, a smattering of books in French and Italian—she claimed to know the languages only as far as dynamic markings and song titles went, but the books were well read, underlined, decorated with a tight looping brand of marginalia.

Jen and her friend Mallory, the mezzo, and another roommate I rarely saw shared a three-bedroom walk-up in Astoria, Queens. When the heat was killing, which was most of the time, the air conditioners made a glistening beaded curtain of falling condensation down the front of the faded building, the gummed dirty sidewalks spattered with water. Pollock drips, Jen's copper freckles—on her cheekbones, the bridge of her nose, everywhere, it turned out. The sex was incandescent—of course it was—and slippery, slick, our bodies greased by the heat. One weekend it was just Jen and me in the apartment— the clothes came off and stayed off, bunched into corners as we wandered in our *Blue Lagoon* innocence. From the bedroom to the kitchen to the little nook where Jen had installed a small green couch cushion beside the piano, the concert perch, she called it. In boxers and bra and panties, respectively, we played and listened and listened and played, taking turns at the piano and the green perch, Jen helping me with the first building sections of "I Am Lost to the World," the notes halting, heavy in my hands.

"Don't think about it so much," she said. "Imagine it's easy, move your hands smoothly over the keys, and the tone will follow."

"I'd like to move my hands smoothly over your keys," I said a little absently, almost out of habit, every phrase an opportunity for innuendo. It was a running joke we'd developed, and yet it worked, too—those early days! Soon enough we'd be back in the bedroom or on the living-room couch with a bathroom towel (that respectful towel) underneath us, or in the bathroom itself, or the cramped grimy shower under weak cold water.

Anything to cool us off, anything to sate us . . . Back at the piano Jen would sway histrionically to Fiona Apple ballads, but the words came out pure, high, in her plaintive, unvibratoed voice, because all this sex made her melancholy, Jen said, smiling her red-lipped, natural smile. Her lips held color in a way I'd never seen before, as if pacing her hair, and at first I didn't believe her when she said she didn't use lipstick, didn't care for it. I chalked it up to some reflex of female modesty, the light deception that says *no lipstick* when what it means is *a little lipstick*. But now we were into our third day together, a long weekend of nonstop seminude time together, and we'd showered together and done what little dressing there was to do together, and the lips still shone pinkish-red, like the cool smooth lining on the inside of an oyster. Or the cartoon idea of an oyster, anyway. With her cartoonishly perfect pink lips Jen sang to me—

And you can uuuuuuuuuse my skin
To bury your seeeeecrets in . . .

"And you'll settle me down?" I said.

"I'll settle you down all right," she said, and back to the couch.

How is it that so much sex isn't tedious? How is it that the body can store so much appetite for so much of the same thing—well, slight variations on the same thing. I'll dispense right now with any misput suggestion that I'm much of a bedroom artist. We talked a lot, Jen and I, laughed a lot during lovemaking, rolled around, groped, joyously struggled, but we weren't breaking records, weren't innovating the *genre*.

And yet we couldn't get enough of each other. Sex felt necessary, essential, like breathing.

During one of our *after* breaks Jen told me about the mint green couch to which the cushion I sat on once belonged. It was in her first off-campus apartment, in Alphabet City, full up like a punk house, except most of the musicians were classical and baroquely averse to mess and sprawl. Too bad for them. The place was overrun with roommates. "The indignities of capitalism, right?" said Jen. I nodded my head, a little smile to match hers, though I knew I was being teased.

"Don't you wish you could take back that C plus now?" she said. "I was a diligent student."

"People in your line of work don't care what you got in Poli Sci 110."

"Not true, not true! Raymond looked at my transcripts that first day and shook his head—he had this very disappointed look in his eyes. The only B plus I ever got in a college class and it comes in the last semester? He must have known I was on a slide. I'm sure it's affected my pay."

This particular Raymond was the musical casting director who'd hired Jen to accompany the vocal tryouts of Broadway actors, aspirants and old pros. Jen liked the job, she said, but considered it a stopgap. It kept her sight-reading sharp, and it was money for music, a rare thing, but it was also a lot of repetitive I-IV-V stuff, a lot of camp. Jen's real ambition was to go on to graduate school in musicology, but her first round of applications in the spring, before I'd really gotten to know her, hadn't panned out. Perhaps the B plus was a genuine sore spot. In my defense, I hadn't actually graded her other two papers, but it was likely that my first hard over-swift evaluation had spoiled the pot for her. Jen seemed to sense I sensed this and took pains to keep the B-plus jokes away from the higher-voltage lines of the grad-school question. When she did talk about the applications she talked about luck of the draw, hypercompetitiveness, a crapshoot. She said she hoped a year of real-world experience in the music industry might help her chances, and that she'd apply to more fallback schools next time. In the meantime there was "Bye Bye Blackbird," "Bewitched, Bothered, and Bewildered," "Mack the Knife," "I Dreamed a Dream," etc.

But back to the mint green cushion. Jen described roommates everywhere, seven roommates in a three-bedroom two-bathroom apartment, and sometimes it was eight roommates, effectively, when the couch-crashing friend of a friend had her boyfriend stay over, the two of them sleeping head to toe on the green living room couch. Jen was the girl's name—she'd forgotten the boyfriend's. The other roommates started referring to her as "bad Jen." Pretty soon she'd taken over a corner of the living room; her toiletries stood brazenly on the crowded bathroom sink alongside those of paying roommates.

"And nobody really knew this girl all that well," Jen said. "I think she'd been in a sorority with one of the roommates, but it was more like a favor you didn't know how to refuse. Bad Jen and her boyfriend were there more and more, and their stuff was there, little piles of clothes and whatnot surrounding the couch and in the corners of the room. Every day looked like moving day. It was getting out of hand. Six girls, two bathrooms, and now we didn't even have a common space we could use? The squatter was amazing if you think about it, her shamelessness—I was sort of in awe of her. How could she just keep smiling at us like that? Hi, how are you, how was your day? If she had a job, we didn't know about it. If her boyfriend had a job, we didn't know about it. The boyfriend's stubble started speckling the sink—you could see where he'd tried to wipe the hairs away with his hand, in a pass or two. It wasn't enough. It was getting totally out of hand. But we couldn't rat her out to the landlord. It wasn't any nobility on our part, we just didn't want to implicate ourselves in hosting a squatter for most of the semester. One day we came home and Jen or her boyfriend had hung a sheet from the ceiling with thumbtacks—it divided off the sofa, it claimed half the room. When we confronted her about it she started crying and said she was just trying to create a little privacy for herself. She said she'd just broken up with her boyfriend and was looking for work but it was impossible in the city, unless you wanted to work crap restaurant jobs, and even then. She promised us she'd leave soon and said she was really grateful for all our help. We were all really good people . . .

"Fast-forward a week. She's still there. The sheet's still up. We haven't actually seen the boyfriend, but the little black hairs are still showing up on the sides of the bathroom sink. We could have had the locks changed, but how to explain that to the landlord? We could have just owned up to the landlord, but we weren't that brave. What we ended up being was in-credibly passive-aggressive. If bad Jen got in the shower, one of us would take down the sheet, another would stuff her clothes into shopping bags. The next day the sheet would be up again, the bags unpacked. We'd try again. All of us were involved by the end, even bad Jen's former sorority sister. She'd get in the shower or leave the apartment for some reason and she'd come back and all her stuff would be packed and ready to go. She must have been getting the hint, she'd stopped smiling at us and saying hello and how was your day, but she still found a way to stay there. It was incredible. Finally she left the apartment one evening and we moved the green couch out of the living room and locked it in one of the bedrooms. We were so paranoid and frightened—I think we were scared of her by now—that we distributed the cushions throughout our different closets, like a mob kill. And that did the trick. Her stuff was gone in the morning. We kept expecting her to come back, but she never did. We ended up getting rid of the green couch, but I kept the cushion in my closet for the rest of the time I lived there, like a weird souvenir. It turns out it's a very comfortable concert perch."

"This very cushion?" I said.

"That very cushion. Unspeakable things were probably done on it."

"It does feel a little stiff in places—call it 'character'?"

Jen guffawed, hid her face behind a curtain of wavy auburn hair. If she washed it and left it to air-dry, it kinked and waved like lasagna noodles. From behind this wavy curtain she said, "Oh Lord. I did wash the cover, but maybe not well enough."

"I'd like to do some character-building exercises with you—bad Jen."

She unparted the hair and smiled a wondrous smile— blessings on those fuchsia lips, those straight white teeth, the cheekbones with their copper freckles. "If anyone ever heard us talking like this, you know I'd die, right?"

"I'd be mildly embarrassed myself, but I think I'd survive it."

"Well, just so we're clear—Naughty Professor," said Jen, and she tugged me back to the couch by the band of my boxer shorts.

In my defense, Jen had turned twenty-three that summer— only five years separated us now, and we'd never once touched during the semester. When people asked us how we'd met, we said "in school," vaguely. I said I was just starting into a PhD program, which was of course the biggest lie of all, and Jen said she was working a little before grad school. The story worked just fine, for what that's worth. Maybe little. Would it help to add that we didn't really think about it much—our accidents of meeting were mostly a joke now, a bit of goofy role-play, fore-play. Anyway, it's not really my purpose here to try to defend myself.

This was the summer of Soline.

One of the brag points of wonky business journalists in those days was that only wonky journalists, and the fraudulent insiders themselves, stood a chance of understanding what was then coming to light about the multibillion-dollar energy company. Nonsense. Read Marx in *The German Ideology*, read Luxemburg, Gramsci, Jameson, or just open your eyes—it's already there in front of you. It was there in 2008. It was there with Enron, of course. (From an article in *Forbes*: "If Enron, operating in a deregulated market, was calculus, Soline and its many-fronted micro-frauds was a kind of *multivariable* calculus.") It was there in the history article I read in my senior year of high school, when I was far from a math whiz, but I didn't need to be, did I? The article described the British land enclosures that yanked the common fields out from under the peasant farmers, the first wave of proto-capitalist consolidation, with wave on wave coming in behind it, a new ocean, a new reality. Rather miraculously, I've rediscovered this article in a social-studies reader in the library here, among the primers and tech manuals, the expurgated novels, old water-warped copies of *Scientific American*, the donated refuse of a hundred other collections arranged sparsely on the blue metal shelves. In the article is an old protest poem from the days of King Henry VIII, a piece of light verse that once wrought heavily on me:

> *The law locks up the man or the woman*
> *Who steals the goose from off the common,*
> *But leaves the greater villain loose*
> *Who steals the common from off the goose.*

Five hundred years later, and what's really changed? The instruments of oppression may have digitized, they may blink and scroll and refresh to the millisecond now, but they're still the same shrilling vacuum hoses that suck from the many and give to the few, and more often under the law's protection than its suspicion. Soline was remarkable in how cleverly it stole, how completely it ended up erasing the livelihoods, the retirements of its workers—but in this it was only an outlier, a sinner in degree, a good citizen in kind. This was capitalism being capitalism. Let the notebook-dumping journalists self-flatter about the arcana of deception, let the Wall Street experts talk a technocratic blue streak about "depreciation timelines," line costs, loans as revenue, "mark-to-market" valuations—it was still some asshole who set the detonator, another asshole who okayed it, and the assholes had a choice. That's the point. That's the *real* point. It's what the Group was saying all along, I think, or trying to: There's a choice. It isn't always easy, or easy to spot: Predatory capitalism has never been more invisible, more inevitable-seeming, more adept at impersonating nature. And how can you fight against cyclical "Nature"? How can you fight a degenerative disease that passes itself off as a mere tremor, an "instability in the market," or worse, a kind of weather system, a system no human hand can control since no hand set it in motion to begin with? The unmoved mover, or some such bullshit.

Sam Westergard had his ideas. He was new and he was brash and when he raised his long lanky arms to serve that summer, he looked like a Moses, a Prospero summoning new powers from the air. He was beating me easily now. Somehow, somewhere he'd turned a corner in his play and I was struggling just to keep things competitive. Sometimes I brought Jen along and we all played a lighter brand of tennis, two-on-one, more relaxed. Other times I took my beating—three–six, four–six if I was lucky—and then Sam and I sat in the beech tree shade, stretching down, rehydrating, planning the revolution.

"We occupy the White House lawn," Sam said. "Or we bring the Hoovervilles back. We find some way to disrupt the Soline trial."

"That's theater," I said. "And insane."

"Or we occupy fucking Larry *Bosch's* front lawn. 'Here's where Soline's criminal CEO lives'—have you seen that palace of his up in Westchester?—'here's Bosch's castle, and meanwhile thousands of his subsidiary workers are scrounging to make rent.'"

"You're going to put that on a sign—'subsidiary workers'? You're going to sloganeer that while you're being dragged away for trespassing? It's just theater, Sam. It's impractical."

"Well, at least it's something. And theater can be useful, can't it? Anyway I thought we were just blue-skying here."

"'Blue-skying'? Dear God, you sound like one of them."

"A joke, comrade, a joke! Give me a little credit. Besides, didn't Mao or somebody say something about knowing your enemy?"

"I'm sure he did."

Sam looked at me with a peaked high face, waiting.

"If you're going to do theater," I said, "you do it small, pointed, with a name and a face and a street address you can access without the National Guard showing up."

"I'm on bated breath," Sam said.

"You're on snark is what you're on. I should have never given you that Eagleton to read."

"But I'm so glad you did! He's actually funny! What's wrong with a bit of levity, huh?"

"Nothing," I said. "But will this levity of yours hold up in one-hundred-fifteen-degree heat?"

The question did the work I wanted it to—Sam blinking, quirking his head a little, a little smile of genuine curiosity on his thin, fleshless lips. He had never even attended an ISO meeting, had wrung his recent "conversion" (his word, not mine) out of a handful of books and pamphlets, ten at most, had a tendency to confuse basic concepts (base and superstructure, say), but he was genuine, I felt, articulate, and a good tennis partner. I felt confident I could get him in on some actual action: a woman named Maria Nava and her two children in a little foreclosed bungalow just off Baseline Drive in Phoenix, Arizona—this was the face, this was the address. We had heard through Alex about Maria losing her job and her benefits and her twenty-year retirement with Alta Gas after that company went down with the great pirate ship of Soline, which had acquired it in the last months of its plunder. Of course I'd read about the "preferred-stock retirement plans" that the employees, new and old, had felt pressured into taking, and how the company froze its workers out of those accounts once the stock began to plummet—these were some of the machinations the journalists most reveled in. Yet the particular details didn't interest me much, if I'm honest. I knew a rabbit hole when I saw one, and I refused on principle to be shocked by Soline's last-ditch tactics, as if there was anything novel in the executive class chucking its workers overboard. The fact was that Maria Nava was behind on her mortgage, the bank was making good on its shameless threats, and Soline was in clean, cool deposition rooms, lawyered to the hilt. If a settlement ever did come down, if it exceeded the legal fees, if it fought its way free of escrow and appeals court, if the burgeoning welter of other *ifs* fell eventually just into place—well, but Maria couldn't wait for that.

"I'm in," Sam said.

"You're in? Don't you want to hear the details first, the money piece?"

"Sure," he said, "but I'm in."

"Have you ever been to Phoenix before?"

"Oddly, no. But I know the desert. I was born there. It's in my Mormon blood."

"Weren't you supposed to be born a tepid Protestant, or a good agnostic, with a last name like yours?"

"One of the many wrong turns we Westergards have taken."

"Ah," I said.

I'd never been to Phoenix either.

From the airplane the city looked more like a scorched cave floor than a city, sere browns and darker browns, beige buildings like stalagmites rising from the flat gridded spread of the valley where it gathered at the downtown. A few sputters of green resolved into trees as we sank back to earth, but mostly the city looked dry, and brown, and hot. Put a chunk of the world in a waffle iron, Phoenix comes out. You understand my bias. A child of the East Coast, I conflate beauty with greenery—I reduce it to that. This was Sam's message to me on the car ride from the airport, with Alex driving. From the backseat he lectured loudly over the loud blowing air conditioner. He said I was making the classic, myopic mistake of enshrining fragile life, green life, as the lodestar of the aesthetic. But what about stubborn life, resilient life, brown and hard and drought-resistant life? Did beauty have to be so exclusive? Above the scrim of tract homes and power lines green scrub poked out of the mountainside like weird eyes, saguaro cacti sliding past with their strange stubby arms outstretched, half outstretched, in greeting. Sandstone scree lay all about, dully blushing, scored, sharing the sloping foothills with the cacti and scrub until the mountain broke vertically, shot up into shelves of dark rocky crag. Those canyon lines were what hemmed us in, what rose above us, our tallest buildings—the utter dominance of nature.

"This really turns you on, doesn't it?" I said to Sam. "This is sexual for you."

For a moment the foreground houses and chain stores abated as an open unfenced lot, a tract of land, really, flashed a closer sea of scrub brush, the sharp dry blooms blurring past like a cloud of anemone, wavering strange life. It was the desert reclaiming its own, or maybe the developers were just biding their time.

"I'm saying I can appreciate the landscape," Sam said. "You just look up a little and it's there."

"Eli tells me you're a poet?" Alex said.

"Not really," Sam said. "I write poems sometimes, I've landed in an MFA for poetry, but I don't really think of myself as a poet."

"Sam and I are on the run from our chosen selves," I said. "It's really quite something."

Whatever that was supposed to mean. If it was bait, Alex didn't take it. She was smiling the smile of a Mona Lisa, cryptic, distracted, beautiful. I'd forgotten how beautiful she could be in her tossed-off, anti-beautiful way: the tomboyish hair that she cut herself, the dark straight bangs that boxed in her round olive face, the large eyes, the strong and aquiline nose, a little ebony stud at the line where the nostril began to rise. Ancient people survived in her face, some of the Aztec blood this country and others had worked so hard to wipe out. Alex's family lived in a town outside Tucson. Her mother had been a small, dark, elegant, slightly jet-lagged woman in teal jewelry when she'd come to visit Alex in New York the previous year, calling her Alejandra, taking me in with a standing, wary smile over the croque monsieurs and mimosas that we ate and drank amid the rowdy Sunday brunch crowd—my foolish suggestion. I thought we might have been riding in an Esposito car now, a Honda, simple, responsible.

"There's nothing wrong with being a poet, is there?" Alex said.

"No, there's not," Sam said.

"You could help us liaise with the media," she said. "Or maybe write press releases, who knows? I'm thinking we should go mainstream with this. Maria is the sweetest woman and she has the most beautiful, photogenic children—I actually thought this—and her neighbors love her. Some of them joined us in the occupying yesterday. Some others brought over a vat of carnitas last night. No one's not on our side this time, no one that matters. We should milk this."

The chain stores and white glowing strip malls had dropped away, the empty scrub lots multiplying. The tract developments with their trailing stucco walls and names like The Sunset, Shangri-La, The Desert Rose—these were soon replaced by the blinding ranches, the chain-link fences, the dead, crisped, yellow-brown lawns. We turned off Baseline Drive onto a smaller street, skirting the dirt field where a lone shirtless bedouin of a teen passed a soccer ball between his knees. In the car you could feel the sun pushing through the windows, compressing the air-conditioned air. You could feel the heat cradling the car. When we pulled up to Maria's house and cut the engine, the heat rose around us like a flood. A pair of green tents had been set up in the front yard and quickly abandoned: They looked like weird shrubbery at either side of a red faded door that hid against the ranch's rosy stucco. A small garage, too, connecting to the house's main façade with its picture window, blinds drawn, the gray bleached segmented walkway curving up to the front door, the sparse hanks of stubborn crabgrass betraying the outlines of the individual concrete slabs. Red Spanish tile covered the roof, reddish gravel lay in the small garden planted with ground-hugging fierce shrubs I couldn't begin to name. Poster-board signs and pickets surrounded the tents, studded the entire lawn. A handmade banner stretched most of the way across the low chain-link fence: SOLINE IS ON TRIAL, NOT THIS FAMILY! Another sign shouted for Soline CEO Larry Bosch to pay Maria Nava's mortgage: LET BOSCH PAY BACK WHAT HE STOLE! PEOPLE OVER PROFITS! another sign said. HUMAN NEED NOT CORPORATE GREED! RIGHT IS RIGHT— COME TO THE LEFT! And several others.

"We need to clean this up," I said, "make the signs more pointed, less generic. This looks like an undergrad protest."

"And you sound like a grad student," Alex said. "We'll see what we can do, but check your hypercritical mode at the door, okay? This isn't academia, thank God. I hear you're dating jail-bait, by the way."

Alex with her brown shining eyes watched my reaction and laughed deliciously, the car struck like a bell. "Yeah, we've got some catching up to do. Are we ready? Leave the bags in the trunk, we'll get them after dark. The last thing you want to do is touch metal here in the middle of the day."

Inside the small house a group of twentysomethings, a few thirtysomethings, sat around the wall-unit air conditioner in the back of the living room, five to a couch, four to a love seat, a few hangers-on hanging off the armrests, smoking, talking in lazy, heat-subdued voices. On the couch I recognized several of my comrades from the New York ISO. We all exchanged greetings, hugs. I introduced Sam around. Out of the kitchen stepped Tiffany carrying a glass of water in either hand. She was unchanged from the grading sessions we'd had together with Hahn. I was surprised to see her, and surprised how happy I was to see her. I hadn't known her to be more than rarely involved in ISO activities. How had she heard about this one?

"From Hahn, actually," Tiffany said. "And I've been following the Soline news, getting infuriated. And then from Ms. Persuasive here, who finally made me—"

Tiffany stopped short, taking in Alex, who'd lifted her finger in Plato-pontifical mode—but now we saw she was actually asking for silence. A car idled outside, and it wasn't Maria's, apparently. Alex tilted her finger floorward to where blue and red light now skittered on the warm tile floor, just managing to penetrate the blinds. Then we heard the quick telltale *whoop-whoop* of a police siren. In an instant our quorum broke and reassembled in the front yard, ranging down the curving walk, standing guard in front of occupying tents, beside protest signs—a number of people from ASU's progressive group, apparently, and Tiffany, Andrew, Dawn, Nate, Adam, Sarah, Ali, all from the New York ISO, and Sam, of course, a few others whose names I've forgotten, but a decent-size group, fifteen of us in all. We all shielded our faces against the sun, blinking and blinking in the sudden ferocious glare. Alex made her way to the front of the staggered group, leading Maria by the arm, or anyway leading a small compact woman I assumed was Maria— Sam and I hadn't been formally introduced to her yet. I moved to within a few feet of Alex, feeling Sam's clammy hand at my elbow.

"What's up?" he whispered.

The police cruiser cut its lights, its engine.

"Not sure."

"What happens now? Should we do something?"

"Just sit tight," I said.

The first officer, a Hispanic woman not much bigger than Maria, stood behind an open passenger-side door. Her arms were held out slightly like a weight lifter's, to make room for the belt riding high on her waist and studded with weapons like dark strange barnacles. When her partner finally unfolded himself from the driver's seat, he rose high above the white wide car roof, a giant of a man. You expected this man to open his mouth and speak with the voice of Elohim. Instead, he approached the low chain-link fence with his partner—it came to her chest, his waist—and kept silent.

"*¿Toda está bien, señora?*" the first officer said, addressing Maria. "*¿Es usted la dueña de esta casa?*"

"*Soy, sí,*" Maria said slowly, a little coldly. "I am still the owner of this house, yes. Everything is fine."

The first officer introduced herself and her partner in English, names I instantly forgot—Officer So-and-so, and "up there" Officer So-and-so. No one laughed at the attempted ice-breaker.

"Are these friends of yours?" the officer asked Maria, gesturing.

"Yes," Maria said.

The other officer's radio sputtered and squeaked in its epaulette pouch; he seemed to startle a little. He leaked a few formalities out of the side of his mouth. His tall dome of a head, bald, stinging white, shone like porcelain except at the sides where the faintest shadow of hair still appeared. He wore mirrored sports glasses, like his partner, gray cargo shorts, a dopey blue polo shirt that hung oversize off him, Sam-like, with the Phoenix Police Department's shield at its breast.

"They've got your tailor, apparently," I muttered back to Sam. "You sure you're not consulting?"

"Huh?"

"What was that?" the giant officer said, lifting his voice across the yard. "Huh?"

Not a giant's voice, it turned out, but a pretty average basso. In brusquer tones the officer repeated his question.

"Just having a conversation with my friend," I said. "I assume that's allowed?"

Alex turned to me and said quietly, "Shut up."

"Why does your cop cruiser just say 'Police'?" put in Adam Carr from deeper in the yard. "Shouldn't it say 'Phoenix Police Department'? PPD? You could spell it out phonetically."

Alex turned around and told him to shut up too—Adam smirking, unaccountable in his white-boy dreadlocks, a Bob Marley from Boulder, Colorado. We'd never gotten along.

"Wow, that's hilarious," the female officer said.

"Very original," her partner said. He pushed his sunglasses up onto his head and took in Maria with his pinkish small eyes, strangely small for the size of the face—acres of cheeks, vast tracts of forehead and skull.

"Ma'am, are you aware that it's against city ordinance to keep standing camping equipment in your front yard?"

"Sir, are you aware that that sounds like bullshit you just made up on the spot?"

Adam again, ignoring Alex's stare.

The officer kept his eyes on Maria. I couldn't see her face, only that she held it very still. From behind me I heard stiff crunching steps.

"Hey!" the female officer shouted. "Hand out of your pocket!"

It was one of the ASU kids—Jason, I later learned—young-looking in his upswept hair, his construction-cone-orange shorts. He lifted a smartphone slowly. "Phone," he said, "only a phone. I was just wondering if you had that ordinance number? So I could look it up?"

"You think we're lying?" the officer said.

"No, no, not at all, not at all. I just want to look it up."

"'Trust but verify,'" Adam said. "That's your boy Reagan."

Maria said, "Please," turning her straining eyes on us.

"That's okay, ma'am," the tall officer said. "We deal with morons for a living."

"If we move the tents to the backyard," Maria said, "would that be okay?"

"We're not here to write you up, ma'am. We just wanted you to be aware."

"We wanted to make sure you're all right," said the other officer. Then she added, quickly and lowly, "*Si tus amigos le dan cualquier problema, avísanos, bien?*"

I'd caught the gist of the sentence, particularly the dubious emphasis laid on *amigos*. I'm sure Alex had too, a real Spanish speaker. Her back was long and motionless in front of me, rather narrow in a pale green tank top, a faint band of sweat, darker green, tracking the length of her spine. The spine straightened in surprise as Maria reached her arm around her, awkwardly, a stiff unpracticed gesture that told in Maria's body language too.

"They're not causing any trouble," Maria said. "They're my friends. They're helping me."

"We understand that," the officer said, "but if that changes . . ."

"Your concern is touching," Adam said.

"They're trying to take her house away from her," Sam said. His voice was reedy, painfully earnest after Adam's.

"Sam!" Alex said, spinning around, throwing her arms out incredulously. "Adam! Everyone! Since when do we talk to fucking cops? Huh? You think these people are your debating partners? They're cops! They're instruments of the state! So let's save our fucking breath, and a little of our dignity, okay?"

Alex faced forward again, the cops stiffening. We'd all stiffened, I think, and Maria especially. It felt like whole minutes before the giant officer softened, scoffing a little, shaking his large high hairless head back and forth, back and forth.

"I take it you're the Occupy leftovers?" he said. "You poor little hipster shits—you guys are all forty years late to the party." He tapped his partner on the shoulder and started backing toward the cruiser. "Real nice friends you've got there, ma'am. Real classy. If they wear out their welcome, you let us know, all right? We'll check in again."

When the cruiser pulled away from the curb, it cleared its throat of a pent-up siren and a burst of blue light, picking up speed as it turned onto Baseline. Maria turned and I saw that her olive face was flushed, glowing with feeling. I don't imagine I was the only one to read second thoughts into those round sweating features, rosy at the cheeks and tip of the nose, the large eyes sharp with adrenaline—or was it anger? Some of us had gathered around Maria, semicircling her. She raised her voice for all of us to hear.

"Please move the tents," she said. "Thank you. There should be room in the backyard. Please do it now."

Alex was herself again, reasoning with Maria in soft, persistent tones. We didn't know if the ordinance was real, first of all, and even if it was, it didn't matter—what were their rules of etiquette really worth if they couldn't protect her, or the town, from the likes of Soline? If they *wouldn't* protect her. It was a power play, Alex said, and we couldn't give in to it. That and the fact that moving the tents to the backyard, slinking out of sight, defeated the purpose, the publicity of the protest—

"Please do what I ask," said Maria, speaking to Alex but also past her. An impressive finality was in her voice. She put her head down and started for the front door, our loose semicircle drifting open like a buoy line, reluctantly, to let her pass.

• • •

That night I called Jen from the close cocoon warmth of the tent I shared with Sam. The heat hadn't broken, exactly, but it had slumped off a bit, lazing away as the long twilight lazed above the distant mountains beyond mountains you could just manage to see from Maria's backyard. The aerial effect, Sam had called it, a photography term he'd picked up from his sister, apparently—that blue on fading blue, that purple on fainter, ghostlier purple. I hadn't even known Sam *had* a sister, and here we were sharing a tent on the edge of the desert. Sam was gone now, giving me my privacy. The last light of the day had gone with him, and the inside of the tent shone eerily from the lantern hung from a hook off the central arcing pole. The light made the roof look particularly striking, green-white, milky, like an inverted firmament with the small buzzing insects on the other side of the canvas for negative stars, little odd-shaped holes to let the darkness in.

"Eerie?" Jen said. "Eerie how?"

"Like ectoplasm eerie—I don't know. This weird green artificial light and the ceiling writhing just a few feet above you. I've never really liked camping, have I told you that?"

"Even with all your Audubon guides?"

"Trees are different. You can study trees from a porch if you want to, through binoculars."

"But surely tent sex is some of the best sex there is."

"Oh, well . . ."

"Are you alone?"

"Not enough."

"Is that why you're whispering?"

Through the green milky canvas I could see the dark outlines of other tents, people in camping chairs, people sitting on blankets. I could hear the steady susurrus of quiet conversation. We were all trying to be polite, well behaved, and maybe we were a little bit cowed too. Unusually for us, there was no weed, minimal drinking—we were conscious of the noise. We didn't want to upset Maria or give the cops the slightest pretext. A wavering world-beat melody wafted up through the campsite from a portable speaker, and of course there were the obligatory boxy chords from a nearby steel string. Nature sounds too: crickets like high violins, a pair of strange keening night birds for woodwinds. For a moment I thought I heard Alex's voice, mellow and confident at the same time, holding forth about something or other, but then the voice changed, modulating higher and thinner.

"You still there?" Jen said. "Sweetie?"

"I'm here. I wish you were, too."

"Does that mean your ex-girlfriend's ignoring you?"

"Har, har."

"How do you know I'm kidding?"

"You'd better be. It means I miss the hell out of you—bad Jen—in all senses. And it turns out I'm a little more alone than I thought."

"Alone and lonely, eh? Should I ask what you're wearing?"

I unbuttoned my jeans, adjusting myself. "A little less than I was a minute ago."

"Oh, really."

"You remember the thing I was telling you about earlier—the aerial effect?"

"I'd like to see *your* effect go aerial."

"Ha! You upstaged me!"

"Why? What were you going to say?"

"I was going to say I'd like to see your *areola* effect."

"Oh would you, Naughty Professor."

"What do you say we add some pictures to this exhibition?"

"*Les sexts?*"

I went first.

"Oh my," Jen said. "Ooh la la. Okay. I see your aerial effect and I raise you . . . just a second," she whispered.

The interval stretched and something in it possessed me to say, "We're like my parents, you know that?"

I wasn't sure Jen had heard me, if she was still by the phone, but then she said, bemused-sounding, "Paging Dr. Freud?"

"I just meant with all the wordplay."

"Wordplay as foreplay—swordplay?"

"I'll stipulate."

"Oh, I'm sure you will."

I laughed. "Do you know what I mean, though?"

"Sure. The son seeks the mother in the lover, in the partner. Was that Freud or was that someone else?"

"It sounds like pop psychology to me."

"And you're saying Freud *isn't* pop psychology?"

"Oh my God," I said. "Jesus."

"You like that?"

"Where did you get a cheerleader skirt?"

"Freshman year of high school. I was briefly a Cougarette. *Aimez-vous l'image, mon chéri?*"

"I'm on the precipice . . ."

"I thought you'd like that. Boys are a bit predictable, aren't they?"

"Permission to land?"

"Wait, wait for me . . ."

I was all the way out of my jeans now, boxer shorts down

around my ankles, going at myself lying back on my sleeping bag. Steps scraped in the burnt grass outside the tent door—I sat up like a cardiac victim, paddles at my chest.

"Eli?" It was a female voice. "Are you alone?"

"One second," I said. "Sorry, so sorry," I said, and I cut the call.

It was Alex, of course.

"Can I come in?" she said.

"Give me a second. Let me just put a shirt on."

"What's this standing on ceremony," she said, as the zippered front flap of the tent began to fall in.

"Alex, seriously!"

When I finally did open the flap from my side, Alex was smiling, wearing that old raffish face of hers. "I didn't interrupt anything, I hope?"

I made myself as comfortable as I could under the circumstances, leaning back on one elbow like a sultan, the other arm placed strategically. Alex sat lotus style, high and straight, boyish in body and manner, on the blue yoga mat I'd teased Sam for bringing along.

"Just doing a little reading," I said at length, matching Alex's smile.

She offered to come back in a minute if I needed one—not a surprising offer coming from her, but I blushed all the same. And here I'd been girding myself for the next round of wisecracks!

I'd forgotten. Alex knew about humor, she could speak that language, but the thing you had to learn about her—the thing you learned to marvel at, if you were like me—was that humor for her was incidental, a little frivolous, take it or leave it. It didn't grease the wheels of the world for her as it did for me, or for my parents: In the Lentz home ("*Lentz*, like the pre-Easter period, but in the plural," my father liked to say. "All the atonement we can get"), in our modest split-level set back from a leafy road, we encountered seriousness only where it was impossible not to encounter it: war, genocide, sickness, death and its grim accoutrements. And even then it was only death joined to specificity—in the abstract, Dad especially was capable of poking fun at mortality, disease. Speaking lightly of renal failure, say, or anthrax scares, he'd stop and announce, "You realize I'll never die of these now, right? Too ironic. Not even your mother's vengeful Catholic God would do that to me."

"*My* God? I think you need to brush up on your Pentateuch, pal. That grumpy mass murderer was your invention, was he not?"

And so on, Mom smiling, Dad smiling.

It was all of life, then, and most of death, love, metaphysics, all tethered to a punch line. It's not a bad way to grow up—don't get me wrong—but imagine Marx on the heels of that, imagine Engels, Trotsky, Luxemburg, all that volubility, all that high-stakes High Church seriousness! Imagine the very *idea* of a confrontational politics. Imagine Alex Esposito and her sharp black box of hair, the way it waved with each cut, slowly, like time-lapse photography, sometimes straight, sometimes slanting down her forehead like a guillotine—imagine me watching her and marveling at her brazenness, her bravery, her sheer *quiddity* as she pressed the *Socialist Worker* on students hurrying to class through Washington Square Park, her loud and unselfconscious sloganeering, the impassioned way she chaired the ISO meetings I'd started attending, I confess, much more regularly, religiously (yes, Sam, I'll say it) after I developed a crush on Alex in my second year at Randolph. A year later she and I had grown into each other's lives like twisting vine, imperceptible at first, then it was a fact, immutable. We had implicated ourselves in the other's affection. I learned everything from Alex, so much. What I called my Trotskyist street voice—that was me imitating Alex imitating Trotsky, I think, though who really knew. I knew I liked the words she chose, and the way she voiced them. Only rarely did they overflow into the kind of anger I'd heard that afternoon with the police officers. It was as if the light gathering sharply on the bald officer's head had blinded Alex to herself.

"Is everything all right?" I asked her. "Are you okay?"

"I think we're okay, yeah. We've got a good core group. We've got our firing group together. Now we just need to make good on it."

I let out a groaning breath, not entirely intentional.

"What?"

"That's from *The Urban Guerrilla's Handbook*, right? Our 'firing group'? We sound like rank phonies when we talk like that."

"Oh, don't be such an asshole," Alex said, yawning a little. "I didn't want to talk strategy anyway. You can be Holden Caulfield tomorrow."

She slid onto her elbows on the yoga mat until she'd stretched out opposite me, our heads at either side of what must have looked satyr-like in shadow, from outside the tent, this strange two-headed beast reclining silently in a green light.

"So what should we talk about?"

"Tell me a story," she said. "Tell me about this jailbait of yours. Or this Mini-Me of yours."

"You mean Sam? The Mini-Me who's six inches taller than I am and can kick my ass at tennis?"

"Eli and his tennis."

"Game of kings."

"I thought that was chess."

"Tennis originated in the French court hundreds of years ago, and who's more regal than the French?"

"You always were taken with that veneer of sophistication, weren't you? That's all the French are good for these days. That and turgid theoretical prose. Where did you find him? Sam, I mean. Is he serious?"

"You and your seriousness," I said.

I told Alex about Hahn and the Marxism seminar where I'd met Sam, Sam there on a lark, at first, an intellectual tourist, the type of thrill seeker Alex and I had seen flit in and out of ISO circles time and again. Was Sam serious? Who could say? I told Alex about the Occupy marches Sam had taken part in. She rolled her eyes. Well, and more to the point, he'd come along to Arizona, hadn't he? Alex asked how he'd paid for the trip, which seemed to me a violation of unspoken rules. When I didn't answer the question, she asked it again, and I told her about the money from my dissertation grant that I'd helped him out with—better spent that way, I figured, than on my fucking dissertation.

"So for all you know he could still be a tourist," Alex said.

"I don't think so."

"But you don't know."

"Of course I don't know. Who really knows anybody, or for that matter anything—"

Alex's hand went up and her eyes, suddenly heavy, sedated-looking, dropped like blinds. No, she said, she didn't mean epistemologically. She hadn't come here for a philosophy lecture.

Outside, one of the night birds kipped and the other, in *responsorium*, kipped back.

What came next? Besides the waiting, I mean—there was never any shortage of that. How long was it before Sam came to tell me about his run-in with Luís and Aida, Maria's children, before he enlisted me in his plan to circumvent the group's plan, the loose "strategy" Alex referred to? It might have been the third day we were there, or the fourth—where memory fails me I'll order by faith, which, as I understand it, means believing in your own cooked books.

Call it the fourth day. Faithful Sam came to me with the sweaty earnestness of a faith healer, a tent preacher. He'd been alone in the darkened hallway off Maria's kitchen, feeling for the bathroom door when he undershot it and opened onto Luís in his bedroom. The boy snapped around owl-like, the whites of his eyes like saucers. He looked much younger in that moment than his sixteen years. Sam gave me the scene in some detail, a good poet—Luís smooth and surprised, swiveled around, his upper body bent over a large brown packing box of neatly folded clothes. Other boxes stood open like mouths around the room. What was he doing? In his own surprise Sam asked the question out loud, as if the answer weren't obvious. All the walls were barren of the pictures and posters that had hung there for years: you could see the naked outlines, vulnerable-looking, on the off-white plaster, where the posters had shielded the sun and dust. To the left of the bed the closet door was open and a pile of old toys, a child's toys, cars and trucks and foam balls, green army men, spilled out.

"And what did Luís say to you?" I said.

"Nothing," Sam said. "I'd asked a stupid question. He was obviously in there packing up his life for some storage facility, and then what? How much does a three-bedroom apartment go for in Phoenix? Or a two-bedroom, a one-bedroom? Does part-time work at a Verizon store stretch even that far, and what if the house goes into deficiency? What's their day-to-day going to be like?"

"Deficiency?"

"It's when the amount you owe on the house is more than the bank manages to sell it for. You lose your house and gain a toxic load of debt in the process. That could definitely happen in this housing market. Tiffany was telling me about it. Did you know Tiffany has a law degree? Did you know she practiced for a while at some fancy New York firm? Anyway, she knows a little about foreclosure law. She and that new guy Jamaal, who was at ASU Law for a while, were comparing notes—a bit of résumé-trading too, hackles up. Mostly his hackles."

"So he dropped out?"

"Huh?"

"Jamaal. You said he was at ASU Law?"

"Too much debt for too few prospects, I guess. Apparently he failed to see the benefits of being institutionalized and un-derpaid and scared all the time. Not like you and me, eh, com-rade?"

"Well—"

"I wasn't done with the story," Sam said. "So I'm in there with Luís, right? I'm in the room when in walks Aida with a grocery bag of packing leftovers, some old trinkets and things.

She was going to add them to the donation pile unless Luís wanted anything. Then she noticed me in the room and went quiet and tight, like she'd just been called on in class. I could tell I was intruding on a sort of intimacy. Luís spread the bag's contents on the floor and started picking through them. It was the kind of stuff you just collect over the years—a snow globe, a little checkers set, that sort of thing. He held up this weathered stuffed giraffe with a long spotted neck and long painted lashes around the eyes, and I could tell it meant something to her, just from the way he held it, like he was asking a question with it. Aida's eyes darted over to me as if to explain why she didn't want to talk about it. Luís said she should keep it—they were keeping it—and Aida just said okay and sort of stood there in the room like she didn't know how to leave. I got down on my knees and helped Luís put his sister's things back in the grocery bag. I handed it to her and I said—I said this to both of them—"

"I think I see where this is going," I said.

"I said that they should both keep all their things. We were going to find a way to help them keep their house. That's why we'd come here."

"Okay."

"I promised them, Eli."

"Okay, look. You're new to this, you're enthusiastic—that's good. I'm just not sure a sentimental attachment is always the most effective means to—"

"What are we doing here, anyway?" Sam said. "We're just sitting on our asses. What 'means' are we employing?"

"Alex and I were making calls just today—the local media needs its 'color stories,' don't they? The pressure's building on the bank, Sam, you know it is—"

Sam waved this away impatiently. "I need you to do something for me," he said.

"Or otherwise we wait for the confrontation on the day of foreclosure—we get the media there for that—"

"Eli," Sam said. "I need you to do something for me. Will you do something for me?"

He called it "knocking doors"—the phrase courtesy of the Mormon missionary work he'd tried for a few months before ditching the work and the church altogether. We'd always just called it "canvassing," but now a religious shadow, a "mission," a sense of conspiracy hung over the day's efforts. At one point Alex knocked on a door, and a white woman in a yellow bandanna, late sixties perhaps, opened and squinted at us—whether from the sun or suspicion we couldn't tell. (I pull this door from a memory trove of dozens, whole hours of them.) The woman, Jan, listened to what we had to say with smiling attention, nodding at appropriate intervals, her expression going sad and chagrined at all the right moments. When she opened her mouth it was a formal, Nordic accent that edged her words. She ran the flat of her palm up and over the bandanna, as if pressing her brain for excuses.

"I think it's terrible what's happening," she said. "I just don't know what I can do to help."

"Ideally you would come and join us in solidarity with Maria," Alex said. "If not full-time, at least on Monday when the bank wants to evict Maria and her children so it can sell the house without her permission. Several of your neighbors have already committed to be with us that morning. We think the presence of community members will send an important message."

"Oh, well . . ." Jan said, and smoothed back the yellow bandanna. "I'd like to be there, but I work in the mornings."

"The eviction notice is for seven a.m.," Alex said. "Many of your neighbors are planning to come before work. Will you commit to that as well?"

"It's just that I run a half-day childcare group and it begins at seven thirty. Parents sometimes drop the kids off early. I'd like to be there. I'll try to be there . . ."

She was averting her eyes now. It was just the two of us, Alex and I, but I supposed we were intimidating enough. I reminded Jan about the name and number of the local congressman we'd listed in the flyer and also the name and number of the home-loans manager at Bank of America. I said we hoped she'd put in a call to them, at the very least, and express her support for Maria. If enough pressure mounted on these people, who knew what could happen.

"Of course. Yes, thank you, I'll do that. I hope everything goes well for her," Jan said, and with a curt quick smile she shut the door.

Out on the sidewalk Alex said, "I wish you'd stop letting them off the hook like that."

"She was never on the hook."

"You don't know that."

"I thought we weren't going to argue epistemology," I said, putting a joshing arm around Alex's shoulder. We bumped along for a few paces like that, our hips knocking together, my palm clammy—I only now realized how clammy—against the warm bare skin of Alex's upper arm.

Alex wrapped her other arm around my waist and said, "You're petit bourgeois, you know that?"

"There are worse things."

"Are there?"

She pulled away and doubled back to the little inlet of another chain-link gate leading onto another cement walkway—an entire street of these, an entire neighborhood of slight variations on this theme. How much longer could this go on? How much longer did it *need* to go on? I checked my cell phone but couldn't quite make out the numbers in the powerful glare. It was pervasive, this glare, palpable, another element. I squinted into it at Alex—a gray tank top today, the same khaki shorts, her legs long and thin coming out of them, dull brown. Today she wore a faded blue Mets cap that cast a brim of darker blue shadow onto her forehead, her sunglasses hung at the bottom edge of it. I couldn't see her eyebrows, but I gathered they were raised.

"We've been doing this for an awfully long time," I said.

"It was your idea, wasn't it?" she said.

"We're going to die of heatstroke."

"Your idea."

By the end of the afternoon we'd collected a few more commitments, none of them firm enough to anchor much hope to, and none of them to occupy with us full-time. It was just as well. The clutter in Maria's backyard had grown by the hour, an almost bacterial expansion, until the half-used ketchup bottles, empty water bottles, rocking beer cans, plastic-bag tumbleweed coated the grass and all the hot-to-touch tarps and towels too, and we decided to create a committee that dealt only with cleanup, and I was its chair.

Alex took a shower when we got back to Maria's, then came

into the backyard to help me and Adam and a few of the ASU crew collect the latest trash, three large Hefty bags full of it. Adam was becoming a little less unbearable—perhaps. In any case he'd joined me in grumbling about the more or less permanent loitering group around the AC in Maria's living room, the group that made the bulk of the overloud, over-messy camp in the backyard at night, then transferred its spirit and sprawl in the daytime to the indoor couches. I'd joined them there a time or two, but compared to them I was Alex-like, Herculean in my commitment.

"Where's Sam?" Alex asked once we'd come in from the backyard. "Where's Tiffany?"

I answered honestly that I didn't know.

Nate from ISO, one of the biggest disappointments of the occupation, a couch occupier, sat watching a video on the laptop that perched on the couch's arm. Dawn, Ali, a few others crowded in beside him, scrolling silently through their phones. Nate didn't look up as he said, "Sam and Tiffany? They left a while back. That Jamaal guy too. They took his car."

"Did they say where they were going?" Alex asked.

Nate shook his head.

"What the hell are you watching, anyway?"

The video showed a younger Larry Bosch in medium close-up, warm lighting, a generic fireplace backdrop—it looked like a *20/20* interview. Fuller featured, less severe than I was used to seeing him in the glare of recent events—the thin bellow-like folds down his neck that you noticed in current photographs were the ghosts of former jowls, apparently. Here Bosch looked comfortable, a well-fed man. His wife, in a collared red blouse, sat a little stiffly beside him, smiling.

"What is this?" Alex said again.

"I don't know," Nate said. "Call it research."

"It sounds like a puff piece to me. The poor rich people."

Bosch was running with a question about his first company's bankruptcy—his sense of helplessness and failure, his responsibility to the investors, to the employees, the sleepless nights, the personal money he'd tried to plug up the leaks with.

"We had to move into my parents' house," Bosch's wife said. Nancy. "Larry was out of work for almost two years. Our kids were in middle school. We were terrified." Midwestern features, a wide high forehead, the pale yellowish skin communicated something honestly strained about these memories.

Bosch rested a chubby hand on his wife's arm, laughed uncomfortably. "That was a very difficult time for us."

"Jesus," Alex said. "Click out of this, will you?"

"What?" Nate said. "I was curious."

"He recovered quite nicely, didn't he, Mr. Rags to Riches? Just remember that this is the same guy who froze Maria out of her retirement account. He cares so much about his employees that he speculates and defrauds them out of a company—not for the first time, it sounds like."

"I hadn't forgotten, thanks."

"No?"

A stalemating silence developed between them, Nate holding Alex's eyes as she stood above him.

Finally Alex said, "Did Sam and Tiffany say when they were coming back? Or Jamaal?"

Nate leaned over the couch side to check his cell phone, mumbling something.

"What?" Alex said. "Nate?"

"No," he said, straightening again. "That was a no."

• • •

It was almost dark by the time they did get back, Sam and Tiffany and Jamaal clod-stepping and swaying into the backyard, where we'd set up an after-meal drink and chat with Maria. Her round face was pleasantly flushed by now. She wore black pants and a red Verizon polo shirt with a little golden name tag pinned above the logo. The sun had dropped below the scrim of dark scrubby mountains behind the house, behind the city, and for once it had taken the heat with it—a watery convocation of pinks and oranges spread out in the lower atmosphere, the desert sky going down medium, medium rare. We were enjoying ourselves, sitting in a circle of camping chairs among the greasy cheese-strewn taco boxes that Maria had brought home for us. When we'd protested she'd said, "I can't eat them all myself, can I?" Her children sat on either side of her, Luís slumped and thin in red soccer shorts, his chin resting on his sternum like a pensioner's, regarding the phone he thumbed expertly at his lap, Aida more compact, hunched over her phone, an armadillo curl to her small back.

When Sam saw us with the Bud Lights he raised an invisible can and called out, "Excellent idea!"

He was the softest on his feet of the three of them, more boneless than usual in a ratty blue polo, each step undulating up his long body like a wave, up his narrow chest and shoulders and his thin putty neck, chin weak, mouth parted—Little Lockjaw no more. Tiffany wore her inebriation better, quieter, true to form, a subtle slackness in her wide olive face, a subtle glossiness in her eyes. Only Jamaal, already relaxed in a bright pink T-shirt—the loose physique, too, the loose dandelion Afro—only Jamaal looked all the way normal.

"You must be the designated driver," Maria said, walking a beer over to him. "Here, take my seat. I was just heading inside."

We all protested this announcement, but Maria said, "Another early shift tomorrow," singsonging the words, falsely cheery. "No, I shouldn't complain. It's what I wanted. It's what we need."

"You can always complain," said Adam. "It's an inalienable right."

"How set in stone is your work schedule?" Sam asked Maria. "If you needed to cancel a shift, or maybe come in late . . ."

"They like you to give twenty-four hours' notice. Why?"

"But if you got sick," Sam said. "You don't need to give a day's notice if you're sick, right?"

"No, I don't think so. Why?"

"No reason in particular."

Maria hesitated, waiting for Sam to continue. When he didn't, she turned to us and put on an easy enough smile. "Thank you for the work you all did today. Thank you again. God bless you. Good night."

Maria's children followed wordlessly after her into the small stucco ranch house. A soft yellow light stood in the sliding glass door, glowing yellower by the minute against the darkness.

"You guys were out drinking?" Alex said to Sam and Tiffany and Jamaal as they settled into the vacated camping chairs.

"Any leftover tacos by chance?" Sam said.

"No. You were at a bar, is that where you were?"

"We went to celebrate. Sort of."

"Celebrate what, sort of?"

Jamaal and Tiffany looked to Sam as if by prearrangement.

He tipped his long white face back in a long swill of Bud Light. A few lanterns had been brought out and set in the middle of the circle to fend off the darkness, and the sharp thin glow of them cast Sam's Adam's apple in stark relief. *Of Man's first disobedience and the fruit of that forbidden tree* . . . What was he stalling for? I honestly didn't know. My only job had been to keep Alex away from the house for a few hours—beyond that Sam had been vague. He was thinking of trying something, he'd said, but it was too provisional to mention, a shot in the dark.

Adam, in the un-Edenic dreadlocks, laid his hand on Sam's forearm when he lowered the can. "What's up?" he said. "Where did you guys go?"

"Okay, people," Sam said. "Open minds." He turned to Tiffany. "You've got all the jargon down. You tell it."

"It's not that jargony," Tiffany said, "and Jamaal should get a lot of the credit too. It was one of his former law professors who gave us the name of a friend, a legal arbiter at the courthouse downtown. The connection was what got us in the door without an appointment, but it was Sam's stubbornness—his asshole-ishness?"

Sam shrugged.

"'I am not moving from this chair until you pick up that phone and make something happen,'" Jamaal said, hunching his shoulders nebbishly, overenunciating in a parody of Sam's clipped voice.

"That was what kept us in the guy's office," Tiffany said. "I think we might have burned that bridge in the act of crossing it."

"At least we crossed," Jamaal said.

"The arbiter called Bank of America and explained Maria's situation, the Soline connection, our occupation of the property, all of it. He was on a first-name basis with the loans manager, with Ned. After about ten minutes they'd hammered out a nonbinding oral contract—which basically means two guys talking on the phone. Maria would need to agree to it to make it real. The gist of it is this: She's not getting out of it. No clemency, no forgiveness of back payments—the bank refuses absolutely, what sort of precedent would it set, and so on. The bank will, however, offer a partial debt forgiveness in the form of a waiver of any potential deficiency judgment after the sale of the house. In a deficiency judgment, if the house were to sell for less than Maria's outstanding balance on the mortgage, which is a very, very likely scenario, Maria would still owe that money to the bank, with interest, and typically these rates are highly injurious. It'd make a bad situation much worse, extend it out for years. But what the arbiter has tentatively arranged is for the bank to let Maria walk away from the sale free and clear, no deficiency, no further debts, nothing. A clean start. The arbiter has also offered to walk Maria through the paperwork tomorrow, which is a bit of a miracle on such short notice and bearing in mind that we basically barricaded ourselves in his office, had no power of attorney, and weren't all that grateful for what he did do. By the end of an hour our relations with this guy were only *amicable* in the legal sense of that word. Here's his card, with Ned the loan manager's information on the back. Ned Chamberlain. My advice would be for somebody to go inside and pull Maria out of the shower or wherever she is and give this to her immediately. The home-loans manager said the papers need to be signed tomorrow if they're going to be signed at all. Come Monday it's too late and the eviction notice stands as is. That was made explicit."

Tiffany held out the business card to no one in particular. At length I took it and brought it to my lap without really looking at it. The crickets had come up, the night birds.

"Huh," I said. "Huh."

Alex took the card from my hand and tore it neatly in two, dropping the halves at her feet.

She said, "Who else knew about this? Did you?"

"I didn't," I said. "I had no idea."

"You think this is good news?" Alex said to Sam and Tiffany. Jamaal was beginning to look chastened already. "Where is there a shred of good news in this?"

"She's going to lose her house," Sam said. "She's out of options there. We're all out of options there."

"That was made explicit, was it?" Alex said. "By Lord Fucking Chamberlain?"

Sam stood up from his camping chair, listed a bit, like a sailboat, a sloop in sudden wind. He moved across the circle with unsteady purpose and gathered up the torn business card at Alex's feet.

"This is *real*," he said. "This is a real option. What do we honestly think is going to happen Monday morning? We chain ourselves to the furniture and the cops just capitulate, the bank says never mind? They'll just dig in harder! This isn't some Marxist theory class, it's reality, and there's a real family that has to live in it."

Sam was looming over Alex's chair, not meaning to perhaps, but looming higher with each breath, like an oil derrick.

"You need to sit down," Alex said.

"I'm taking this inside to Maria. This is a real option."

Sam stepped uncertainly toward the house and Alex caught a hank of his shirt and hauled him back, levering herself out of her seat with the action and pulling Sam down into it in a move so swift and efficient it might have been choreographed. Alex crossed the circle toward Sam's empty seat, tossing back over her shoulder that I should talk to my protégé, talk some sense into him.

"Why didn't you tell us about this?" I said. "Something this important you should have told the group beforehand."

"Not to mention Maria," Adam said.

"Not to mention Maria. If I'd known this was what you were planning—"

"You knew about this?" Alex said. "I thought you just said you didn't know."

"I didn't. Not specifically."

"He knew," Sam said. "Oh, he was in on it. His job was to distract you while we made off to try something practical, something real in the real, material world. We didn't know exactly what, and we didn't know if it would work, so we didn't advertise our plans, least of all to Maria. We didn't want to get her hopes up."

"Eli?" Alex said.

I was shaking my head, shaking and shaking it.

"Is that true, Eli?"

"It's true," Sam said, "but it's not the issue. The issue is this card you tore up and the opportunity attached to it. A hundred thousand dollars in debt forgiveness is real—whatever we're playing at here is not."

"We spent four hours canvassing in heatstroke heat, Eli,

and the whole time your Frankenstein is out trying to undercut it all? The whole time it was just a decoy?"

"That's not the issue," Sam said.

Alex said, slowly, "You need to stop telling me what the issue is. We'll decide that as a collective—that's how this works. You think you're swooping in to the rescue like some action hero? Debt Forgiveness Man?" She turned to the group. " 'Debt *forgiveness*'? Is that why we came here? Soline detonates an entire town and we come in in our hazmat suits offering *forgiveness* to the victims? Guess what, Maria, we're aiding and abetting the bank in taking your house now! We're apologists for predatory capitalism, we're 'reformers'—we would have told you sooner but we didn't want to get your hopes up!"

"I live on earth," Sam said. "Maria and her family live on earth, in the real world, and what you're talking about is some ethereal kingdom come—"

"You need to stop fucking telling me what I'm talking about," Alex said. "I know that a lot better than you do."

"You're waiting for the revolution to come and in the meantime a family's about to lose their house and gain a toxic load of debt in its place."

Sam stood up again, wavered again. ASU Jason was there to block his path, then Nate from ISO, then Dawn and Adam.

"These aren't eggs you break to make some grand omelet," Sam said.

"That's true," Nate said.

"That's true," Adam said, "but sit down."

"We'll decide as a group," Dawn said.

At length they all sat down, smoothed their hackles back into place. Another silence came over the group, night-pricked, humming, and in the middle of it you could hear Tiffany's slow, deliberate intake of breath.

"There's one other condition we should have mentioned," she said.

In the end we put it to a vote, a grubby circle of dim-lit buzzing parliamentarians. Sam and the ayes narrowly carried it, but with a rider provision from Alex's noes tacked on: We'd wait till the morning to tell Maria about the offer.

In the tent Sam and I were silent, avoiding each other's eye, each pinned to our opposite corner as if we'd fallen into a centrifuge. You could hear Alex outside going from tent to tent pressing her case for appeal. At one point Sam looked up from his Nietzsche and said, "Tent canvassing," and I managed a little smile. Minutes more passed like this, the crickets out in force now, the kippering night birds, not much else to compete with them since our camp was unusually subdued tonight. Our last.

Finally I said, "I wish you hadn't done that."

"I'm sorry," Sam said. "Really. That was shitty of me."

"Do you even know what I'm talking about?" My meanness again, my Trotskyist bark.

"Well, what I'm talking about is what I said to Alex in front of the group, about our arrangement."

"Oh it is, is it?"

"Yes. I am sorry about that. That was childish of me."

"I suppose that's what I meant too," I said. "Gratefully your other disclosure upstaged it—a little flesh wound in the back, then the grenade."

"I've murdered The Occupation," Sam said, flourishing his

hands dramatically, "capital *The*, capital *Occupation*. Will I ever forgive myself?"

I shook my head, turning away from him, turning back to my reading.

"You voted for it too," Sam said. Then softer, "We're doing the right thing."

I had voted for it too. The other condition Tiffany mentioned was that the occupation disperse immediately—the bank didn't want a scene at eviction, didn't want protesters at the house or at the Bank of America offices. Tiffany had let out this news in little hesitating winces, waiting for the blow that never came. No one was much surprised by then. Shut the blinds, turn the lights off—par for the course.

It would be a sorry way to go out, but Sam and Tiffany and Jamaal were probably right. The risks were too great, and in the end it wasn't our decision to make. It never had been. If Maria wanted to take her chances with our occupation, leave the deficiency waiver on the table, then by all means let her. But she wouldn't. Somehow I knew she wouldn't, and apparently I wasn't alone in that intuition. The camp was quiet now, and weirdly tidy—towels and tarps had been folded and gathered in in preparation for tomorrow's teardown.

Outside, Alex's voice rose loose and relaxed, lark-like. Then it came to the door of our tent.

"Are you boys decent?"

I opened the flap onto her grinning face, the curt bangs and the strong Roman nose and the ebony stud catching the lantern light—she looked like Caesar. She leaned her upper body into the tent holding a half-full dime bag of dry flaky weed—it could have been pencil shavings, or birdseed—and in the other hand she held by its plastic scruff a cluster of Bud Lights.

"I've come to either smoke or drink a peace with your Frankenstein," she said to me.

"I thought Frankenstein was the scientist," Sam said. "Isn't the monster just Monster?"

"Don't get fresh or I might change my mind. Do you want lowercase bud or capital Bud?"

"I'm not much of a weed guy, actually."

"Of course you're not."

"Repressed habits die hard."

Alex turned a goofy, kinking, tight-lipped, high-browed smile at me. "No wonder you two get along." She slipped into the tent and assumed a cross-legged slouch beside me, flopping the slim bag of weed into my lap. "You're welcome to as much or as little of that as you'd like. It's not as bad as it looks. But please go smoke it somewhere else. Maybe on a cliff edge, or in traffic."

"At least one of those beers is mine, isn't it?"

"No, it isn't, Eli." Alex blinked at me.

It couldn't have been more than half an hour later when I heard the first laughter sounds coming out of the tent. They were laughing together, their twinned silhouettes leaning in close like conspirators. Maybe it was a trick of my hearing, a deception of the greenish light or my green, wasted state—I observed them from a distance, a stoned voyeur orbiting the yard with the skunky weed in a small glass bowl—but I doubted it. I called Jen and got her voice mail, only realizing the time difference (it was almost two a.m. in New York) after I'd left a message about how much I missed her and how I wished, although of course I was happy for her and her job, but I wished she were here with me now, things were going well, but then again not really, not if I was honest, etc., the message dropping down through descending levels of lugubriousness to match the descending clauses. I didn't trust myself when I was high—it was true I liked control. In general I distrusted states of consciousness I couldn't re-create out of my own innate tool kit. *A very Boy Scout answer from a very Boy Scout boy*, Alex would say, *had* said—something very nearly like that. Didn't a good book or film or piece of music induce states of consciousness you couldn't get back to on command? Didn't love? Didn't sex? Consciousness, like the reality it pilots, is a contingent thing, and I should learn to embrace that. I should learn to do a lot of things. I should learn, I should learn, I should learn, I should learn . . . What were they talking about in there? What were they laughing about? How were they laughing just a few hours after they'd shouted each other down like drill sergeants? One more loop around the yard's perimeter, stepping stealthily, observing all the time the green tent with the two twinned shadowed bodies shifting against the canvas like the shadows in Plato's cave, the parallax effect, young Marcel and the spires of Martinville aligning, disaligning . . . But I was tired of literature, tired of philosophy, tired of ideas and the whole sham show of it. Tired of action, tired of inaction.

Something buzzed in my pocket, and again. My phone.

"Hello?"

"Hey, sweetie, is everything okay?"

"Oh, Jen . . ."

"I got your message. Is everything all right?"

"I woke you."

"That's okay."

"I'm sorry I woke you."

"That's okay. What's up?"

"Petty politics. It's nothing, really. I'm sorry I bothered you with it. I do wish you were here, though. I wish I could hold you."

"I wish that too."

"You know I love you, right? I guess we've only really said it in a jokey playful way—'Oh, I love you, you're so funny,' that sort of thing. I mean it, though. Absent irony, absent hedging. You're perfect for me, Jen—you're perfect. A lot better than Alex ever was, if you really want to know. Not that I'm comparing you, not that it's a competition—"

"You're not comparing us?"

"Or if it is, you win by a mile, that's what I'm saying. What I'm saying is I love you, Jen, and I miss the hell out of you."

"I love you too, Eli."

"You do?"

"I do."

"You really do? Really truly?"

"Are you a little tipsy, *mon amour*?"

We said good night while I was at the far side of the yard, over by the ASU quarter, and by the time I'd circled back to the green dome tent Alex's shadow had slipped out. The sleeping bag was warm and fragrant with her body when I settled heavily down on it.

"You two sounded like you patched things right up, huh?"

"She already had the votes to overturn it when she came to the tent," Sam explained to me. "That's what accounted for her chipper mood."

"And what accounted for yours?" I said.

"Huh?"

"You'd always be second in her ledger, you know. Not to skip ahead too much, but there it is, comrade—a warning. That one's married to the revolution."

"Huh?" Sam said.

see that a certain zeal is at work in my recounting of everything bad, wayward, careless, mean and destructive that marked our last days at Maria's. It's a masochist's zeal, a self-punishing one, perhaps appropriate, but it does leave a lot out. The night after his shouting match with Alex, and the subsequent makeup session, Sam displaced me from the tent altogether—or maybe I volunteered to move? Who can remember from this distance? It was easy enough to see the writing on the tent wall, anyway. I'd talked to Jen on the phone again, self-pityingly floating the idea that she come out to the occupation. It turned out she'd already booked her ticket. By the time she arrived on Saturday evening, the bank's offer to Maria was dead and buried, and Maria had never even known about it.

On Monday morning the police came. Adam Carr got himself flex-cuffed and taken in for "resisting an officer"—no real surprises there. ASU Jason ended up joining him in the holding cell, which surprised me a little more, and Alex and Sam did too, which surprised me not at all. I can still see Sam flushing out of the tent behind Alex on that last morning, like some ridiculous desert bird, the loose folds of his oversize T-shirt flapping against his thin upper arms.

• • •

One more moment in Phoenix, or really in its shadow, its aftermath.

Jen and I had rented a car and were driving up to northern Arizona in gloomy silence. This was according to the plan we'd made, though of course we hadn't planned on any of the preliminaries: getting kicked off the property so roughly, the rushed awkward goodbyes with Maria and her family, the collection we'd had to take up to bail our comrades out of jail—my comrades, anyway. In the back window of the rental car Jen's giant pack hulked, complete with the yoga mats like scroll ends and the hiking sticks that had hung down from either side of Jen, like holy tallithim, when she'd first arrived on Maria's front porch. She said she'd hoped we might get in some Americana on the back end of the trip. I'd said why not.

Quickly to the Grand Canyon, then—above miles of open, carved-out, calcified sky, like loss embodied, a present absence, and where was the vast spiky mold the land had been imprinted with? Taken up into heaven? I really was sounding more and more like Sam.

"Well?" Jen said.

"Well what?"

"Do you like it? Isn't it impressive?"

"Of course it is."

Sienna on darker sienna, burnt umber, ocher, a riot of reddish browns, a vast layer cake of them, and the aerial effect stretching back and back through the dipping receding endless wedges of canyon. It was one of those sights that no amount of pre-seeing could quite prepare you for—I had to admit it—and I had to swallow yet again some of the flippancy I'd reserved for the West with its hard-hewn landscapes, its ancient absences. *Take a freeway excavation, take a foundation dig. That's a newborn canyon, isn't it? Close enough . . .* My father liked to say that forty years wandering in the wilderness had been plenty—he wasn't a camping man either, and my mother didn't press him. Mostly our experience of the outdoors was the woods around our house, the little footpaths cut through brambles and thorns and undergrowth that we walked for exercise or relaxation, or a bit of Frostiana in my poet phase. If serious Jen in her thick hiking boots and spider-bottomed canes had showed up for a walk in the woods south of Boston, she would have felt distinctly overdressed, I'm sure, but the pitch and difficulty of the going would have matched the Grand Canyon rim trail, if not exceeded it. I don't remember breaking a sweat during the hour or two we walked the trail, most of it paved. Large oak and juniper roots sometimes clawed through the pavement and buckled and broke it, but other than that Jen's hiking sticks weren't needed, were merely decorative, something rhythmic to do with her arms. No matter—two-thirds of American sporting was buying the sporting gear, wasn't it?

"A little barbed," Jen said to this, "but I'll take it. At least it's words. At least you're talking."

"I'm sorry. I am sorry. I think I'm still back in Phoenix a little."

"I can tell."

It was then, at a scenic turnout from the trail, in front of an easel-like topography display that showed the Colorado River eating away at the ancient plateau over ages and ages, it was then that I told Jen about the loan manager's compromise we'd left on the table. The evening sunlight was climbing down the rough terraces of stone, the light thickening to orange, moted, honeyed. Jen was silent for a long time, looking out beside me long enough to watch the light change again—it was granular now, arced, the sun slipping down behind the western shelf of a horizon and tipping its last rays brilliantly into the sky like teetering cables. Then the edifice collapsed altogether. I reached for Jen's hand in the sudden chill; she allowed it to be taken, squeezed my hand in turn, but I sensed a certain reflex in the gesture, a certain loyalty.

"Of course I regret it now," I said, "in retrospect. I'm sure everyone does . . . But there it is. Anyway, I wanted to give you a little context for my mood."

Jen asked, "Why didn't you tell her?"

"The group decided against it. It was a collective action. You can't go in there with one set of procedural principles, then switch them on a whim, an individualist whim."

"I see."

"I feel awful about it."

"Would you say you did more harm than good in the final analysis?"

"In the final analysis?"

"Don't do your semantics thing. You know what I mean."

"I think it's a little hard to say at this point."

"That's an academic's answer. That's the kind of hedge you hate."

"Yes," I said. "Yes, I think we probably did more harm than good."

The sun was down now, the canyon fading before us, an absence ebbing away into the general absence, and there was another chill in the air, the evacuated high air. The mood had broken, though, like a fever, and on the coarse starchy hotel bed that night Jen and I made love, gently, full of need but careful of it, too, careful of ordinary need—it was strange and lovely. Coming down from those heights the blueing light of the TV played over our bodies. We settled into each other's arms, my shoulder blades cold against the faux-leather pad of a headboard, but only for a moment. In the upper channels we found an old episode of *Columbo*, one of Jen's mother's favorites, one of Jen's favorites, and we drifted off to sleep to the sound of the bumbling, dissembling, charming detective who always gets his man.

We kept on in the morning, up and around the big broad rim of the canyon that looked like a green shifting weather system on the rental car's GPS. Up through piñon forests, the trees bristling from above, roughly uniform, as if a huge sponge of green paint had been dabbed over the land. Up through climbing mountain roads with the sharp rising banks of pinkish earth on either side like geologic cutaways, rocky fins. The land was bunching up, smoothing out again, accordion-like, uncertain. Finally we crossed into Utah, into Sam's old stomping grounds, and the desert sky lowered like a boom, the power lines running eternally up into the high mesas. A rust-red promontory rose in the distance and soon signs were announcing the little town of Kanab. Gassing up there, driving through the gridded downtown, I half expected to see sober bearded men in formal dress, prophetic distraction, leaning their arms out of pickup trucks or trailing their much younger wives behind them in heavy braids and long calico skirts. In the end I saw only a few people, and mostly they were tired-looking, on the older side, and dressed for the heat. In Zion Park, too—this was our destination, the other stop Jen couldn't not stop for, and I was game now—but in Zion it was more of the same. Normal people keeping their outlandish ideas to themselves, apparently. The most foreign experience we had was overhearing a troop of bronzed chatty Germans with their packs and sticks—they looked like Jen, like us. We were doing real hiking this afternoon. The sun was broad and flat and strong and in its light you had to squint through sunglasses to make out the signs and wonders: ANGELS LANDING, 3 MI. Up ahead a giant saddle of red-rock mountain broke from the assorted pines and rose and rose. We stood at the foot of all this, the start of a gradual, switchbacking, rock-walled trail—slow and steady, etc. I wasn't intimidated, but I asked Jen just to be sure.

"Sure I'm sure," she said. "If those Germans can do it, and they have at least twenty years on us."

"They're genetically modified, bear in mind. *Übermenschen.*"

"Here, take one of my sticks."

"It's the Moses look. I'm Charlton Heston."

"Let's go, my people."

A few minutes later, in good breath still, I said, "I'll let you take one of my sticks tonight, if you know what I mean."

"I was hoping you'd say something like that. It's nice to have you back."

The first mile of the hike was easy, or easy enough. The next mile we had to lean into more, the switchbacks narrowing, steepening. All around us vast striated hunks of rosy stone shot up from the green-dotted canyon floor well below us—it was officially intimidating now, and, yes, very beautiful. In the last half mile or so the switchbacks fell away altogether and a long, thin, steadily rising ribbon of blushing stone trail traced the spine of the mountain up to its top. Here the pin oak and piñon didn't range up the sides of the mountain to cast thin shade over the trail—these trees *clung*, they were smaller and sparer, bonsai-like, clinging impossibly to the steep rocky sides of the mountain, their roots like grappling hooks.

"Jesus Christ," I said, looking over the side. "Don't look over the side."

"I know. I know that."

There was a slight tremolo in Jen's voice—I was relieved to hear it, comforted somehow. She had stowed our walking sticks back in their pack-side holsters, the sticks swinging on certain steep boulder-high rises and clacking behind her like giant castanets. In a few minutes we were holding on to cordons of anchored chains, a feature the park had added, Jen informed me, after too many hikers had slipped to their deaths. The steps were of hard uneven red rock, planing away at odd angles, smoothed slick by weather at points, by too many hikers. I stopped to rest for a moment and realized my hands were shaking. When I'd recovered myself a little, I asked Jen how she knew so much about all this anyway. How had a Western yen cropped up among the piano books and conservatory studies of a central New Jersey childhood?

"It was at Randolph," Jen said. "I went through a Messiaen obsession. Do you know him? *From the Canyons to the Stars* is a musical ode to this place."

"It must be terrifying music."

"It's beautiful. A lot of ondes martenot. I've got some on my phone if you want to listen." She looked up and behind her. "Maybe at the top? We should probably concentrate on this last part, huh?"

A rock-hewn stairway the height and pitch of a rollercoaster climb, maybe three feet wide all the way, the little trees down to shrubs now, weeds, mosses, the kind of life that clings to life, and that barely. Five minutes without talking, without breathing, really—all the faces tipped down in seriousness, deep concentration. At the last steel pole anchoring the last length of chain I allowed myself to look up. Jen was there with her out-stretched hand, her smile beautiful, heat-blushed, almost sexually relieved, and all that thin blue air behind her.

I rendered my verdict over a lunch of peanut butter and honey sandwiches, gas station trail mix. "I never want to do this again—ever—but I'm glad we've done it. Half of it anyway. And I like the view better than the soundtrack to the view," I said, removing the earbud that piped in Messiaen's high, windy sounds. "Maybe when we get back down to terra firma, huh?"

We were eye level with the high brontosaurus humps that cast everything else in ridiculous relief: the pygmy river below, the pinpricks of large spreading trees, the scrub brush on the river's banks much smaller and vaguer than model train foliage, a kind of mere greeny smudge.

"I don't even want to take pictures," Jen said. "Pictures wouldn't do this justice. I just want to try to remember."

She brought the back of my hand, calm now, to her dry, warm lips. "This is good," she said. "This is a good, good thing."

"I'm glad we did it."

"Do you know what I mean, though? When you wouldn't change anything? On the phone a few nights ago you said you loved me. I think you were a bit buzzed when you said it—"

"I meant it. I mean it."

"I mean it too," Jen said, tipping back her hat brim, lifting the shadow off her white freckled face, smiling. Her mouth was warm and sharp with the taste of peanut butter. It was a long kiss, too long under normal circumstances and in public, but in the hard thin light at the top of Angels Landing, in the gusts of wind that made you brace the stone underneath you, though you were a hundred feet from any edge—in all this a certain inhibition dropped away and an honesty born out of exhaustion came up to take its place, an honesty of the body. We kissed for a very long time. You felt this was a person you could crawl inside of and rest in. This was a person in whom you could find shelter, warmth, affection, understanding, counsel, gentle reproof, love, all good things in good supply.

No one was paying much attention to us anyway. The middle-aged Germans had circled up closer to the edge, passing around clear bags of flax, it looked like, and behind us a regular stream of hikers crested the summit with a rush of relief to blind them almost completely to the amorous couple sitting cross-legged and centered at the summit's rough table, whispering and kissing by turns. Really it was only the little birds that watched us, hopscotching toward our set-aside meals, fearless, darting for crumbs. Yet whispering felt right. It was a fragile thing we'd found, a sudden thing, a kind of secret we'd discovered between the two of us and we were nervous to let it loose in the rough bracing air. Jen said she'd had some recent good news at work to match the good things that were happening in her life with me. When Raymond had learned of her grad school ambitions, he'd taken it upon himself to disabuse her of them. It was a gentle, joshing process, conducted over the course of several weeks of strategic compliments, strategic jokes (*I heard that key change you added—really beautiful playing. Imagine how much better you'd play with eighty, ninety thousand dollars in extra student debt . . .*), all of which culminated in a sit-down lunch a few days ago at a Greek café within view of the Guggenheim, just the two of them. Raymond told her it hadn't been as easy as she might think in New York City to find a gifted sight reader, a gifted musician, who would show up dependably, coax the best out of each of the auditions, and put up with the industry-standard slave wages they paid her. Not to mention the transcribing and arranging she'd volunteered to do in her after-hours.

Here Jen interrupted her story. "Raymond talks as if that kind of thing is drudgery, but it's just because *he's* tired of doing it. I love it. You think the natural medium for composition is the instrument itself, and it is, but it also isn't. Until a piece moves from the keys to the staves it's just this fleeting, private, unstable thing."

"So he's got you composing for him?"

"Not for him exactly. He works with a network of composers and songwriters, some of whom pride themselves on being 'intuitive' musicians. That's code for theory illiterate. Sometimes he'll just give me a songwriter's practice files and it's my job to try to make something out of them. Then last week he sent me a raw score, something he was co-writing, 'toying with,' he said. It's a reworking of *Kiss Me, Kate*, and it's a mess. It's just placeholders, vague ideas. My job was again to punch up what was there, make it more rigorous, more complete—"

"Are you getting paid for any of this, Jen? Did Raymond really call them 'slave wages'? If he's only paying you with compliments, he's underpaying you."

"Easy, Engels, easy. I'm getting there."

"But the upshot is you're not applying to grad schools again? You're quitting?"

"Eli, let me finish the story. We're still at the fancy Greek place, square plates, several forks—you see where this is going, right? Raymond loves the work I've done on the score. Everybody who's gotten back my work, whether it's transcribing or 'organizing,' quote-unquote, everybody says great things, you know? I'm really good at this, Eli, and Raymond recognizes that. He gave me a substantial raise, and I see what you're thinking—you'll just have to trust me that it's substantial. But he gave me a raise and a week's vacation—hence this trip, this view—and he also said he's going to get me a co-writing credit on the score if he can scare up the funding to produce it."

"Why is any of this exclusive of graduate school? I thought that's what you wanted."

"It's what I thought I wanted. But I didn't know what I wanted. I was frightened. I'm a classical musician in the twenty-first century, I'm always worried about where the next rent check's coming from. But this could be a good thing, you know? Eli? I thought you'd be happier for me."

"I am, sweetie," I said, "I am. Of course I am. Come here."

Everyone was dropping out of graduate school. It was a sinking ship, with the true believers stuck in steerage. I limped along for my sixth year at Randolph, picking up courses through Hahn's generosity, her forbearance, really. I wasn't much more diligent in my acquittal of duties than I had been before, showing up to meetings with papers half graded, or very, very loosely graded, intending to go back to the batch once I'd survived the norming sessions and do the students the justice they deserved. It didn't always happen. I tried to imagine in each student a Jennifer Daugherty banking on her grade in Poli Sci 110 like she banked on a scholarship disbursement, or a meal—it didn't always help. Hahn and I still met occasionally for dinner, usually at the Moroccan café near her apartment, which really was excellent. It was as if a certain region of my palate had been waiting and waiting for the taste of tagine, like the soul's lost half that Plato describes, and now it had found it and needed to binge. Hahn usually paid, despite my halfhearted objections. "Don't embarrass yourself," she said once. "If you had the money you wouldn't be TAing for me, would you?" She also knew not to ask about my dissertation or the grant money I'd frittered away in its name. I knew not to ask about Stephen, her dying husband. I had seen him a time or two more—he wasn't squirreled away, Hahn wasn't embarrassed of him—but the effect of the brief encounters was chilling, if I'm honest, a constraint on the rest of the night. Steve spoke through an electrolarynx now. The thing had attacked his very vocal cords—ravenous, ravenous appetite, devouring him wholly, cutting him off from the world of friends and acquaintances, who could only smile so long in the presence of his world-weary jokes, his self-deprecations, crudified now by the stiff toneless voice entrusted to deliver them, as if his mind had been switched out for a hard drive. I said none of this, of course, not to Hahn, much less to Stephen, not to anyone. Yet they both sensed it coming off me—they must have—like a scent. Steve leveled his weak whey face at me one day and said through the electrolarynx, "The trouble with living death is that the party goes on without you, doesn't it?" And Hahn, pushing me to the door, said, "Please, honey. I'll be back in an hour."

What was happening with Sam and Alex and the rest of the Phoenix crowd? Not much that I observed. I knew Jamaal and his willowy Afro and his bright, loud loose-fitting clothes had come east from Arizona. I saw him around at a few ISO meetings—he stuck out pleasantly from the somber gray-clad masses of Manhattan. I knew he was in Queens now, with Sam and Alex and a few others from the occupation. Sam had invited me out to their rented house in a couple of tepid text exchanges, or in the post-tennis banter that began to feel forced, sparse, windy—and pretty soon months had gone by without us seeing or communicating with each other. We'd never really talked about what we'd done together in Phoenix, only about the heat and the fucked-up politics of the place. They didn't even celebrate Martin Luther King Day, Sam informed me.

One day in the middle of my seventh year at Randolph—and believe me that that number could sometimes catch me up breathless—but one day I left Hahn's office after yet another norming session and set a course walking due south. It was late afternoon and I was on my way to meet Jen and her parents for dinner at an old, dark-wood-paneled place I hadn't heard of, but apparently it was swank and soaked through with history, a holdover from Melville's Manhattan. *There now is your insular city of the Manhattoes*, the poet of the sea had written, *belted round by wharves as Indian isles by coral reefs—commerce surrounds it with her surf.* I'd been rereading *Moby-Dick*, some of Beckett too, tacking on to Steve's obsessions, or maybe just avoiding my dissertation. What this meant in practical terms was that I now carried thick books in my shoulder bag that thumped against my side like an unwieldy externalized heartbeat. The books were giant, world-swallowing, absurd, but of course their very absurdity made them necessary, and their necessity made them absurd (this is from Beckett's *Watt*, I believe). In any case, I found comfort in this course of reading, a comfort I tried to draw on now as I headed south toward the commerce-racked Wall Street of my destination. Silly to say, I know, but lower

Manhattan often put me in a gloomy, End Times mood, as if it weren't just the edge of the island I slid toward but the edge of the world, a fifteenth-century seaman, superstitious, scared of sea dragons and usurers, evidently. That my fiancée and her quiet hippie parents waited for me at the end of my journey made it a little less treacherous, but only a little.

Away from the noise and harry of the avenues, I was cutting through Washington Square Park when I heard a familiar voice. It was high, insistent, straining against the wind, shouting out rhythmic, rising lines about billion-dollar cables going into the ground to help the rich get richer faster, about the rising compensation for the top one-tenth of one percent—we weren't the ninety-nine percent anymore, we were the ninety-nine-point-*nine* percent, the vast democratic many against an oligarchic few, and the oligarchs were winning! And why? The rest of us didn't care enough, we weren't mad enough, we weren't *organized* enough! Alex waved a rolled-up copy of the *Socialist Worker* at passing head-bowing students. They leaned forward under their heavy backpacks like Sherpas, or stared at their phones all the more intently. Alex looked like she might just whap the shy passersby with her newspaper, like an owner to a dog that shits the rug. Her hair was jet-black, India-ink-black, much darker than usual—she must have dyed it—and against that sharp-cut contrast her olive skin looked flour-white. It was as if Sam had rubbed off on her too. I should mention it was March, the sun was dead and buried beneath a thick slate sky, the streets constantly dark and wet. Everyone's skin seemed to luminesce a bit more, glowing dully or brightly pale as the case might be—we were a city of deep-sea invertebrates. It was still a little startling to see Alex's pallor, though, seeing her unseen as she shook her head after another slip of undergraduates. She looked geisha-like, a little thinner, too, around the jawline and the long pale neck that descended into a gray wool scarf, a long peacoat. The small stud was gone from her nose, I noticed, only a blemish-like dot where the piercing used to be. I was almost on top of her before she saw me.

"You," she said.

"You," I said. "You're still alive!"

"I'm still alive."

"Where have you been? How are you? I hear you and Sam moved in together?"

"Something like that," Alex said. "We're all keeping a low profile for now."

"What does that mean?"

She didn't answer me.

I said I hadn't expected to see her out paper-driving and sloganeering. I was under the impression she had more or less quit the ISO. It was almost a year since I'd seen her at meetings.

"Those meetings are a joke," Alex said. "They're just masturbatory grad students and undercover cops. And this stuff"—she gestured wand-like to the square with a rolled-up newspaper, as if she'd be content to make it all disappear—"this is mostly a decoy. We're not going to find anyone for the Group here."

"Come again?"

"We're not going to find anybody for the Group we haven't already found."

"*The* Group?" I said. "I thought Jamaal was joking. The Phoenix Group? You guys have a name now?"

"Mostly just the Group," Alex said, "and Sam wanted a name. I don't particularly care one way or the other. It's just—"

She cut herself off, stiffening the shoulders she'd lifted

lazily. Her look had changed; her eyes stared past me, wide, walleyed. I turned to see a tall man in a bloated dark parka, dark sunglasses, and a pulled-down beanie sprinting toward us with long swift windmilling strides. Something flashed in his hand, metallic, shearing light—he was right on top of me, swerving at me, and I still hadn't put together who he was—and now the shiny something punched hard and flat against the open V of my jacket, right against my shirted sternum, shocking me. The blow pushed me back several steps, took the wind out of me less with the force of it than the shock.

"Move!" the man said in Sam's voice, but deeper, gruffer, and he took back his arm and pushed past me, sprinting on. I felt the hard weighted thing slide down the front of my shirt inside my coat, lodging at my waistband, as a late teen in a blue ski jacket broke out from behind a crowd of other students. He was red-faced, yelling after Sam. "Stop him! Stop him!"

The student rushed past us before I could get a good look at him, but he went with the reckless, splay-footed stride of a non-runner, a non-athlete. This was Sam's salvation, apparently. Alex was pulling me away. She had the paper-drive samples tucked under one arm, her other hooked through mine and pulling me in tight. We moved briskly but not too briskly.

"What the hell was that about?" I said.

"Don't look back there," she said. "Come on."

We exited the park and sought refuge in a dark Irishy sports bar a block south of NYU—mounted TVs showing *SportsCenter*, a scrum of freestanding tables beside the bar, a wall-hugging row of high-backed vinyl booths, unaccountably sticky, each with a dim green hanging pool lamp over a thick slab of dark-wood table. It was against one of these that I slapped the weighted rectangular packet I'd removed from my waistband. An encased iPhone. It looked new, newish. Alex plucked it off the table.

"Turn it off," she said. "They've got these tracking things now. Oh, wait, oh wow, this genius didn't even set a passlock."

"What the fuck are you doing, Alex?"

"Restoring to . . . factory settings . . . now . . . and now . . . done."

The screen that had dimly etched the lines of Alex's face went dark and the face with it. She put the phone in her pocket and laced her fingers together on the tabletop.

"You know what I meant," I said. "What are you guys doing?"

"Yes," she said, "I know what you meant."

Again her eyes shot away from me and I followed them to the door of the bar—it closed slowly and heavily, restoring the gloom as a middle-aged man in a ponytail shuffled over to the barstools. A minute later Alex's eyes did the same wary tracking and this time the door admitted Sam in blue jeans, a thin gray sweatshirt, the top half of long johns, it looked like, and a rather bulging backpack that slung off him like a reverse kangaroo pouch. He'd lost the sunglasses, the pulled-down beanie, and in their place he wore a crooked, triumphal smile. He slid into the booth beside Alex and kissed her on the temple.

"I get your adrenaline up?"

"You're such an amateur," she said, fighting a smile of her own.

"Proudly, proudly." He turned to me. "Old buddy old pal, how have you been? Jamaal told us about your engagement—congrats, mazel tov, many happy returns. Oh, and thanks for the help back there. I didn't hurt you, did I?"

"What are you guys doing?" I said again. "You're common thieves now?"

"Common thieves," Alex scoffed. "Do you hear this guy? At least we have a cause to expropriate *for*, Eli. What do you have—mood swings? Judge not lest ye be judged, am I right?"

"Good God. Sam really has worn off on you, hasn't he?"

My old friend looked taken aback at this, pulling his head back, literally, on his neck, turtle-like. The progress of the last several months seemed to have pushed the tide of his hairline noticeably farther up his forehead, hollowing out the pool of his cowlick bald patch that much more, the place where his cowlick used to be. When he looked up from the table I could see his jaw sharpening, the small fibrous muscles twitching through a swallow.

"We haven't seen each other in a while," Sam said. "Some things have obviously changed, but it's good to see you. Congratulations on your engagement."

"Thank you."

"What else is new? How's the dissertation coming? Sensitive question?"

"Sam," I said, "Alex, I need to know why you're stealing phones from hapless undergraduates."

"They'll be fine," Alex said. "Send an e-mail to Mom and Dad and a new phone's in the mail same day. These trust-fund kids . . ." Alex's face went bright with remembering and she turned to Sam, taking his hand with a thoughtless easy intimacy. "Your Doogie Howser today didn't even set a password lock on his phone."

"You already wiped it?"

"We can post it tonight."

Sam reached under the booth and from the squeal of zippers produced three more phones. He dealt them neatly onto the table in front of him, one beside the next beside the next, bracketing them with his forearms.

"A good day then," he said to Alex, though really he was looking at me. "One of them's locked, but let Jamaal work his magic and who knows . . ."

"Wow," said Alex. "Impressive trawl."

Sam hadn't removed his eyes from me when he said, "We can get up to four hundred for a phone in good condition. Jamaal jimmies with the ones we pick up locked. Tiffany posts to an online marketplace from a safe IP address—she knows computers too, apparently."

"Tiffany's in on this?"

"You haven't seen her around campus much either, have you?"

"Adam's in too. ASU Jason came out last summer after he graduated," Alex added.

"Why are you telling me all this?" I said. "What happened to mooching off family and friends, getting *our* parents to put money in the mail same day?"

"That's not adequate anymore," Sam said. "And for me expropriation is the only way I can contribute. My folks haven't exactly been openhanded since my first arrest."

"Your *first* arrest?"

Sam looked to Alex, raising his shoulders and eyebrows in subtle tandem.

"The reason we're telling you this," Alex said, "is because we miss you. We really do want you on board. What are you accomplishing with all those motions and sober discussions at ISO meetings, all that impotent talk? We've got actual plans in the Group," she said, tossing the stack of *Socialist Workers* to fan out on the table. "A lot more than hocking dead trees at NYU students, that's for sure."

"Like what?" I said.

"Are you in?" Alex said. "You could still keep on at Randolph if you really wanted to, though I don't see why you'd want to at this point."

Sam put in, "We've collected a decent little group out there—they're all serious, good people. You'd like them."

"Vanguards," I said. "You guys sound like you're putting together a party of amateur vanguards."

"Which of those words is a dirty word?" Sam's face approached another thought, then backed away from it. "You know what? We're being way too sober about this. Let's get some beers in us, catch up a bit—we are at a bar, aren't we? First round's on me?"

Sam raised his arm to flag a server as I reached my own across the table, slowly, with all the energy drained from it, with old battery acid sludging up my veins. I picked up one of the stolen phones, pressed the power button at the top and brought up a screensaver photo of two twentysomething men, lovers by the look of their smiles, their two smooth faces pressed together at the cheeks, their eyes tipping up for the camera.

"The happy couple," I said, pushing the phone back to Sam, who fumbled quickly to turn it off again.

"Looks like we're leaving," he said.

"You'll be sorely missed."

"You're a real prick sometimes, you know that?" Alex said to me.

I'd started into a slow clap, just loud enough. "Excellent work, guys. Really noble, important work. Hey guys?"

At the door they didn't turn around.

• • •

I stayed on at the random sports bar for a beer or three or four—it was only polite to the server who'd arrived with his ordinary face to take my order. Probably a trust-fund face in disguise, in poor face.

Adrenaline must have propped me up, like a laboratory monster, to get me the rest of the way to the dinner with Jen's parents that night—they were just sitting down when I arrived—but now when I think of the meal I remember almost nothing from it. Jim Daugherty survives as a pair of beige broad cheeks looming up from across the table, Evelyn Daugherty, paler-complected, gray-haired, a wavering smile at her lips . . . I remember the smile beginning to crack a little as I turned aside the questions about my dissertation, with bluff practiced quips, about the academic job market I was assumed to be preparing for, about the wedding Jen and I were assumed to be planning—

"What *can* you tell us, Eli?" Evelyn said at one point, or something like that. "You're awfully slippery tonight."

"I'm against positivism," I think I said. "Just say no to the positive, no?"

On the train ride home Jen said to me—and this I remember distinctly, her voice a sort of jump-start to the stalling apparatus—"Are they such outlandish questions to ask? Are they really so prying?"

I heard the threat of water in her voice, a bed of hard stony gravel underneath it. "What?"

"It's like you're giving a deposition: 'We can neither confirm nor deny that we've set a date. Those discussions are ongoing and private.'"

"Is that really what I sounded like?"

"They were making polite fucking conversation, Eli! They're trying to get to know their future son-in-law!"

"I've had a really shitty day, Jen. I don't want to talk about it right now—"

"Oh *you've* had a shitty day?"

"No, look, I'm sorry. That's not what I meant. Jen?"

She'd already turned her face away as a couple in their rain-sheened winter coats sat down beside us. Was it raining outside? I might have seen a tearful rivulet, too, in the L train's dark reflecting window. I tried to talk to the back of Jen's silent, unyielding head, leaning in close to that forest of scented hair. She never turned around.

When we got back to the apartment it was Mallory's presence that now intervened—politesse like a gag order. Jen didn't want to talk in the privacy of our bedroom. What if Mallory heard us? Didn't mortified voices cut through walls?

Or maybe she'd just finished talking for the night.

For the next several hours, with the lights in the room dropping off one by one, all I heard was the buzz of intensifying rain through the open window. It was Jen's long habit to leave the window at least a little ajar, rain or shine, night or day, winter, spring, summer, fall—much more important that the air should "circulate," the thinking went, than that the heating or AC bills should stay low. I'd made the mistake of challenging this custom early on, a Daugherty ritual, apparently, a *trait*, deep-sunk in the family gene pool. She'd just always done it that way, she said. She couldn't imagine getting to sleep in a shut-in room. And I should be grateful she wasn't her father, known to put up a full window fan in full winter. Things could always be worse.

I sat at the foot of Jen's bed—our bed—fully clothed, while

Jen's sleeping form hardly disturbed the smooth covers. I hadn't been banished here, exactly; it was more like a self-exile, a self-quarantine. I needed to understand my own mind. How often had Jen hinted at a date herself, or tried to joke her way into the conversation, and how often had I diverted it to other topics, diverting her with a quip or two about bourgeois respectability, the race for a bread maker, a new dish set. Of course none of that actually accounted for my hesitation—I knew that much about myself. Nor was it the mulish, dumb-male commitment paralysis. On nights like this I felt closer to the truth as I narrowed my inward vision to that sludge of old battery acid climbing up my veins, rising like a dark hardening *stuff* through the tubes and byways to stuff up my heart. A hemlock of self-loathing, a sense of waste, in both senses of that word. I knew Jen could do better than me.

A rill of cold air sank in from the windowsill, pebbling my skin at the thought. In spite of precedent I covered up Jen's exposed arched feet; she'd kicked off the covers again a moment later. On a typical night, I imagined that the bottom hem of the covers and sheets must have looked like a tangled trapezoid, slanting up sharply from left to right—left was my side of the bed, right was Jen's.

A sudden panic seized me— *If I should ever lose her . . .*

I moved to the little alcove of Jen's side-sleeping body, reached my hand out to her shoulder.

"Please don't," the voice said, quiet and crystalline.

"I thought you were asleep."

"No."

"Oh . . ."

She rolled away from me, facing the other side of the bed.

I said, "What were you doing if you weren't sleeping?"

"I was thinking."

"What about?"

I said, "Sweetie? Talk to me. Please."

"Do you have any idea how much you embarrassed me tonight? Showing up like that, obviously drunk, slurring your words, and then what you actually did say—or didn't! All your evasiveness, like you'd been forced to submit to a police investigation."

I rested my hand again, almost imperceptibly, on Jen's shoulder.

"Please, Eli."

"I want to explain myself. I want to feel close to you . . . It's like—I don't know—you want your life to be worthy of the person you love. You want an equal exchange, an equal merger of lives going into something like this, and I'm just not there right now. I'm not even close. I have these days where it all becomes painfully apparent to me, how much time I've wasted, how little I have to show for what I've done. Today was one of those days. It's not an excuse, I know, and I am sorry. Genuinely. I'll write a note to your parents tomorrow."

"Don't. That'll just bring more attention to it."

"Tell me what to do then. Tell me what to do."

"Why did you even propose to me, Eli? Why did you let me say yes?"

"A girl like Jennifer Daugherty you've got to lock down."

"No. No quips. If you can't say it straight—"

"This is a lifelong relationship. I wanted you to know that. And it is—*it is*. You do know that, don't you? You have to. Jen?"

At length she reached up and took my hand. I got under the covers as she gathered it to her breast, the steep rise and fall of her back against my shirted chest. We'd be okay, I told her. I promised we'd be okay, pulling her in close to me, being pulled, my arm held to Jen's waist with a sudden animal force, a boa constriction to force our love out into the open air where we could catch and keep it, trap it alive.

"Do you promise?" Jen was whispering. "Do you promise me?"

"I promise," I said. "I promise we'll be okay."

One other point to pick up from the dinner that night, with Jen's mother asking the questions—Evelyn, who'd also wanted to know about my dissertation and my plans for the academic job market, and who'd balked when I turned her questions aside so glibly, something I regret now. The truth is I'd given up on academia altogether. I'd started looking for other jobs, halfheartedly at first, in the short term, with my grad school funding running down. I knew an eighth year at Randolph was basically out of the question, and when Hahn confirmed this to me I took it more or less in stride. I did get a little chippy with her, which is something else I regret.

"I thought you knew the end was nigh," Hahn said to me, at lunch this time. "I figured you must have known."

"No, I didn't," I lied.

"Well, are you even close to finishing?"

"You know I'm not."

Hahn explained that if I could somehow finish my dissertation over the summer the department might just see its way clear to a final extension of funding while I went out on the academic market. But just that phrase in Hahn's mouth—the academic market!

I was all the more determined to seek my money elsewhere—

skipping ahead to the stopgap economy, then, to the indignities of a job search in the late-capitalist city. I'd applied already to the Strand and McNally Jackson, and later I tried Greenlight Bookstore, BookCourt, WORD, Housing Works Bookstore, Barnes & Noble (four of them in two boroughs), Kaplan Test Prep Center, Central Park Tutors, Huntington Learning Center, Brooklyn Roasting Company, the Queens Kickshaw, Ninth Street Espresso, Applebee's (three of them in three boroughs), TGI Friday's (two in two), Mike the Glazier, Sasha's Framing and Supplies, Gotham Carpet Cleaners, Starbucks—a month, a month and a half of my life, not to mention the job applications I'm probably forgetting. I did get a quick call back from a slow-voiced Starbucks manager, but I let the message languish. I was waiting on too many others, I told myself, but really I could see how it would go: the studious distance on the faces of the mock-busy clerks, their neutral smiles as I described my long-ago experience in retail, leaving behind my applications just in case. Thanks, sure, they'd see what they could do . . .

Apparently tip jobs were out, too. You needed to know somebody, Mallory said. She knew that much from experience. One night over takeout Indian I asked her about her job as a paralegal at a midtown law office, the job that had helped her afford the nicer place she and Jen now rented together, the two-bedroom in Greenpoint, Brooklyn, the sometimes fortress of politesse. If we'd gone straight three-ways on the rent, I'd have come up empty-pockets in no time. Not that Jen had asked me to three-ways the rent, and not that I'd made my discomfort explicit—another long story, ages long, I suppose, stretching back at least as far as Abraham and Isaac and all the other patriarchs. How that foolishness clings to a man!

I was asking Mal about her paralegal job. What exactly

did it entail? What did it pay? Did she like her boss—bosses? What?

"Oh, no, I'm not laughing at you," she said, "I'm laughing at me. The pay's pretty bad when you think of all the work you take home, all the extra hours you put in. Your boss is pretty much anyone in the office with a law degree, which means you work for a wide and impressive variety of assholes. I'd say the best preparation for paralegal work is a major in vocal performance and a crushing amount of student debt. Or maybe a gambling problem? That could work too."

Impish and thin-faced, her brown-green eyes spaced just a breath too wide apart, or maybe it was the way her long nose spread out very suddenly into the broader delta of her brows— but there was something slightly alien in Mallory's look, over-evolved, knowing. Mal Mallory. She was bad cop to Jen's good on most nights, and on most nights that took some doing. They goaded each other to heights of greater and greater outrageous-ness.

"You *like* when they treat you bad," Jen said. "Don't you?"

We sat at the high table on high wooden stools in Jen and Mallory's kitchen alcove. I didn't place myself on the posses-sive deed after three months of living there—I wouldn't after four months, five, not even after another round of lowlier ap-plications finally turned up a job at Tommy's Pizza and Subs in Astoria and I started paying something, meager somethings toward the rent. I knew I was an impostor no matter how much Jen tried to reassure me to the contrary.

"Well, maybe I like it a little," Mal said. "I do like a few spanks from those paddles they've all kept from their prelaw fraternities."

"Sororities too."

"Of course. They hit the hardest. More to prove."

"On your bare ass, I hope."

"Where else? Undies at my ankles, bent over one of those big, hard, ergonomic chairs—"

"Wow," I said, "you're really going for this, aren't you?"

"You're uncomfortable? He's uncomfortable again," Mal said to Jen, with her sideways smile, the knowing look that at once acknowledged and excluded me from the long-held rhythms of their friendship. I didn't begrudge them these moments—I understood them, took a certain comfort in them. Why shouldn't they feel comfortable enough to look around me at times, through me?

Our tri-sided dinners became little islands, little points of reprieve for all of us soon enough. In the evenings I was now coming home with the smell of flour and marinara sauce like some aural tattoo on the inside of my nostrils. This is still the abiding impression of my time at Tommy's: burnt flour, the insidious, crystalline spread of it, an unstoppable osmosis. It mixed almost festively with the red sauce on my pine green apron, speckled and spattered—Pollock comes to mind too, and again, except that here the artistry consists of mindlessly circling sauce onto eight-inch disks of personal pan pizza dough. Better that, I figured, than working the firing range at the front of the kitchen. It wasn't just that the range sat in plain view of impatient customers, or that the stinging bits of boiling cheese and meaty grease jumped up and bit your soft inner wrists, the feel of fire ants—it was also Marco, it was *mostly* Marco, the beak-nosed ponytailed manager who ran the register and policed the grill like an Iron Guardist. From behind, the short gathered rump of his ponytail looked like a cowering rodent through the gap in his pine green hat. Then snapping around, he'd bark at you about the order on your left, the order on your left was burning, it was drying out, and the one on your right, you'd forgotten the cheese, and the one in front of you you were taking off already? Hold it, hold it, here, *wait*, and he'd motion for Rodney with the tattoos like smudges on his thin black arms to take over at the register. He'd shoulder me aside, literally, with a line of customers looking on, scoop up the offending brown sizzling mass of meat and vegetables and cheese, flip it, redice it in expert time, the spatulas blurring, drop one of the spatulas to grab a squeeze bottle of water to prime the grill, drop more cheese, prime again, and scoop up the salvaged sandwich into its waiting roll, just so.

"Impressive," I said once.

"It's not that impressive, Stopgap. Mix the ingredients together, heat them up, put them in a fucking roll, and fast. It's not rocket science. You don't even need a PhD to do it."

"Good thing, too, since I don't have a PhD."

"Shut up, Stopgap."

By the time I got home from a shift and showered and dressed, and went out for pickup perhaps, I could feel a little of my humanity beginning to return, like the skin of my fingers that eventually smoothed and re-plumped when I'd been on dish duty. (I still carried the sharp smell of burnt flour in my nostrils, though, always, always, as if I'd been snorting the stuff.) After dinner Jen usually retired to the piano and I took up my spot on the brown suede couch under the gooseneck reading lamp. I read Beckett or Melville or one of Jen's mystery novels, whatever I wanted now, reading to the sounds of Jen's evolving score for *June vs. Hurricane*. After the modest Off-Broadway success of the *Kiss Me, Kate* reboot, Raymond had secured enough funding for an original musical comedy that he and Jen had now collaborated on for a year: Raymond was the words man, Jen the music. It had taken no small effort on my part, but finally I'd convinced Jen to unplug the headphones and let the apartment listen in. She was in the final stages, she said, fine-tuning, which was the only reason she'd agreed. And we shouldn't get used to it: In the blank-page phase of composition she'd rather sit stark naked on the piano bench than unplug her headphones. In that case, I said, I wouldn't mind.

One night Jen was playing and playing again through a spare but rising, plaintive recitative section. I asked if recitative was the right word for it in a musical.

"Good question," Jen said. "Let's say yes? Why not? Wagner called his operas 'musical dramas.' He didn't mind mixing terminologies."

"Shall I get you a Wagner bust for your electric piano?"

"Have him scowling maybe."

"My frowning baby's frowning muse."

She showed the real thing at this, or a hammy simulacrum of it: the pursed mouth, the diving brows . . .

In truth her composing face looked less like a frown than an all-face furrowing, an intense gathering in of the features as if by some inward centrifugal force. She didn't like me watching her as she worked, but I'd done enough surreptitious observation to get to know and love this muscular squinch. I think she may have needed glasses, too.

Jen returned to the music, waiting music, spare but rising, quietly yearning. In Raymond's draft of the libretto (why not?) the main character, June, wanders a Jersey Shore boardwalk as the light fades. (Raymond, like Jen, was a New Jersey native, and this was another point of bonding between them.) The music rose only to drop down again, wavering, foraying down into the muddier depths of the piano as something brooded, something took shape. It was Hurricane Sandy. On this particular evening Jen had Raymond's lyrics up on the stand, sometimes singing them under her breath. *What can I do when there is nothing to do? What can I say when there is nothing to say?* A little moody for a romcom, I said from behind her. I'd moved over from the couch—hovering, yes, but then the words weren't her words. I hadn't realized that the title of the musical referred to a literal hurricane, but there it was looming up in the stage directions: [*storm sounds rise, winds, rain . . . whatever the budget can manage!*]. I made a comment about this too and drew a swiveled rebuke from Jen—her pressed-lip smile, an abridgment of a smile.

"How's Beckett coming? Or Melville? Or who is it you're reading for your dissertation these days? How's that coming along?"

It wasn't. I'd abandoned my dissertation once and for all, as I've told you, and I'd been meaning to make this clear to Jen for weeks now, months. For now I said, "I know I'm being annoying—I just thought it was lighter fare, a sort of coming-out comedy."

"It's light and it isn't," said Jen. "I don't know. Raymond's changed things around a bit."

"June's still in high school, though, still struggling to tell her parents and her boyfriend?"

"On leave from college now. Her father's sick."

"Her father's sick?"

"Colon cancer."

"Jesus."

"Well, people get sick."

"Does she still come out to them?"

"It's harder now. There's more at stake. They're strict evangelicals."

"Strict evangelicals on the Jersey Shore?"

"Please, Eli. I'm trying to do this."

"It's too much," I said. "Sexual repression, religious fanaticism, colon cancer, a devastating hurricane . . . Are you guys sure about all this?"

"Sure, *we're* sure about it," Jen said, suddenly fierce and reaching for her headphones on the stand.

It was around that same time that I started meeting up with Sam again, too.

It's a kind of admission to say it, to recall it, and almost as unflattering to me as the ham-handed incursions I've showed myself making into Jen's evolving musical. (It wasn't really hers to evolve, I soon saw.) But the truth is I enjoyed seeing my old friend again. He'd somehow found out where I worked and was now coming into Tommy's on Tuesdays and Fridays, our ancient tennis days, buying Gatorades from the little counter refrigerator and sitting at a table with *Flesh as Collateral*, say, or *Us vs. Us: Corporate Schismatic Strategies and How to Combat Them*, or some such awfulness that he'd diligently read and take notes on as he waited for my shift to end. For my part, I'd started bringing a duffel bag to work.

Into the back comes Marco one slow afternoon, the shop cavernous in its post-post-lunch-rush silence. I was washing the counters, the dishes done. Rodney was on his phone in the break room, really an alcove with a mini fridge and a stool. When I heard Marco's step, I turned around and tried not to grimace. He was smiling nose-first, as he always seemed to do, his close narrow lips curling up and around the crooked totem so that it looked like the nose had leveraged the smile, winched it up by pulleys. His eyes were small and dark brown. With his hat off, the pulled-back slick of his hair looked flat and dully grooved, like a record.

"Your boyfriend's here, Stopgap. Looking hornier than usual, I must say."

"That's good. Very good. That'll do nicely in the harassment suit."

His smile widened.

"Speaking of which," I said, "why 'Stopgap'? Have I ever said anything about this job being temporary?"

"Your face says it, Stopgap, your slow-ass work says it, the way you talk—everything about you says it."

"I see."

Marco mocked the phrase back at me Britishly, then lifted his chin at the wall clock and told me I could finish up the counters and head out at the top of the hour. Some thirty minutes early.

"Let no one say you're not a broad-minded, magnanimous man," I called after him.

"See you tomorrow, Stopgap."

At the top of the hour I went to the back room to change into my tennis gear and retrieve the personal effects Marco made us store in a bank of blue lockers the size of several shoe boxes stuck together. An old-school gesture. He didn't want us out front with our phones, zombie-eyed and head-hung as customers came in. I found the rule equal parts repressive and endearing, a bit old school myself, obviously, but now I found it merely tempting, especially in my present mood, since managerial Marco, efficient Marco, stupid Marco had somehow left his locker's padlock unfastened in its catch. The little arm of the lock hung free just above the joining place. Was this hubris or accident on his part? Was it a cosmic Dare? Inside the locker I saw a wallet and a Samsung phone—I took both of them, leaving only a pair of keys behind.

Outside, I followed Sam toward the subway, shaking. Summer lay heavily on the city, the damp heat and the sick-sweet garbage smells rising, the sheets of light coming off the mirrored buildings. At an intersection a crosstown breeze brought a moment's relief—the sun went behind clouds, the glass storefronts revealing their wares again. For a moment people seemed to speak softly on the sidewalks, soothingly, for my benefit, but my hands still shook. I told Sam I was quitting my job at Tommy's.

"Oh yeah?" he said. "What happens after you quit? You got something else lined up?"

I pulled out the cell phone and the wallet to present to him—a puppyish gesture. I'm embarrassed of it now.

"What's this?" Sam said.

I told him.

"Are you kidding me?"

"What?"

"How fucking stupid are you?"

"From your glass house you throw stones," I said.

Sam started back the way we'd come. "Come on, we're going back."

"What the fuck are you talking about?"

"We're going back, moron! Come on! Do you know how traceable you are? Hurry!"

We walked double-time back to Tommy's, where Marco

was manning the register with a bored, slack expression that wavered into a smirk when he saw me. I'd just be a minute, I'd forgotten something in the back room.

"Couldn't keep away, eh?" he called after me. "You like us that much, Stopgap? Awww, Stopgap . . ."

Morose Rodney was still on his cell phone in the back, still on break. He looked up as I passed into the little room with the lockers. "Forgot something," I said, half choking on the word as I saw with an all-body clench that I'd shut up the padlock, or someone had. I pulled down on the lock and nothing happened. I yanked down—quietly, quietly, but I yanked—and nothing happened. I rotated the first of three crenellated number strips and pulled down at steady intervals. Nothing. Hot breathlessness filled my body. I could hardly hold the lock for shaking. How long had I been in here? Shaking, I tried the leftmost strip again, forcing myself to go slow, stopping at each crenellated break in the silver number line, rotating, stopping and pulling, rotating—

Pure liquid feeling broke open in me as the catch fell suddenly open.

"You okay?" Rodney said from behind me.

I whirled around—"Shit!"—feigning shock, tearing wallet and phone from my pocket and throwing them clanging into the locker, falling against it. My shock was genuine enough, come to think of it—only the laugh I faked.

"You scared the shit out of me!" I said.

Rodney stood in the doorway. He made no response, only slid his eyes left toward the sound of approaching footsteps.

"Where'd your boyfriend go?" Marco said. "I'd hate to think we offended him."

I grabbed my duffel bag and started for the door. I said I'd accidentally taken my phone charger with me the first time and decided to come back to drop it off. Bad battery on the phone, probably needed a replacement—

"Your locker's open," Marco said, nodding.

Idiotically I followed his eyes to where the blue metal door gaped open and dark as a mouth.

"Wait, isn't that my locker? What the fuck is my locker doing open?"

He looked from me to Rodney, moving quickly to his property, checking his phone, rifling through his wallet.

"I saw him throw something in there."

"It was an accident."

"I don't see any cell-phone chargers," Marco said.

"It was an accident. You can stop looking. I didn't take anything from your fucking wallet, Marco."

"And I should take *your* word for it?" Marco said, suddenly turning on me, chesting into me. "The fucking thief?"

"Am I? What kind of thief brings the stuff back, asshole?" I tried to sound angry, affronted, but my body backed sheepishly toward the door.

"Don't you dare move. Rodney, keep him there. Who do I even call for this? Do you call 9-1-1? Jesus God—Rodney, keep him there, keep him while I find a fucking number for the cops."

"Oh, that's perfect: 'Yes, hi, 9-1-1? I wish to report that nothing at all has happened. Nothing was taken from me. I'm just a paranoid bigoted piece of shit.'"

Rodney grabbed halfheartedly at my forearm, but I broke past him into the open store.

"You don't think the cops care about attempted robbery?"

I was backing through the dining room, hip-checking tables, ready to run if Marco pursued me out of the back.

"I've got your name, I've got your address," he shouted, "I've got your work address, you fucking thief! Where you *used* to work—"

I crashed out of the store and fell into a jangled run-walk, a jittery dance that could have fooled no one. Sam stepped out from under his prearranged awning, his face like a moon reflecting mine, white and taut. "Good Christ, are we running?" he said. "Should we just run?"

By the time we got out to the courts in Sunnyside and into our warm-ups, we'd mostly calmed down. We tried out a few lame jokes to prove to ourselves we could joke about it. Our *second* warm-ups. I remember how fast the court played that afternoon, notwithstanding all the cracks and weed patches that made me pine secretly for gentrified Hoboken. I felt loose-limbed and live-armed with the racket, unusually loose, unusually alive. Free and uncalculating. Did I litter up the stat sheet? I must have. Did I lose? Of course. But I remember I also hit several clean winners past Sam charging hard at the net—he was experimenting with serve-volley tennis of late. I felt invigorated, rattling with angles and possibilities, the air wet but clean in my lungs. Sam looked like a wrestler at the end of his sweat-suited training run, a large oval of dark gray dropping down from his neck and spreading through the middle of a Randolph Athletics T-shirt almost to the navel. I hadn't realized those shirts were for sale: I recognized its kind from the Randolph locker rooms, recalled its stiff itchy embrace. You handed the gym people your student ID as collateral, they handed you a graying T-shirt made from burlap.

"Not exactly for sale," Sam said, "but I wanted a little souvenir of my time there. They could keep my student ID. What did I care?"

"So when you steal it's a souvenir and when I steal it's, what, suicide?"

"That was a suicidal move you pulled back there, yes."

Onto the grass now, drinking our Gatorades and stretching. The grass felt stiff and crabby under my thighs, sparse, like patchy stubble on the underlying dirt that turned to mud with the sweat seeping into it, but at least we were cool in the shade of a courtside oak. Sam was getting abstract now, moving from the particular to the general, like a good Marxist. I watched his face as he spoke: Little colonies of silvery sweat beads still perched on his narrow upper lip, on the high jutting cheekbones, rosy with sunburn, and all along the long jutting jaw. His eyes were more recessed in their sockets than they'd once been—he too had lost weight—and his tall slick forehead stood in the shadow of a black Federer hat, a new addition. He looked like a skeleton with skin stretched over it. (We were all that, of course, but lately Sam reminded you of it more.)

"Anyway, I assume you've heard about old Larry?" Sam said to me.

"Larry?"

"Old Lar—the disgraced Soline CEO, just got off scot-free in the trial, to no one's great surprise? We're on a first-name basis now."

"Of course, yes, sorry."

Larry Bosch, man of the hour again. At the start of a forced but rich, a very rich retirement, he was readying his forty- or fifty-odd million in cashed-out, apparently untouchable stock to take with him to the gated obscurity of Westchester County, or maybe over to the Hamptons or the Vineyard, down to Florida. No one quite knew his final hiding place—reports differed—but the general shape of it we'd seen enough to lift our shoulders, most of us, with something less than shock. The captain of industry sails off into the sunset in his looted ship, leaving behind crowded raftfuls of lawyers on huge retainers to continue muddying the waters. The plausible denials must be kept plausible for the appeals process, a few of the lower-downs appeased in their country-club prisons—*le capitalisme americain.* I'd seen and read plenty about it in the news—you couldn't not—yet the heart that hung under the head registering all those nouns and verbs was already gamy, contracting, already packed tight with its own troubles. Life was then pizza dough and stinging flour and gray scalding dishwater, as I've said, and now it was also a fiancée whose first foretaste of professional failure had pushed her so deep into herself that for all my attempts at comfort I must have looked like a sea lion awkwardly battering an oyster. (The show was rumored to be losing backers, and initial rehearsals had gone disastrously. Raymond had moved things to a smaller venue, pushed back the theoretical opening, etc.) Nor could I get Jen to dissociate herself at all from a production that she herself had called a hijacking—she was merely taking orders now, "shaping" again, doing damage control. The depression she'd sunk to also belied, frankly, what she'd once told *me* by way of comfort, roles reversed. All jobs suck a little, on Broadway or in the academy or on a grill line—most of the time you're doing someone else's bidding, biding your time, and the important thing is to keep your perspective. But now?

Some blogger for *New York* magazine writes a glorified gossip piece ("*June vs. Hurricane*—And the Hurricane Appears to Be Winning"), and Jen prints it out and pins it to a corkboard hung above the desk in our bedroom, double-underlining the worst parts.

Failure! Failure everywhere! More than enough failure to go around! In between long pulls on his fruit-punch Gatorade, the gulps like live squirming worms moving down Sam's throat—out of this vivid grotesquerie Sam produced even greater ones from a seemingly endless store of facts and figures about the Soline result. Eight cents on the dollar, he said. That's what the thousands of Soline victims could expect from the compromised settlement more than two years after the fact, two years after most of them had lost their savings or their retirements or their homes or all three: The prosecutors would get their generous cuts, the victims would get the leftovers.

"I know. It's depressing," I said.

"It's *accepted*," Sam said. "It's basically unchallenged—Lazarus under the table waiting patiently for the scraps to drop, only now there's no afterlife to make it up to him in. Do you know what eight cents on the dollar actually means for these people? One source I saw estimated that each family will get less than three thousand dollars apiece, whenever they do finally get it. That's eight fucking cents on the fucking dollar."

"Jesus," I said.

"It's a joke. It's disgraceful."

"Well, what is to be done? That old, depressing question."

Sam stood up. "Are you coming back to the House today?"

• • •

I still had a little caked dirt clinging stubbornly to the backs of my thighs when we arrived at the Phoenix House. The other times I'd visited, Alex had been out, but now here she came down the front wooden stairs like a fifties housewife in her blue-checkered dress, supple and smiling. She looked a lot better than Sam did, anyway. Her color had returned, and a healthy bit of flesh. I was tempted to greet her as the Italians do—*You've gained weight!*

Or not really. And the Italians don't actually prize plump edges anymore, do they? It's the imaginary idea of Italy, the ancient idealized *idea* of a thing that clings to the mind.

"Comrade!"

This was Alex's greeting to me, a happy one. I gave it back in kind, with a pair of impromptu European air-kisses—and all was forgiven.

From the outside the Phoenix House looked unremarkable, a faded yellow semidetached at the end of a street full of faded semidetacheds, just another homely tooth in the long gappy smile of the block. Only on the inside did the House distinguish itself as the sort of punk pad–cum–commune it aspired to be: Trotsky beside Lenin beside Baraka on the sagging weathered built-ins, a few novels and flimsy chapbooks to ward off the suggestion of narrowness, a mess of washed-out Persian rugs on the hardwood floors, tacked-up festoons of Christmas lights on the walls, and beneath them several unframed photos and handmade signs: Polaroids of the Group members, the obligatory red fist, a Sharpied encouragement to FUCK THE POLICE! There was also an apparently working record player overhanging the salvaged end table that stood next to a quadrant of dirtied, deeply used couches . . . It was the signature decor, the feng shui of another, older time, only now it belonged to our time, too, by sheer insistence. Past and present together. Not dead, not even past.

I thought of Florence again—helplessly. At any moment it seemed the present world could drop away and sunstruck tangerine-colored Firenze could float up to take its place: the patched stucco walls, narrow cobblestone streets, the chilled frescoed chapels, the green-and-white canvas restaurant awnings that rippled from across the piazzas like sails. Only a week in country, but it was more than enough time for Alex and me to put on a little Italianate flesh of our own: We ate meals of pasta and pizza and risotto, minestrone, mozzarella di bufala, or sometimes straight gelato, affogatos galore, espressos at all hours and in all weathers, great quantities of cheap wine, stinging grappas tossed back in one go, Hemingway-style—all that wonderful peasant food. *Il cibo poveri!*

We loved the taste of the language too, though we understood so little of it, spoke even less. We went to our guidebook for relevant words and phrases that we practiced like vaudevillians in the privacy of our little *pensione* room. *Il cibo poveri!*—the local lilt leaping up and jumping down each word, each syllable a seesaw, with the pinched swirling hand flourish too, of course, that we inevitably let slip into our real interactions with real Italians. You asked directions of a kind-looking man in uncomfortable-looking shoes, the classic nose—must be a native—but at the end of your question about *un ottimo caffè* your hand floated up and circled as you looked helplessly on, too late, like a Tourette's sufferer.

"I can't believe you did that," Alex said the first time it happened.

"You think he noticed?"

"Of course he noticed!" She threw her head back, laughing,

the beautiful white horseshoe of her upper teeth exposed. We laughed together. I don't believe we ever did find that *ottimo caffè*—we made do with another guidebook-recommended gelateria instead, more ice cream for dinner.

But I return, a little reluctantly, to the Phoenix House.

I'd sunk down into a low gray couch opposite Sam and Alex, Sam stretching out his pale thin legs, stork-like, his tennis shorts riding high on his thighs. I noticed the downy white hair there, and Alex's hand coming casually to rest. I thought of the undersides of my own legs. Should I put a towel down? Or was there a bathroom I could freshen up in?

Alex craned her head behind her past the kitchen, half open above a yellow laminate island, the matching counters with the stands of opaque vodka bottles, cereal boxes, a coffeemaker, more photos on the fridge.

"Give it a minute?" Alex said. "Or maybe more than a minute? I think there's a bit of a happening in there."

She didn't elaborate further, only lifted down the record player's arm onto Sam Cooke's haunting, beautiful song "A Change Is Gonna Come." The famous keening voice rose up out of timpani and big-band strings—

"Nice call on the music," I said. "Your namesake, Sam."

Sam was looking at Alex. "He could use the bathroom upstairs, couldn't he?"

"Downstairs is community space, upstairs is for House members," Alex said, as if speaking only to Sam.

"I know that."

"Okay, then."

"He's an honorary House member, isn't he? He's basically here on a trial basis."

"Is that true?" Alex said, turning to me.

"I just don't want to dirty up your couches."

"They've seen worse."

Alex looked into Sam's long face again. She turned back to me slowly. "Here's what you do. Go take a shower upstairs. Make sure the little window's open or you'll die of mold ingestion. Dinner's in an hour, maybe two. Everyone'll be here. Okay?"

Sam Cooke was singing out from the depths of his gloomier bridge—

Then I gooooooo-ooooo to my brother
And I say, "Brother, help me pleeeeeaaase . . ."

The nearer Sam, meanwhile, looked satisfied, nodding, not quite meeting my eye.

I climbed the stairs with my duffel bag and came down several minutes later to find the music changed, and everything else in the House too. Several people buzzed in the kitchen, talking loudly and knowingly about things I could just miss the meaning of, or just miss the larger meanings behind the smaller ones, I suppose I mean. Jamaal in a bright pink T-shirt that said THIS IS WHAT A FEMINIST LOOKS LIKE said, "Anyhow, how touching, right? How hopeful! Democracy! Bipartisanship! Reaching across the aisle! Eli!" He side-armed me into a hug when he saw me standing there, holding up his other hand ashine from a bowl of tossed salad on the counter. I eventually gathered that Jamaal's sarcasm—I'd heard it dripping from the first—referred to a private-jet-setting consortium of American billionaires, mostly New York–based but with a few outliers in Chicago, Houston, Silicon Valley. Democrats and Republicans, Yankees and Southerners, men (and they were all men) who spanned radically different industries and "cultures," but they'd all come together to promote competitiveness, free trade, unfettered innovation—or really ballbusting tactics to compete with the ballbusters abroad, exploitation, and death to all regulators. Touching and democratic indeed. I kept hearing the name "O'Bannon" bandied about, particularly in Jamaal's mouth, and with a kind of odd pride, as if O'Bannon were a horse Jamaal had put money on.

"The man is a flat-out evil genius," Jamaal said. "You know he's being investigated, right?" Sam and Alex at either end of a wooden cutting board nodded; Tiffany rifling around in the condiments shelf of the open refrigerator sent up a blasé "Figures." "Yup," echoed Greg—Greg from the old norming sessions, bow-tie Greg, at the stove, sautéing onions. Jamaal must have noticed the look of confusion on my face because he lifted a pontificating finger as if to explain his point, then he shook the hand out. "In short, he's funneled money to every Tom, Dick, and Harry in his fucked-up nepotistic Irish family, but since they're all on the payroll, and since they all have some inscrutable Orwellian title like IT Product Design Overage Underage Manager, as wide a brief as they need to cover their asses, basically—oh, and they've all got their own shell companies! That's the thing! They've shell-companied the fuck out of this steaming pile of till-stealing until the investigators can hardly move. The latest is they tried to subpoena one of O'Bannon's son's hard drives but O'Bannon claimed the computer wasn't theirs to give away—it belongs to the shell company, a separate legal entity, no provable paper trail connecting the two. It's a fucking free-for-all."

"Bravo," said Tiffany wearily.

"But he's still in New York?"

This was Sam from the opposite counter, still slicing off coins of what looked like cucumber.

"I'm pretty sure," said Jamaal.

"You're *pretty* sure, pretty boy?"

"Well, what about your boy? What's the latest on him?"

"Oh he's here. He's still around. His greed keeps him close."

Somewhat absently, a little hard to hear (I'd been drafted to set the table in the other room), Sam took up the conversational line and described Larry Bosch in the late nineties, early two thousands, several years after he'd filed for and recovered from bankruptcy. Now at the cutting edge of a union-busting movement, he'd secretly hired a PR firm to slime the union bosses at the Jersey-based petrochemical company where he worked in the front office. Portraying the bosses as two-bit Castros but just as greedy—how they lined their pockets with members' dues, drove Lexuses, sold their charges downriver for discreet bonuses, etc., etc.

"He was basically calling them class traitors," Sam said, "and the thing is these fucking guys sort of were—huge salaries, lavish vacations and conferences that the workers they represented couldn't possibly afford. They basically handed their own prosecution to the executive class on a silver platter. You wonder what the Madison Avenue guys got paid for."

The conversation had spilled over into the communal meal of French bread and salad and some kind of baked vegetable medley—a ratatouille?—that tasted powerfully of the Pam some two-bit chef had slathered the cooking dish with. I didn't much mind. A general bonhomie more than made up for it. We caught up, reminisced, gossiped. (I shouldn't suggest that all the House talk, or even the bulk of it, revolved around questions of social justice or strategy or one-percenter excess.) At the end of the meal I'd relaxed enough to try out a quip about Maoist self-criticism sessions—when would ours begin? I was ready. All this felt too pleasant and freeform to be trusted. When would we draw blood?

"I bet you'd like that, wouldn't you," Alex said. "A little Stalinist circle jerk?"

"I was kidding, I was kidding!"

"So was I," she said. "You can relax, Eli. You're welcome here."

I got back to the apartment in Greenpoint very late that night, begging a ride from Sam. Jen was awake upstairs. She asked where I'd been and I told her everything. Or almost everything. I didn't mention the job I'd unofficially quit (or the doctoral program I'd quit months earlier). I didn't mention the wallet and the phone I'd tried to steal from my boss, the jerry-rigged atonement I'd tried to make at Sam's insistence, all the shouting that followed. I talked about Sam instead, the visit to the Phoenix House, the reunion with the old cohort, some of whom I hadn't seen in almost two years, and how much the same they seemed and yet different, some of them scarily different. In the blue-black dark of Jen's bedroom—this was still how I thought of it—I lit up the air with my talk, calm and clinical but also a little wondrous, too, like an anthropologist's talk. Each member of the House contributed not to an individual quota but a general goal, and not just toward rent and food (these were cheap when you considered how many people were crammed into a two-bedroom two-bathroom house) but also toward an action fund. I couldn't get anyone to pin down exactly what action they were building toward; they didn't know themselves, they said—

things were fluid, evolving. Sam was still stealing and selling phones with the help of Jamaal and Tiffany, who also had side jobs. ASU Jason worked graveyard shifts at a 7-Eleven, Alex did a little bartending, Adam and Greg had rich and trusting parents. All the House members cadged what they could from friends and family, honed hard-luck stories, lied shamelessly. And all for a cause no one knew anything about—what it was, what its goals were, who would lead it. I never even found out who was in the downstairs bathroom or what they were doing in there for seven hours, closer to eight. I'd been granted a little access but no real access. I'd gotten information but no answers.

"I know the feeling," Jen said, not bothering to hide whatever it was that seeped up into her voice.

I thought to keep going, pretend to the normalcy I'd pretended to more and more lately—normalcy at three a.m., on a work night, in another shared anecdote, since we shared everything with each other, didn't we? I started to tell Jen about the Bank of America ad Sam had pulled up on YouTube to show me. This was much later in the evening, much deeper in our cups. Picture Maria's round face resolving out of the PBR fog and smiling gamely over small white script that read "actual Bank of America customer"—a well-lit room in soft focus behind her, a soundtrack of feel-good acoustic music underneath. She described how she couldn't have gotten back on her feet without the help and understanding of her Bank of America mortgage broker and the debt-forgiveness plan they'd drawn up together. Cut to a brief slow-motion of Maria and her children playing in a green backyard, gamboling around like cartoon sheep.

"That's not their backyard, is it?" I asked Sam.

"Of course not. You think they let them keep the house?"

"I just didn't think a bank could do that sort of thing,"

Maria was saying as the music went tonic, the screen fading to white as the words stood out in simple black script: "Caring. It's what we do." The bank's logo faded last, of course, outlasting everything, tattooing itself on the eye.

"If not the house, what are they talking about?" I asked. "You think she's talking about that deficiency-agreement stuff?"

"Who knows what the small print actually covers," Sam said.

"I guess that's good, though, right? That the bank was still open to something? I guess something's better than nothing."

"Well, she has her reward," Sam said coldly. "God bless, and fuck off."

Jen looked at me hollowly now, peering out from behind dark lusterless eyes set into her darkened face. She didn't acknowledge the story I'd just told about Maria, or half told—the abortive power of her gaze. I laid a gentle hand on her shoulder and felt the strong plane of muscle slip under my touch, a noticeable recoil. Persistent, I moved around behind her on the bed and leaned my weight into a massage that she eventually responded to, leaning back or falling back into my working hands. I slid down the straps of her nightgown and reached for the lotion we still kept on the bedside table. From soft strokes at Jen's warm, smooth back I moved to the sides of her torso, the sides of her small breasts, pushing the nightgown down to her waist and rubbing to the gentle catch of her hip bones, the hem of her underwear.

Jen's voice cut above the white noise of the fan in the window. "They announced the cancellation today."

"What?"

"The cancellation was announced today."

"Of the show? Of your show? What happened?"

"Yes, the show. The money's gone."

"All of it?"

"Why, do you want to chip in?"

"Oh, sweetie, I'm sorry. I'm so sorry . . ."

"Are you?" Jen said.

"What?"

"Are you really sorry?"

I could tell she was looking right at me, and I felt convicted in that darkness and silence. It was true I'd looked forward to the end of *June vs. Hurricane*—I'd looked forward to the mercy kill, I suppose—but I'd never breathed a word of this aloud to Jen. Cautiously, perhaps cravenly, all I'd dared do was mirror her mooning expressions back at her in a weak pantomime of sympathy. When she'd asked my opinion of a rehearsal, or a blunt e-mail from an investor, I'd focused on tone, narrowly, dodging and weaving around content, getting in and getting out with practiced feints, less a boxer than a politician. I told careful half-truths when pressed, general truths. How could the theater establishment expect daring productions, bristling productions, if this was how they greeted them? As if you couldn't experiment in a one-tier experimental theater on West Fiftieth Street . . . No wonder Off Broadway was looking more and more like its lumbering overweight parent, predictable, complacent, risk-averse, tired. It might be that failure in a climate like this constituted a kind of distinction, a badge of honor, a *better* failure, if I could adapt Beckett . . . But I couldn't. I shouldn't have. I'd overplayed my hand.

In the dark bedroom Jen recalled to me the choicest of these comments. Hadn't I meant them?

I said I had—more or less.

"Then why are you sorry?" she said. "You said it would be

a good thing if it failed, didn't you? And you said it was over-stuffed."

"I said it was 'bristling.'"

"A euphemism. An obvious euphemism."

Jen slid out from under my hands, replacing the straps of her nightgown. I heard the white voice of the fan murmuring out from the window again, getting louder.

"Jen, what are you doing?"

"I'm just trying to understand why you'd be sorry that the show's called off. You said you'd be glad when it was all over."

"I was only agreeing with you!"

"Good. Okay, good. And what I was saying," Jen said, "what you were agreeing with was that a piece of work I'd put my name to, that I'd worked on for over a year, was a fucking train wreck. It was a fucking train wreck and I just wanted it to be killed—I wanted everyone to go home. Is that what you were agreeing with?"

"What do you want me to say, Jen?"

"Say what you mean for once. Tell the truth."

"I agreed with you."

"You agree that it was a fucking train wreck of a show?"

"Sure."

"Say it then. Say it."

"I agree that it was a fucking train wreck of a show."

"Wonderful," she said. "Thank you. My dear fiancé."

She got up and crossed the room to the small chair in the corner, conjuring a cream blanket from out of the darkness, snapping it up unfurled from the chair, a kind of magician's trick, as if all the moves had been planned out beforehand.

"This is ridiculous," I said.

"Is it?"

"You're being ridiculous."

At the door Jen said, "Good night, dear fiancé, sweet fiancé."

"Please don't go out there, Jen. Sweetie, please come back to bed. You want Mal to know we've been fighting again? This is awkward for her."

"So considerate all of a sudden."

"I don't understand what's happening right now. I feel like I walked into an ambush."

"You don't think Mal already knows we're in a fight? You weren't here for dinner—you think she missed that? Where was my considerate fiancé for dinner? Where was he all night? Why didn't he call? Why doesn't he ever call anymore? Mal's not stupid, Eli. Neither am I."

"You don't have to go out there," I said.

"I really do."

"No, I mean I'll go. It's your fucking bedroom."

"How considerate," Jen said, handing over the blanket as we passed in the doorway, our bodies not touching.

I once heard an ex-Weatherman say, a penitent, that he and his friends had been downright cultish to go about sacrificing their lives and livelihoods, their relationships, on the altar of some low-level war against the United States, as they thought of their work then. How blinkered they must have been, how beady-eyed to imagine that their cause would inspire others to join it, that with their rallies and their bombs they had set something real in motion, and so on. And this from the same man who'd once said, famously, *If I die in a beautiful cause, so be it* . . . From one extreme to the other—a familiar enough tactic, a retrospective tactic. The past is a foreign country and I was a stranger there, a stranger to myself, and so on. This is one of the avenues of interpretation now open to me, I realize, an escape route. Yet the afternoon I'm thinking of now—skipping ahead once again—has me sitting contentedly and a little bored in Sam's rusted brown Buick. I have no desire to get out, not really. And I can easily recognize myself on that afternoon. I can get from the me who sits here writing now, remembering, to the me who sat there jogging his leg in the front seat, waiting for something to happen.

Eventually I got out of the car to feed the meter. A quarter only got you ten minutes here, but I supposed we'd been lucky to find a parking spot at all. Lower Manhattan, late September. The air studiously neutral, at last emptied of the humid frenetic energy that had made of the city a kind of particulate snow globe in the last few weeks. There was even a slight cool breeze issuing down this uniconic stretch of Wall Street, so narrow and dark with shade that the breeze might have been a low whistle through a pair of pursed lips. The city moved vertically here, two-dimensionally, with the buildings dragging cornices and pretentious friezes up their long gray lengths, and lower down chunky iron lanterns jutting out like uncovered limbs— again my doomy imagination in these nether realms of the city.

Two middle-aged men in shirts and ties, black shoes and pants, gelled hair, moved past me under the temporary construction pavilion that hugged the building to our left across its entire length and gave the Buick that much more protection. One of the men gave me a quick incurious look. When he and his colleague were farther down the street I heard a rapping sound behind me and turned, Sam cranking down the window.

"What the hell are you doing?"

"Stretching, I guess. Breathing."

"Just go feed the meter, okay, and get back here. The more time you stand there, the more people see you, the more likely one of them is to remember you. Put an hour in, forget the time limits. This is taking longer than usual. And Eli?"

"Yeah?"

"Hurry? For fuck's sake?"

"Okay," I said, "okay—"

For a moment I had to stifle a laugh. There was an uprush of pleasure in me (or was it pride? relief?) to think that Sam might be more nervous than I was. People would remember me doing what exactly—standing by a car? And for what reason? And who would ask them to remember? This was the easy part, the least risky element in a hugely risky, evolving plan, a plan that evolved more risk with each after-dinner strategy session at the Phoenix House. Other big-shot businessmen, other deposed kings of industry kept their names in the conversation (Jamaal still talked a lot about O'Bannon, for example), but Bosch and his unpunished crimes, his local address, made him the frontrunner for retribution. One night in an excess of beery courage Greg gathered his pale pinched features under the overhang of his brow and said we should just kill Larry Bosch, shouldn't we? Make an example of him? The collective intake of breath around the table gave way to nervous laughter, with Greg leading the charge, assuring us he was just kidding, just fucking around—we all knew that, right? Not murder, then, but it didn't have to be. Political theater could be high stakes enough. If we couldn't hold our nerve standing outside a car under a plywood construction awning, or use a credit card instead of quarters to secure a parking spot (Sam worried a card would be traceable), then what hope did we have of abducting a millionaire dozens of times over, probably a bodyguarded millionaire, and then holding him—what?—for ransom? For a publicity stunt? For the hell of it? The plan was still evolving, we told ourselves.

At the green box of a parking meter I slid in the last of my quarters, coming up well short of an hour. We'd been here since two o'clock, it was almost five now, and I'd emptied a bulging pocketful of change into this mute dumb machine. Up ahead on the sidewalk, just past the construction awning, an old-fashioned hot-dog vendor stood under a plain blue umbrella.

He was short and compact in a clean white apron, wearing a black Yankees cap and a mustache, working what looked like a large chrome icebox with a grill attached to it. I started toward him, my eyes casually lowered. I remembered the sunglasses parked atop my Mets cap, put them on. At the stand itself I kept my head bowed, pretending to deliberate over the row of prismatic water bottles, sodas, Gatorades, iced teas, the bottles catching the light as the sun leaned into view at the far end of the street. The man's grill was clean and tidy, with little mounds of white onions caramelizing in one corner. Old Marco from the sub shop, unmissed Marco—I hadn't seen him in two months though I'd come home to Jen and Mallory with many fabricated stories about his micromanagerial zeal, his Napoleon complex—old Marco would have been impressed. To Jen and Mallory I'd started paying a slightly larger share of the rent, by the way, from my parents' largesse. (I claimed the money came from the extra hours I was working at Tommy's.) I'd had a birthday recently, complete with a surprise visit from my parents, a trip to the U.S. Open with Jen, then a chance at a private dinner to lay on my parents a true enough sob story about job-market difficulties, rising rents, falling grad school stipend levels, etc. I came away from that night with a ten-thousand-dollar check—a loan, my parents stressed, though they'd been thinking about something like this for a while. I think they worried I wouldn't accept the money if it were presented as a gift—I think of this queasily now, guiltily.

"Two hot dogs with onions, please," I told the vendor without lifting my eyes to him. I watched the spatula expertly slide under one of the caramelizing mounds, then another, then drop the confetti-like brownish onions along the length of the buns.

"Actually, add these in too," I said, taking two Gatorade

bottles down from the row and passing along a twenty-dollar bill. "How about three dollars in quarters and you keep the change?"

"Thanks, boss," the man said, fingering the coins from his small metal safety box.

I thanked him for the food and the quarters and started back for the parking machine.

"You guys don't stand a chance, you know," he called after me.

In my surprise I turned around and took the man in directly, his wide dark face and the high-peaked cap, the darker mustache like a sea creature under his nose, thick and bristled, slightly shining.

"Come again?"

"You guys don't have a chance. Face it." He gestured at my hat.

"Oh, the Mets!"

"You were lucky to get out of the division series. I take Atlanta in four."

"Well, we'll see, we'll see," I said, and turned away. I'd all but soaked through the thin waxed paper cradling the hot dogs by the time I got back to the car, my sweat glands stoked at an instant and not to be calmed anytime soon.

Sam did nothing to hide his anger. "Did you give him your driver's license? Your Social Security number? A DNA swab?"

"You could see all that, huh?" I handed over the hot dog and the fruit-punch Gatorade. "You're welcome, by the way."

"You learn how to use your mirrors when you do this enough. And how not to be flagrantly stupid."

"I figured we needed more change, okay? We need to eat too, don't we? You're *welcome*."

"Sure thing, comrade," Sam said through a mouthful of hot dog, the bite bobbing in his cheek like a mound of chewing tobacco, unmannerly and crude. It would have seemed out of character for Sam, except that lately Sam seemed to be permanently out of character. For now he kept his blue-gray flat eyes trained on the high-mounted small rearview mirror. He wore the same black Roger Federer hat—blackish gray—with the sweat stains wavering along the brim and the faded edges as if the hat had been dipped in salt water. Of course it hadn't been dipped in any water—that was the problem. Personal cleanliness, like notions of private ownership and space, tended to fall off at the Phoenix House, as if that cliché of communal living had to be cultivated and brought up into pungent bloom. Add to that the House members who smoked—Tiffany, usually opening a window in the second bedroom, but not always. Greg too, I gathered—a sympathetic smoker. My own sympathetic responses moved quickly to squinting and headaches in the presence of cigarette smoke. I was crashing on the sunken gray couch at the House every now and then, but most nights I still returned, gratefully, to the clean cool neutral-smelling uncluttered apartment in Greenpoint.

Sam's eyes flinched at the rearview, suddenly straining.

"What is it?"

"Don't turn around. Use the side mirror."

"Is he in there?"

A trio of suits, a quartet, young men by the looks of them, paused on the sidewalk in front of an ornately arched entryway not far beyond the hot-dog stand. The men in their fine-cut clothes and the entryway with its inlaid squares of stone carving, a lip of twisted stone running along the inside of the arch to look like mooring rope, the thick morbid lanterns, the large flags—all this announced the grand ambitions and haute airs of the offices inside. And the ambitions and airs of the men who worked there (they were almost all men—in two-plus hours we'd seen only a handful of women emerge from the bank of glass doors). Haute airs, haute heirs—one of the synapses I'd glued together over the course of this long, tedious afternoon. Somewhere in Ortega y Gasset I'd learned that *patrician* was the Roman term for the man who could afford to make a will and leave an inheritance. The rest were proletarians, the vast remainder.

Another man had joined the group on the sidewalk and now, decisively, all five of them started away toward Water Street.

"That wasn't him, was it?" I said.

"Assholes in suits," Sam said, "but not our asshole. What's taking him so long today?"

"I kind of have to use the bathroom too—don't hate me. How long does he usually stay in there?"

"This is my point, comrade. You know I love you, but I'm not sure these junkets play to your strengths. You have to be able to sit—still—for a long time."

"You don't have a bladder? Alex doesn't have a bladder?"

"You leave my girlfriend's bladder out of this," said Sam, suddenly enjoying himself. "You've lost all privileges there."

"Jesus."

"What?"

"You tell me," I said.

"I think that's him."

"Who? Bosch?"

"Don't fucking turn around," said Sam.

In the spotted side mirror I watched a small, gaunt man, the top of his pate shining powerfully, step to the same curb the suited quintet had just occupied. In a loose coat, tieless, he lifted a phone to his ear and looked tired, shifting his weight from leg to leg as he talked, listing over to one side or the other of his body's y-axis. Two other men stood nearby, taller than Bosch, better dressed. None of them looked any bigger than an inch in the conjuring medium of my side mirror—a simple bringing together of thumb and forefinger could have snuffed them all out.

We followed Bosch's town car at a length of three or four cars, sometimes more, never less. Sam knew the route well. Up Water Street and onto the FDR with the infinitesimal low river like a diamond slick running off to our right, the Brooklyn Bridge's giant legs in the rearview and the Manhattan Bridge's looming up ahead quick and gray. Then the long flat climb to the top of the island, the Art Deco monuments on the Brooklyn side, the low row houses of Queens, ferries on the water, the black whir-ring freeway rails. At the entrance to 278 Sam split off and let the town car continue on its way. We doubled back into Queens and started for the House.

"You're assuming he doesn't have pressing business in Yon-kers," I said. "Or maybe White Plains?"

Sam didn't acknowledge the joke. "Anyway, you know the rest," he said.

"He never stops off in midtown for any business?"

"Not that I've seen. He's persona non grata at Soline headquarters—they've had to purge him, or appear to have purged him. No, it's just Wall Street to home now, Wall Street to home . . . He was in there a lot longer than usual today. I don't know what that means—if anything."

"Do you know how much Bosch pays on his house in property taxes alone?" I said.

"Half a million."

"Oh, come on! You guessed too high! You're supposed to guess something semi-reasonable—remember, we're just talking about property taxes."

"Fifteen dollars."

"Three hundred grand, wise ass. On property taxes alone."

"You got that from the *Architectural Digest* piece?"

"The real estate website—there are all sorts of stats on there, more photos too. Rooms the size of ballrooms. I think there might actually be a ballroom in there. They've got a perfect blue lake that backs up to their land and a little stream that runs through it with a little bridge over it like something out of a fucking Jane Austen novel. Who knows how blue the lake actually is—these photos are like soft-core porn with all the lighting and the touch-ups. The colors are like the Platonic ideals of colors, the Platonic ideal of a blue lake or a red Persian throw rug in front of a fireplace the size of a Studebaker. Do you know how many bathrooms he's got in that place?"

"Thirty," Sam said.

"Fuck you."

"Zero," Sam said. "No bathrooms at all. Just a porta potty out front that they have to share with the construction workers."

"Seven! Seven bathrooms! What the hell does an empty-nest couple need with seven bathrooms?"

"Seven's a biblical number, as I'm sure you know. Maybe he's a spiritual man."

"I think we can assume Larry Bosch is a deeply spiritual man," I said. "Anyway, now what?"

"Now we do it again."

"You mean tomorrow?"

"Maybe."

"What does 'maybe' mean?"

"It means maybe."

"Well, what are you thinking?"

"I'm thinking he's trying to move his money, do something to shelter it, protect it. Three hundred grand is a lot to pay for property taxes, but in the scheme of things, in the scheme of Westchester County and all that criminal wealth, a ten-million-dollar house is middle-of-the-road. I think he's plenty liquid and getting ready to be more liquid."

"You meant you and me when you said 'we' a second ago, right? About doing another junket?"

"You'll have to arm-wrestle Alex for it. We'd be taking her car. And I think she kind of likes this stuff. Makes her feel adventurous, she says. She says it ironically, but you can kind of tell."

"Then there's her famous bladder control . . ."

Sam smiled vaguely ahead at the windshield, cryptically, a shadow of sadness passing over his face. "She says it makes her feel a little like Bonnie to my Clyde."

"Is that right?" I said.

We called these outings "junkets," by the way, since "stakeouts" sounded too Hollywood, and too blunt a reminder of what it was we were actually planning, contemplating, kicking around. How serious were we about an abduction? I wouldn't have been the one to ask. I'm sure some bad ideas do hatch in haste, and out in the open, with a group's enthusiasm or insanity running ahead of itself and in loose hurling concert. Our bad idea was different—secretive, tentative, jolting into a new stage of evolution without the Group being notified of it, with only a few insiders putting their heads together in the shadows. This was the problem with Sam now, too. When he looked through a windshield and smiled a vague little half-turned cryptic smile, or when he disappeared for days on end and no one could tell you why or where to, you realized you'd lost the bead on this friend of yours. This strange, ever-thinning friend, this angular insect of a man with his mandible jaw—who was he? Was he a paranoid now, a sudden introvert? Had I somehow lost his trust? Was he testing me? He ran hot and cold sometimes in the space of a single sentence, and the cold could stop your heart, as if you'd swum out with him into the warm shallows of his old enthusiasm, his old joie de vivre, only to feel the bottom drop out at the continental shelf's edge: Suddenly you're in bottomless, dark, updrafting, freezing water.

By contrast, Alex at this same time became more solicitous of me, teasing, probing, more intimate than she'd been at any time since our relationship—more intimate than she'd been at times *during* our relationship. We still prepared our potluck ramshackle dinners *en famille*, and if it was Alex's turn to spring for the protein or the booze, or if it was mine, we walked together to the greened sooted copper stretch of Roosevelt Avenue where a bodega, a Korean market, and a liquor store all huddled within a block of one another in the latticed shade of the elevated 7 train. A simple shopping trip could take us hours, slowed by the sense that something was being rediscovered, something unearthed in our long walk-and-talks, like the knowledge from a past life that Socrates apparently drew out of his pupils as they walked beside a river. By the time we got home, Alex and I often met with the recriminating stares of hungry House members, some of them asking outright what had taken us so long.

When I asked my own questions of Alex, she usually turned them aside, Sam-like, turning us back to less pressing subjects, gentler subjects. She recalled the time we'd spent together on top of a green mountain in Vermont, at an academic conference overrun with academics—somehow we hadn't prepared ourselves for that. A floating enclave of Morningside Heights, it set down on top of a rural campus and sent Alex and me scurrying off into the woods. Did I remember that? Into the woods to live at least a little deliberately, to suck out the marrow of a misconceived week! By the third day of the conference Alex and I had thrown away our name tags and all the scheduling material. We skipped a panel she was supposed to be on (how did I not see that she was crashing out of academe?), spending the day instead on the dappled dirt paths Robert Frost used to walk during his summers on this same mountain. Copper plaques stood at elbow-resting height in the sunlit clearings along the trails. Some of the chiseled verses you could just make out ("Something there is that doesn't love a wall"), but many others were too effaced, worn out by weather and time, burnished a dull gold in the sun. The bare plaques were like open invitations to add our own verses. You got to contribute at least one, if you believed Whitman. One late afternoon with the sun through the trees turning grainy and thick, honeyed, the golden hour, Alex and I spread a blanket over the low ferns just off the trail and made love.

It surprised me a little to hear Alex recalling all this now, but it probably shouldn't have. My instinct in her presence was always to excise, to gloss over the year of romantic love that had interrupted and rather complicated our friendship, but this was never Alex's way. Today on the shopping run it had been my turn to cover the meat and the booze—I sprang for lean ground turkey and two cases of Blue Moon, pricey beer—and now I felt Alex's hand graze mine as we meandered back to the House. We were wearing matching Mets caps, as it happened, large sunglasses, with late shadows like masks over our faces. I could make out Alex's mouth going lopsided again, happy air through her nose.

"And how about my almost-date with Lyme disease?" she said. "You remember that, don't you?"

On the last morning of the conference she'd come to me in our little cabin/dorm room, her hair wet from the shower, in her towel, raising her left arm to reveal a small unplump tick that had rooted at the edge of the armpit's concavity. Alex's eyes and lips were flat and, I thought, faintly accusing—I remembered that the first trips into the woods had been my idea, that I'd dismissed Alex's concerns over ticks as citified, paranoid.

"It wasn't an accusing look!" Alex said. "That was all in your head!"

"I am a bit of a worrier sometimes, aren't I?"

"A *bit*? You were apoplectic! So now *I've* got to worry that this little fucker in my armpit might be transmitting an incurable disease and I've also got to stop my boyfriend from throwing himself in front of a speeding pickup as some sort of honor suicide. 'Oh Jesus! Oh Jesus! I'm so sorry, I'm so stupid—fuck! Fuck!'"

"I don't remember being *quite* like that."

"Exactly like that," Alex said. "Heaping ashes on your head, rending your garments—it was biblical."

"You really are starting to sound like Sam," I said.

"I say Puritanical, he says biblical. We happen to be in

agreement about you, comrade. You've got a guilt complex, you're an emoter, a loose cannon. What's the opposite of a stoic? That's you."

"Are you being serious right now? Does Sam really say that about me? The both of you?"

Alex must have seen the change in my face, or anyway she looked at me with a changed expression, the puckering eyebrows pulling down beneath her sunglasses.

"Eli, learn to take a joke."

"Does Sam say that about me, yes or no?"

"You can ask him yourself," she said. "He's back tonight. Get right up in his face—I'm sure he'll like it as much as I do."

"I'm sorry," I said, "but Jesus, Alex . . ."

I continued with the bit in my mouth for the rest of the way home, softening my words a little but mostly just slowing them down, drawing out the silences around them like so much difficult taffy. I was persistent, though—I wanted answers. Where had Sam been for the last week, anyway? What had he been doing? And why was it that Alex seemed to know about it and no one else did?

"Alex?"

She kept her face pointed steadfastly east, a rictus smile on her lips. At the turn onto our street a homeless man in a nest of grimy blankets held out his sign perfunctorily—Alex reached into the grocery bag I carried, pulled out a Blue Moon, and handed it off to the man without a word.

Back at the House, Sam had already arrived home, just in time for dinner. He looked at ease setting the table, catching up on the latest with Greg and Tiffany, Asshole Adam (who wasn't so asshole-ish anymore), ASU Jason (now two-plus years out of ASU). I realized I needed new names for these people, new versions. I'd tried especially hard to reconcile the Greg Baxter I'd known through Hahn's norming sessions, pedantic, begrudging, bow-tied Greg Baxter, with the Greg who'd apparently come aboard the House through Tiffany's persuasions. I'd had to adjust what I thought I knew about Tiffany, too. More than once I'd watched her and Alex interlocking hands as they climbed upstairs for the night, Sam following behind a little sheepishly, uncertainly—a cocked eyebrow to me once, on the couch, conspiratorial, a lucky libertine's smiling acknowledgment, but he didn't pull it off. I sensed he was surprised and unsure of his role now. Did this account in part for his distances lately, his sudden silences? His absences?

During dinner I saw that I wasn't the only one being kept in the dark on Sam's recent whereabouts, and not the only one chafing under this ignorance either. Jamaal got up at one point for a second crack at the fajita bar, floating into the kitchen on the helium power of his Afro, bigger and looser than ever, like a flowing electrostatic field around his head. He'd complained of the sweat soaking his hair like a sponge throughout the hot hot summer, but here we were in October now, the home stretch, or so we hoped.

In the kitchen Jamaal reached into a cupboard only to jerk the hand back as if stung. "Fuck! These roaches!"

He detoured on his way back to the table to lift the record player's arm off Sam Cooke, copacetic and soft.

"Just a minute, Sam," Jamaal said. He turned to us. "Black Sam, I mean, Sam with the soul."

"How do you know I don't have soul?" said our Sam. "You've never heard me sing."

"How do you know I'm talking about that kind of soul?"

"I have as much soul as you," Sam said, looking suddenly very pleased with himself, "and full as much heart."

Then his face sank a little when nobody got the apparent reference.

Jamaal sat down opposite Sam but addressed the whole group, leveling a long forefinger like the barrel of a gun. "First order of business: We need to do something about these motherfucking roaches. Next person up for grocery run, get some real traps, not these cheap-ass motels where the fuckers can rest up and watch free cable. Second order of business—" He jutted another finger out under the first, the hand like a two-pronged pitchfork pointing at Sam's chest, a Black Mass of the peace sign. "Second order of business is where the fuck were you and why can't we get a straight answer about it out of anybody? I mean, you must have known," he said to Alex, "but it's like the goddamn Manhattan Project the way you guard it." And turning to Tiffany, "And you too—what's with all the Stalinist secrecy around here? Do we have to join this triad of yours to get answers? Do we have to fuck our way to the top?"

"Wow," Alex said. "What a charming reactionary you make."

Tiffany said, "Nobody told me anything."

"I went to visit my sister is all," Sam said. "She just had a kid, a little girl. I wanted to meet her. Do I need to run my travel itineraries past everyone in the House?"

"Honestly I didn't even know to ask. I didn't realize I'd been excluded from a secret." Tiffany again. "I must have missed that memo."

"It was a secret because you all *made* it a secret," Jamaal said. "'Where'd Sam get to?' It's a simple question, with a simple fucking answer."

"Okay, okay," Greg said, holding up a papal hand, apparently casting himself in the role of sainted moderate. He pointed out that we were supposed to be in the middle of planning something pretty big, weren't we? If only for that reason we should probably do a better job of keeping each other abreast of things—"updated," he corrected himself.

"Well, actually, on that front," Sam said. "On that front we might need to slow down for a while."

"Says who?" said Jamaal, and the lines quickly redrew themselves. "Who's deciding all this anyway, and behind what closed doors?"

When Jamaal finally shouted that it was Phoenix all over again, only roles reversed—another cabal had been formed—Alex handled the accusation calmly. "Not a cabal, no," she said, "but a leadership group? Well, if the shoe fits . . . Weren't Lenin and Trotsky, Luxemburg, Guevara—weren't these people all part of *led* factions? We wouldn't know about their movements otherwise—"

"So which one are you?" Jamaal interrupted. "Which one is Sam? You're Lenin, he's Trotsky, is that it? You're Bonnie, he's Clyde?"

Sam did another of his startled turtle-jerks backward on his neck, cutting a hateful look at me—Alex slower to respond, comprehending.

"Why *shouldn't* he tell us?" Jamaal said. "We're either an open organization or we're a bullshit hierarchy, in which case Eli's down here with us, in the shadows of the Great Leaders. Solidarity of the also-rans."

Alex spoke very quietly now. "Here's what I know. Sam takes off for a week and everything basically stops. When he and I hang fire, you all hang fire. No one decided this, no one announced it, but it appears that, yes, a natural hierarchy has emerged."

"That's good to know," Jamaal said, scraping back his chair on the way to the staircase, where he turned and gave a deep, faux-subservient bow.

When he'd slammed a door upstairs, I noticed a new hand-made sign hanging on the wall where Jamaal had stood. It was a black-and-white printout of an old-timey police officer—think James Cagney in his later period—complete with brimmed shining hat, the bared teeth between bulldog jowls, the dark glowering eyes. I recognized Alex's handwriting above and below the image: WHAT SHOULD YOU DO IF A PIG AP-PROACHES YOU???

- DO NOT LET THE PIG SEARCH YOUR PERSON OR BAG OR VEHICLE—OR ANYTHING—UNDER ANY CIRCUMSTANCES!

- DO NOT VOLUNTEER ANY INFORMATION ABOUT YOURSELF OR ANY OTHER HOUSE MEMBER!

- MAKE THE PIG STATE CLEARLY THE REASON FOR HIS APPROACH . . .

A little word balloon grew out of the "HIS" in this last direc-tive: "Or 'HER'? Hmmmmmm?"

Pretty soon the conversation had relaxed again, spreading out delta-like as we all moved to the couches. I noticed Alex slipping back into her casual-intimate mode with me, with Sam and Tiffany looking neutrally on. I didn't know how to feel about this. I felt Alex's smiling judgment settle over me like a fallout, gentle and familiar. I'd never understood her, had I? I was a Puritan, an athlete of repression, etc. And maybe that shoe fit as well. I certainly did perk up a minute later—mentally, bodily—when Alex came up from behind me on the couch and ran her hands down the front of my chest. I covered them with my own hands, instinctively. Alex's face soft and close, her cheek to my cheek. She whispered in my ear, side-kissed my temple. The other House members lazing nearby looked discreetly away, I noticed, all except Tiffany—Tiffany with a cautious, warming-up smile. She'd seen this before, perhaps.

And Sam? Sam's eye I carefully avoided, though later I could hear his distinct, heavy tread following behind us up the stairs.

"*Et voilà*, as you'd say, with your stupid French envy," Alex said to me as we crossed into the bedroom.

A little odd to consider, in a House so skimpy on boundaries, but I'd never actually set foot in this room. It surprised me. Out of the roil of things in my body, the muted roar in my head, I chose to focus on the stylish, spare decor, the room glowing like a darkroom from the red-shaded table lamp. Above the table, a red-framed circular mirror floated the reflection of a large, goateed, beret-wearing man on the opposite wall, a marked intensity in his gaze. If I was meant to recognize this face, I didn't. It looked a little like a Lichtenstein print presiding over the constellation of smaller frames, carefully arranged to look uncareful: a gold-winged dragon, like something off a Roman crest; a trio of men and a raffish underfed-looking woman in Bolshevik long coats and peaked hats . . . As for the bed, as for the sleeping situation, this too rather startled in its contrast with the haphazard threadbare sprawl of the rest of the

House. What lurid imaginings I'd allowed myself about Alex and Tiffany and Sam usually involved an unwieldy sultan's bed, as wide as it was long. But here a tidy queen with a white headboard, a simple flower pattern on the comforter, tucked into the far corner of the room, and in the other a narrow bunk bed was made up with clean, cool bedding the color of Easter eggs—pale blue, pale green. Sam took a seat in a black wooden chair beside the table, and Alex and Tiffany sat together on the bottom bunk, taking me in a little coolly now.

Finally Sam gestured to the iPod dock on a bookshelf behind me and said, "Why don't you choose a little music for us, Eli. Anything will do. And turn it up."

In the iPod's artist list I came almost immediately to Fiona Apple, perhaps Jen's all-time favorite pop artist. I hesitated, then chose one of Jen's favorite songs—"I Know." Let it serve as a reminder. The flat porous speakers began pouring out the buzzing piano line and the canny unsentimental voice—

> So beeeeeee it, I'm your crowbar—
> If that's what I am so far . . .

"You guys know I have a girlfriend, right?" I said. "A fiancée."

Leaning back on the bed, Alex raked her hand across Tiffany's hair like a chime. She laughed. "You really thought you were being seduced, huh? I give you the bedroom eyes and you obey, hey?"

"Here we go," Sam said, "okay." He carried his chair and another nearby to the bedside, motioning for me to sit next to him. We were close around the lower bunk, leaning our heads in like the conspirators the rest of the House probably still suspected us of being, speaking under cover of Fiona Apple's rainy love songs.

"I can trust everyone in this circle," Sam said. "I do trust everyone in this circle. All right?"

"Me too," Alex said.

"Me too," Tiffany said.

Now they were looking at me. "Sure, yes," I said. "Sorry, I do too."

"Okay, good," Sam said. "I'm not sure about anyone else, though. Or not sure enough. Are you guys?"

We started working through the others one by one—what we knew about them, how they'd come to us, how much exposure we felt they could bear. A slow, methodical probe, a little too slow, perhaps, since after several minutes Sam started getting noticeably twitchy.

Alex laughed at him.

"What?"

"You want to show Private Lentz your new toy, don't you?" she said.

"I think we've made a good start, don't you?"

"Very."

"We can come back to this, of course. We will."

"Of course."

Alex toed out from under the bed the worn navy blue backpack Sam used for his cell-phone trawling. Once again it dipped tellingly when Sam held it upright. Fiona Apple was still going on the player, jazz brushes on a snare like rain against a window. It wasn't a squeal of zippers this time, just a slow, careful reaching into the bottom of the bag's main compartment, Sam's arm half gone, as if he were birthing a calf. When the gun came out it was wrapped in a white linen kitchen towel. Sam displayed it on his lap, the pointed ends of the towel like the blooms of an opening flower. The gun looked that much blacker and blockier—it looked fake, shining a little too brightly along the barrel and stock, or handle, or whatever you called it, a fine waffling down the side of the grip. Only when Sam offered it across to me on tray-like hands, like a deadly hors d'oeuvre, did I feel its authenticating heft. It was real all right. I didn't touch the trigger—I didn't dare to.

"It isn't loaded," Sam said. "And it won't be. But we need it."

"We need it?" I said.

"We need it."

"And this is what you were really doing last week?"

"I really was at my sister's in Pennsylvania. They live out in the sticks, hunting country, not far from a truck route, and they're paranoid. They've got three or four of these things. I doubt they'll miss one for a while. Anyway . . ."

He went off into other talk, shop talk—about the gun, its make, how to use it, how his brother-in-law had taken him out shotgun hunting and told him always to aim low, always lower than you think. And how different could one of these be? He was looking at the pistol resting heavily like a talisman in my palm. We were all looking at it, falling to silence now. It was mesmerizing.

One other thing we discussed that night around the lower bunk: my sleeping situation. I was made to understand that I would now be a visitor to the apartment in Greenpoint, a mere checker-in, a keeper-up of appearances. This was one of the conditions of my remaining in the leadership group, or at the House at all—I had to commit. I had to be all in. I can't pretend that at the time I really struggled with the decision.

Within a few days Adam and Jason had quit the House and only Greg and, to everyone's surprise, Jamaal remained. Sam and Alex set Greg to more cell-phone trawling, with Jamaal and Tiffany continuing to help with the wiping and posting—cell phones, iPods, tablets, laptops, whatever Greg could lay hands on. The Group needed the money more than ever, Sam said, but he and Alex needed to concentrate their energies on planning. Not the old plan, we said, but the new plan, which needed to remain secret until it shaped up more. It was grunt work for Greg particularly, and also a loyalty test. Why the long-faced former bow-tie wearer insisted on passing it, his bushy brows unbent, I still don't know.

As for me, I made good on an offer to pick up the rent slack Adam and Jason had left. There went November, December, January. By the end of February I'd drawn down my checking account to eight hundred dollars, all the tough-minded generosity of my parents gone to seed my double life. I'd stopped paying more than token sums to Jen and Mallory, claiming my hours at Tommy's had been slashed. I was afraid I might get fired, I said, but then again who cared, right? Good riddance! Maybe getting fired would jolt me out of my complacency and depression, send me back to my dissertation, or to a better job, or something, anything!

It was after one of these performances, all variations on a theme, the sputtering fugue state of my life with Jen, that Mallory patted me on the shoulder and said, " 'Good riddance!' Right!"

The obvious sarcasm in her voice brought me up short. It was just after work hours, late evening, with a dandruff of snow falling out of the blue-black darkness through the window. I realized I'd forgotten to ask where Jen was.

A moment later Mal emerged from her bedroom still in her heavy peacoat, moisture glistening on the coarse sleeves. She emanated the cold she'd brought from outside, sitting beside me on the piano bench. Up close I could see that the chill-deepened circles of red at her cheeks and nose tip, around the curve of her ears—she looked suddenly like a Raggedy Ann doll—were not pure but mottled, points of white and red in minute alteration, like a Seurat painting. Her wide-set eyes were long and brown and the wedge of forehead skin between them, the thin incurving brows, the top of the long nose sent your attention swinging out into the ski-jump air in front of her face. Mal was looking at the score I'd stopped playing out of shyness.

"'Lost to the world,' huh? I'd say that's appropriate. Play this part again," she said, underlining the section with a long rosy fingertip, the nail unpainted.

I did as I was told.

"Now sing along to it."

Hesitantly, very quietly—

"Louder."

I did as I was told.

"Yup," she said, "yup. That's what I heard. This passage here," and she sang it herself with soft, brilliant clarity, a low-to-high figure, effortless. "Do you hear the difference? It's not a trombone slide. Mahler's not crooner material. Move up crisply to the next note but hit it soft—transition with dynamics, not your hammy glissando. You try," she said.

I tried.

"Better. That's a little better. You have a decent voice, you know that? You've got a decent mid-tenor. You could do something with it if you took some initiative."

"Thank you?"

"It's a compliment."

"Thank you."

"You want some more advice? I know you didn't ask for any, but do you want some more?"

I could hear in her voice that it wasn't really a question. I might have been squinting, bracing myself.

"You're really fucking up with Jen, you know that, don't you?"

"I know," I said, "I know it. It's all this stuff at work, and some other stuff—"

"Shut up, stop it. Just stop. I know you're lying."

"What? I'm not lying."

"Last month Jen went by your work to surprise you. She was going to take you out on a date—remember dates? It's this thing where two people who love each other, who are still technically engaged, go out and spend time alone together? Anyway, she talked to your friend Marco, got the whole story. He said you're lucky he hasn't pressed charges yet. What are you doing, Eli?"

I took this in for a minute. "When last month?"

"I don't know. Pretty early."

"Early? So she's been sitting on this for six weeks—more than six weeks?"

"Look, I don't know what your deal is, I don't particularly want to know, but I can tell you that you're fucking up royally. Do you know where Jen is right now?"

"I was going to ask."

"If you tell her I told you this I'll kill you. I'll never talk to you again."

"Where is she?"

"She's out with a guy she met through work. Some random guy auditioning late in the day, doesn't make the cut, but sticks around to ask your fiancée out for coffee."

"She's seeing him tonight?"

"This isn't the first time either. I'm telling you this because I like you—I'm not sure why. You're a ghost lately, but you're a friendly ghost—how's that? Anyway, that's my advice."

"I'm not sure I caught the actual advice."

"Stop fucking up."

This was the intelligence I'd received from Jen's closest friend. For several days I carried it around with me like a secret scar—a secret of a secret. It was a button I could push to make my heart go tight, instantly pinched and smarting. It was a kind of penance to push it; I pushed it often. I thought of it that way, too, that Sam-like way—evacuated religion, a giving in to the forms, the temptations of dogma, as I think Derrida puts it somewhere. Sam had influenced all of us, of course. He was the common virus we'd all caught.

I didn't like myself for being jealous, regretful, mournful, whatever I was. I didn't like to think that Mal's information had activated feelings in me that had lain dormant for months, that competition could do what love and loyalty could not, that pitifully ordinary machismo sat so near the seat of my motivations. And I think this is why I did nothing for several days, then a week, then two, staying away from the apartment more and more. On nights when I did stay over Jen came home late,

sometimes very late, never disclosing the details of her night—
and I was careful never to ask her to. We acted like casual
friends more than lovers now, unfailingly polite, a little distant,
closed off to each other brick by brick—though it was true we
sometimes still made love, sometimes held each other as we had
before. This was my resolution: I would do nothing different.
With Mal's insider information, with this pen-tip hole in the
ceiling that gave on to Jen's double life, I would still play the
hand I'd been dealt; I would honor the ignorance that should
have been mine. Each day I put on Mal's secret to me like a hair
shirt. I pushed the button again and again.

But plot caught up to me. Plot, as they say, is character—
which means I might do better to say simply that character
caught up to me. I sat in the melting weather on a flight of
stone steps stained white with the memory of winter salt, like
a recessed sea. The sky over the narrow mid-rise buildings was
gray, uncertain, wispy—you could see the atmosphere slipping
the lower clouds under the higher ones like sheets of paper. This
was Tribeca, not far from Canal Street and Chinatown, where
the commercial rents were cheaper, apparently. You had to go
downtown before you could go up, Jen liked to tell people about
her work—downtown to the light-filled hot creaking hardwood
loft they used for auditions, uptown to whatever Off-Broadway
venue the lucky few would start rehearsals in. Jen always talked
about luck, never talent, as if talent were simply assumed and
assumed to be copious, vast, sprawling, hanging out undirected
most of the time in the gutters of modern capitalism. Luck
mattered more, or unluck—of course they did. How lucky had
some striver been to show up for an outside chance and leave
with the phone number of a woman like Jen? How lucky had I
been?

Well, but here she came. I could hear the freight elevator being drawn back into the raspy lungs of the building as Jen made her way out of the black steel door and down the steps, Raymond following. I was a ways off, but I recognized Raymond's slight frame with the square shoulders, the bleached boyish hair that swirled upward like a cap of soft-serve ice cream. Jen wore her shorter, lighter peacoat with the white Amelia Earhart scarf loosely coiled around her neck, one end of it hanging off the back of her shoulder like a casual hand. Her hair was up in a loose ponytail—she was proud of her cheekbones, I'd learned, justly proud, and easily annoyed with the auburn strands that broke free of her ears and fell into her face. At the tail end of winter the hair had returned to its natural red-orange, much starker than the strawberry blonde it lightened to in the summer months. I liked it better this way—sui generis. Here was a woman you could pick out of a crowd.

If Jen had turned left, in my direction, I was prepared to stand up from the stoop all smiles, surprising her. We would go out for dinner. I would press out the dregs of my bank account to pay the tab at a noodle bar, or whatever she wanted. In a way I wanted this to happen—in one version of these memories, this *is* what happens: Jen and I hang our faces over steaming white porcelain bowls of ramen, talking little but sitting close, side by side, as if the steam could heal us. In one version it does heal us.

But now Jen and Raymond turn right toward Lafayette Street and the uptown trains, and I have to follow.

From the far corner of a 6 train car I watched the two of them reflected in the glare-warped window, my hat brim pulled to my eyebrows, my love with her face tipped delicately down at her cell phone, looking up and smiling at occasional comments from Raymond. She left him at the Union Square stop with a squeeze of the hand, getting off into the throng of rush-hour bodies that I swam in gratefully, anonymously, until Jen cut out of the current that pushed us toward the L train connection. Upstairs in the streets I nearly bumped into her—she'd stepped into the leeward draft of a newsstand just past the railinged maw of the subway stairs. It was another text, I assumed, her thumbs dizzying the screen, that saved me. I took cover under a Best Buy awning across the street, pretending to check my own phone as the glass double doors ejected shopper after laden shopper like tottering clay pigeons into the open air.

The white tents of the green market lined the perimeter of the square, gray-green in the waning light, wet-looking, tentative. People moved in twos and threes, coats open, inspecting the wares piled bounteously, colorfully on the folding wooden tables. The hemming-in buildings looked down on the scene with mute dull faces, blank-window eyes. It was a few weeks since thousands of protesters and activists, some of them our old ISO comrades, filled this square in a show of outrage over the latest in a pile of black bodies that New York's finest had heaped into the mortuaries: a stop-and-frisk gone bad, or worse than usual, a twenty-year-old breaking for his Bronx apartment entrance, reaching for his keys, five bullets in the back. Initially the police made much of the fact that a dime bag of weed was found on the body. Our group chose not to participate in the march—too much exposure, and what was the point? Marches and protests were the release valves a militarized state let the people pull. That was our position then, anyway.

When I looked through a break in the traffic at the spot where Jen had been a moment before—empty air. I found her on a bench in the center of the tent market, recognizing her from behind, that spout of orange-red ponytail. Just then she put her phone to her ear; she stood up, turning all the way around once, twice, smiling, raking her happy gaze past me like a lighthouse beam. Finally she found him. He'd snuck up in plain sight behind a woman with a double-wide stroller and a green puffer vest—Macduff in the moving grove. A kidder. I hated him instantly.

This particular kidder, this interloper (I couldn't help thinking of him in that way) had longish dark hair that swept messily over his ears and low over his forehead, curtain-parted—Al Pacino circa *Serpico*, slightly. He might have looked a little like me, if I'm honest, but of course I couldn't be honest. I couldn't be expected to be, could I? Objectivity is too heavy a cross to lay on the jilted.

The next several times they met up it was more of the same. They'd find each other at Union Square and set off for a meal or a drink somewhere within a few blocks. They were forming routines, traditions, memories, the kind of things you'd tell your kids about when they slid one after the other into your neat and ordered lives: *Your father used to sneak up on me every time we met here, and the thing is I knew it was coming, I knew to expect it, but he always found a way . . .* I remember the day Jen got off the 6 train early, at Astor Place instead of Union Square, and by the time I'd poked my head aboveground they were kissing. The repeating arches of the Cooper Union building stretched off behind them, dull pink in the late-winter light, or early-spring light—I couldn't have told you the difference just then. Young Macduff with his carefully messy hair had joined his stupid face to Jen's, his stupid fingers lifting the hair around her temples out of place. Jen's hands were on his hips, lightly, a little awkwardly, I thought—I hoped. I followed them onto St. Mark's Place, passing the high cluttered brownstones with the fire escapes like strange zippers down their fronts, ready to open up the buildings in zigzags and spill their privacies gruesomely into the street. I couldn't have noticed this at the time—memory labors to fill in the scene. What I noticed was that Jen's new boyfriend had taken her hand. More gradually I became aware of the near darkness, the last light clinging with stubborn fingers to the luminous strips of crosswalk paint, the serpentine coil of graffiti down the side of a corner mailbox, the luster of the stone in the white-stoned apartments. When we passed Hahn's building, blue-white in the gloom, I saw that her living-room light was on, the yellow glow in a window set half below street level. How the mighty were fallen—though I didn't have time to think about Hahn now, either, or dying Stephen.

I had just watched Jen lead Macduff down the stairs to the nondescript entrance into Cafe Mogador.

Cafe Mogador! It took the air out of my lungs to see it—Jen, with this interloper, casually entering what she knew was my favorite restaurant, the one Hahn had first taken me to, the one I'd introduced Jen to, and my parents, and all my friends, the few remaining to me, anyway. I couldn't quite believe I'd seen it. I set up at a spot on the patio with my back to the restaurant's large picture window, not quite daring to look inside. For a long time I watched the mysterious switchboard of the opposite buildings activate, permutate, the lights blinking on and off, shifting, sending mysterious signals. Halfway through a bottle of pinot I couldn't pay for I started to mourn each window light as it went out, each quick soundless fade. I felt no corresponding joy or relief at the windows newly lit. Nightlife was beginning, carving itself out of the ageless dark. At my next backward glance I picked the two of them out of the far corner of the restaurant, the lighted patchwork insubstantial and glossy on one side of the glass and on the other, at a shrunken candlelit table, Jen and Macduff leaning over their plates, stretching their necks like sunflowers. When they kissed again, I stood abruptly and a little unsteadily, rattling the untouched plate of tagines at my place. I passed down the steps and through the tinkling front door and into the close field of tables, past friends and colleagues, couples laughing and talking unawares, into one such couple with a wayward lurching step, the loud scrape of a bald man's chair—I apologized quickly, slurring my words, but it was too late. Jen had looked up with the noise.

In no time she was at the bar side, intercepting me. "What the hell are you doing here?"

Her eyes gleamed in the candlelight fiercely, her face distorted by the shadows, and she said again, "What are you doing here, Eli? You need to leave. You need to leave now."

"What are *you* doing here?" I said, but weakly. Jen and the rest of the room looked shrunken down in the wrong end of binoculars.

"Go home, Eli. Eli? I'm not talking to you like this."

"Our home?"

"I'm done talking. I'm going back."

"You're sure you don't want me to join you two? I'm a famous wit."

"Famous shit," she muttered as she turned away—or something like that. I couldn't quite hear her.

Really, I can't be sure she said anything at all—she was turning away from me, in a loud restaurant—but here again "memory" fills in the gaps: Let it be one last punning exchange between us, however sharp. I turned to the bartender at the bar, the big-bearded Dodgers fan I'd seen when I was here with Hahn. He nodded familiarly and with kindness in his eyes. I ordered a shot and drank it down and brought the glass smarting loudly to the bar, like an Old West chump.

"Add that to my tab, will you?" I said, and turned and headed back out to the patio and out into the night.

At breakfast the next morning, at the Phoenix House, Alex asked, "And where have you been lately?"

Tiffany was at the table too, looking listlessly into the face of her instant coffee, a toaster waffle untouched on the plate beside it.

I told them everything—or almost everything. I left out Macduff. I left out my private junkets following Jen through lower Manhattan. Alex asked about the money I'd stopped contributing to the House.

"All gone," I admitted. "All of it. I didn't even have the money for the train fare out here—jumped the turnstile like a punk."

"That's great. That's great to hear. Take more stupid risks like that," Alex said.

"You sound like Sam," I said. "We all do. Where is Little Lockjaw anyway? Sleeping in?"

Alex told Tiffany to go upstairs and get me some "train money." Alone in the room with her now, smiling fatuously, I told my ex how much I admired her talent for mixing business with pleasure. A column of gray moted light leaned in from the little window above the kitchen sink, spotlighting the small table, warming the tips of Alex's hair that slanted artfully down around her cheeks, like the flaring jawbone guards on a Roman soldier's helmet. Apparently Tiffany could cut hair, too.

"Take the money," Alex said, "and use it to get more money. You need to contribute to the House if you're going to live here."

"On the double, captain! Yes, captain!"

"So this is the Jen situation talking?" Alex said. "That's your moodiness lately?"

Tiffany returned to the kitchen with a timeworn, almost velvety twenty-dollar bill.

"I thought you were wrapping that up," Alex said. "I thought that was the deal."

"Yup," I said. "Yup. Yup."

With House money in my pocket I wandered around for the rest of the day, eating by-the-slice pizza, ducking into used-book shops. I jumped a pair of turnstiles to get over to Greenpoint that evening, using the rest of the cash to buy a supermarket bouquet of drying-out irises, a hint of brown at the delicate tongues, the purple of the petals a fading memory of purple—the best I could do.

I put the flowers in a vase on the high kitchen table and waited for Jen. I went to the piano, playing through the first fragile sections of "I Am Lost to the World," singing along where I could, recalling Mal's advice. I wasn't sure where Mal was at this latish hour. When she did come home I was already in bed, reading in the placid yellow light of the bedside table, like one half of a long-married couple. I remember perking up, puppyishly, until I heard that it was Mal moving around in her room on the other side of the apartment.

Then it was later, the room was dark, and I was vaguely aware of Jen getting under the covers beside me.

"Oh," I said, rousing. "There you are."

"I didn't expect to see you here."

"Did you see the flowers?" I said. "I got you flowers."

Apparently she hadn't seen them.

"Can I ask where you were tonight?" I said.

"I don't think you can, no."

"No?"

"I don't think you should, Eli. Not anymore."

"No?"

I saw now that she was lying not under the covers but on top of them, fully clothed, her dark hair spread over the pillow as if it were floating there—Ophelia-like, lake-borne. She looked straight up at the ceiling.

"What am I doing in your bed, then?" I asked. "Why do I still have a key to the apartment?"

"I don't know," she said. "Why do you?" Then she said, "Do you remember my roommate with the boyfriend who crashed on the couch with her? The green couch that the green cushion comes from?"

"I remember."

"What was he still doing there? What was either of them doing there?"

"You're just trying to hurt me now," I said. "If you really felt that way you'd have said something—you're not twenty anymore. You're just trying to hurt me."

"Maybe," she whispered.

She took a long breath—and something in it wanted out, I sensed. I sensed the magnitude of this moment rising up around me, suddenly, another of the tiny white open-topped rooms that made up the rat maze of Experience, Memory, Sea

Change. You stood inside the little room and above it at the same time, watching yourself scrabble desperately around.

"I brought you flowers, Jen. I came with my hat in my fucking hand."

"Thank you for the flowers," she said.

"But what—my presence isn't required anymore? I should just drop them off and leave? Out the servants' entrance?"

"If you're going to be ridiculous you should just leave."

"Why am I being ridiculous?"

"And I'm not doing the talking here, Eli. I'm not the one who needs to explain things."

"What should I be explaining?"

"Please leave, Eli. I'd like you to leave."

"You mean the PhD stuff? The Tommy's stuff?"

"I don't want to have this conversation anymore. Please just leave."

"Look, I'm sorry. I am sorry. I shouldn't have lied to you about that stuff, but it's just—I don't know . . . You have a calling, Jen. Do you know that? You've been lucky. Sometimes I think you don't realize how lucky you've been."

"Sure. A calling to play I-IV-V over and over again for strangers. To have my first and probably last collaboration just absolutely tank."

"Speed bumps," I said. "I promise you—speed bumps. You're brilliant, Jen, and you're beautiful and you're driven and you have something to drive *toward*, something to get you out of bed in the mornings—and that makes you lucky."

"And you don't have that? Is that really what you're saying?"

"I think I do now, but it takes me away from you sometimes."

"That's bullshit."

"Why is that bullshit?"

"Because it's bullshit! Who proposes to someone and just disappears? Who does that?"

"Sweetie." I reached across the comforter for her hand. "Sweetie, please."

She allowed it to be taken. "I'm going to miss you a lot," she said.

"What?"

"I'm going to miss you, Eli."

"Don't say that."

"It's true," she said.

At some point you start to lose, and lose, and lose again. You become practiced at it, connoisseurial. What's the line again? *The art of losing isn't hard to master*? Yet it's mastery without any of the feelings of mastery—there's no pride in it, no point to it, nothing pointed at all. It's a numbness that comes to you, a muted, white-noise, wandering-through-the-airport-at-midnight kind of feeling. Your skin begins to harden like a mold, and underneath it, moldering, wasting away, Pompeian, is your personality, your little lode of certainties and plans, and your backup plans, too, every one of them, the last handholds on autonomy. You begin to grope, you flail at things. You surprise yourself with the force of your sudden demands. If Bonnie and Clyde are going out on another of their nighttime junkets, you sure as shit are going along. You're not asking. You're tired of sitting around and waiting for the pearls of wise direction to fall from their lips. You're more than a bystander.

"What the hell are you talking about?" Sam said. "It's just a grocery run."

"You're taking the car on a grocery run?"

"Who said we're taking the car?" Alex said.

I slapped my cupped hand over the spidery bulge in Sam's jean pocket—a metallic chirring.

"We're out of everything," said Alex. "It'll be more than we can carry. How's the money search coming, speaking of expenses?"

"You're out of bullshit?" I said. "You're going on a bullshit run?"

Sam laughed a little, shrugging his shoulders. "Do you need to use the bathroom before we go?"

Only a few miles north on I-87 and the high-rises of the city start to sink behind you. The row houses thin out and disconnect, the land spreads out, becomes land. Green within green rises around the highway, mounding into the lower air, hemming in the view. A thick apron of grass rolls up to the tree line like a dais. You see neon golf links flash through the gaps, country clubs, small flickering lakes. Past Yonkers, past Bronxville, past Tuckahoe, Hastings-on-Hudson, Dobbs Ferry, Irvington, past White Plains off to the east, past Elmsford and Tarrytown and Sleepy Hollow—all these soothing names on the square green exit signs, their letters faintly glowing as the sky's fader drops, a gray sky going grayer with the promise of night and rain. The towns themselves tick by invisibly, always out of reach, out of sight behind a screen of trees. Only when you turn off the small highway to seek an address—it is a hamlet within a hamlet—do the white clapboard stores crop up awkwardly, belying the wealth of the people who shop there, or have their shopping done there. Stoplights droop from wires hung like holiday festoons, the telephone lines disappearing into the trees. A gravel shoulder skirts the road, replacing sidewalks. The light fixes milky and nacreous to the low-hanging sky—late light, summer light, though at the bottom of this well of woods it's hard to tell.

Now the mansions begin to arrive, slowly, at long stately intervals. They break through the trees with the bore of a driveway mouth, a place for a mailbox, a fleeting glimpse at a mini Versailles, a mini Buckingham, a faux Parthenon—"old wine in nouveau riche bags," Sam remarks, glancing at me in the rearview. "These people are not imaginative."

Alex rests her tapering hand on Sam's long thigh and I see that the fingers of the hand, the arched fingertips, shake a little.

"Still light out," she says to him.

"It's okay."

"Is it?"

"It's okay."

"Since when is it okay?"

We drive on. The road narrows and turns, dropping down into a gully with the dark ferns and saplings and low branches scratching the side of Sam's Buick. The light is weak except by contrast with the dark teeming trees spinning by, a strobe effect, chiaroscuro, and suddenly the road and the tree scrim swing around close to an open, lighted space beyond it.

"We're at the lake," Alex says. "We're already at the lake."

Through the whirring dark branches the lake comes to life, stop-start, like the action in a flipbook. It shimmers and turns with the road like a great gray disk.

"We need to slow down," Alex says. "We need to pull over somewhere and wait till it's darker."

"We've come at this time before."

"Not at this time of year, though, Sam. Sam, please."

Sam lets off the gas a bit but motions with a careless sweep of his hand to the overgrown roadside spinning like a slot machine, no shoulder at all. Another turn sends us reeling against the door panels like parts in a centrifuge. Finally, with the road straightening, a break in the trees gives on to a little inlet of gravel, a makeshift small parking lot—the slow pop and groan of rocks under our tires. Cutting the engine and the lights, we adjust our eyes to the blue-gray evening. A stand of maple and oak crisscrosses in front of Bosch's Lake, as Sam and Alex call it, though they've seen other mansions spaced generously along the water's edge. From here we can't actually see Bosch's property, that sprawling Austen-scape, but it can't be far. A narrow dirt trail with tree roots like protruding veins feeds into the parking lot at the right side, feeding back out of it and into the woods at the left side, curving away toward the lake. Trees rise all around us, shielding us from the road. Traffic is sparse— only a few cars hum by as the Buick's engine ticks down and the sounds of birds and the night's first crickets fill the car. Alex's hand has relaxed on Sam's ropy thigh, I notice, but now the leg itself bucks and tenses.

"That's him," Sam whispers. "Fuck, I think that's him."

"What?" Alex says. "Where?"

"That's fucking him."

An old man with his pale bald head uncovered, a brown mackinaw hanging open down past his knees, just now emerges from the trail mouth at the right of the lot. He glances up at our car—the same short gaunt face, the freeze-wrapped former jowls, the little eyes. He turns back toward the trail, whistles pure and high. A compact yet long-haired tawny dog trots out of the gloom, unleashed, his old belly swinging low and close to the ground. At the trail mouth the dog pauses to sniff and piss on a cluster of ferns. A hot-dog collie, if a collie at all.

"Yup," I say, "that's him all right. I pictured the dog being taller."

"Look down," Alex says. "Don't look at him. Look down."

Bosch is crossing at the front of the gravel lot, heading for the trail connect. He trails his coated arm behind him and snaps his fingers, whistling again. It occurs to me that the mackinaw is overkill in this warmish weather, an old man's habit. Not ten feet from our hood he gives the car a once-over, notices us, pauses, another up-and-down glance, then he turns down the lakeward trail. When the dog catches up to him, Bosch bends a little stiffly to rake his fingers in the collie's fur.

"He recognized us," Sam says. "We were just sitting here looking suspicious and he saw us."

"Let's go," Alex says. "Let's get out of here."

"How do you know he recognized us?" I say. "Why would he recognize us?"

In the front seat Sam is silent, still, the white tonsure of his bald spot showing above the headrest. He stretches out his arms on the steering wheel; his right leg starts going, bouncing fast and tight like a jackrabbit's.

Alex puts a hand out to calm him. "We really should go," she says.

"He saw us," Sam says. "He looked right at us. He recognized us."

Alex leans across the gearshift and turns the key in the ignition, the old bathroom fan of the Buick's motor belatedly catching and sputtering to life. Sam is doubled over in the front seat like he might be sick. A hollow *pock* sounds behind me as the brown trunk fills the rear window. Sam is out of the car, the air livid with the open door's *ding-ding-ding-ding-ding-ding-ding—*

"Sam?" Alex says. "What are you doing?"

In a moment she is up and out of the car too, opening her arms as if to shepherd him back inside, or block his way. She notices something. Her eyes go wide, pleading. She says airlessly, "What the fuck are you doing?"

Sam has the gun. He tucks the black blocky thing behind his shirt into his waistband. He folds Alex's arms like umbrella spokes to her side, holding them there and saying, "Relax. Wait here. You too," he says, suddenly turning at the weight of my hand on his shoulder.

"Sam," I say.

"It's fine," he says, "just wait here," and he starts toward the trail at a wolfish trot.

For a moment I obey him, I stay put, Alex and I both, stuck to the spot, and then suddenly we're running, suddenly we're sprinting down the trail. Up ahead in the latticed dimness Sam has picked up his pace, not turning around. "Sir?" he calls after Bosch. "Hey, sir!" The man in the too-large mackinaw turns his head at Sam's approach—I see him darkly, distantly, rolling up his shoulders in an instinctual flinch. The voice that comes out of him is defiant. "No press. No press!" Something menaces in Sam's movements, his footsteps breaking, rattling in the dirt. "What do you want?" the man says, almost quietly now—not a yell, not a plea. The yell of pain comes from Sam as the collie sweeps in from off the trail and latches on to his ankle. You can hear the dog growling, grunting as it rips and pulls. A single pistol shot, a loud *pop*, makes the dog lie down.

Now Bosch makes a sound—"God," it might be, or maybe "Gus," a dog's name. Bosch is running away from Sam, with Sam running after him—we are all running now—with Sam shouting after him to stop, wait, stop, *wait*, and now the old man has pitched forward, jerking forward and to the side as if bitten by the sound, then another, then a third loud pop. The last move is decisive but very slow, or perhaps it just seems that way from this distance, this catechized remove. Sam stands above Bosch as the old man rotates slowly on the ground, Sam tracking him with his gun, following his movements, as if stirring something in the air.

The report stops me cold—Alex too. After a few seconds she inches up beside me on the trail, staring straight ahead. Her look is small, white, mindless.

"He shot him," she says.

"Who? Who shot him?"

"Jesus Christ he shot him."

I must have looked mindless too. No light on upstairs, I'm sure of it. All of a sudden I was all feeling, the sum of automatic commands, but I couldn't seem to catch my breath. I was taking in great brimming mouthfuls of air, great gulps of the stuff, and it did no good. A sharp pain was in my chest now, an ocean in my ears. The body on the ground hadn't moved in several seconds—the man on the ground. Fish-mouthed, streaming, gasping, I turned again to Alex, searching out the face of this blank-faced woman who used to raise an eyebrow at me, quirk her pink playful mouth in the middle of a conference talk that had gone off the rails, gone ridiculous somehow—the look acknowledging this and diffusing it. I think I was looking for that look now, if I could be said to be doing anything in this mute, popped instant. Sam was standing twenty feet away from us, checking his clothes, I realized later, for blood.

He put the gun back into his waistband and broke into another trot. Alex put out her arm to stop him, the stile of her arm, and this time he let himself be checked.

"The shells," she said.

"What?"

"The shells."

"Shit."

While they collected them, I was moved on a watery conveyor toward the bodies, unconscious of my steps, my pained breathing, the sweat running down my face and into my eyes, the body asserting and erasing itself in rhythm, a sort of tidal flow. Here was a dog tipped over on its side—forelegs sprawled, a modest swell of dark cranberry blood slicking the hair down the neck and upper back. The whitish tongue lolled sideways in the parted mouth below flat, dark, crow-like eyes. I was distantly aware of a conversation about footprints. Alex was off the trail trying to wrestle a low leafy oak branch from its trunk while Sam, lanky Sam, muttering, bent and bent at the waist like an oil derrick as he scoured for the last shell, he couldn't find it, it wasn't there—

"Here," I said. "It's here."

A lucky penny catching the light, a gold doubloon, it hid half under the dog's back leg, in the wispy sandy hair running off it. The shell was warm in my hand, dully shining. Something burnt hung in the air, something wet underneath it. I was less attentive to Bosch, or really more afraid of him, but now here he was too: on his back, one side of the beige mackinaw fallen open to reveal the swell of gut pressing out against the pale blue button-up blooming with black-red spots, black galaxies of blood. His legs twisted awkwardly away from him, in mid-stride. The thin bellows of his neck stretched out under his chin, his face cast back, eyes open and full of shock—a bronze expression, cast. The mark on his forehead sat too high for a Hindu's bindi, but this is what came to me even then. What blood there was pooled darkly in the little well just below the vanished hairline, the skin around it bruising already, and under the eyes. His color was changing.

"For fuck's sake," Alex said, pulling me out of my crouch, throwing me backward toward the car. She had the leaf-rake in her hand. "Follow Sam!"

In the car Sam drove at speed, taking turns that pushed and rattled me like a loose cracked egg from one side to the other of the cavernous backseat. I was leaking something, emitting strange sounds. When I looked up the trees were streaming fitfully by in the window, another chiaroscuro, more dark than light now, a nauseous-making darkening strobe. I closed my eyes and opened them again and the scene hadn't changed.

"Sit up," Alex said from the front seat, turning around. "Put your seat belt on. Be quiet."

I obeyed and obeyed. I was waiting for sirens, roadblocks, helicopters lowering down to block our way—I knew with perfect clarity that someone was coming for us, and then no one did. Perhaps no one had heard the shots in that isolated wealthscape, or if they had they'd mistaken them for hunters, teenagers playing with leftover Fourth of July noisemakers . . . Apparently we'd been lucky. Then, a little above Yonkers, our headlights began to mist over, lighting like amber the first drops of rain, little flecks of it, mote-like, then the long limpid lines. From the elevated highway through upper Manhattan the lights of the city appeared crazed, schizophrenic, trailing down the windows in long prismatic strips and cracks—a smell of rain mixing with the urine (my own, I realized) and everything else the rain kicked up, ammoniac, sweet, sulfuric. In the front seat Sam had the window cracked. I heard him breathing in that watery shearing air.

"You think this rain is getting up into Westchester?" he finally said.

When we got back to the neighborhood Sam parked the car a good mile from the House—we didn't question his judgment on this point, but Alex was saying, almost whispering at first, her voice just rising above the million fingers of water on the car's broad roof, "Nothing planned, nothing fucking planned . . . No message in it, no meaning in it, nothing organized, nothing fucking *planned* . . ." she said, with the litany rocking her up into a hoarse scream. Sam rolled up the window. Alex rocked forward and back in her seat, rocking the car, rattling visibly. I was on a wavelength with her, on the horrible conveyor again going past the horrible features of the dog in its false sleep, Bosch with the cast-back neck turning ashen already, the birdlike sheen in his eyes.

"People know who he was, what he did," Sam was saying. "They'll put it together."

"Oh they do? They will? So that was your plan all along? That was your plan all along? That was your fucking *plan*?"

"He saw us," Sam whispered. "He recognized us."

The bullet hole was high and to the right on the forehead, the little shining well of blood with the dark bruising all around it, starlike, an explosion of nerves.

"You think people are going to remember what some corporate asshole did two years ago? You think people are going to care? Joe Six-pack wearing a hole in his fucking couch?"

The bruising around the wound looked synaptic, a new decaying life, like the bruising on a pear.

"Tell them I did it on my own," Sam said. "The police. Tell them you had nothing to do with it, it was only me, and it was. I didn't mean to, but it was. He wouldn't stop. He saw us—"

"Shut up."

"He recognized us. Tell them you tried to stop me. Go tonight, right now, go right now and tell them—"

"Shut up! Just shut up!" Alex said. "Just shut up and shut up and shut—*up*!" Alex said, lifting off on the last word into another scream, soaring on it.

Sam reached for the driver-side window handle and cranked it down again, gasping in the rainy air.

In the backseat I reached for my eyelid, my left, suddenly. A sudden something, a larval something had hatched and was beating its stiff wings unceasingly under my eye. I'd begun screaming too, matching Alex decibel for decibel.

In other versions of that night Alex and I do go to the police. Who knows what we say there—I haven't worked that out. The catharsis, the resettling of gravity in the seat of the stomach, is simply in turning up, trudging into that harsh-lit room, linoleum floors, maybe a chain-link gate at the intake desk. We are soaked and shaking, but we are there.

D id you see this?" Tiffany said the next morning.

She put the open laptop in front of Alex at the dim-lit breakfast table, gently, with a kind of reverence. The *Times* had the story, the *Post*s, the TV news stations with their helicopters hovering over the lot where we'd parked, now marked off with police tape. I didn't know what Alex was pretending to see for the first time exactly, but I knew enough. My eyelid twitched and gathered, an involuntary puckering. I felt the pores of my forehead yawn open. I hadn't slept. I hadn't had solid food in nearly twenty-four hours, and I had no appetite.

The computer's pale glow lit Alex's features from underneath, making cavities above her chin and eyebrows, dark raccoon circles of her eyes—she looked stricken but to me utterly staged. She wore a carnival mask.

"What is it? What's up?" Sam said, bringing a cereal bowl over from the counter, hovering at Alex's shoulder.

Tiffany watched them reading the screen; I watched Tiffany watch them. She wore an oversize, Sam-like T-shirt that said "Lifeguard" on the front of it, with a large red cross underneath the word. The shirt made her look younger, more naïve, washed up on the far shore of a teenage sleepover. She frowned a little, a perplexed searching frown that took Sam in as a smile grew around the corners of his lips—a sliding scale.

"Wow," Sam said. "Is this for real? Is it my birthday today?"

"What are you talking about?" I sensed it was my turn.

An early-morning jogger had discovered the body and alerted police—no search party had been organized, no alarm sounded previously. It made you wonder about the state of Bosch's marriage that no call should go out to the police when he failed to return home from his evening walk. Maybe the dog was mostly Bosch's, maybe he had another apartment, a pied-à-terre in the city to work and play in. Who knew how the other half really lived—their intrigues, their secrets, the array of their enemies. All the articles we'd seen so far had been variations on the AP story and basically useless. Tiffany's article too: a few brief facts about the body's discovery, and lower down a brief paragraph of background on Bosch and Soline, Soline's "violations" (sickeningly toothless word), the subsequent bankruptcy and trial, Bosch's ultimate exoneration. The police were investigating all possible leads—a piece of boilerplate—and asked anyone with information to come forward.

In another version of these memories the mad heartbeat in my eyelid, the fluttering wing pushing out of my eyeball carries me off to a private corner of the House, out into the bright glaring streets, anywhere. I make the call myself. I tell the police what I know. Which means what—a plea bargain? Immunity in exchange for testimony? I call a lawyer. I call my parents with their lawyer friends. I take Jamaal aside, I take Tiffany, the local Juris Doctors. Or else I climb up to the third-story roof of the House and contrive to leap headfirst for the sidewalk.

Sam turned to the table now, addressing us with a clownish, overextended smile. "Somebody beat us to it! Where should we send the thank-you card?"

My skin slipped under its hardening layer, like a shudder of water under ice. It was the glee in Sam's Grand Guignol style—

"Jesus," Alex breathed.

"What?"

"A lot of good it does Maria Nava and everybody else," I said. "The eight-cents-on-the-dollar crowd."

"Fuck Maria," Sam said. "I thought we'd established that. As for the others, well, yeah, I guess you're right. It was always going to be hard to get back the money Bosch stole from them, but I guess you're right."

"Since when do you read *The New York Times*?" Alex asked Tiffany.

"I saw it linked."

"Linked where?"

"On Twitter."

"Twitter?" Alex said. "I thought we weren't doing Twitter—any of that corporate-troll bullshit. We're supposed to be limiting our exposure."

"I don't *send* tweets, I just follow a few friends and old ISO people."

"Deactivate the account," Alex said, and turning to Sam and me, "You guys too. Or no, don't deactivate, just stay off it. Keep quiet online. Even this Bosch story—keep the searches to a minimum, don't establish any patterns. I don't like to think what Big Brother can swipe from the ether nowadays. And another thing: No more sticky fingers, no more trawling for cell phones, laptops, whatever. We need to cut all that out for the time being, shrink our exposure to zero."

Alex's look, roving slowly across the table, dared us to disagree. Tiffany held her face perfectly still, I noticed, like a bell jar.

"And the money piece?" I said.

"We'll figure something out. You'll help us figure it out, Eli."

"Shrink it down like a tightly puckered asshole," said Sam, looking at me as he curled shut the fingers of his right hand into a fist, making a sealant *schloop* sound. I can't be sure but I think he might have winked at me then.

He was coming unhinged. I suppose we all were.

"Is this really so funny to you?" Alex said. "We haven't exactly been discreet in our opposition to Soline and Bosch. We could be suspects in this."

"Suspects in what?"

We all turned at the sound of Jamaal's voice, a little groggy coming out of him as he filled up the kitchen doorway. He wore a V-neck undershirt, loose basketball shorts, rubber sandals. Greg was behind him and apparently showered and fully dressed, his wet bangs icicling down toward the bunched bushy brows that seemed to repeat Jamaal's question.

"Come check this out," Sam said excitedly, waving them over to Tiffany's computer. I couldn't tell if the flapping-pennants tone came out of Sam genuinely or not. I think now that it did. And why shouldn't fake enthusiasm at someone else's murderous work shade into real enthusiasm, as if the work really were someone else's? Wasn't that what was happening to me? Each time I flashed on the scene—each time the scene flashed on me, broke in on me—I felt less and less attached to it, less attached to my life, my body, the conveyor belt lifting me off the ground until I floated above the trail, silently, above the bodies laid out underneath me like bones in an archaeologist's dig, the wasted fragments calmly waiting for some magical touch to piece them back together again, wire them upright.

We lay low in the House, all of us, for another two days. No one had had to tell Tiffany or Greg or Jamaal to stay inside—they just followed our lead, crouching when we crouched. Our faces shone with strain, everyone squinting indoors, communicating through private signals what strategies they'd worked up to cope with the minutes like hours, hours like slow carving knives against the skin.

For my part, I thought of Jen. I sought her out in the whited-out, shocked spaces of my mind, trying to re-etch her there. Stray moments obliged me by reappearing, brief scenes, pale figments that I managed to hold, tremblingly, like water in my cupped fragile hands. In the foolishness of my passion I'd deleted all photos of Jen from my phone, all videos, text messages—all the sweet banal e-mails going back to the first tentative weeks of our relationship. Passion's passionate inverse, really. It was the storm I'd carried with me out of the calm, quiet breakup. All keepsakes I'd trashed too—down the garbage chute in Jen's apartment complex went the small cardboard moving box silted with romantic notes, movie tickets, theater tickets, concert tickets, the playbills that featured Jen's name just inside the front cover, the creased trail map we'd used to navigate Angels Landing in Zion Park, the single-sheet program from Jen's senior recital with the baroque embroidering notes in the margins, the doodles I'd made during the Liszt and Gouldian Bach pieces that bored me, the other notes, complete with rapturous underlines, that I'd made during the long John Adams piece and the Mahler lieder that enraptured me (_remarkable tone_ . . . _eerie yet beautiful_ . . . _beautiful_ . . . _BEAUTI-FUL! . . ._).

It was more than the idea of Jen I loved, I'm sure of it now, much more than her talent and her beauty. The deleted e-mails I mourned the most were the ones in which she'd massed all the sweet silly punny texts we'd exchanged over months and that her phone could no longer hold. Intending to file them away in her computerized journal, Jen was typing them out one evening at the high wooden dining-room table. I snuck up behind her, hovering my chin near her shoulder and whispering some hammy accusation about what was _zees_, incriminating notes from her _paramour_?

A little ridiculous to have to clarify this now—I am the source, I realize, the _fons et origo_ of this ridiculousness—but at the time Jen and I were still buzzed on our recent engagement and Jen's actual paramour, her Macduff, was more than a year away. On that evening at the table Jen slapped shut the laptop, refusing to show me what it was she'd been copying down. It made me wonder. I teasingly asked about it several times in the following days. She only assured me there was nothing to worry about, they were only good things, but they were private, bound for her journal . . . The next time I caught her compiling the notes I abandoned all subtlety and snatched the computer away from her. I promised a full-body massage if she'd let me read, holding the laptop at stiff arm's length (negotiating from a position of strength). And I didn't mean the half-assed foreplay massage, either, but the real, arduous thing, the kind of massage that would make us both sore. More and more Jen complained of the knots that formed near the graceful wing-bases of bone in her upper back (Neruda: "fever or forgotten wings") and that came from sitting upright at the piano, her arms outstretched, hour after hour, day after day.

I did the lower back too that night, the backs of her arms, glutes, hamstrings, calves, the sensitive soles of her feet. And eventually I did get to see in e-mail form a long run of compiled text messages that read like sloppy unguarded haiku, or the transcript from some blissed-out surrealist trial.

Hey there bear. Just sitting here and missing you.
Do you swear?
Didn't your boy Jesus say you must NOT swear?
You're my only boy!
Correct answer
Ach, gotta go
Raymond giving you the lipless smile again?
Talk soon, mon amour

Mon cher?
Here!
I really miss you today
Early period or late period Cher?
The one with the tone warbling. My voice is boxy with love of you.
Hurry home to me then! I'm dead inside in this empty apartment
Soon!

Fuck if I can put a single sentence right today
It's all right, sweetie. Come back to it later

Actually it's all wrong. Aye, there's the rub.
I'd like to rub you a little later on
Deal

Miss my heart
Ditto! A thousand dittoes!

These are reconstructions, of course, earnest best guesses. It soothed and distracted me to write them down in the marble-covered notebook I'd labeled "Notes on Something, Anything Else." Later, I changed this simply to "Notes," a placeholder title for a project that felt at once more and less meaningful, more and less urgent, more and less confused. What was I writing about? What was I writing for? I filled several of these notebooks, eventually, with stories, scenes, recollections, meditations, litanies of regret, things I thought I might be able to make some end-run sense of, but to what end? What good could understanding do me anymore? Here were unbudgeable facts: Life had changed irrevocably, once and for all. Nothing and no one could be brought back from the dead. Not a man with a field of blooming red flowers for a chest. Not a relationship you'd killed.

Yet it soothed me, it did distract me to make my notes, sitting at the kitchen table late into the night or at the red-lit desk upstairs, always writing privately, surreptitiously. I got down all the text exchanges I could remember, some of them specific, miraculously recalled, most loose and representative. I tried to get down some of the late-night conversations, too, all the talks about music and literature and politics we'd had, Jen and I, in those first heady weeks. You're trying to find out if this is a person you can find rest in, and give rest to yourself, that vital shelter. You're trying to find out if this is a person you can make a life with. Very much contra Engels and his anti-monogamy arguments, of course, but who really cared about those anymore? I certainly didn't.

Other details, other realities that cut through the overgrowth of theory—

Jen had a pattern of small orange freckles across the bridge of her nose and onto her cheeks that sometimes looked constellatory, little suns lit up and burned brighter by the light of the sun overhead.

There was something slightly waxy in the skin of her face, not false, not over-tight, just a certain paraffin sheen at the shelves of her cheekbones, the curve of her forehead. It may have been the soap she used, a brand I'd never heard of—Newpeau, something like that. How oddly touching it could be to see the blue-and-white squeeze bottle sitting squat on its cap beside the electric toothbrush—Jen swore by that, too—in the bathroom. You felt you'd penetrated some mystery, or really that some vital door had been opened to you: Here was true intimacy, quotidian, routinized, unembarrassed.

"I used your foaming face wash," I told Jen one day.

"You what?"

"I hope that's okay."

"Why? Your skin is perfect."

"I wanted to feel what it was like—those little scrubbies are like microbes or something? Or what's in there?"

"Who knows. I've been using it since I was thirteen, fourteen. Force of habit."

A decade of the same face soap! More! At the time I figured that boded well and I went about inspecting other signs and talismans in the bathroom Jen shared with Mallory. This was the two-bedroom place in Astoria, where the air conditioner dropped a shimmering bead curtain of condensation down the front of the building. I learned Jen had fierce opinions against antiperspirant—not just sticky and gross but cancerous—and that she took a rather French view of deodorant in general: A little went a long way, she said, even in a New York summer. More than once she came home to my ravenous, rooting embraces and kisses that sought out her breasts, of course, but also the faint musty resin on her inner arm and armpit, the hint of salt there that I licked with bovine earnestness and languor. At first she squirmed under these caresses, giggling, but soon she must have sensed what they did for me, and real passion ensued. It's difficult to describe. The body is equipped with so many delicate buttons and levers, wondrous and variable. But this was more than bodily, certainly more than a mechanical reaction. I think the real excitement lay in the mutual taking down of barriers, guards, insecurities, uncertainties, hesitations, fears.

It was around this time that Jen told me about the handsome young priest she used to masturbate to, the thought of him sitting there perversely aroused in the latticed darkness of the confessional. These had been the last days of her observance— eighteen years old, a new freshman at Randolph, and like most of us she'd borne the accidents of birth through her childhood and into young adulthood, the dying sparks of them anyway, the last scuds of momentum. Within a year she'd made peace with her agnosticism ("Taking off God was like taking off my clothes at night," she said. "It felt natural and honest"), but for now she was still a confessee, a penitent. In the darkened box she said the words she had to say, mentioning the sins of the flesh she and her first college boyfriend had shared in. I knew very little about this boyfriend and never found out much, never asked much. These were the limits of my own inhibitions—and to think that in exchange for this comforting ignorance I took a measure of pride in my sophisticated restraint! (My faults have been obvious enough, I suppose, but here I confess them outright. Let the four corners of this page, and the next and the next, make up my belated confessional.)

Jen knew her confessor by voice and by sight, the thirty-something recent seminarian sent to palliate the Gospel to the college set. Father Otto's sermons floated down from the pulpit like wafted balloons, lightly, religion as self-help and inspiration, but in the confessional booth his manner changed. He asked Jen how many times, how often, and how recently. He asked if and how often she'd initiated the sinful encounters.

"He really asked you that? He called them 'sinful encounters'?"

"Yes."

"So much for softening the Gospel."

"He was a Ratzinger disciple, soft in tone, hard in everything else. You learned that youth was no guarantor of progress. Or not in any predictable way. Sometimes you need whole generations to die out before it's safe to come up for air."

"And what did you tell this guy? What did you say to him?"

"About my boyfriend? I told him everything. It was dozens of times, sometimes two times, three times a day, and I initiated plenty."

"And he was titillated? You could hear it in his voice?"

"Oh no, no, I doubt it. Not like you," Jen said, "Mr. Raring to Go." She cupped her hand around me through the bedsheet and pretended to downshift, dropping her voice. "We'll take care of this in just a minute. Let me finish my story, okay?"

"I know, I wasn't trying to . . . I couldn't help it."

"I wouldn't want you to. But in a minute."

It wasn't until several months later that Jen came back to the image of the young priest sitting straight-backed and tempted on his side of the filigreed partition. Jen and her boyfriend had tumbled out already, not much to say to each other in the postcoital moments, or ever. When she pictured Father Otto sliding his hand under his habit, it was a conscious blasphemy, and this is what titillated. It was all about her, though, it was about her and for her, a gesture of freedom. And this freedom was now in everything she did—how she thought, how she talked and wrote, and how she played, with a new looseness, a new dynamic boldness, a new disregard for the inevitable small mistakes (or big mistakes) that marked the way to real progress.

For her senior recital Jen called on Father Otto to let her use the beautiful white-pewed chapel for her performance. She remembered the low-hung crystal chandelier, like something out of a European great house, and the Art Deco flair of the white-and-black-checkered linoleum at the front of the space, the inverted bowl of a ceiling, the white balcony that circled not far underneath it like the upper tier of a wedding cake. It was a little girl's fantasy of a wedding cake set down in the darker, stranger dream space of a Lewis Carroll story—she could think of no better place to hold a recital. The acoustics, too, were surprisingly good, though this was almost an afterthought. I pictured Jen as the little dark figurine planted plastic-feet-first in the cake's lower tier, a little stiff and nervous-looking in her long black scoop-necked dress, her hair in a brassy chignon, her hands clasped together at her front as she made the littlest bow after her Liszt piece, still early days. The grand piano was behind her with its broad black wing stuck up in the air and threatening to whirl up like a wind-borne maple pod (we called them "helicopters" when I was a kid and stuck the split sticky ends to our noses). The concert grand was something Jen had to master, tamp down, and at the beginning of the concert and from my vantage at the back she looked slight to the task. At the keyboard, though, something changed. She seemed to grow and grow, Alice-like, filling the room with huge confident sound, sitting straight-backed and commanding at the bench, her arms outstretched and moving hypnotically. Watching her play like that again in my mind, I realized how this slight pale frame could hold enough brazenness to approach Father Otto after her private desecrations of him, and after four years of absence.

"It wasn't quite four years," Jen said. "I'd turned up once or twice more for sentimental reasons—Easter, Advent, the high pageantry stuff. I hadn't actually spoken to him, though, and I'd never gone back to confession."

"What did you say to him when you asked about the recital? He was at the concert, wasn't he? Salt-and-pepper hair, cool-guy goatee?"

"You were sitting in the row right behind him. Handsome, wasn't he?"

"Wow," I said. "It's masturbation as thought murder."

"I didn't *kill* him, Eli."

"You killed his relevance. You'd killed his magical authority over you."

"All I said was that I wanted to play beautiful music in a beautiful space and he said of course. He didn't hesitate. Father Otto was a nice enough man with the keys to a beautiful building. It was that simple. No more magic than you brought to it yourself."

It was that simple. We lay in bed naked and simple and

conducted our lives for each other, our pasts, our desires, everything—or almost everything. We didn't go in for total disclosure, honesty as blood sport. We weren't foolish enough to think that the heart's dark corners look good under a klieg light. Some secrets you carry around forever, like scar tissue. Later on, of course, there were secrets I could have unburdened her of if I'd been paying better attention, if I'd been present in mind as well as body, and later there were secrets I could have unburdened her of if I'd been present at all. Jen was right about that too.

These were secrets that wouldn't have needed to be *secrets*, I wrote, *that wouldn't have existed at all* . . . And here I stopped my note-making, checked my pen. I was at the edge of another counterfactual no-man's-land, a field littered with what-ifs. What good did it do to imagine how things would have been if they'd been different than they were? The body was there now, irrevocable, unbudgeable. It wouldn't be reanimated. It wouldn't move again.

In the last of the kitchen cupboards there were half-empty bottles of cumin, chili powder, coriander, onion powder, nutmeg, and cinnamon stacked in a maladroit pyramid. There were two cans of Campbell's bean and bacon soup in another cupboard, a folded packet of taco seasoning at the terminus of a red powdery trail through the sawdust and filing-small cockroach droppings. There was an old roach motel in another cupboard, dry and ineffectual. And that was it. Nothing to speak of in the refrigerator or freezer—greasy condiment bottles, frozen peas hard as rock salt, a box of stale Cheerios on top of the fridge. No bread, milk, meat, cheese, nothing to sustain a person past dinnertime last night, and it was breakfast now, on the third morning, and there were six of us.

At the breakfast table behind me Greg Baxter sat folded forward with his head in his arms, his shorn, affronting head. He'd come down by himself while I was surveying the food, grunting a hello and slumping down into his seat, and it was then that I noticed the disappeared hair.

I placed a quarter-full bowl of dry Cheerios in front of him, wordlessly, and sat down with my own bowl.

"Thanks," he said, looking up bleary and unfocused, un-showered. When he saw me staring he said, "I needed a change. We're also out of shampoo."

The caterpillar brows looked starker than ever in the sudden moonscape of his upper face and head, pale white, with only the faintest shadow of former hair, the sloping forehead running up into an almost geologic baldness. It gave him a startled look.

"What?" he said.

"Did you Bic it or something? It's impressively smooth."

"Not much else to do around here, is there?"

I thought I might have heard an accusation, a tremor of fear in Greg's voice, but I ignored it.

"The skinhead look," I said. "Very classic."

"Don't be so predictable," Greg said.

I set to my bowl of stale Cheerios, but slowly—you had to make it last.

"A king in the morning, a pauper at night," I said. "Do you know that phrase?"

Greg didn't answer me.

It was the dietary folk wisdom of some Latin American

country—Peru, maybe, or Venezuela. You ate heartily in the morning and lightly, poorly at night, if you wanted to keep thin. And solvent, of course. This was the political subtext some writer had picked up on and expounded. "It might have been Trotsky, or maybe not," I said, holding forth to Greg in his waxing, weighing silence. He could see the object lesson in ideology, though, couldn't he? Out in the rural hinterlands where bread and milk and coffee cost less than the typical dinner foods, you learned to do your real eating in the morning, and you learned to valorize this, looking down on the fat late-dining rich in the big cities. In the same way, medieval Catholics learned to look up to Lazarus, wretched on earth, like them, but now rich and sitting at a heaped heavenly banquet—*Ave Lazarus*, patron saint of political quietism. In certain moods I could almost admire the elegance of this sham thinking—

"This is sand," Greg interrupted me. "These Cheerios just collapse into sandy sludge the second they hit your molars. I can't eat this shit."

"Yeah, sorry," I said. "It's no good."

"Why are you sorry?" said Greg, taking me in squarely now.

"Huh?"

"Why are *you* sorry?"

A long silence filled the kitchen.

"Why don't we just go out and buy some more food?" Greg said. "There's a novel idea."

"Do you think we should? Alex is probably right that we should be lying low, don't you think?"

"Do I think we should starve? No. I don't think we should starve."

"Well, how much money do you have? Because that's the other thing. I've only got twenty-eight dollars to my name, and twenty of it is in an account I can't access without an ATM."

"We can go to my ATM," Greg said. "Are you coming? I could use the help carrying the bags."

Outside, I squinted with what felt like my entire face—I felt the warmth of the sun on my teeth. I shook at the knees, sometimes dipping like a lunge stretcher when a step didn't hold and I had to struggle for balance. An instant oil was covering my face, and the eye flutter was back, sudden grabs and contractions that I couldn't predict or control. We made it to the Chase ATM, Greg and I, and continued on toward the Korean grocery in the blue shadow of the 7 train's hulking tresses. I found I kept calmer with my eyes on the sidewalk, the sun skittering off the little deposits of shine in the cement, going dull at the gum spots, in the sudden shade of a box tree. I saw the people of the city from the waist down: suit pants, jeans, shorts, skirts, a color-wheel menagerie of bony knobby hairy lower legs ending in running shoes, high-tops, loafers, sandals, high heels, boat shoes. One lower leg in particular arrested my attention, pale and hugely swollen at the ankle, the white sock stretching to hold its bulbous load. I left the ankle behind at the edge of a crosswalk, following Greg's New Balance trainers until a bass voice shouted, "Hey, hold it! Stop right there!"

I jerked up instinctively to see a plump traffic cop holding his palm out to us. A trio of men in green reflective vests and white hard hats bent over an open manhole behind him. Into the subterranean darkness I could see a hooked stepladder descending alongside a dirty segmented yellow hose, wriggling wormlike with strange pressures. It suddenly horrified me to think that a grown man had to go down there, tucking in his shoulders to get past the hose, breathing in the tangy decayed stench that came up to us a step delayed. We were back on the sidewalk now and I was suddenly nauseous.

Afterward, in the Korean grocery, I leaned my head into a freezer case. Greg asked if I was okay.

"Did you make eye contact with that cop?" I said.

"No, I don't think so. Why?"

"That scared the shit out of me. I haven't caught my breath."

Quickly, unobtrusively, we split up to fill hand baskets with the kind of food that could last us a week, two weeks, a month if we needed it to—bunker food. Pastas and soups, beans, canned vegetables and fruit, a goldbrick stack of ramen noodles, rice, bread, peanut butter and jelly, a trio of on-sale boxes of corn-flakes, milk, a flat of bottled water that I tucked under my arm and labored toward the front of the store with. Greg inter-cepted me and reasoned that the water was too bulky to carry home and not exactly indiscreet, either, if that's what we were going for. I granted the point, but instantly I thought of the electric-looking orange water that stank in the bowl after my recent urinations. ("You're supposed to pee pale," Jen had told me—another intimacy.) I went back to scour the shelves until I found a box of Kool-Aid powders to help the tap water go down.

"Apparently I'm eight years old," I told Greg outside. "You sport a blinding neo-Nazi haircut for the cause and I can't even drink plain tap water."

Greg snorted a little, surprising me. A car slowed as it passed us in the street, pulling up to the curb, idling, a pair of brown legs getting out and a female voice calling "Yeah, you're good," apparently to the driver. It took me half a block to restart my breathing.

Greg said, "It'll be nostalgic. Like summers of old."

"What?"

"I used to drink that sugary crap every day."

"Oh, the Kool-Aid. Yeah. Thanks for buying that," I said. "Thanks for covering all this."

"Sure," Greg said, but now he was the one hesitating. At length he asked how much longer I thought we'd be lying low. I said I didn't know. He asked about the House's plans now that things with Bosch had obviously changed. A ponderous weight on that last word—"changed."

"I really don't know."

"Well, what are Alex and Sam saying about it?"

"I don't think they know either. I haven't actually asked them. Have you?"

Greg snorted again, but now it meant something else. I realized he and I were in the middle of the longest conversation we'd ever had—mostly I regretted it. The sun, late morning now, came down like a physical presence, a hot hand on the nape of my oily neck, the prickly crown of my head. The moving shadows that moored to the feet and legs of passersby crisscrossed on the sidewalk. Certain nips of quartz or marble, shiny somethings in the gray poured concrete, caught the light and seemed to lift from their places into the lower air, hovering, like fireflies, or the spirits of the dead.

"Can I ask you something?" Greg said.

"Okay," I said.

"And you'll answer me honestly?"

"Why wouldn't I?"

"Did we have anything to do with this?"

"No."

He looked across at me. "You're sure we had nothing to do with this? None of us? None of them?"

"No," I said.

"No you're not sure or no we had nothing to do with it?"

"Fuck you, all right? You asked your question, I answered it. I think I liked you better in bow ties, Gregory, your fucking cardigans—at least we knew where you stood."

"What's that supposed to mean?"

"You asked your question, I answered it."

We kept on toward the House with our grocery bags heaped in front of us, weighting us down. A few blocks shy of the House I started to feel it in my legs—not the groceries, not the first stint of exercise in three days. It was a sort of muscular dread that came over me, a resistance, a force field that the House put off and that my body couldn't penetrate. Ocean surf in my ears again, and underneath it a reedy whine like you'd hear after a loud bang. Something swooped at the corner of my eye and the eyelid clutched horribly. You felt the drag of surf against your ankles and legs, thighs, stomach, chest, slowing you now, floating you out past the breakers, out into the currents that carried you away from land. I could just hear Greg's voice coming over the sound of these swells, these *vagues* that pushed me back—

"All I'm saying is that if any of us are involved, in any way, or even if we're not, staying put is not necessarily a good idea. An investigation like this starts at the scene and goes out in concentric circles—family, friends, neighbors, anybody in the area who may have harbored a grudge, anybody, let's say, who may have gotten arrested on a disorderly at a Soline protest in Phoenix—"

"You seem to know a lot about this," I heard myself say, but distantly, drifting back.

"Yeah," Greg said, "I do. My stepdad's a cop. Okay?"

I was drifting back, wavering, floating away from my life and somehow dreading it at the same time. What I know is that I stopped short of the House's high cement stoop, set the groceries down on the sidewalk, and made an excuse to Greg. It wasn't a convincing one, I'm sure. I didn't need it to be.

When I was little, my parents embarked on a fitness regimen that consisted largely of charity 5Ks, a little gym work, and their first outings to the local high school's complex of under-kept tennis courts. To these last I tagged along. The thick grain of the courts came from a mixture of sand and other anony-mous grit that the court makers must have added to slow the playing surface down, or perhaps just out of thrift. In any case, it suited our family's debutante needs, keeping the ball high and hittable. We darted and swooped around the courts on Saturday mornings (I was aping my parents then, a preteen's carefree prerogative), pretending not to care what happened to our shots, reveling only in the fun of it, the exercise, suppos-edly, and the fact that we really were debutantes now, twirlers of tennis rackets bought at a proto–big box store called Pilgrim's Progress. We were playing the gentry's game not far from the spot where the *Mayflower* spilled its first WASPs! I recall my mother in bright red cargo shorts—the late eighties must have had another name for them. My father wore gray sweatpants and an Andre Agassi–esque windbreaker, a study in greens: neon, olive, pine. The courts were far from pristine, as I've said, and my parents looked much too much of their time to really threaten the timeless Wimbledon-white purity of the game, yet here was Dad unselfconsciously experimenting with top-spin and here was Mom, on my side of the court, hopping back to return the shot with a laughing *yip!* She regathered herself, mimicked a skirt-pinching curtsy as the yellow ball dribbled into the net.

"I say, Joseph!" Mom called in her best grande dame. "A cracking shot!"

"Oh you flatter me, Susanne-Anne!" Dad said.

My mother's name is Sue, my father's Joe, and in this memory they're laughing with the color high in their faces, the wind in their ridiculous outfits. Merciful forgetting has spared me any notion of what I must have worn on those outings, but I do recall the feeling of confidence gathering in my strokes as I hit the ball flat, then obliquely, then with slice (I caught on to the sport faster than either of my parents), and I also recall the uneasy dawning sense that my parents' rapport had come before me, developed independent of me, and perhaps had survived a little in spite of me. I was quickly very serious about tennis and often glum, throwing rackets and shouting what curses I'd learned in middle school. Not long after this my parents eased off on the family-style tennis dates, enrolling me in private lessons and sometimes jogging the perimeter of the courts together while I sweated and grunted and swung from my shoelaces.

It wasn't until the advent of my idea of myself as an intellectual that I learned to take pleasure, fitful pleasure, in sports. My first girlfriend, born in Korea, adopted into a family of looming Irish Catholics, believed she saw things differently from most people, and I believed her. She was certainly an unabashed scofflaw at Plymouth High, if the law there was to take Eagles football and basketball seriously, as it was. I recall Stephanie's ringing voice in the cafeteria: "Oh my God, will the ball go in or will it not go in? Will the ball cross the net/line/fence or will it not? The suspense is killing me!"

And this blasphemy was heightened by the fact that Steph, in the year we dated, danced in the JV cheer squad that took the court or the field during halftime and hurled its members high into the air—they looked like solar flares in their orange skirts and tops—and afterward returned to the bench or the sidelines to cheer on the boys. "All that clapping and rah-rah-rah-ing is just contractual," she often said. A contrarian by nature, she reveled in the eclectic image she knew she presented: short shorts that rode high on her white thighs, dizzyingly high, and the navy blue NPR tote bag that slapped against her side like a bulky constant companion. Years earlier, before I knew her, she'd made the local paper by exhaustively estimating the weight of our town—buildings, houses, cars and trucks in driveways, driveways, streets and roads, graveyards, the putrefying dead, trees, forests, rivers, beaches and marshes, and a hundred-odd-square-mile layer cake of topsoil and subsoil, roots, aquifers, sand, all the way down to Plymouth bedrock.

With Stephanie, in other words, you had to find a way to *justify* sport—pure purpose and grace in action, I argued on the shoulders of Aristotle, not so different from the pleasure of seeing a gymnast-dancer tossed in the air. In college I darkened and expanded this view with the help of Nietzsche and Schopenhauer, Derrida, Stevens, Larkin and Hardy, Woolf and Plath, and a handful of others who persuaded me, indirectly, that sports were no more or less meaningful than anything else. If all was *vanitas*, I would latch on to the things that advertised their emptiness, their artifice, the things that took a certain healthy pride in their self-created image—literature mostly, and games. My deepest scorn was reserved for the institutions and virtues that refused this kind of honesty. I mean religion, of course, but also, a little later on, "work" as a faux religion— its various altars to "value," "productivity," "efficiency," etc. I began sprinkling my breakfast cereal with scare quotes, seeing them everywhere, seeing them riding on the backs of every dust mote, every particle of "reality." After several brief but involving love affairs with Marxist writers ("Food first," Bertolt Brecht wrote, "then morality"), it seemed I'd become a Marxist myself.

It's a common enough rest stop if you're trying to take the long way around nihilism. You see the alternative there through the trees, flickering and turning like a sunless lake. You start to wind up and up through pine forests, high mountain roads made entirely of words, and wills, a vertiginously high mountain that you build yourself on the way up it. A wrong move, a sudden buffeting wind, and it's darkness all the way down. One night in the loosening of nerves just before sleep I'd asked Sam what he thought we'd really accomplished in killing Larry Bosch. "Maybe nothing," he said, and a part of me shuddered with recognition.

I got these thoughts down in note form in my phone, in the absence of my notebook, with the intention of transferring them later on. I'd need to go back to the House for the notebook at least, a change of clothes, a few other essentials—I was waiting outside Jen's work, but waiting with the manic, rattling feeling of a man who can see a giant countdown in the noonday sky.

Nada y nada y pues nada—from the Hemingway story, I noted down. The sky's whiteness blinded and obliterated. It meant nothing. I couldn't feel my right leg from the position I'd taken on the stoop. I didn't care enough to move. When Jen finally came down on her lunch break I lurched after her down the street like a zombie, a Frankenstein—or Frankenstein's monster. I meant the monster.

"Good grief," Jen said, turning. "You're out of line, Eli."

"I really need to talk to you."

"This is totally out of hand."

"I just really need to talk to you, Jen. Please, okay? I just really really really really really need to talk."

Jen started away from me, turning onto Canal Street, weaving through the fissures of onrushing humanity, running me off them expertly. She wore the pale yellow sundress with black polka dots that I'd loved her in, the pink shoes on her feet quick and light like ballet flats. I couldn't keep up with her, and now I heard that I was crying. I was streaming tears in the middle of Canal Street, crying in loud gasping jags and shouting Jen's name.

"Please, Jen! It's not what it looks like. Please! Oh my God, Jen, please!"

Abruptly she slowed and stopped, sidestepping into the lee of a McDonald's entranceway, but now I couldn't get the words out. She looked embarrassed for me, sour and squinting, confused, angry, repulsed, uncertain, all at once. She brought me into the suctioned-off airlessness of the restaurant's breezeway, the noise of the city dropping off as the outer door resealed.

"What? Eli, I can't . . . What?"

I was blubbering.

"I can't understand you."

I collapsed into her arms—literally. It wasn't a ploy, a coy gesture. My legs simply gave out in that quiz-show glassed-in

booth that looked out on the bristling passersby, the Hieronymus masses of Canal Street. I met their eyes as Jen swung me
around, struggling under my weight. The jury of my peers.

"My life," I stammered.

"Here, here . . ." Jen propped me up against the glass, put
her hands on my shoulders to pin me there. "Speak slowly. Slow
down."

"My life is over."

I said it again through halting breaths. I really felt it now. I
knew it in my body.

"Your life isn't over, Eli."

"I think it is."

"Look, hey. Look," she said, dipping to meet my eyes. She
swam up in my vision—beautiful Jen through my tears, with
the auburn bangs falling into the white round face, the smear
of freckles.

"You can't follow me anymore," she said. "You can't do it,
Eli. You understand that, don't you? Eli?"

On the other side of the breezeway a tableful of teenagers
sat staring at us, cupping their enormous drinks—

I felt like a worm slit open and pinned to the tray of the
world.

When I got back to the House I saw the brown paper grocery
bags slumped haphazardly on the kitchen counter, with one in
particular bowed and wavering with a dark low water stain. I
discovered the gallon of milk gone warm to the touch inside
it. Sam was already screaming at me—he'd followed me from
the door—but I went about calmly putting away the milk and
other perishables in the fridge. Where the fuck had I been?

Sam wanted to know. What the fuck was my problem? Where was Greg?

I said I didn't know where Greg was. I said, "Don't sweat the groceries, huh? Don't mention it. Your gratitude is so obvious," I said, but my voice was shaking now.

Sam took my shirt in fistfuls and threw me back against the fridge door, scattering magnets and papers all over the floor. A printed photo slid to rest upright: Alex and me and a gaggle of others in stages of pale undress, in the packed dark sand of a Long Island beach. We crouched around a giant FUCK THE POLICE that Alex had spent the better part of an hour carving out of the sand with a child's sand-castle trowel.

"This is funny to you?" Sam said.

"Yes," I said, "yes it is. Isn't it to you? Not even a little bit?"

The strength of his grip surprised me. I felt the hard sharp knuckles of his fists going into my sternum, pushing the breath from my chest, but I laughed all the same. I couldn't help laughing now. A late Saturday afternoon at the beach with Alex and some of our ISO cohort, with the beige wafer sun low in the sky since we knew our limits, UV-wise, or at least I did—Alex tanned, of course. It must have been her first outing of the season because her legs above the invisible shorts line looked almost milky in their whiteness, the tone below them starkly different, as if my girlfriend of only a few months at that point had been dipped halfway into a giant vat of root beer. It was an afternoon of swimming, reading, and half-assed sand-castle building until Alex hit on her whimsy and we just sat back and watched her work, laughing, shaking our heads, giving occasional pointers. Who had brought their phone? She wanted the angle of the photo just right, politely but insistently prodding a zinc-nosed man to try it again, if he didn't mind, a little wider, try to get us all in if he could. In this one the FUCK was partially cut off, in that one the POLICE. Would he mind trying one more time?

From that afternoon to this—could anyone have plotted it? I was almost crying for laughing.

"Hey! Hey!" Sam said, marking time with my shoulder blades against the freezer door.

"Okay," said Alex, "that's enough." She was just behind Sam now, bending to pick up the photographs of flyers and postcards on the floor.

"What are you going to do, Sam? Are you going to do to me like you did—"

His eyes warned me off it. He tightened his grip on my shirt and pressed hard until Alex said again, "That's enough." With the stack of papers and magnets in her hand she tapped Sam on the shoulder, gently, a gentle little gesture to embarrass him out of violence.

Tiffany and Jamaal, like plaintiffs at the bar, had come up to the chest-high island that opened onto the kitchen.

Alex's face was close to mine at the fridge, intimately close, unreadable, stoic. The words leaked out of her mouth. "Where were you, Eli? Where's Greg?"

"Gone, apparently," I said. "You know as much as I do."

"And you have no idea where?"

"No."

"Okay. Okay," she said, speaking softly, seemingly unaware of the audience drawing in around us like a buoy line. I answered the next questions with the forethought of only a few seconds. I'd gone to see Jen, yes, but only to say goodbye. On our walk home from the grocery store Greg had convinced me that we needed to move, all of us, that the best way to ensure we didn't get caught unfairly in the police dragnet was to get as far as possible away from it. I said in retrospect it did seem curious that Greg should empty his checking account to buy a few groceries.

"Only in retrospect, huh?" said Sam.

He turned on Tiffany and asked where Greg would go. He was from Connecticut, right? Where in Connecticut?

Unprepared, startled, Tiffany flinched a little, her face bowed. It was the effect Sam had on all of us lately—you couldn't not sense it: his new volatility, the dry-leaves crackle he gave to the air as he passed. Certainly Greg had sensed it.

"Where in Connecticut?" Sam shouted.

"Greenwich area? I'm not sure." Tiffany mouselike, resentful, shrinking back.

"Didn't you say you guys used to fuck? And you don't know where he's from?"

"He just always said the Greenwich area. I never went with him there."

"Fine," said Sam, "fine, fuck it. Fuck everything."

He took the stairs with bounding steps that we heard overhead like furniture crashing. When I went to the bedroom half an hour later I saw that some of the furniture really had been crashed—the black scarred chair overturned and the desk on its narrow side, the single drawer lolling out of it like a dead black tongue. On the floor Sam had spread all the papers and books Greg had left behind, rummaging roughly through them. In the middle of this mess I found my marble-covered notebook gutted and torn, all the pages ripped out, all the notes I'd made to remember Jen and the other good times, the bad times too, memory's ungovernable overflow, all of it lying like the dirty end of a ticker-tape parade on the bedroom floor. I'd reached down to gather what I could when Sam's scarecrow form darkened the doorway—I turned on it viciously. Sam shoved me back into the room, shouting at me. What the fuck was I thinking putting all that incriminating evidence to paper? What kind of a fucking sentimentalist was I? I charged at him. He waved me past him like a toreador and ran me headfirst into the wooden bunk-bed frame. For a second my vision exploded black and spotted, my legs gone limp. Sam caught me in his arms. He laid me down on the lower bunk bed like a father, or a lover.

When I woke up all the way it was morning and everyone's bags were packed.

In other versions I'm back at the gravel lot. Sam is there by the open car door tucking the black blocky thing into his waistband when I come up behind him and grab it away. I empty the clip into the gravel, one loud sharp bang after the next after the next after the next—

Or else I empty it into Sam.

I was in my bedroom in Plymouth now. My childhood bedroom.

A new notebook lay open on the blue-painted writing desk where I'd spent my first derivative efforts in high school, where I'd stared long and blankly into the thin wood-paneled wall that let in the ground moisture and the winter cold. It was supposedly summer now. Above the desk a small window gave on to a half pane of loamy soil, a buzz cut of pale green grass. You could see the tops of the spare beachy trees where my neighbor used to hide a Rubbermaid container full of ripped-out pages from his father's *Penthouse* stash. For five dollars he showed me where it was and for the space of a summer an equivocal friendship was born. One day Sean was righteous with anger over another boy in the neighborhood, Tim Sheehan, a grade below us, a small runty fighter who would wield just about anything, even his bike, as a weapon. Sean had the red livid marks on his calf to prove it, a bright perforated line where the tire treads had bit. "This *fucking* kid—he doesn't know when to stop," Sean said, thrilling to the word we'd both started adding to our sentences to season them, mature them. The woods behind my house connected through a long sloping rise to the Sheehans' property. One of the last things we did in that shape-shifting summer, Sean and I, was steal the offending one-speed and throw it down a broken cistern.

My *Confessions*. This was how I thought of the notebooks now, not that there was anything particularly Rousseauean in my tone or purpose—no dogma, no redemptive plan informed the scenes and memories I instinctively reached for. Into the notebook went Sean and the weightless falling bike, the leaf-composted bottom of the old cistern receiving it like a dark orange maw. Into the notebook went Bosch too, eventually, but not yet. I was getting down the life as I lived it, living to get it down—the other stuff would keep, the sequenced explosions that had sent me down into this bomb-shelter basement for cover. There was a hoary dampness to the light I now wrote by, a permanent evening suffusing the air. The room had been meant for a finished basement suite, I should mention in fairness to my parents. I believe they envisioned it as a potential rental space, but at fourteen years old I was desperate and pushy, impatient to be out of the upstairs bedroom that shared a wall with my parents' master. It wasn't their proximity to *me* that discomfited—I have no unsubtle love sounds to report, no Freudian primal scenes. No, it was much more about my proximity to them. Fourteen is a strangled peat fire in the stomach, and lower, of course. It didn't matter that several odd-shaped squares of industrial gray carpeting had yet to be cut and laid for the downstairs room's perimeter. It didn't matter that the new drywall partitioning the old flooded basement into a bedroom and an entertainment room remained unsanded, unpapered. What mattered was that I be left alone with the lurid pages I'd filched from Sean's filched stash. What mattered was the twenty-inch TV-VCR in the entertainment room and the Lentz family copy of *Schindler's List*, cued up to the brief early sex scene (such was my pre-Internet blasphemous despera-tion). Within a few years Henry Miller, Joseph Heller, Updike, Roth, and all the other artful bawds had rather koshered my libidinous fugue state, elevating it into art—the art was the art, rather, and I was brought to this limb-littered table, a starve-ling, to feast. Was it any wonder that I managed to ignore the damp musty smell that hung like a curtain in the room? Or the slick chill patches of wetness that seeped up into the bare ce-ment corners in the mornings and startled my bare feet? Small sacrifices, really—small then, small now. I just needed the pri-vacy. A few words to my buzzing stricken confused parents and I was back in the room where I'd spent my burning years, as I thought of them now.

In terms of the notebook chronology, I came first to the scene with Hahn and the craven petition for money on the way out of town. Travel funds, we called them, emergency funds. Sam was there to ensure my compliance. He sat beside me on Hahn's stiff couch, the brown high curtains drawn in mourn-ing, I assumed, giving the room a cave-like air. Stephen had passed just two days before, Hahn informed us. The apartment looked swept and bare, as if it hadn't been lived in for weeks—a pile of mail crowding onto the fireplace ledge. I remember feeling touched and a little disoriented by Hahn's choice of words: "passed." A greeting-card word, a word for Congregationalist pastors. Where had this lifelong atheist passed on to, and where did this surviving atheist, a fresh widow, imagine he had gone?

"I'm so sorry," I said. "I had no idea."

"Our condolences," Sam said.

Hahn nodded with her lips tight. Behind her glasses with the dim light playing on them, striping them, her eyes were unreadable. Quiet hands on her lap, overlapping—a ridged vein stood out on her top hand and ran up through the fragile wrist.

"It was a long time coming," Hahn said, setting her tone down like a subject at a norming session, transitioning to a new subject. "What can I do for you two?"

She had no illusions about our presence there.

A strange formality filled her face, narrow as ever, framed by the dark blond bob grown nearly to her shoulders—and the sort of light I'm tempted to call *metaphysical* limned her features, the face's dips and prominences, the faint parenthetical creases at either side of her drawn mouth. It was a dim light, crosshatched with shadows, and it coaxed her out subtly, gently, like a Rembrandt subject.

In the end Hahn asked very few questions and led us down to an ATM at the corner of her street. She took out three thousand dollars, the maximum her bank allowed, and placed the neat stack of hundreds in Sam's outstretched palm, demurring his quiet thanks. I couldn't say anything.

At the foot of her apartment steps she hugged us goodbye, each in turn, and wished us good luck. I asked Hahn when the services would be and she told me. "Services"—another God-tainted word, smelling of camphor, old men's robes.

"You'd better have asked about that just to be polite," Sam said, lifting his arm out on Fifth Avenue to hail a cab. This wasn't the least inconspicuous mode of transportation, perhaps, but it was the fastest.

I didn't answer Sam's threat.

"Eli?"

"Don't worry," I finally said.

"Now I am worried. You can't just show up at a public funeral, Eli. I'd think that's pretty obvious."

"Don't fucking worry."

"Are you going to Hahn's husband's funeral—yes or no?"

"No."

"Don't turn liability on us."

"Wow."

"What?"

"Wow," I said.

In the cab back to Queens we were silent, angled away from each other and looking forlornly out the windows, each to his own side. I was forlorn on my side, anyway, slack and glassy instead of twitchy—detached, floating ghostlike past the blurring rails up FDR Drive, the East River a broad tarnished china plate. It took me a minute to realize we'd turned off onto the Midtown Tunnel and by then it was too late. I touched Sam's narrow knee. He flinched, looked up, squinting.

"I think this guy's taking us the long way," I whispered, almost mouthing the words.

"So let him take the long way. We're good for it." Sam turned back to the window—the city had pivoted to the left, running off behind us. To the right stretched the skinny docks and low red warehouses, the green park-inlets waving up the Brooklyn coast. "City of Whitman," Sam said.

"That's right," I said. "That's right—you're a poet."

There was wonder in my voice. I meant no sarcasm. It's just that it was easy to forget how we'd first met, where Sam and I had come from. He'd rarely talked about his poetry back then, and when he did it was with an embarrassment and a sort of guilt that his baptism into Marxist politics only sharpened, intensified. He'd been thieving all along from the common stock, he said, gobbling up Pell Grants, subsidized loans, and for what? A few tepid sonnets, a villanelle sequence, everything metered and cozied and rhymed. He was a fucking *formalist*, he said, with self-loathing. But he was too hard on himself—I can say this now, definitively, with Sam in the ground. He had real talent, grace of line, enough earnestness to choke you sometimes, but sometimes it did fill you up.

The one poem of Sam's I still have he read one evening, appropriately enough, at KGB Bar in the East Village—red-light-district decor, Soviet schmaltz on the walls, high stools around a cramped gleaming bar, and a patchy PA system, of course. I didn't catch the title of the poem the first time I heard it read, but the rest of it I liked enough to ask Sam for a paper copy afterward.

The Good Life

I despair about where/if it is, this mushroom land,
dun carpet in a stand

of dunny trees
(nutrition in a sun-blocked world)

I feel quite stuck in cosmic waiting
rooms,

the brooms of systems sweeping me out
with dust toward dust. I must

get my shit together, I must come good
after twenty-eight years of grace, period.

But who do I ask for directions?
The gurus are cheats, assholes,

exes,
and I've never really known my Father.

I've only my two thin hands to break brush with.
Tell me: should I bother?

At the House Sam divided up the money five ways. We all exchanged curt hugs before retreating to our separate cars—Sam and I to his old broad Buick, Alex and Tiffany and Jamaal to Alex's Honda. No one knew where the other was going, exactly, and no one asked, though we all had our ideas.

"Do you think we'll see Jamaal or Tiffany again?" I asked Sam in the car.

"I hope not."

"They have their suspicions, you know, just like Greg did."

"Let them suspect. They don't know anything, and they're scared. Productively scared."

Sam dropped me at Grand Central with my single lean garment bag—amazing how little you really need, in the end, how much of a life can be abandoned—and I started away toward the station. With a shy honk Sam called me back to the passenger-side window he had leaned across to crack open. Not then, but on the Amtrak home I recalled the day more than three years earlier when I'd slipped a Marxist primer through the cracked-open window of the same front seat, though on that morning the conspiratorial shtick had been just that—a little shtick, a joke. What a horrible joke that Sam and I should be playing out this scene in nervous earnest now, cutting our eyes left and right, lowering our voices.

"Where were you on that night?" Sam said, testing me. "What were you doing?"

"Sam, I've got it."

"What were you doing?"

"Diner, fishbowl, long way home—I've got it."

"What diner?"

"The Peter Pan."

"And when the rain got bad, where did we pull off?"

"Sam, I'm going," I said, and I headed for the bank of brass-gleaming doors without turning around.

During the three days I spent at my parents' house I surfaced to the main floor only reluctantly. Base appetite had driven me to my basement lair years earlier—only appetite could drive me up again. I made ham and cheese sandwiches in the kitchen, quickly, efficiently, or else PBJs (my taste buds regressing to high school too, apparently), trying to ignore as best I could the professional speculators piping in from the TV in the living room. Nancy Grace had the story now. I tried to block out the segments squeezed cheek by jowl between Pepto-Bismol ads, Viagra commercials, shills for the newest heart medication. Mostly it was Bosch's name, that primal noise, that broke in on me—*Bosch . . . Bosch . . . Bosch*—like explosions from a distant battlefield.

Since when had my parents watched so much twenty-four-hour news, anyway? How had they learned to watch Nancy Grace?

"Oh, you don't really watch it," Mom said. "It's just a noise to keep you company."

"It's *unbearable*," I said. I felt my eye, the insistent something under my eyelid beginning to jump and grab with each *Bosch*.

"Is it unbearable? We're so used to it by now."

Apparently the "news" as a kind of aural nightlight began shortly after I'd left for college. I'd never complained about it on visits home before, Mom told me. I'd never seemed to notice. Dad, especially, coming in from the corporate cold of an insurance brokerage in downtown Boston—asshole boss, tetchy clients, bad commute—didn't care for the added insult of an existentially quiet house. Mom needed the constant burble less. Thirty years into her high-school math teacher's stride, she'd started singing in an ecumenical choir that met several nights a week to practice Bach masses, old Negro spirituals, the whispery haunting pieces that you couldn't quite locate in time or space.

"Why not play some of your music?" I said. "Why not run the fucking dishwasher? It'd be better than *that*, surely."

"I could turn it off if it means that much to you," Mom said, moving toward the set.

It was the second week in August and she would soon be back in school. She had the rosy capillary blush about her cheeks that suggested inveterate drinking in some Irish, but in my mom it just meant a recent visit to the beach. She'd lost weight where my father had gained it—at the sucked-in cheeks, at the under-chin with its sharper smoother drop-off. When she showed her white teeth they looked whiter, wider, with a plasticky tensile sharpness in the lips. Her nervousness made her look younger by several years. Yet I sensed that any conversation with her reappeared son made her feel older, too, more fragile, as it did me.

I heard familiar music coming out of the TV, then Maria Nava's voice.

"Wait," I said, "that's okay. You can leave it on."

It was the Bank of America ad Sam had showed me on YouTube. I hadn't heard the sincerity, somehow, the genuine relief in Maria's voice the first time I'd seen the ad. Now Maria spoke through her wide soft face into my mother's living room, shots of Aida and Luís horsing around on the grass. "I was afraid," Maria said. "I really was afraid for me and my family when all this was happening. I was looking around for any help I could find. I didn't think I'd find it with someone at a bank, you know, but then I met Ned." Cut to Ned, hair parted at the side, anodyne, friendly-looking. He looked harmless. Ned began to talk about the "debt-forgiveness plan" he'd created with Maria. Hey, he had a family too, he said, and he knew how hard these times were for hardworking people like Maria. I realized I was watching a more extended version of this commercial, an ad that was also a penitent genuflection that was also and always an ad. The cozy acoustic guitar came up on the young family gamboling around in the green green grass—fade to white and the final tag line in black: "Caring. It's what we do."

I waited for the old ire, the sense of rightness in my cause—I suddenly wanted it, needed it—but it wouldn't come. Nancy Grace filled the screen, with a harry of legends and tickers and crawls all around her. I'd caught a little of this loop out of the corner of my eye before, but now it assaulted me head-on: pictures of Bosch and Bosch's family, and now Nancy Bosch at a lectern with two adult children at her side, all of them red-faced, swollen, as Nancy struggles to read prepared words about a loving husband and father, a good man, who never deserved this. Cut to another snippet of video as the suited executive squints and raises his hand against the strobing gale of camera flashes—cut to a large black Escalade pulling past a corridor of metal police barriers that holds back the angry protesters with their signs. The chasm widened in my stomach and I began to fall through it, Alice-like, falling into nothingness, blackness. I rushed back to the kitchen counter and grabbed my plate, scurrying back downstairs to eat alone.

"Son?" Mom called after me. "Eli?"

At the writing desk all my recollections read back like horrible stalls, feints, repetitions. I'd started practicing my statement to the police, too, writing it out like the fool I was.

Where was I on the night of August 21? Out for a little drive with friends, Officer, and I think a stop-off at a diner—what night was that again? A Thursday? It must have been the Peter Pan Diner, and I must have ordered from the breakfast menu since I remember the hash browns tasting like wood chips soaked in oil. An overrated place, we all agreed, and yes, cash only—we paid in cash. Then we took the long way back to the city, pulling over to the side of the road when a rainstorm made a mockery of our windshield wipers . . . Then we drove the rest of the way home without incident.

What a fool I was! What a rank coward to cling so hopelessly to this thin little filament of a chance! If the police came digging, circling back, prodding my story for inconsistencies,

I was supposed to volunteer that we'd actually stopped off in those dark rainy woods to smoke pot, fishbowling the car. This was Sam's invention, his pièce de résistance—it explained why we'd taken the toll road up (they'd have the footage available) and the out-of-the-way way back. It also gave off a little whiff of criminality, ergo plausibility—ergo problem solved.

I confess that I'd briefly felt flattered that the group should choose me for this subtler role—the fool!—this character who withholds a minor infraction, then confesses it shaking and racked. And then I felt genuinely racked, genuinely shaky to learn that Sam had been keeping weed in the bowels of his old-school glove compartment all along. (If the cops checked for traces there, he assured us they'd find them.) The fact astonished me: All the time we'd been out on "junkets" in Sam's Buick, chasing and tailing Bosch around the city, or out trawling around for unguarded cell phones, laptops, iPads—all this time Sam had carried the classic pretext for an arrest in his glove compartment.

This moving target of a man—when had I lost the bead on him? And had I ever really had it?

In the late afternoon I heard someone on the creaking stairs descending, hesitating. The wooden planks lulled their song momentarily, but now the song resumed and gathered tempo and purpose. I was at my bedroom door before Mom could get into the entertainment room. She saw me, startled back.

"Oh," she said. "I was just coming to talk to you."

"I figured."

The room glowed bluely with light from another cutaway window against the wall, a lighted band of blue-white sky above a narrower band of dark loam. The house was set at an angle, you remembered, dug into a slope that slowly rose toward the back of the property. In heavy rain I used to watch the black dirt gel and burgeon at my bedroom window, half daring the earth to come through the glass and bury me, sink me struggling in that black grainy sea, a white hand sticking out in sudden desperate protest—*Of course I didn't really mean it!*

"Do you have a minute?" Mom said.

"Actually," I said. "Maybe not quite yet."

"Let's pretend you do, okay? As a favor to me? Call it a trial run."

"A trial run?"

"You pretend you're the kind of son who still comes to his mother when he needs help, I'll pretend I'm the kind of mother who can still help you. Okay? A trial run."

She sat at one end of a plaid couch against the wall and patted the spot next to her with her small white hand. She wore blue argyle socks and the gray corduroys, narrow-waled, that Dad liked to run his fingernail across at speed, making a sharp little *zeep* sound. A thin black sweater, narrow with white stripes, like a fashionable take on prison garb. She'd cut her brown hair to curl tight around her ears and upper neck, having taken inches off her pageboy too. She opened her mouth to speak but changed her mind, dropping back into a not-quite smile.

"Why am I here, right? That's what you want to know?"

"We assume you're here because you need to be here," Mom said, "but yes, a little detail would be nice."

I leaned my back against the armrest, slipping my feet under Mom's warm thighs as I'd done throughout childhood, the two of us reading, say, or watching TV, with Dad off in his study or away on business. Sealed away in our respective minds but close, connected, touching.

I started into the lie I'd prepared for this conversation too, another alibi—things souring with Jen, the engagement called off, the ultimatum from Hahn to finish my dissertation or else, the job I'd gotten, the job I'd lost, the money I'd borrowed from them and all but squandered . . . I could see the concern in the long smooth lines of my mother's face, but I couldn't tell whether or not she believed me. For some reason I felt that the money was the sticking point—ten thousand dollars wasn't easily sneezed away. I described what I'd spent to appease the people I'd crashed with for too long, how quickly large sums can disappear in New York. I said I was sorry—and I was.

"I'll pay you back," I said, "I promise. I want to pay you back."

"How much of it do you have left?"

"About four hundred."

The money was Hahn's, but the figure was accurate.

Unfazed, Mom nodded, but then she said, "Who are these friends you owe money to? You owe them rent, you said?"

"I don't owe them anything anymore. I didn't mean that. They're not really my friends, either."

She looked calculating now—doing the numbers, carrying ones across multiple lanes of numerical traffic. You saw it happen at parties sometimes, family gatherings, a vacant look while she went somewhere behind her eyes and peeled back the weeks and months and years of your time on this earth. Tell her your birthday, she'd tell you the day of the week you were born on—a trick she'd learned in graduate school.

Mom said, "Is one of these friends you owe money to Alex? Your old girlfriend Alex?"

I looked at her without cover, without preparation.

"She called the house this morning while you were in the shower. She asked if you were here."

"She did? What did she say?"

"She just asked if you were here. I said you were but you weren't available, could I take a message. She didn't have one. I think she might have been calling from a pay phone. It was a strange call."

"You're sure it was Alex?"

"I recognized her voice. She seemed shy to be talking to Eli's mother. Do you owe her money, Eli? Does she need money from you?"

"Does Alex need money? How should I know?" I said. "What the hell are you talking about?"

"I'm just asking you a question," Mom said. "Are you in trouble?"

For the rest of the afternoon I waited for Alex to call again, or text—or something. What did she want from me? Why was she calling my parents' landline? I waited through the evening and late into the night, cycling through the old CDs still arranged in the sideways wooden cubby on the brown dusty ledge above my bed. The old bulbous CD player still worked, with the cutout picture of Robert Plant, curled at the edges, yellowing with age, hanging on the wall with a red thumbtack through one of Plant's iconic golden curls. In the picture he is quiet, eyes closed, holding the microphone tenderly with overlapping hands as if he just might kiss the thing instead of sing into it— an older man's gentleness, his face lined. "Going to California" was on the player now, 3:00 a.m. by the red glowing numbers

of the clock display. I sang along to the chorus distractedly, as I
had fifteen years ago, more—

> *Made up my mind to make a new start*
> *Going to California with an aching . . .*

The words stretched on Plant's ghostly tenor like a canvas, an
otherworldly skin. Perhaps it was here that I'd picked up the
crooner style Mal chided me for when I tried to sing Mahler.

I'd never been to California. I'd only gone as far west as
Maria Nava's backyard in Phoenix, Arizona, it occurred to me
now, and now I thought I didn't stand much chance of com-
pleting the journey to the coast. Eastward, against the course
of empire, I'd gone as far as Europe after college—London,
Paris, Brussels, Munich, Berlin, Vienna, Florence, Rome. For
a month you run along rail lines and rutted tourist trails like
a neuron passing unthinking through the automatic brain, the
vast cerebellum of western Europe. The sameness of desire is
humbling, occasionally comforting—very occasionally. When
I think of that trip now the first thing to resolve out of the
gray blur of monuments and mansard blocks and other generic
beauties is the talismanic head of Karl Marx, at his gravesite in
North London. You wend back through the unpruned green-
ways of Highgate Cemetery and suddenly there it is, looming
up hero-size—Marx's great gray bust on a high granite base.
The forehead sat hugely above prow-like brows, great recessed
pits for eyes, the round nose riding high on a prodigious sea-
foaming wave of mustache and beard. He looked like Poseidon,
Zeus, a menacing Santa Claus. Years later when I sold my car
to fund a weeklong trip to Florence with Alex, I made a special
arrangement for an eight-hour layover at Heathrow so that Alex

could visit the grave too. The afternoon was misting, I remember, and Marx looked changed, less inspired and inspiring, his eyes prosaically visible in the gray even light. He seemed to be looking down on us, weighing us in the balance.

"Done ticked this box, haven't we?" Alex said in a sudden chirping cockney.

I couldn't tell if she was joking to mask her disappointment or to lighten mine, or maybe both. *Done tixed is box, aven't we?*

The gilt lettering of "WORKERS OF ALL LANDS UNITE!" looked faded and a little chintzy, but Alex posed underneath it and smiled in her pink zippered hoodie that doubled as a raincoat, the water beading and pilling on the soft fabric.

I tried to keep these memories with me as I journeyed into sleep, fitful sleep, but I couldn't hold on to Alex or rainy disappointing London for long. In the morning I walked outside into birdsong and bright light, letting myself feel shocked. I walked up the long sloping rise past the Sheehans' property, past the stand of thin trees where Sean and I had huddled over crumbling pink body parts, the limbs shoveled haphazardly into our gaping id furnaces, the doors of superego standing wide . . . Eventually I looked around me and saw that I'd wandered far beyond the woods near my house, uncertain of where I was anymore, with no bread crumbs in sight. Then a woman on a horse cantered into view, slowing to a walk as she approached me. What a tall, broad-chested, proud-maned animal she rode! I gave the horse a wide berth as it passed, the woman high in her saddle in white riding pants and a light brown shirt with a darker silhouette of a palm tree on it. She looked distinctly out of place in Plymouth, Massachusetts, but she did match her horse, mocha-colored with white streaks in its mane and lower legs so that it might have been wearing tube socks. I nodded a hello to the woman, who looked off beyond me, battening down her eyes in sudden confusion.

"Me?" the woman called out, pointing. "Or him?"

I knew it was Alex before I'd turned around. A hundred yards off, not far from where two trails joined in a sandy confluence, a small figure waved her arms against the brightness of the trail mouth. Familiar in her tank top and shorts, familiar in the voice she lifted up against the tree sounds and wind—I saw Alex's Honda, too, parked a little ways behind her in a cul-de-sac. A pickup with a horse trailer attached to it curved into view as I picked up my pace, running. A strange sense of calm was coming over me, an inevitability like the movement of an airport conveyor belt. When I got into the car beside Alex I tried to get her attention, putting my hand on her hand as she reached for the ignition.

"Hey," I said. "What are you doing here?"

Alex started the car. "We should go. We're drawing attention to ourselves."

"You weren't exactly discreet a moment ago."

The woman on horseback came to the trailhead, descending her mount with a swift athletic swing of the legs, holding the reins at her cheek like a child with balloon strings. Alex and I must have looked like quarreling lovers in our dumb show, my body at right angles to hers. I needed to know what was wrong.

"What's wrong?" Alex said. "What's wrong? I don't know, Eli, what could possibly be wrong? I was looking for you!"

"Why were you looking for me?"

Alex pulled away at speed. Mailboxes shot past us, cracked driveways, modest white houses through the trees.

"Where are you going?" I said. "Do you even know where you're going?"

"They questioned Sam," Alex said. "The police questioned him."

"What? When?"

"The other day."

"Yesterday?"

"Fuck, Eli! How should I know? He didn't give me a detailed timeline on the phone."

"He called you? From jail?"

"He didn't call me from *jail*, moron! You think he'd call me from jail?"

Alex jerked her head back and forth, back and forth again, as if trying to shake off my naïveté, my preening moronic questions. Yet I didn't know anything. How *had* he called her? Where was he? How had the police found him? Where had he gone?

"I don't know any of that," Alex said. "I just know we have to find him. He's obsessed. We have to find him."

"Wait," I said. "Wait wait wait wait wait wait—"

Through the window the shapes and colors of my childhood spun past—past Ames Way, tree-lined Marshland Street, past Carolina Road, past the O'Briens' and the Delanos' and the Sheehans'. The fixed point of the mailbox at the top of my family's drive rushed toward us—past us.

"Alex," I said. "Alex, where are we going? You just passed my house. What are you doing?"

She was shaking her head again, muttering bitterly through tight-set teeth.

"What?" I said. " 'Fucking' what?"

"Fucking amateur! He goes to his parents' house to hide!

Probably the easiest place in the world to find you, Eli, and that's where you go."

A blue minivan shaped like a great sleek nose sped up Standish Drive as we shot down it, a brief sucking *boom* as we passed.

"Jesus Christ, Alex, will you slow down?"

She leaned forward and to the right with the sudden swinging pressure of the car, arcing us left onto Webster at the bottom of the hill, barely slowing at a three-way stop.

"Oh the discretion!" I sang. "The discretion!"

At the next stop sign, a four-way intersection, Alex slowed just enough for me to jimmy up the power locks and jump out of the car. A crazed operatic scream chased after me, the noise stretching and yo-yoing back as Alex turned the car around and tracked my progress up the hill, making a running recitative of abuse through the open window: "Goes straight to the first place anyone would fucking think to look, the shit for brains. Get the fuck in the car, Eli! This is serious! Do you doubt it?"

When I looked up again she was showing me the gun. It was shinier than the other one, all-around shiny, snub-nosed.

"Wait," I said, slowing. Alex's Honda kept pace beside me.

"Just trust me when I say this is serious," Alex said. "Okay?"

"That's not the same one, is it?"

"What do you think?"

"No."

"No, it isn't."

I broke around the back of the Honda and flew up the little bank of grass that the Teague family never kept mowed—past the fishing boat on its side in the side yard, the lichened blue aboveground pool that Mr. Teague once threw me in to teach me how to swim, my rigid little body like a mute white stone sinking straight to the bottom. The oldest Teague girl broke into our house a year later and stole petty cash, a little jewelry, leaving a sort of calling-card note on our fridge's message board—the cops compared it to the handwriting on her homework. Half a mile straight ahead, then, through backyards and driveways and copses, clouds of ghosts, bursting through them like a cannonball through its smoke. I came out of these last woods with a crosshatch of thin red lines down my arm, a long pearling streak down my leg. The skin of my face felt tight, the sweat prickling at my hairline. I saw Alex's car in the driveway, Alex's form through my fogged-in glasses going soft at the edges as she stepped into my house, my mother holding open the front door.

When I got upstairs I did nothing to hide my heavy breathing, the red stripes and scourges on my arms and legs from the neighborhood's brambly woods. Mom blinked at me. I was bent over my knees.

Alex said, "Speak of the devil . . ."

We told my mother we were going out for an early lunch to hash some things through—vague like that, and I think she sensed we were lying.

She said, "Is this the type of lunch place that charges money for their food?"

I put a hand on Alex's shoulder as we dropped down the stairs, to make a better show of it. When we turned the corner away from the front door Alex muscle-bucked my hand away.

"Where'd you get the gun, Alex?"

Back in the car she volunteered a little more information about Sam—less affronted now, driving slower. He'd hung back in the city looking for Greg while the rest of us returned to the leafy suburbs we'd spawned from, apparently. Not that Sam had shown much acumen, either, asking around about Greg at ISO meetings, around the Randolph campus, sleeping at the House or in his car—but that was Alex's point: Sam was losing it, a danger to Greg, a danger to all of us now. He'd kept it together enough to tell the cops the story we'd agreed on—he was out again, not enough to be held on—but now he was probably out redoubling his search for Greg. An obsessive, a liability.

"So he called you from a pay phone?" I said.

Alex nodded.

"Do you know if he mentioned the fishbowl thing to the cops?"

"I don't."

"What were the questions they asked him? How did they find him?"

"I don't know," Alex said. "I don't know any of that. It was two minutes on the phone and most of the time he was asking *me* the questions, trying to find out where Tiffany or Jamaal had gone, if I knew anything about Greg, anything about you and where you might have gone."

"Me? What have I got to do with anything?"

"We just need to find him," Alex said, "or find Greg. Find Greg and maybe we'll find Sam. He won't be far behind."

"And you have no idea where he is?"

"You mean Greg?"

"I mean Sam! Your boyfriend Sam!"

"Is that what he is?" Alex said softly, a little amused. Then she said, "Why don't you tell me where he's gone to—he's your best friend, isn't he? No? You don't know?"

She appeared to take brief satisfaction from this little touché, if that's what it was, but now her face dropped back into olive-sallow slackness, her hair wet and luminously dark from the shower she'd taken in the downstairs bathroom, the first she'd had in three days. I'd showed her how to work the wonky taps in the shower, the bathroom unfinished like my bedroom, unadorned, the shower stall a mere plastic husk of a stall, a placeholder, the white bowl of the sink sticking out of the wall with its gray throat exposed—provisionality abandoned to permanence.

Past Alex's window a row of light-topped silver stanchions ticked by like the measure lines of a sonata, a sudden pastorale. Green within green again, a scrim of trees running behind the unlit car dealership at the edge of town. Up ahead I saw the interstate and signs for Middleborough, Taunton, Norton, each name an echo, a ghost limb. There were years when those place-names would have brought nothing to mind so much as the locker rooms attached to the high schools in them, the dark linoleum hallways after school hours, the spread of fenced-in tennis courts we played on, the meager crowds, mostly parents. Now the names put off a fresh-cut grass smell, reeking mulch, the hiss of sprinklers, the sensorium of suburban wealth that got weaker as you moved out of Boston's powerful orbit, stronger again as you came into New York's.

On the interstate the sky lowered like a shade, darker grays within gray, suddenly, the furrowed white brow of a thunderhead pushing out here and there from the newly installed mass. We were headed toward Greenwich and the millionaire ZIP codes of neighboring Westchester County. Somewhere nearby Bosch's ghost would be hovering in the air, like a seagull on the wind, a plane in a holding pattern over JFK or Newark. I was up there with it now, seeing the bodies from a bird's-eye view when I saw them, the eye of memory slowly turning in the air, hovering, half presiding over the bodies, a man's and a dog's, in their final loneliness.

I realized that the car—coming back to earth—was bending away on an off-ramp.

"We're getting off?" I said to Alex. "Why are we getting off?"

I saw her subtly check her phone. I noted the blue illuminated bars showing gas levels on the console stacked four or five high above the glowing red E. A group of faded, sad-looking picnic tables slid by on our left, a widening apron of grass. Then the low-slung rest stop came out from behind trees, a group of small brown shacks with a lodge aesthetic that the gas stations and fast-food chains roughly matched: a restrained set of golden arches, a Dunkin' Donuts sign in muted earth tones . . . The main building's low roof ran up shallowly, its peaked overhang like an amphitheater shell to an audience of cars. The sun was still behind clouds, but enough light seeped through to reflect the slate sky in the prodigious span of windshields coming into view on our right, recalling a super-image spread across a bank of tight-packed TV screens, the sky in the million microdomes of a bug's eye.

"This is the lunch stop we promised your mother," Alex finally said, parking. "To hash things through, right? I'd love to know what you told her."

Inside the main building a line of vending machines and a grimy blue pay phone filled the space between the men's and women's bathrooms. I came out before Alex, scoping the layout—a convenience store in the right-hand trench, a fluorescent food court–style expanse at the left, white square tables and chairs all welded together and bolted to the floor as if road-warped travelers might try to pry them up for souvenirs. Just then Alex came in through the front entrance again, the glass doors sucking shut behind her.

"I thought you were in the bathroom," I said.

She nodded at the small leather carryall looped over her shoulder. "Forgot this in the car," she said, and disappeared into the ladies' room.

For a good twenty minutes we sat across from each other eating Quiznos at a table in the corner, a casualness sinking into our skin, like exhaustion, and at the same time, with our guard down, an old-times intimacy coming up, an old-times routine.

"Guy in the corner," I said. "Other corner. Don't stare! It's like riding a bike, Alex. How are you so rusty at this?"

"In the Patriots jersey?"

"The very same."

"Half empty or half full?"

"Whichever you prefer."

"Whose jersey is he wearing? Is that Brady's?"

I craned my head to try to make out the numbers spread across the man's spreading gut under the table. I couldn't quite see them, but then I wouldn't have known Brady's jersey number anyway—my taste in sports ran admittedly to the genteel.

"Not mine," Alex said. "I'm a woman of the people. I know all about the Boston Football Patriots."

"Of course."

"Actually, I do know a little about Brady from the tabloids. Let's assume for the sake of this exercise in"—she hesitated, neck bent, squinting—"in glass half fullness, let's assume the gentleman in the corner, our friend Rick, let's assume, is wearing a Tom Brady jersey. Now, understand that Rick isn't one of those big-boned stocky guys of—what, English stock? Irish?— who seeks some vicarious existence in his favorite righty quarterback. Brady's right-handed, right?"

"No idea."

"Pretty sure he is. Rick is too. But here's the thing: Rick doesn't get off on thinking he *is* the quarterback Tom Brady, fucking the same supermodels and paying out the same giant alimonies when he gets tired of them—or maybe it's child support? I can't remember. But Rick's not interested in that. He just likes the way the guy passes the ball, the way he runs out of the pocket, the way he squeezes a water bottle a good foot above his head on the sidelines, very casual-like, you know? Rick loves that. He loves Tom Brady, but he doesn't actually want to *be* Tom Brady. Tom Brady doesn't get to just relax and eat a Big Mac at a middle-of-nowhere rest stop. Tom Brady can't eat Big Macs at all. Tom Brady probably has to suffer through an endless stream of minimally plated nouvelle cuisine dinners, often working to make conversation with people he doesn't know or particularly like. See, Rick doesn't want that. He likes being alone with his thoughts—he can handle that. Do you see him checking his phone every two seconds? You don't. He likes to relax and enjoy a Big Mac, which he enjoys a lot better, frankly, than whatever bastardized European fare they serve at those overpriced bistro pubs, whatever the fuck a bistro pub is. If there's a meaningful distinction between a bistro pub and any other mid-price restaurant with a liquor license, our friend Rick doesn't see it. He doesn't get taken in by marketing, he's not one of Pavlov's slobbering dogs. The man likes his Big Macs, so what? He likes a shamefully rich football player playboy who's probably delinquent in his child support payments, so what?"

With a grimace-smile I raised my index finger like a referee's yellow flag.

"Too much projection at the end there?" Alex said. "Okay, I'll withdraw it."

"Why should he feel the need to defend football and Big Macs?"

"A little splash on the entry, granted, but pretty good otherwise, no?"

"Eight out of ten."

"Who's rusty now?" Alex said, slapping the table. "Okay,

your turn. Who who who who who?" she said, roving her gaze across the room.

In Florence Alex and I had played this game daily, obsessively, at every meal, every snack stop. The first half of our trip was filled with glass-half-full speculations about soft-eyed gelato-shop owners, amateur artists with their easels at the banks of the glittering Arno, French tourists in their stylish dress, uncomfortable-looking shoes. Then came the midweek announcement that Alex and Columbia were finished, the academic life she'd lived, goodbye to all that—and with it, curling silently, sourly in the air, the suggestion that she and I were probably finished too. From then on the trip had all the lilt of a funeral march and all our speculations about the people we saw went glass half empty, decidedly. The pruned woman kneeling down with her eyes closed at the cordon line before Ghiberti's golden door? A religious zealot first, an art lover second or third or tenth, or not at all. The glum-looking man at an alfresco café table, staring at the tourists over his thin empty glass? Stood up on a date, or maybe just out of work, swallowing his savings one grappa at a time. The classical guitarist with the long dark braid that hung down her chest like a ferret? Unemployed too, basically. A hobbyist. What else did twenty years of careful study in just about any art make you? I recalled for Alex a line of Saul Bellow's: The best humanists would be called in to pick out the wallpaper for humanity's crypt. The guitarist was good, too, very good, subtle and soulful in her playing, and lonely. She set up nightly on the steps of a little stone church a few streets from the Ponte Vecchio. In the distance you could hear the more popular buskers with their acoustic-electric American Top 40 on the famous lit-up bridge. We'd passed these talentless young men before, seen their open guitar cases glittering like treasure chests. How simple it was, sometimes, to hate the world. You just opened your eyes.

On the other side of the table Alex had come back to herself—playtime over, apparently. Clouds moved in over her face, her eyes unblinking through narrowed lids. At her neck a tendon stood out like a long fin, running down through the clavicle and making a line against which the gentle bait in her throat dropped and rose again.

"You see that pay phone up front?" Alex said, nodding. "That's our ticket."

"Ticket to what?"

"Don't say anything incriminating on the call, just find out where he is. Do you have his number?"

"Sam's?"

"Greg's. He's the priority. We need to warn him, but we obviously can't do that over the phone."

"Warn him against what? What's Sam going to do?"

"How would I know that?" Alex said. "All I have are worst-case scenarios."

She took her phone out of the carryall, a pen, an old grocery receipt, and copied down the number for me to call. She'd tried herself several times but Greg hadn't picked up, and frankly she didn't blame him. She was linked in Greg's mind with Sam, and Sam hadn't exactly been subtle in his suspicions of Greg, his late hostilities to him. I was different. I'd earned Greg's trust enough to elicit advice from him, borrow money from him—I'd been the last to see him.

"I tell him it's important that we talk to him, but we have to do it in person," I said.

"No 'we,'" said Alex. "Don't even mention me."

I took a handful of quarters to the pay phone by the entrance. The doors behind me rang open and sucked shut, sounds of sneakers on the floor mat, the thwack of flip-flops, the traffic noise from the interstate rushing over the cement partitions and coursing in on the breeze. For long seconds I heard no dial tone, no meaningful clicks—I was on the point of fingering down the receiver when a staid single beep signaled Greg's voice mail. I said the words. I tried to keep my voice low and calm, but a tremor of genuine worry must have ghosted through the message. I don't like to consider where that fear came from—that Alex's concern, a concern about what all this might mean for *us*, is what accounted for the frightened vibrato feathering the edges of my words. Yet it's also obvious, isn't it? Self-interest presided over all this, that bugaboo of Marxism and all utopianism, that black beating heart of all genuine interaction under capitalism. *Of course I mean it! It involves me!* Maybe Greg heard something of this in my message to him—I can't be sure—but a few minutes later when I tried him again I heard his voice on the phone, his live voice, tinny and far away, trembling, breathless, cowed.

It had to be in person, I told him. "Not over the phone. In person. Trust me, okay?"

He gave me the address. I wrote it down. I lied and said I was calling from New York. Two hours, I said, maybe a little under. It was that simple.

I returned to the table, smiling, an idiot vanity on my lips, idiot vanity on my face, the way it pulled up my brows like a marionette's, the puppyish, golden retriever's pride in my eyes . . . That was me. That was the face I wore to the cliff's edge.

"You got it?" Alex said.

I pushed the paper across to her. "You should have timed me," I said.

"Maple Court, huh? In Stamford? That sounds about right—the obligatory tree fetish. I'll bet he's at his parents'."

"Maybe so."

"Quite a group we put together, isn't it?"

"What did you expect? We're a bunch of grad school drop-outs."

"It's okay," Alex said, standing, looking quickly past me. "It'll be okay." She crossed to my side of the table and hugged me tight around the neck, leaning into my ear, saying, "Please don't be mad at me, Eli. This'll all be okay. Okay? You know I love you," and she pushed her lips hard into my cheek.

I wheeled around, tracking her sudden steps to the door. Sam was just inside the entranceway, tall and pale, his thin frame loose in the soiled white giveaway T-shirt that hung from his shoulders as if off a coat hanger, the concave chest, the sharp jaw that bent to receive Alex's hasty kiss. He pulled her to him, holding her in an embrace, the subtle exchange of the receipt, and now Sam's eyes were on me. He carried a sagging blue JanSport backpack over his right shoulder as he stepped into the harsher light of the food court, an overhead light that filled him out, lit up the pits and hollows of his face. He was nakedly what he was.

"Don't be mad at Alex," Sam said as he lowered himself down across from me. I retain the image of a green wispy road-runner on the front of his T-shirt, an impressionist figure sliding past—I was staring straight ahead, making a fixed frame for Sam to drop into.

"Eli?"

"You needed the address?" I said. "Is that why I'm here?"

"For what it's worth, Alex didn't want to do it this way, but it had to be done. It was my idea."

I looked up at Sam. "All you've got weighing down that backpack is your dirty laundry, I assume?"

A faint smile crossed Sam's lips, minnow-like—there, then gone.

"And what's to stop me from walking out of here right now?"

"And hitching a ride back to your leafy Boston suburb?"

"Or anywhere."

"Common sense," Sam said, rising slowly back out of the frame. The runner in stylized outline, his limbs like wisps of green smoke, rose too—low cacti in the foreground, a few deft lines to hint at canyons in the background. "Cedar City 10k— Fun in the Sun Run," the shirt said. It moved out of view and trailed after it a belated fug of body sweat and overmatched Old Spice. Sam whispered in my ear, soft and low, dovish, like Alex from a moment ago.

He loped to the front entrance and turned and waited for me there, feigning interest in a Coke machine that he almost matched for height. He wore the tight dark jeans I'd rarely not seen him in, the ones with the white threadbare outlines in the fabric like salty leavings from his front-pocket wallet, the rectangular cell phone he still used in a pinch, I gathered, and here we were in a pinch. He wore the same flat loafers, too, that he used to slip on after tennis, furred and moccasin-like with wear—or if not the exact pair, a close descendant. He was not one to change styles quickly, Sam Westergard. A man of deep habit. A man of action with the habit of repeating his actions again and again, clinging to his talismanic routines. I later learned that Sam had made a near nightly ritual of his trips up to Bosch's neighborhood, sometimes late-night trips, sometimes trips that must have shaded into very early morning, the pale light in a few of the tollbooth photos covering Sam's tan Buick in a purple shroud, covering over the car's dents and rust spots, taking years off it, but never quite obscuring the license plate or the jagged New Jersey–shaped hole shaping the glow of the left brake light. The sexual politics of the House's upstairs bedroom being what they were, I never really wondered why Sam should move from mattress to mattress, rarely waking in the same one consecutively, as if the darkness of night hid nothing so much as a silent game of musical beds. Upward of forty trips, I learned at the trial. An obsessed man, Alex had called him—and I'm convinced that that much of her performance was genuine. I could see the burning points of Sam's personality emanating off him by the Coke machine, unfurling like plumes, like a peacock's spread of manifold shimmering secrets. For the bird it's an automatic gesture, an upwelling out of deep, primordial springs. I wonder how much different it was for my friend Sam.

At length I let him catch my eye. I let him nod me to the door. Outside in the lot the tan Buick overhung the parking spot just opposite the one Alex's Honda had been in.

Sam spoke once we pulled back onto the interstate. He told me we were doing the right thing, the smart thing.

"I'll be the one to talk to him," I said. "That's a requirement. You don't even come near us. Promise me that or I'm out right now."

"Of course," he said. "That was always the plan. Why do you think we needed you?"

"You don't come within a block of the address. I keep the address, actually. Hand it over."

At length Sam did as I asked.

"You drop me at a place where I can get a taxi. He thinks I'm coming up from the city—it should look that way."

"Of course."

We dropped back into silence while the green overtook us at either side, closing in on us. It dulled the senses, doing to the eye what the tires' steady keening through the car's thin floor did to the ear—white vision, white noise. I remember perking up as the steepled clock-tower sprawl of New Haven came and went, the red-brick city like the miniature landscape in a model train set. I perked up more when the road dipped down and hugged the shore and a great infinitesimal light danced over the water—a late sun had come out—and curved Connecticut, staring, ran out across the molten Long Island Sound. It occurred to me that Sam was probably a fugitive.

"Let's not get dramatic," he said.

"Let's not get dramatic? You were just questioned by the police about a murder, weren't you? Are you supposed to be crossing state lines? Aren't the cops keeping tabs on you?"

"It's not a drunk tank, Eli. They don't take your keys."

"What did they say to you? What did they ask you? What do they know? Sam? Will you cut the fucking sphinx routine already? Aren't I basically your accomplice now?"

"Relax," said Sam. "Relax. I don't know what Alex told you, but you can relax, okay?"

It was suddenly all I could do not to leap across the wide leather console and yank that grief-counselor calm off Sam's face. He knew everything except how to keep us out of prison! He knew everything except how to put out the fire we were presently dying in, our bodies chucked in for meaningless tallow. Sam told me again not to be so dramatic, almost whispering the words now, shaking his head—I was shouting—staring ahead at the paying-out road and shaking his head like a disappointed father.

"Tell me everything the cops said to you, right now," I shouted, "and I'll decide whether or not it calls for drama. Right now, you sphinxy fuck! Aren't I here? Aren't I in the car with you? Haven't I given everything to your fucking suicide march?"

"Not everything," Sam said. "Not everything. You can't pretend you haven't had divided loyalties."

"What the fuck does that mean?"

"In the world, sometimes, but never really of it, huh?"

"Will you put your fucking New Testament Greek away and speak—English!"

"You were a member of the House but never all the way. You were there on a trial basis, a need-to-know basis—it was all over your face. It still is, Eli. And what you need to know now is that the cops found me. Somehow they found the House. How did that happen? Do you know?"

"I have no idea. That's what I'm asking you."

"Oh I have an idea," Sam said. "I have an idea. His name is Greg. Your buddy Greg. Anything physical, anything solid and the cops would have never let me go. They wanted to talk about the Bosch protest, in Phoenix—two years ago and on the other side of the country? How would they know about that?"

"You think Greg informed on you? You're saying *he* sent the cops to the House? Why would he do that?"

"I'm not saying he did that. I'm not saying that."

"What *are* you saying? What are we doing right now?"

"I'm just saying it'll be good to talk to him. I just want to talk to him. Maybe he's confused. Maybe he's scared. Maybe he thinks he knows something he doesn't."

"*I'm* talking to him," I said. "I'm doing the talking."

"Sure," said Sam. "Of course, sure. We just need to remind him that he doesn't know anything. None of us do. We hold our nerve, this goes away. That's the message, all right? Stamford five miles." He nodded to the sign.

He took out his phone and handed it across to me. We could use it to navigate the last stretch, he said. He was planning to destroy it anyway.

"Shouldn't we stay off cell phones altogether?" I said. "Don't you have some kind of map in here?" I reached for the glove compartment's handle that didn't give, noticing for the first time the small round lock in the handle's corner.

"No map," said Sam. "Sorry."

"You're sure?" I said. "I could check it for you. Which one of these opens door number one?"

Sam arrested my hand, violently, just shy of the ring of keys hanging off the ignition. "There's no map in the glove compartment," he said. "Trust me on that. And look—let's be realistic for a second." Slowly Sam unfastened his grip on my wrist, the blood surging. "I'm going to need to know where you are, and I don't think tailing a taxi into quiet residential streets is a good idea. Just put the address in the phone, Eli."

"Let me out," I said.

"No."

"Let me out. I'm serious, Sam."

"You're welcome to try—that'd be, what, the drop and roll at seventy miles an hour?"

I was suddenly desperate. "Sam, please, come off it. Let me out! Please let me out!"

"And where would you go?"

"I'll hitchhike. I'll go to a bus stop. You'll never hear from me again."

"I need to talk to him," Sam said, "and I need to make sure it's done right, okay? Say you're worried about me—say I know where he lives, I could be close, say I'm crazy and unhinged and all the stuff you probably do say about me. Say you'd feel a whole lot better if you two were on the move—a talk in the car. Or maybe you're paranoid about wiretaps, whatever. Say whatever you need to say to get him in a car and away from his house. Okay? Then you park somewhere—maybe you need to pee or you thought you saw a cop. Make him park and I'll take it from there. That's the plan. That's all you need to do, Eli. Then you're free. Okay?"

In the taxi now, numbness spreading—

Nothing twitched or grabbed anymore, nothing troubled the glassy surface. It was a new phase in the sensorial Tilt-A-Whirl of the last several days. Now the surgeon put the knife in but all you sensed was the blunted pressure of it, the smell of blood like copper in the air. It could have been anyone's blood.

I felt the dull weight of the gun through the JanSport bag in my lap. I'd insisted to Sam that I bring it with me—not that I'd use it, not that I knew *how* to use it. It was a lucky rabbit's foot, merely, a dark charm, the prospect of rhetoric by other means. This is what I'd told Sam—Sam in his loose road-race T-shirt, in his police-evidence car, with something locked away in the glove box, Sam with the whitish dark rings under his eyes like pats of butter melting down his face.

Through the broad tinted windows of the taxi I could make

out Greg's town unspooling like a straight solid line. The manicured hedges, the narrow drives, dormer windows cut out of the gray shingled roofs, the ineffectual white wooden fences and stacked stone walls—it was Norman Rockwell's America, privilege koshered by quaintness. I'd seen this town before. I'd seen it before I'd ever laid eyes on it—a sin, yes, a violation of etiquette, but not a falsehood. You're brought up to believe that the world will always slip your stereotypes of it, resist your generalized ideas about it with the force of its *thingness*, each snowflake unique, etc. How disappointing to realize that this myth too has been debunked—I think of the Cheever story in which all the husbands and wives of a town turn up to a costume party in football jerseys and wedding gowns. A whole slew of humanity playing to type, uncoordinated, unplanned. It's all they can do to laugh about it.

And my type? What was the role I was trapped in? I walked down the slight decline of a driveway to the house I'd written down the number for, the numbness lifting, dispelling like a sun-chased fog, a certain brightness churning out of the motion of my legs. The taxi hummed off up the road, and underneath it I thought I heard Sam's Buick cutting its engine through the trees. A stone wall rose in sliding scale with the driveway—it ended at the garage at the side of the split-level green-shuttered house, pine green against the whitewashed clapboard. You could have taken my parents' house in Plymouth and set it down some two hundred miles away and there you'd have it. Here you had it. A mulched garden at the level of the retaining wall with pods of green topiary bushes, a black-brown wooden fence at the side yard, dark with weather and age, a line of maples and oaks foreshortening the backyard, mooring to their shadows that stretched like prison stripes across the roof. I rocked myself up into the garden, noticing the inset stairway only a few feet ahead, feeling the gun at the bottom of the JanSport rebounding against my back. A sudden rapping from somewhere behind me—a storm-window rattle. I backed up enough to see the twin glass slits in the white garage door, like robot eyes in their darkness and narrowness. A moment later a jack-o'-lantern light came on in the windows and there was Greg's face looming up baldly, smoothly, wide-eyed in the left-hand glass.

I could hear the heavy breath coming out of him as I scooted under the lifted garage door. I saw the boat shoes he wore, the navy khakis capping thick white legs, an almost comic self-impersonation.

"What's with the paranoia routine, captain?" I tried to sound bluff.

"What?" said Greg. "What you said on the phone, the way you sounded—"

"I know, I know. Okay, look. Why are we in a garage?"

Particleboard lined the walls, a suite of power tools hanging off hooks in the switchboard of holes. There was a small gray Jetta with rounded edges like a cocoon just behind Greg, who faced me again.

"My little sister's upstairs," he said. "I'd rather talk down here."

"Whose car is that? Is it yours?"

"Not really. I use it when I'm here."

"Okay," I said. "I want to show you something."

I brought the JanSport bag around to my front and peeled open the zippered compartment to Greg's view. Like a wounded man, I uncovered my spleen to him, dark and shining, lit at odd angles—a spill of black blood, it could have been, a squid's ink filling the bottom of the bag.

"What is that?"

"It's what you think," I said. "It's not mine, it's Sam's, all right?"

"What are you doing with it?"

"I need your car. I'm not stealing it—I just need it." I closed up the bag. "Listen to me."

When I laid my hand on Greg's arm he flinched dramatically, thrown back against the car's back window, a stuntman's reaction.

"Hey," I said. "It's okay."

"My sister's upstairs," he whispered.

"I just wanted to show you what we're dealing with. Sam's nearby, okay? I need your car. I'm going to leave it at the train station—look for the keys under the wheel well. Sam wants to talk to you but you don't want to talk to him—trust me. As soon as I'm gone, lock your doors. Call the police. Tell them everything I just told you, okay? Greg?"

He stared past me, a sudden porcelain doll, the white skull and forehead and cheeks, the great brown Marxist eyebrows unmoving. I wondered if he'd heard me, if he'd taken any of it in. Then he whispered, "In the ignition. I leave the keys in the ignition."

"Call the police," I said.

I took the turn out of Greg's driveway smoothly but at speed, expecting a certain restraint from Sam, a discreet following distance that would have kept my hapless passenger in the dark, if I'd had one. I was the passenger now, the passenger and the driver, the doubter and the doubt—I was the lure. And discretion had never been Sam's style. The big rattling boat of the Buick came up in my rearview as the town quickly gathered the line it had cast—picket fences blurring by like clouds of spirit, the spirited measure-marker progress of lampposts and telephone poles, the trees, the sky, everything, all of it respooling.

Sam was half a block behind me. When I looked in the mirror I could make out his mute stern features hovering there, his face like the face scrawled onto a balloon floating above the steering wheel. It gave nothing away. Could he see who was driving? Could he tell that the passenger seat was empty? The Jetta's windows tinted the last of the daylight through the car, making a vacuum of deeper purpler dusk inside—was it hiding me, protecting me? Could Sam really not see what was happening? What was to stop him from just turning around?

I paid little heed to a stop sign out of the residential blocks, turning onto a larger hilly street that still looked small, quaint in the way the stores and red-brick buildings cozied it, but big enough for a traffic light at the bottom of the hill—red, of course. I was a mile from the train station, more—*Keep straight*, an automated female voice directed me from my phone. Maybe Sam couldn't tell I was alone from a distance, but now his Buick nosed up and over the same hill, cresting it like a Viking ship over a gray wave, a steady speeding up as gravity did its work. With the crossway traffic speeding smoothly through the intersection, Sam's face filling the mirror again, bearing down on it—just as the front of Sam's car disappeared into the back of mine, the mirror's trick, I stuck my hand out the window and hooked it right, over the roof, pointing largely, frantically, gesticulating with all the subtlety of an air traffic controller, all subtlely abandoned now. I peeled right onto the shoulder to avoid a speeding car, the Doppler wail of its horn as it swerved into the oncoming lane to pass me. I cut left and into the rush of traffic, cutting off a green sedan and another car behind it—a moment's relief—before Sam could make the turn. I didn't know where I was going, where this road was leading us. Panic filled up my veins, made my chest thin and weak. When the green sedan dropped off behind me it was to turn into one of the long, obscured driveways that sudden remoteness had scarced—we were in deeper woods now, green covering every-thing, thickening everything. Sam was coming up behind me. The other car had gone. I felt the gravity lift in my stomach as the Jetta turned hard and we slalomed, the car and I, down the first narrow street that came to hand. Why I sought out this isolation that could only jeopardize me—a sandy clearing up ahead on the left, an abandoned construction site set back from the woodland houses stretched like grimy gray pendants on the little string of road—I couldn't say. I couldn't access self-preservation just then, or maybe I was still trying to keep up the ruse.

I was out of the car, in any case, before Sam could cut his engine. A reddish mound of heaped crusted earth stood off to one side of the clearing, a scatter of tree stumps like excised moles on the rocky land around it. Something was supposed to have been built here, but who knew how far back that supposing stretched, how many years of waste this clearing represented—I think of this now with a coroner's objectivity.

"Playtime's over, Sam," I was shouting, "playtime's over." I had the empty JanSport slung over my shoulder, the gun in my hand. "Give me your keys."

In the wedge of the open door Sam shook his head woefully. "You stupid fuck," he said.

"Fuck *you*, Sam. Give me your keys."

"I was talking about myself," he said. "*I'm* the stupid fuck. He's not in there? Just to confirm?"

"Give me the keys, Sam. This is ridiculous."

"Maybe I'll see you around, Eli," Sam said, and he got back in the car.

"I'm pointing a gun at you!" I shouted.

"That's right. You are." Sam sprang up and out of the front seat, a sudden lilt in his movements, in his voice.

"Why don't you give that back to me," he said. "It doesn't belong to you. You really don't want it."

"Give me the keys," I said.

The snub-nosed pistol trembled horribly in my hand. Looking around I saw a snatch of a shack-like house through the trees, an old car on blocks—strange rustification.

"You look ridiculous with that thing," Sam said. "I should have listened to Alex. You're an amateur."

"Give me the keys."

"You're going to shoot me, Eli?"

"Give me the fucking keys!"

"Might want to rack the thing first, you fucking amateur."

I pulled the top of the gun toward me like you see in the movies—a sudden terrifying *clack* filled the air.

"You might also want to load the thing," said Sam, stepping toward me, his palm outstretched. "There's no ammo in it." He said again, "Give me the gun, Eli. This doesn't involve you anymore."

He lowered his head and shook it once, disgustedly. When he lunged for my arm the gun bucked and Sam folded forward like a briefcase. He dropped to the ground bent forward and holding his side, screaming. He was screaming my name. It took me a long time to understand it but the noise, a blue peal in that clearing, was forming itself into words. I could make out my name. "Eli! Fuck, Eli! What did you do?" The ringing came up in my ears then, in my emptied-out bell-struck skull, the ringing canceling out everything, pushing me back, staggering me back toward the getaway car.

"Where are you going, Eli? Eli!" Sam shouted.

I was driving by pinpricks, just trying to avoid the trees, aiming only for blankness. I could hear Sam's screams reach a new desperate pitch behind me, rising up through the ringing like an aria. "Eli, help me! Come back! Eli! Eli! Eli!"

This is the picture I'm left with. This is the scene I come back to again and again, more helplessly, more joltingly than the one with Bosch. I've presented it here by way of reconstruction, a first-time recording—my notebooks leave off just before Alex's arrival at my parents' house in Plymouth.

Anyway, you don't forget something like that. At the trial Sam's death at my hands was taken for a kind of confession from us both, a bodily confession, with the signature in Sam's blood like a long rough stroke from where he'd dragged himself back to the Buick. He called an ambulance but didn't know where he was, didn't know who'd shot him. On the 9-1-1 tape they played at the trial his voice is weak already, drained: "I didn't recognize him. Never seen him before. Please hurry." The lead prosecutor, a vain man despite his lumpy baldness and rough, pitted cheeks, argued for an interpretation of events that made Sam look amateurish, thoughtless, careless, stupid, blind, and very lucky. The state wanted it both ways—Sam was a bumbling, raw, instinctual Raskolnikov whose obvious left-behind clues required a table of crack lawyers in smart suits to decipher them. When a reporter asked this same prosecutor, post-trial, how the three of us had evaded capture for nearly two weeks, he replied, "Beginner's luck."

Nothing I have to say here will match that for crassness—I regret everything we did. I regret the deaths, of course, but more than that, prior to and larger than that, presupposing it, enabling it, I regret Sam's projection that incubated and grew, with our help, and became flesh and blood. The zealot's heaven imposed on earth, in the little patch of dirt where Bosch lies turning and turning still. For what it's worth—and I do know how little it's worth—I wish Bosch were still alive. I think Sam wished that too. Whatever access of panic or nihilistic drive overcame him in that moment by the lake in the woods, I have to believe it was momentary, unplanned, and uncharacteristic. I want to believe that. I had seen Sam's gentleness overlaying his sharpness, the lubricating skin, the kind gestures, the gentlemanly niceties. And weren't they more than mere gestures, mere niceties?

On the Long Island Rail Road train into New York that night, with Greg's Jetta left behind at the station just as I'd promised it would be, I saw a text message from Sam. It must have come in only a few minutes after the 9-1-1 call: "You didn't mean to, did you? I believe you didn't. S." It took me almost an hour to respond—was he all right? was he in the hospital?—and by then he wasn't responding at all. Alex, too, got a message from Sam that night. She admitted as much at the trial, but no more. "It was of a personal nature," she said in the affectless tone she adopted during those weeks, her brown eyes flat and withholding, and not once meeting mine. The evidence of the message was buried along with Alex's cell phone in the East River silt. Sam's phone had been destroyed with a well-placed bullet to the memory card—an arduous task. All that blood swathed over the Buick's leather seats, the thick console, the wide glove compartment that he finally unlocked to take out the gun. The

rest of the evidence in the car remained intact, preserved carefully, lovingly, a diorama of Sam's guilt—he was a Christian to
the end. His final recidivism was to try to take upon himself all
the punishment, all the sin. In the Buick's trunk: another hand-
gun, an unscrubbed laptop, a scatter of books, and a handwrit-
ten note that read "I alone killed Lawrence Bosch on the night
of August 21. —Sam Westergard."

There were four guns in all, and all of them purchased
through an Armslist page sourced to western Pennsylvania.
Sam's name and details had been changed for the purpose, the
seller's too, presumably, but the IP addresses matched. The
story about Sam's sister and the new baby, the hunting tag-
alongs with his brother-in-law—all bullshit. A lie for my benefit, and apparently for Alex's too.

One of the books found in Sam's trunk was *The Urban
Guerrilla's Handbook*, perhaps the most incriminating of the
documents he'd taken from the House. It was complete with
Sam's careful underlinings, his sparse but telling notes. "Yes,"
he had written at one point, a simple *yes* floating up the mar-
gin like a trial balloon, the word tied to a double-underlined
sentence about how the imperialist giant is known by his toe,
how that single prominence foretells the great gathering bulk
behind it. "Start your attack, therefore, at the toe . . ." Sam had
written at the bottom of the page. On another page he'd written: "Phoenix as our Moncada?"—Moncada, the military bar-
racks where Castro's forces had suffered a defeat that paved the
way to future victory. All this was introduced as evidence at the
trial—Sam's pipe dream, apparently. His pipe-bomb dream. I
can see that now. I think I might have seen it then—had I chosen to see it. At the time I pushed any hard-stop realities out
of my mind—we were only talking, weren't we, no matter how

earnest or daring the talk, how thrilling? Also, I had no idea Sam was building up a small arsenal. The section in the *Handbook* on munitions was particularly well underlined.

Four guns. One to Sam, one to Alex, the gun I had taken with me to Greg's, and the gun in the Buick's incriminating trunk. The black blocky pistol Sam had shot through his phone with was the same one he'd shot through Bosch with—it bore only his fingerprints. When the paramedics finally arrived they found Sam's dead body in the driver's seat, with the glove compartment unlocked and hanging open like a mouth, its secrets spilled.

I still don't know what to make of it all. What was this threatening "talk" Sam had planned for Greg, and would he have done more than just talk? Why *should* that gun have been loaded? Or did Sam know the jig was basically up—playtime was indeed over? He'd pre-prosecuted himself with the left-behind clues, cast the narrative of his guilt (*I alone killed Lawrence Bosch . . .*) in the amber of his ancient Buick. At the trial the police photographs of the car looked Hollywood-ized, klieg-lit, flooded with annihilating light—for each line or feature the photographs carved out, another was lost in the glare. Sam's giveaway T-shirt was deep crimson down to the bottom hem, the jeans stained and wet through the crotch. His face, as I can't help but see, had the same death wanness I'd seen on Bosch's face, the vital color drained from it, the skin like parchment. I can see the slaked tilt of Sam's head and neck against the car's side beam, and the long, sharp, locked jaw—all lurid. And all of it for nothing. You wonder if Sam's Christ would have climbed down from his blood-slicked cross if he'd known just how little his sacrifice would matter. The state wanted its heads in the end, live ones, and only Alex and I had ours to offer. Thirty years for Alex, thirty-five for me—parole on the distant edge of that horizon, on "good behavior," but what does that mean? What does it mean today, or tomorrow, or twenty years from now? Twenty years is an epoch, an endlessly receding mirage, like Sam's heaven.

But I have gotten ahead of myself.

On the train back to New York, with Sam's text message catching me up more breathless than I already was, a sudden spasm, a contraction of the lungs like you see with whole cars getting flattened like beer cans—I looked out at the night and saw only my reflection in the glass, dull, haggard, shocked. I fixed on the long regress of my glasses reflected in the window reflected in the glasses . . . I suddenly wanted to see Jen. I needed to see her. I remembered that Stephen Hahn's memorial service would be held tomorrow morning—I wanted to see Hahn too, and I wanted to see tomorrow morning. The night slid darkly by beyond the window, darkness foreshortening the world and framing me inside it, a complicated image, diffuse, spirit-like, as if the soul I devoutly doubted had slipped from my body to hover over and observe me, judge me, sending invisible currents of thought and disdain from that world to this, a synaptic tentacling. In high-school physics it was Dr. Zeke who'd lit up a pale crystal ball like a miniature sun. It radiated spikes and zigzags of energy until you laid your palm on it and drew all the molecular action to yourself—narcissism at the level of biology, at the level of the cells. "Chemists want to be biologists," Zeke often said, loose with his students, seigneurial, smelling powerfully of the Marlboros he smoked in the room's equipment closet. "Chemists want to be biologists, biologists want to be physicists, physicists want to be gods."

Strivers everywhere. "That's the hierarchy," Zeke said. "That's life." Endless striving. I thought how odd it was to be through with all that, through with life in the middle of life, in my body and out of it, observing. All I wanted now was to see Jen, then Hahn, then I'd lift my hand from the buzzing ball for good—I would turn myself in. This plan in its seeming modesty reassured me as I stepped out again into the open air. New York City surrounded me, the great masses with the neon lights covering them in a fish-tank glow, the Hieronymus masses with their plain handsome wide narrow black white faces passing, a strobe effect of them, shifting, merging.

The cabdriver on the way over to Brooklyn spoke to me in his deep sonorous accented voice, from Elsewhere. He asked me where I got my news from.

"My news?" I said.

"All the mainstream outlets are owned and operated by one company only, did you know that? You have to go online to find the real truth."

I'd never heard of the website this earnest chatty man mentioned to me—I've forgotten it now—but the worldview he espoused was instantly familiar. I could have been listening to a member of the Group, unsung, unremunerated, a professional truth teller who'd heard and answered the call. Multinational corporations were set up above governments, whole countries, shaping world events to serve their quarterly profits. Russia, Ukraine, Israel, Palestine, Egypt, Sudan, Syria—all of it could be resolved in a month if a handful of billionaires got together in a room and decided on it. But why would they? It went against their vested interests. The military-industrial-technical complex, the haves and have-nots, depressed labor, rarefied tax evasions, elections bought and sold.

I tipped the man handsomely—I had $300 of Hahn's money to my name, in cash—but on the sidewalk outside Jen's apartment I felt coated in something, some new contaminant. The taxi pulled away down the dark empty car-lined street trailing its brake lights, turning and disappearing. A cold blue light filled the window in Jen's living room, the white pleated curtains riffling softly in the air conditioning. It was cool now, but I remembered how hot Jen's apartment could get in late summer. I felt the weight of brackish river water in the air, an expectation of fall. When I buzzed the number, it was Mallory's voice that answered—to my relief, I realized. She came downstairs in black formal pants, high to the navel, and a white blouse that billowed and overflowed the waistband like a pirate's shirt. Mal pinched and released the excess fabric and said, "Work, Eli. Damned work. I just got home."

"I see."

She stepped out onto the gray cement stoop that a canvas awning overhung, dividing the shadow from buzzing streetlight. Mal's face was in the gloom, the finer features obscured, but I could make out easily enough the look of chagrin rising up, the preemptive apology.

"Is she here?" I said.

"I think maybe you should come back, Eli. Or could you call?"

"Is he here with her?"

She nodded.

"I'm in trouble, Mal. I need to talk to her."

"You're in trouble?"

"Please tell her it's important. I know it's awkward for her."

"Not just for her."

"I'm sorry," I said.

"Well," Mal said, holding open the door behind her, "you might as well come on up. Make a clean belly flop of it."

In the open living room Jen sat on the mint green sofa cushion. Her crossed legs were drawn up like an ascetic's, her arms hugging her knees, her upper body pressed forward under the kneading hands of her boyfriend on the longer couch. Macduff looked harmless and smaller than I remembered him, boyishly intent on his ministrations, a pink bud of tongue sticking out of the side of his mouth. He saw me first—surprise and caesura, interrupted in the middle of this quotidian intimacy, *quotidius interruptus*. If I'd had the ability to feel pain at this scene, a silent shard sliding into the palm I held up to the man—I still didn't know his name.

Now Jen looked up at me, making sense of the change in the room's atmosphere. She wore blue Randolph gym shorts, mesh and loose, pooling like water at the base of her white thighs. I'd have ached to see this, too, though not with desire. Wasn't it months into our relationship before she'd felt comfortable enough to lounge in this gym-rat comfort in front of me?

"Mal?" said Jen, looking over to her friend. She had her palms out too, pleading helplessness.

"I'm sorry," I said. "I am sorry. I made her do it." I addressed all three of them.

For a moment Jen's face was uncertain, wavy—concern overtaking the anger. How wrong had she been about me? Was I dangerous? Her mute eyes slid slowly past me like a satellite dish readjusting. She exchanged silent signals with Macduff. "What are you doing here, Eli?" she asked, not looking at me.

Nothing could have sounded hollower than the vague euphemisms I'd prepared about "trouble," "mistakes," "consequences"—like a high-school guidance counselor to a truant. I chose silence instead.

Jen looked up at me and repeated her question. Her summer-light hair was parted casually and fell in waves past her shoulders. She was waiting. The room felt suddenly cavernous, running away from me—I caught myself against the doorframe. Mal reached out her hand. Was I okay? I fought something back for a long minute.

For all this, Macduff kept silent beside Jen. I felt suddenly grateful to him, indebted. How easy it would have been to cut me down, to make some macho taunt, but instead he followed Jen's lead.

Finally I said, "Professor Hahn's husband, her husband, Stephen—he died. The memorial service is tomorrow morning."

"I'm sorry to hear that," Jen said.

"I have nowhere to stay."

Macduff was on his feet now—not abruptly. He rose with an attempt at casualness. He might have glanced at his watch.

"Derek," Jen said.

"It's fine," he said. "I'll call you tomorrow morning, okay?"

I stepped aside to let them pass together out of the apartment, sending another apology like a weak paper airplane down the stairs. It fluttered, sank. Childishly, sheepishly, I clung to the wall inside the door with my hands behind my back, the loose diamond of my elbows, slouching, avoiding Mallory's eyes.

At length she said, "What kind of trouble, Eli? Are you not going to tell me?"

"If it's all right with you, I'd rather not say."

"Of course," Mal said. "Of course. Don't put yourself out for me." She went back to her room.

When Jen came upstairs I was alone on the couch, staring at a rerun of *House Hunters International*, another comfort measure it had taken Jen longer than this, I thought, to begin in my presence. At first it was all PBS opera broadcasts, art films, classic musicals—it all had to *mean intensely*, as I think Robert Browning put it. That was our model, whether we knew it or not—the Brownings, the *Sonnets from the Portuguese*, Mahler and Mozart, high love and high art rising together like a winding staircase. Only later did we let down our guard and take off our finery around each other, confiding guilty pleasures in pop country music (me), Agatha Christie novels (her), reality TV shows (both of us). For a while our favorite after-dinner fare was the show that flashed aquamarine and pale-sand white across the screen just now: young Americans, mostly, grand locales, big dreams and plans and sometimes the budgets to make them happen, mostly not, but we never tired of it—that blue-and-white dream field, that vicarious expanse.

"You sent Mal away?" Jen said to me.

"No, no. Not really. I didn't mean to."

Without breaking her stride she passed out of the living room and returned with a load of bedclothes—sheets, a pillow, a red-and-orange Mexican blanket we'd once picnicked on in Central Park, I remembered. I thanked Jen again, apologized again, looking off at the screen now, past it, out of cowardice.

"Do you remember this one?" she said from behind me. "I'm pretty sure we watched this one. Young couple leaves New

York to live simple in Costa Rica. They want to live by the beach."

"But they can't afford it. They're crestfallen with the prices. I remember."

On the screen a curving wedge of hourglass sand ran up to meet the couple in their pastiness—the young husband in a Hawaiian shirt, the young wife in a loose pink blouse flapping behind her like a sail. The next scene shows the couple in a low darkish room with the windows cut directly from the stucco; the room has the stoic, unformed air of a monk's scriptorium, but with green spiny palm fronds waving from outside. The Hawaiian-shirted husband is slouching, squinting as he takes in the space, the kitchen, living room, and dining room all combined, apparently. Can they make it work? The woman is shorter by a head and a half, her sail-shirt sagging. What does she think of the place? It's hard to know. The couple is unfailingly polite in front of the plump man with rawhide skin, a bone-deep tan, and a real estate license on the side. If they have hesitations they whisper them, careful of the agent's feelings, perhaps, but careless of the conventions of reality TV. There was a flash-forward to the next segment as the show went to commercial—another apartment, cleaner edges on the inside, a more traditional floor plan with the kind of built-in bookshelves that Jen and I had always oohed and aahed over. Then a shot of the couple out in front of the apartment, squinting into the gale of downtown traffic.

"This isn't the one where they make a shoe stand out of the bookshelves, is it? And the guy forbids his wife a piano because it takes up too much space?"

"You think these two would do that?" said Jen, taking a

seat on the edge of the couch, the bedclothes sitting chaperone between us. "I don't think they're capable of that. Maybe this is a new one?"

Her glass half full for these strangers—of course. It was Jen's default mode. How I'd missed this woman! How I'd miss her again. I decided to tell Jen everything, and plainly, but not yet. I'd tell her on the way to Hahn's husband's memorial tomorrow morning. I didn't want this moment to die too, fragile, flickering in the light of a car commercial.

As it happened, I dressed in a pair of Derek's gray khaki pants the next morning—I'd survived the night—khaki pants and a navy blue button-down that he'd left behind at Jen's apartment, the items pinching and pressing at my chest and middle. It felt like a final insult that our proportions should more or less match, but with the *more* on my end. I'd tried to trim my edges with tennis, hone myself, make myself a proper vessel for something, but not even the House's privations could thin me much. Out on the street I told Jen the story all at once—or I tried to, but she kept telling me to go back, wait, was I serious? Waiting for the punch line that never came, slowing to a stuttering walk, almost to a standstill.

"You're serious?" she said again. "You're serious?"

Against her somber outfit, a black skirt and a black, unseasonably thick sweater, her face looked parchment pale, drained but impervious, refusing to take in the vital facts. I didn't help with my delivery, I suppose, speaking the words automatically, distantly, as if they had nothing to do with me.

Finally Jen stopped altogether on the sidewalk, turning me

to face her. People I have no memory of pressed by on either side. We were feet from the stairs of the Greenpoint Avenue subway station, a great cavern underneath us.

"Are you serious?" Jen said to me. "Are you being serious?"

"I'm just trying to tell you what happened," I said.

"And what are you saying happened? Tell me again. Tell me slowly, Eli."

I told her again. Then I said, "I'm writing it down for you."

You get more used to it over time, but never all the way. No image of your dead brings them back to you, of course, or changes what happened to them, and yet you can't help searching out the magic icon, the potent imagining. Take the effort to remember Stephen Hahn before he shrunk down so vividly into his wheelchair. It's just that—an effort. You feel the uselessness of it in the strength of your wishing for it. That's God, too, I think. That's any heaven you can pin the name on.

I do regret that I didn't get to attend Stephen Hahn's memorial service, or see Hahn again. Jen took me directly to the Ninety-fourth Precinct building off Lorimer Street, a gentle frog march. She insisted on calling around for a lawyer for me. She held my hand at the intake desk.

I would have liked to apologize to Hahn that morning, however obliquely. Any outright disclosure would have only added to her grief, but a hug, a grateful word in her ear . . . I can imagine the gathering: an older, dignified, gray-haired group, with a smattering of students and perhaps a few former patients, all of us in nighttime colors under Hahn's high ceilings, a photograph of Stephen, pre-sickness, handsome and gently arch, smiling out from a frame on the fireplace mantel. Maybe

Hahn can bring just such an image to mind when she thinks of Stephen—I hope so. My image, as I said, is set. How could any framed photograph compete with the live man trembling at the top of a minivan's ramp, listing to one side in his motorized wheelchair, the face gaunt and plastic, the body at the edge of a great darkness, with only the eyes showing clear? And how, for that matter, could any other picture of Larry Bosch dislodge the last one I keep of him, that bird's-eye view of his body on the path, the legs twisting away, trying to take him somewhere but never actually moving him?

And yet I find I can picture Sam as I want him—small mercy to have driven away from his death so blindly. Small mercy to have known him best and least. Perhaps at his core, in his essence, I didn't know him at all—perhaps he eluded himself in that way—but bodily I knew him. Bodily I can conjure him—his long, pale shape, his square jaw cutting the air, cashiering out against the backdrop of a green tennis court. I can see him at the service line, long and gaunt but somehow doughy, too, in his giveaway T-shirts, his baggy basketball shorts, his pale unmuscled legs descending out of them like gym ropes. Where does all his power come from, his speed and agility? He is beating me easily now. He is rounding into form. The arm rises to the toss, crane-like, regal, the spinning yellow ball in the air like a sun at its zenith.

ACKNOWLEDGMENTS

John Adams never wrote a piano piece called "The Radicals," but I'd like to think my made-up John Adams piece isn't too out of tune with the austere, hauntingly beautiful works he has written—*Hallelujah Junction*, *Shaker Loops*, and *The Gospel According to the Other Mary*, to name just a few of the pieces that coursed around in my apartment or in my head as I wrote. Also, while New York University students did stage a protest a little like the one Eli describes, it didn't get as violent and it didn't take place in the post-Occupy moment I placed it in. And these liberties appear just in the first chapter or two—I've taken many others, of course, incurring many debts along the way. Books like Mark Rudd's *Underground* and Larry Grathwohl's *Bringing Down America* helped me riff and extrapolate a little more intelligently, as did many of the writers and pamphleteers the characters in the book read and reference.

For their conversation, critique, and kindness on and off the page, I'm particularly indebted to Hugo Aguayo, Aimee Bender, Vanessa Carlisle, Gil and John Gould, Paul Heideman, Officer Tom Loughran, Mike Turner, my agent PJ Mark, my editor Alexis Washam, her assistant Jillian Buckley, and of course Sharon McIlvain, first and best reader, without whom nothing of this—nothing at all.

RYAN McILVAIN's first novel, *Elders*, was longlisted for the Center for Fiction's First Novel Prize in 2013. His work has appeared in *The Paris Review*, *Post Road*, *The Rumpus*, the *Los Angeles Review of Books*, *Tin House* online, and the *Believer* online, among other venues. A former Stegner Fellow in Fiction at Stanford University, McIlvain now lives with his family in Tampa, Florida, where he is an assistant professor of English at the University of Tampa.

the
Sum of my
Happiness

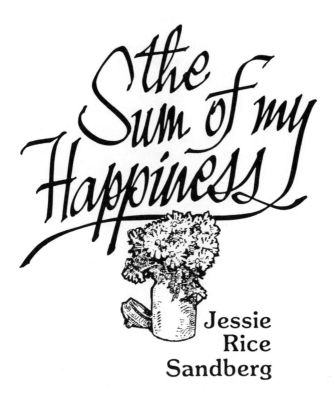

the Sum of my Happiness

Jessie
Rice
Sandberg

SWORD of the LORD
PUBLISHERS

P.O.BOX 1099, MURFREESBORO, TN 37133

Printed and Bound in the United States of America

Don and Jessie Sandberg

Mrs. Jessie Sandberg is the fourth daughter of Dr. and Mrs. John R. Rice. She received her bachelor's degree from Wheaton College and a master's degree from the National College of Education in Chicago.

Jessie is a fine artist and a talented author of several books, including *From My Kitchen Window; Fill My Cup, Lord!* and *With Love . . . and a Pinch of Salt.* She has made a number of cassette tapes dealing with women's problems, writes the popular "From My Kitchen Window" column in *The Sword of the Lord,* and is a contributing editor to the magazine for Christian women, *The Joyful Woman.* Mrs. Sandberg also carries an extensive speaking schedule to various women's groups across the country.

Her husband, Don Sandberg, is music director at Southgate Baptist Church, Augusta, Georgia, and is also active in the ministry of Southgate Christian Schools.

Don and Jessie have four children, all graduates of Tennessee Temple University, and all dedicated to the Lord's work. It is about them and to them that this touching book by Mrs. Sandberg is written.

My dear and precious children:

A mother never gets to specialize in her profession. It is true she may choose to put off the dusting for awhile to cut out paper dolls, or she may decide that baking homemade bread is a better love token to her children than electronic toys, but sooner or later she's got to face all the petty and repetitious trivia, all the profound and unknowable, all the funny and miserable and delightful and frustrating and mysterious elements that are required of a lifetime of motherhood.

Lawyers may decide to go into corporate law or criminal law or to become specialists in divorce cases, but a mother is simply a mother.

Doctors may decide to be gynecologists, cardiologists or anesthesiologists, but a mother is just a mother.

She is a mother of babies, toddlers, young children, or teenagers— each in respective order (and sometimes all at the same time), and no matter how much she may prefer small babies to teenagers or vice versa, she gets the whole package when she becomes a mother.

Because we mothers are particularly vulnerable to self doubts and feelings of inadequacy (and don't tell me you didn't notice!), we can't always tell whether we are being successful or not. We read articles and books, ask advice of the experts and compare notes with our friends, in our concern to become good mothers. In spite of the shocking stories of mothers who have been criminally negligent, I really do believe most mothers hope they are doing a good job.

It is when our children get ready to leave the home-nest to take responsibility for their own lives and to start families of their own that we begin to worry about the missing ingredients in our teaching and nurturing abilities. We wonder if we have said everything that needed to be said and if we have lived out every principle we professed to believe.

I remember that when my sister Libby, dressed in her "going away" finery, reached over to give my mother one final kiss before leaving on her honeymoon, my mother whispered anxiously, "Libby, is there anything you need to know?"

This is my anything-you-need-to-know gift to all of you. I don't pretend that it is "enough" or that you couldn't teach *me* some things about life and love and marriage. Still, it is the best I have to give you from the limitations of my own experience and feelings and knowledge of the Word of God. I hope it helps.

I love you all,
Mom

No doubt you would all have different opinions about the happiest experiences of your growing-up years together as a family. Your school activities, your feelings about yourself and your changing relationships with others, would give each of you different high points in your memory.

Whatever . . . we did have some wonderful, rollicking times together in those early years with a houseful of pre-teens.

I know it was sometimes hard on you having both your parents in graduate school, living in an old house badly in need of repair, having no money to spare, and never enough time to get everything done. Still, we all learned to be resourceful and flexible, and life was sweet . . .

Reflections . . .

I'm happier than
a woman has a right to be
on an ordinary Tuesday afternoon.
And the sum of my happiness is a
collection of little things
hardly worth mentioning . . .
For instance, one order of hamburger and fries
shared furtively with my husband
at 3:00 o'clock this afternoon
in a little restaurant—
Because neither of us
had time for lunch.
Number two reason
is Carol
whose dentist appointment
turned out to be
an adventure
Because the doctor gave her
laughing gas—yes, really—
laughing gas.
A new dental technique, he says.
(There's nothing new
under the sun!)
Reason three—
A busy kitchen at suppertime.
Little Don mixing up custard pudding . . .
Jimmy and Carol
making play dough
(Why suppertime?)
from a recipe in the Children's Activities book
someone brought from the library.
And in the living room
my husband is playing the piano
"My Cup Runneth Over"

from some musical
appropriately called "I Do! I Do!"
Appropriately, I say,
because day after tomorrow
is our 16th wedding anniversary.
(Will he remember?)
And this morning I saw
the first robin of the year—
fat, saucy, and red-breasted.
Even if it's a little cold and bleak
outside
something feels like spring.
Still—why should I be so happy?
It's only an ordinary Tuesday afternoon.

—J.R.S.

You will remember how important books always were at our house—perhaps even more important than food some of the time.

We started an early tradition of making sure that whatever you got for Christmas or for birthdays, there would always be a book as well.

Carol, your first and favorite "bookie" was the story of a little girl named Karen Kay who discovered one day that she was the owner of a rather large family of cats. Your dad and I still sometimes nostalgically quote lines from the book.

. . . But whoever heard of a poem book called *A Gift of Watermelon Pickles?* . . .

A Book Called " . . . Watermelon Pickles"

Her eyes were shining
When she came in the door.
    She was eleven then:
"I found just what I want . . .
    for Christmas
    or for my birthday
    . . . or both . . . "
A poem book:
"A Gift of Watermelon Pickles"—
    Improbable title!

We looked everywhere
    department stores,
    hole-in-the-wall bookshops,
    musty old used-book stores,
    libraries.
But clerks were mute or amused;
Librarians shrugged their shoulders.

We began to know their questions by heart:
    "What publisher?"
    "Out of print?"
    "Privately produced?"

A sudden impulse
visiting a London bookshop—
    "Do you have the book,
    "A Gift of Watermelon Pickles?"
"English don't write books
    with titles like that."
The clerk was brisk:
    "Must be published in America."

And so it began to be a family joke.

"Have you ever seen
　　　'Watermelon Pickles'
　　　or the Loch Ness monster
　　　or the Holy Grail
　　　or the Missing Link
　　　or the ghost of Frankenstein?"
Such things don't exist.

But one learns to be stoic
　　　and Carol grew.
Twelve, thirteen, fourteen,
　　　fifteen, sixteen, seventeen—
　　　and one day—
A perfectly ordinary day
　　　We found it
right there on the bookshop shelf,
looking as if it belonged.
For four-fifty it was ours—Carol's and mine—
　　　and we were eleven again.

　　　　　　　　　　—J.R.S.

Birthdays were always important at our house—with the inevitable cake and ice cream, the gifts, balloons, and special meals. Remember Don's birthday trip to Yerkes Observatory, the big celebration we had for Carol's birthday at the puppet theatre, the picnics at Lake Chickamauga . . . ?

We loved the planning and participation in birthday events probably more than you, remembering as we did, how it felt to be a birthday child:

> *Everything's been different*
> *All the day long,*
> *Lovely things have happened,*
> *Nothing has gone wrong.*
>
> *Nobody has scolded me,*
> *Everyone has smiled,*
> *Isn't it delicious*
> *To be a birthday child?*
>
> *—Author Unknown*

Reflections . . .

The significance of life is often marked in terms of events—birth, marriage, graduations, promotions, moves, successes and sorrows.

Becoming a teenager is just such an event—not significant because of visible changes—but because it is a kind of signpost in that rite of passage toward adulthood.

Your impression of the transition you made to becoming a teenager will probably be different from mine. Adults would say that a thirteen-year-old is hardly capable of understanding himself and his own changing emotions, much less understanding how to handle important relationships with other people. One poet has said cynically that "thirteen's no age at all . . . . "

However, my own memory reminds me that thirteen-year-olds are dreamers, full of idealism and capable of great aspirations.

Knowing how I felt at that point in my own life, I wrote these letters, first to you, Carol, on your thirteenth birthday, and two years later, to Jim . . .

To Carol, With Love

My Darling Carol:

I know you have been looking forward to today for a long time. It is always exciting to have a birthday, but this 13th birthday—which gives you the official title of "teenager"—is doubly special.

Parents always say this kind of thing, you know, but it really seems like such a very short time ago that you were a tiny pink-faced baby with large blue eyes, exquisite little fingers and toes and a voice like that of the archangel! I remember how thrilled your daddy was to have a girl and how earnestly he prayed that we would know how to bring you up to serve the Lord.

When you were not quite two years old you suffered a fractured skull and as we watched beside your hospital bed, we promised the Lord again that we would do all we could to train you in a way that would honor His name.

Then, almost before we expected it, you had developed a sensitivity to sin, and just before your fifth birthday you came with tears, asking how you could tell Jesus you wanted to be saved.

In the years since, you have been the "blythe spirit" at our house with your enthusiasm about every family project, your contagious giggle, and your delight in the front porch "school" which kept your little brothers and their friends happy for hours. (It was worth all the Kool-aid and cookies you dispensed as a lure!)

We have listened with pride to your first piano recital and your first flute solo. We have watched, misty-eyed, as you and your fellow sheet-draped angels sang the sweet "Children's Prayer" in a fifth grade production of "Hansel and Gretel." We have watched you participate in innumerable Sunday school programs, choir and band concerts and somehow, no matter how often we go to another one, we still get goosebumps everytime.

Now you are beginning a new stage of your life. I hope you won't be too quick to rush through this lovely in-between stage when it is

Carol and Roger Parks

still perfectly proper for you to enjoy your little old-fashioned doll furniture or to play a game of football with your brothers. There will be people who will try to make you think that you aren't really living until you've had your first high heels, your first tube of lipstick, or your first date. Don't believe it. Rushing into adulthood when you haven't had time to be a girl is like turning to the conclusion of an exciting book to see how it ends before you've read all the chapters in between. It is one way of finding out how everything ends, but you miss the fun and suspense and beauty of the chapters in the middle.

I know you will receive some special birthday gifts today. If I could wrap up the three gifts I'd *most* like to give you, they would be things a little hard to tuck away in a drawer!

First, I'd give you courage—to be the special kind of person you want to be and ought to be; courage to stand up for your Lord when it is easy and when it is not; courage to be an individual rather than a carbon copy of all your friends at school; courage to take a stand on issues of right and wrong.

Second, I would give you a confidence in the Bible; confidence that God can be trusted to keep His Word and fulfill His promises to those who love and obey Him.

Third, I would give you a positive commitment to the Lord—to keep yourself clean and pure for whatever calling He has for you, to be genuinely interested in winning your friends for Christ, to be concerned about serving Him wherever He leads you in the days to come.

May this be a happy, happy birthday, dearest Carol, and may each succeeding year be better than the one before. You are more precious to your daddy and me than words can tell!

With deepest love,
Mom

A Letter to a Teenage Son

Dear Jim:

Even though I'll see you at the breakfast table tomorrow morning, I wanted to write this special note to place on your pillow tonight to tell you privately some of the things I would have a hard time saying face to face.

First, let me remind you again that I think you are tremendous. I never look at the new paint, paneling and carpeting in your room without feeling enormously proud that you did the whole job yourself. You relieve your dad of a real burden by cheerfully acting as family handyman. Even beyond the help your skills provide for the family, I am constantly pleased to discover how your mechanical and creative skills have developed in the last year or two.

Another thing I appreciate about you is your genuine interest in people—babies, young people your own age, and wonder of wonders—even adults! Not having grown up in a family with boys, I am always surprised to see you playing happily with your baby cousin Melody, and I get a great deal of pleasure seeing you follow Mr. Martin around Grandpa's farm to see what you can learn about horses, tractors and field work.

More than anything, I suppose, I am pleased to see the way you have grown spiritually in the last year. Your deliberate and careful adherence to a regular schedule of Bible reading is probably the most important habit you've developed in your whole life; and I'm so thrilled that this is the year it began—your first year as a teenager.

You are coming to a stage in your life where individuality and personal liberty will begin to seem very important, and it is a fact that a sense of self-worth will be an important factor in your accomplishing all the good things in life which God has for you to do.

You will notice—all too soon, I fear—that the world associates self-worth and personal liberty with a rejection of all authority. All around you there will be voices saying, "You don't have to listen to your parents anymore. You are practically an adult!" "If you don't agree with a rule or law, just break it. The older generation doesn't understand anyway!" "Why should you listen to a bunch of old fogies who have made such a mess of the world?"

You've grown up knowing that our family policy has always been to explain rules and standards when they can be explained, but with the understanding that every rule and standard is to be obeyed by every child in our family WHETHER HE UNDERSTANDS THE REASON OR NOT! You already understand, I know, that God's system is an authoritarian system. A man is responsible to his government, a wife to her husband, children to their parents, and so on.

God does not impose such a system to be mean. It is the only way there can be any order in a world of sin. And it is only by learning to obey those whom God has put in authority over us that we learn to obey Him and do His will.

If the Lord continues the good work begun in your heart, you will discover in the next few years that the greatest freedom in all the world is to be completely and entirely in the will of God. When you want to please Him more than anything else, the rules and restrictions, no matter how petty they seem, cannot chafe or irritate. Your individuality and self-respect will not then be damaged by submission to any authority God has placed over you.

Your dad and I crave for you that special liberty in the Lord. May God keep your heart tender and courageous and strong, and may He fulfill in you all the good promises in His Word!

"Being confident of this very thing, that he which hath begun a good work in you will perform it until the day of Jesus Christ." — Philippians 1:6.

Fondest love,
Mom

Reflections . . .

You grew and the texture of our lives changed. The tinker-toys were replaced by soccer balls, tennis racquets and smelly sweatshirts. The dolls were packed away to make room for cosmetics, formals and high school yearbooks . . .

. . . and always there were questions, thousands of questions, important questions needing answers . . .

Is this the sum of motherhood?
> . . . the smell of bubble gum?
> . . . a muddy footprint on the kitchen floor?
> . . . the minutes, hour-long until
>> a waited child comes in the door?

> . . . a sudden fear . . . the feel
>> of hot dry skin and fever in the night?
> . . . to stop a childish fuss and then decipher
>> who was wrong—or right?

> . . . a thousand questions, such as,
>> "Where does wind begin?" and,
>> "Tell me how birds fly."
> Whose answers from the birth of time
>> have puzzled wiser folk than I.

No, there is more . . .
> . . . a quiet confidence
>> shared when all the house is still.
> . . . self-conscious hopes and fuzzy dreams
>> and yet—a firm resolve to do God's will.

> . . . to watch the choices made—
>> "Is this the girl, the school, the work for me?"
>> (Such weighty choices for so young a heart!)
> . . . to wonder at the future, bright yet hard to see.

TOMORROW:

> . . .these are the arrows I will send abroad.
>> Each day these precious shafts
>> have been within my care,
>> will count somehow—for time and Heaven, too.
> My deepest longings as a mother will be met
>> if I have kept them polished, straight and true.

—J.R.S

Soon we could see how our arrows were "shaping up." We had given each of you to the Lord when you were born, but we found this was an act of sacrifice that had to be repeated time and again in the years that followed . . .

Lord, here are my children
        I give them to You.
        Do what You will.

I dare not give them lightly.
They are the most precious possessions
        I have.

Carol —our own bright spirit—
        Quick step and lilting voice;
        flying fingers on the piano;
                That swinging, shiny golden head—
Designer of projects, dreamer of dreams,
        Slender grace,
        a smiling face,
and lately—the glow of lovelight
        in her eyes.

Jim —with heart set like a flint,
        toward goals of power
        in the prayer closet
        and in the pulpit.
I see the gentleness and grace
        in those grease-stained fingers
        as they work magic
                with plumbers' and mechanics' tools,
        and ruffle the hair of a baby.

Don —who gathers friends around him
        like ants are to a picnic drawn . . .
        Teaser, comforter, mimic
                and sometimes all three at once.
        The student with the look of teacher
                in his eye;
        Steady as a planet in the orbit of his day
                toward dreams unexpressed
                and thoughts unspoken.

Mark —whose childhood visions of sea captains,
of hobbies and valiant kings
still linger on the fringe of college
routines and schedules.
Quiet, calm and self-contained—
Efficient in his studies . . .
Proficient in his sports . . .
and underneath beats the heart of the romantic,
the poet, the statesman, the missionary.

—J.R.S.

Reflections . . .

Sometimes we get so caught up with the very dailiness of life, meeting deadlines, paying bills, answering the phone, keeping the house in order, fulfilling the responsibilities of outside jobs, church work and neighborhood obligations, that we lose the point of what it is all about.

This was written at a point of rediscovery . . .

A Tired Mother's Prayer of Thanksgiving

Thank You, Lord
> for church spires and lavender mountains,
> for exuberant forsythia,
> the smell of morning,
> the laughter of friends.

Thank You
> for college boys who open doors,
> for curious envelopes in the mailbox
> and dear, familiar ones as well.

Thank You
> for English trifle and old books,
> for birdsong and rich, black earth,
> for silly poodles with red bows.

Thank You
> for the feel of clay on a potter's wheel,
> for polished shoes
> > and squeaky new leather purses.

Thank You
> for colored pictures in magazines,
> for a corner of my own,
> a pot of red tulips,
> young voices singing.

Thank You
> for a car that runs,
> for help in the kitchen, unasked,
> for sisters who understand,
> for clean linens on the bed.

Thank You
 for the comfortable banter
  of children at the breakfast table,
 for morning kiss of my husband
  flavored with after-shave,
 for the unpredictability of another busy day.

Thank You
 for the box of seashells
 collected by a friend,
 for Debussy and Beethoven
  and Tennyson and Donne.

Thank You
 for the Bible verse
  that changed my puzzled grief to gentle sorrow
  at the death of a friend.

Thank You for answered prayer, for promises kept.

Thank You most of all, Lord, for forgiveness
 when I awoke this morning, grumpy and ungrateful
 for all these blessings that are mine today.

     —J.R.S.

Reflections . . .

The day actually came when life began to settle into a comfortable routine, with you children turning out to be surprisingly handsome, interesting and civilized human beings. Your dad and I began to reflect on the worthwhileness of all the struggles of early parenthood. The dirty diapers, the dentist's bills, the trips to the emergency room of the hospital, the unending need for new shoes for feet that eventually grew to sizes bigger than our own—all these were compensated for in the fun of having the house filled with the laughter of you and your friends, the serious heart-to-heart talks over cups of hot chocolate in the kitchen after midnight; the thrill of hearing Jim ask, "Is that true, Dad?"; the sweetness of Carol's grateful kiss when I had made a new dress; the frequency of Don's compliments, and the predictability of knowing Mark would always do as he was told.

Just when we had begun to feel we would like life to go on forever like this, we discovered a new look on Carol's face, a new quiet sweetness in her voice. We could tell, Carol, that you had given your heart away even before Roger came to ask your hand in marriage.

Longfellow sums up the feeling of every parent losing a daughter in his "Song of Hiawatha":

> *Thus it is our daughters leave us,*
> *Those we love, and those who love us.*
> *Just when they have learned to help us,*
> *When we are old and lean upon them,*
> *Comes a youth with flaming feathers . . .*
> *And she follows where he leads her*
> *Leaving all things for the stranger . . .*

. . . And so it was with us.

I remember thinking when you were all small babies, "I'm never going to do anything significant with my life but change diapers, wipe noses, and clean up messes!" But oh, how quickly those baby days were gone!

. . . And then, even as we longed and prayed and worked toward the day when each of you would finish college and begin your own specific ministries for the Lord, it somehow came as a shock that you were grown.

This was the point at which I realized that anything I had failed to say to you, Carol—my beautiful daughter—as you prepared for your wedding, needed to be said quickly. And so I wrote you a whole set of letters which I addressed "To my favorite bride" . . .

Dear Carol:

Yesterday, when you and Roger came bounding into the house with the latest developments in your wedding plans, the glow on both your faces brought a lump to my throat.

Your long courtship has given your dad and me more time than most parents have, to get used to giving you up, but still I feel I must drink to the fullest every single minute of your last three months at home. In spite of the kidding your three brothers give you about how nice it will be to have more closet space, more time in the bathroom, and more food (as if the amount you put into your 110-lb. frame could compare to the masses of food they manage to put away!), everybody knows what a great emptiness you will leave behind you.

We are proud of your choice of a husband. Roger's godly heritage, his gentleness and good common sense, his faithful hard work in long years of studying, and his desire to be a great preacher of the Gospel are as good a set of credentials as any set of parents could hope to find in a prospective son-in-law. We're glad, too, that Roger has always been a good friend to your brothers and seems to genuinely enjoy being with the family. In spite of what some modern marriage advisors would say, a person who marries, marries a family.

Most marriage counselors make a great deal of the importance of communication in marriage, and I would not deny the value of being able to talk over one's needs, dreams and frustrations with one's husband or wife. It is certainly true that we do not have the capacity to understand what is important to another person, or what is irritating, if there is not a free exchange of feelings and impressions.

I think you know, though, that in our times there seems to be too little restraint in saying whatever one thinks. How often have you heard someone say, "Well, I'm sorry but I just had to get that off my chest!" Never mind how much that unloading may have hurt someone else; only my feelings matter! We are in an age when "letting it all hang out" regardless of the consequence is considered acceptable behavior.

Recently I read two rather ancient volumes: one was a book of sermons on the home by Dr. T. DeWitt Talmage (written about 1893, I believe) and the other was a small book written for young women around the turn of the century called *Beautiful Girlhood*. I was rather

32

intrigued to discover that neither book said anything about the importance of communication but both said a great deal about understanding and tenderness and love.

Words are wonderful things when they are used in the right way, but they can be terrible and damning too. We can use words to express love, to comfort, to exhort and to lead someone to the Saviour, but we can also use words to cut and hurt and to destroy. How important it is that we use them right in marriage!

The Apostle James gives us the following warning about words, and it would probably be a good idea for every married couple to write them where they can see them often:

"But the tongue can no man tame; it is an unruly evil, full of deadly poison. Therewith bless we God, even the Father; and therewith curse we men, which are made after the similitude of God. Out of the same mouth proceedeth blessing and cursing. My brethren, these things ought not so to be. Doth a fountain send forth at the same place sweet water and bitter? . . . Who is a wise man and endued with knowledge among you? let him shew out of a good conversation his works with meekness of wisdom. But if ye have bitter envying and strife in your hearts, glory not, and lie not against the truth." —James 3:8-11, 13-14.

It's kind of scary, isn't it? The secret is, of course, to keep the fountain sweet so that there are no regrets and no hurts.

Your proud Mom

Reflections . . .

Remember the list I put together to remind myself that there are times when every woman needs to close her mouth? . . .

When to Keep Your Mouth Shut!

Don't open your mouth:

1. In the heat of anger—Proverbs 14:17.
2. When you don't have all the facts—Proverbs 18:13.
3. When you haven't verified the story.
4. If your words will offend a weaker brother.
5. If your words will be a poor reflection of the Lord or your friends and family.
6. When you are tempted to make light of holy things.
7. When you are tempted to joke about sin—Proverbs 14:9.
8. If you would be ashamed of your words later—Proverbs 8:8.
9. If your words would convey a wrong impression—Proverbs 17:27.
10. If the issue is none of your business—Proverbs 14:10.
11. When you are tempted to tell an outright lie—Proverbs 4:24.
12. If your words will damage someone's reputation—Proverbs 16:27.
13. If your words would destroy a friendship—Proverbs 16:28.
14. When you are feeling critical.
15. If you can't speak without yelling.
16. When it is time to listen—Proverbs 13:1.
17. If you may have to eat your words later—Proverbs 18:21.
18. If you've already said it more than one time. (Then it becomes nagging.) —Proverbs 19:13.
19. When you are tempted to flatter a wicked person—Proverbs 24:24.
20. When you are supposed to be working instead—Proverbs 14:23.

Proverbs 21:23: "Whoso keepeth his mouth and his tongue, keepeth his soul from trouble."

Letters to My Favorite Bride

Dear Carol:

I've been thinking about your question the other night: "How can people who really love each other get bored with marriage?"

I gather you had been reading the article in a current magazine, "Ways to Keep Your Marriage from Becoming a Bore" or some such title. I'm sure it does seem odd, from your glorious, exultant, soon-to-be-married point of view, that anybody anticipating a lifetime with your Roger could be bored.

The truth is, of course, that boredom does not come from circumstances, from other people, or from a lack of exciting activity. Boredom comes from a failure to use our own inner resources to be happy, to be usefully occupied, to be a joy and delight to others.

You've often heard me quote Proverbs 14:14, and this is a situation where it particularly applies: "The backslider in heart shall be filled with his own ways; and a good man shall be satisfied from himself." People who look to marriage as a source of self-satisfaction, either in terms of personal comfort, constant attention, total security, or perfect anything else, will find boredom at best and sheer frustration at its worst.

A good marriage—yes, even a good Christian marriage—does not evolve naturally and easily out of ecstatic, romantic love. Like anything good (cakes made from "scratch," a beautiful garden, a college education, skill in swimming or tennis, the writing of a good poem, a dress of one's own design, successful motherhood), marriage takes a great deal of work and thought and prayer and planning.

Mind you, love is important (not only in marriage but in baking, gardening, schooling, athletic development, creative pursuits and motherhood) because love is what makes you willing to work. An Olympic contender learns to relish the very pain of endurance for the glory of the prize.

And so, marriage, as a chosen, lifelong, joyful responsibility, is never boring to the one who is committed to the glory of the prize.

A woman who is constantly crying, either verbally or in her actions,

"Make me happy! Make me feel good! Make me comfortable!" is going to be sadly disappointed and, yes, bored to death! A constant pursuit of self-gratification does eventually become a drag.

Unless we have become committed to claiming the blessing of God, to doing right and doing it cheerfully when it is hard and when it is easy, repeated tasks become tedium, unnoticed effort suggests thoughtlessness; unspoken gratitude becomes neglect; differences of opinion become emotional barriers; delightful mannerisms become annoying idiosyncracies, strength of character becomes stubbornness; yielding becomes weakness, and intimacy becomes intrusion.

Proverbs 24:3,4 says: "Through wisdom is an house builded; and by understanding it is established: And by knowledge shall the chambers be filled with all precious and pleasant riches." This no doubt refers to literal, physical things, but it also refers to a home which is filled with spiritual and emotional treasures as well.

Proverbs 14:1: "Every wise woman buildeth her house: but the foolish plucketh it down with her hands."

God bless you, my darling Carol, and help you to make your marriage the exciting, fulfilling experience you expect it to be!

From one who loves you —
Mom

All marriages have great moments, but they cannot be sustained; all marriages have bad periods, but they pass. . . . Don't expect to get everything you want from marriage (or at least not all at once). Total satisfaction is no more guaranteed in wedlock than it is in any other area of life.

Marriage has been called man's most difficult, if not impossible, enterprise. The demands we make upon it, the expectations we have for it, the rewards we hope to get from it—these are enormous. . . . In the long run, though, it seems that Abraham Lincoln, of all people, had the common-sense answer to what people want and get from their marriages. "Most folks," he said, "are as happy as they make up their minds to be."

—Norman M. Lobsenz
(From "What Do You Want From Your Marriage?"
Woman's Day, July 1973.)

Dear Carol:

Since you already know what a hearts-and-flowers kind of person I am—quick to get a lump in my throat and a tear in my eye at all kinds of sentimental experiences—I'm sure you know how much I have enjoyed watching you fulfill so many of the little romantic notions mothers get about their daughters.

I have enjoyed seeing you as a baby dressed in those adorable outfits with which you were showered as a baby. I remember the ruffled "flower girl" dress you wore at Aunt Joy's wedding when you were five. I remember your "angel" gown worn in a 6th grade production of "Hansel and Gretel," and the outlandish fish-scale dress when you were a youthful Cleopatra in a college performance of "Caesar and Cleopatra."

Now, of course, I look forward to seeing you as a bride. I enjoy all the exciting elements of your wedding plans, and I warn you ahead of time that I will no doubt cry over the flowers, the soft candlelight, the love songs, the gleam of satin, the sweet and holy vows, and that special glow which invariably beautifies every bride.

If we are not careful, we are apt to assume that love is perpetuated through a continual renewal of candlelight-roses-soft-music experiences. The fact is, I believe in observing regularly the romantic traditions that are important to all women. Still, it is true that the major substance of life and love is not moonlight-and-roses, but rather a commitment of the will to behave in a certain way whether we are feeling romantic or not!

A commitment to marriage is not a starry-eyed allegiance to one's partner as long as it is comfortable and happy, and an easy abandonment of the whole project when one is not entirely comfortable and happy. On the other hand, it is not a hopeless resignation to a marriage where love is no longer an important element, either. A girl can literally and actively choose the kind of marriage she will have. It is not just some surprising and uncontrollable quirk of fate that some people have good marriages and some do not.

Among other choices, you decide: (1) to marry in the will of God or not to marry at all. This includes not only marrying a man who is unquestionably born again but who is also actively concerned about using his life to serve the Lord. You choose (2) whether or not you will be obedient to the Word of God in every aspect of your home and personal life. You choose (3) whether or not you will serve others or insist upon being served, whether you will consider it more important to love or to be loved, whether you will be a giver or a taker, whether you will be more concerned about your own comforts or the needs of others.

A woman is not at the mercy of other people or of circumstances when it comes to marriage. She can make prayerful, careful decisions ahead of time and she can determine how she will respond afterward.

Your proud mother

What you want, O man, in a wife, is not a butterfly of the sunshine, not a giggling nonentity, not a painted doll, not a gossiping gadabout, not a mixture of artificialities which leave you in doubts as to where the humbug ends and the woman begins, but an earnest soul, one that cannot only laugh when you laugh, but weep when you weep.

There will be wide, deep graves in your path of life, and you will both want steadying when you come to the verge of them, I tell you. When your fortune fails, you will want some one to talk of treasures in Heaven, and not charge upon you with a bitter, "I told you so."

As far as I can analyze it, sincerity and earnestness are the foundation of all worthy wifehood. Get that, and you get all. Fail to get that, and you get nothing but what you will wish you never had got.

—T. DeWitt Talmage.

(From *The Sermons and Autobiography of T. DeWitt Talmage: 1893*.)

Dear Carol:

I suppose you have already thought about what you will use in your wedding to symbolize:

Something old, something new;
Something borrowed, something blue.

Actually, you have already been collecting "old things for a long time—many of them too valuable to discard now! For example, you've been collecting a lifetime of old values.

Among the most important values are those which relate to the family. Hopefully you've observed your parents' feelings about the importance of family life—meals eaten together with love and laughter as the primary items on the menu; daily family worship (you are used to our custom of having it right after breakfast, but you and Roger may find that another time works best for you); family discussion on every subject, from theology to politics to poetry; family vacations (remember the hilarious two days we spent in New York City?); and family work responsibilities. ('Nuf sed!)

And then you have been collecting standards. Up to now, the standards you've followed have been, in a measure, imposed ones. People will have assumed that you did whatever you did because you *had* to, either because your parents made you, or because you didn't want to hurt our feelings by breaking the rules.

Now, what you do will be based on your *own* study of the Word of God and your obedience to His will. Because your dad and I have watched your growth in the Lord and the consistency of your testimony (and Roger's) through the years, we are not at all concerned that your standards will be contrary to the Word of God. Thank you for giving us that confidence.

No doubt you have been collecting traditions too, and it will be exciting in the days ahead to see how you and Roger will fit together the pieces of tradition you have brought from your childhood to build precious new ones of your very own.

You will have to work out how and where you celebrate holidays (and hope that you can keep both families happy in the process). You will develop unique ways of celebrating birthdays and anniversaries.

42

I do hope that whatever you do, you will never let them go unobserved. The world is a pretty lonely place and everybody needs a special day to have people say, "We love you and think you are important enough for us to celebrate this occasion in honor of you!"

Some of the patterns and traditions you begin will be accidental, fallen into without thought or plan—such as bedtime hours, who will use the bathroom first in the morning, and who will do which various chores related to the family. Be sure you are flexible enough to change where changes are needed, and open enough to talk out family habits that may not be working out comfortably for everybody.

Last of all, you will be taking with you old memories—most of them, I hope, sweet ones.

These happy memories are the ones you will want to hang onto and treasure forever. Forget all the bad ones—the misunderstandings, the irritations, the hasty words, the disappointments, the failures. Make up your mind that you will bury forever any bitterness that would destroy your joy and your relationship with each other!

Hebrews 12:15 says: "Looking diligently lest any man fail of the grace of God; lest any root of bitterness springing up trouble you, and thereby many be defiled."

Well, that's enough about old things! We'll discuss some new things later.

Much, much love,
Mom

Reflections . . .

I was just thinking that collections add a lot of fun to life and they don't have to be the usual kind of thing, such as stamps or antiques. They don't even have to be expensive, and they may not even be the sort of collection that you would put on display.

Here's a new list for you:

A COLLECTION OF COLLECTIBLES

1. A prayer list typed on 3 X 5 cards.
2. Missionary prayer cards (also part of prayer list).
3. Favorite poems.
4. Favorite quotations.
5. "How-to" books.
6. Words to favorite songs.
7. Bibliographies of books that have been a blessing.
8. Giftwrap and greeting cards.
9. Miniature bottles.
10. Letters from people I love.
11. Newspaper clippings of historic events.
12. Lists of "Pebbles of Joy"—things I am grateful for.
13. Pressed flowers.
14. Seashells.
15. "Malapropisms"—funny verbal blunders of my favorite people.
16. The punch lines of old jokes.
17. Historical trivia about favorite artists and musicians.
18. Colored pencils, colored magic markers, colored paper— anything that can be turned into a lovely design.
19. Small cartons, boxes and tubes—anything that can be turned into a toy for a small child.
20. Jars of decorative candies.
21. Collections of answered prayer.

22. Clever sayings of children.
23. Old needlework.
24. Funny cartoons.
25. Pretty soaps.
26. Scripture verses on special themes.
27. Memorized Scripture which is mine forever.

Dear Carol:

" . . . something new . . . "

Planning a wedding certainly does involve lots of new things, doesn't it? It has been fun watching you carefully examine all those bright and shining, never-been-used pots and pans, china, and linens. Speaking from my twenty-five-year encounter with married life, I find a special delight in surveying your treasure of dishes without chipped edges, linens without stains, pots without scars!

I'll have to admit that I felt a moment of pain as I watched Renee make the first scissor cut into those vast yards of white satin which will become your wedding dress. The shining newness of that wide expanse of material will soon be cut into all sorts of shapes, and some of it will be discarded into the wastebasket as scrap.

There are so many new and wonderful experiences in marriage. You and Roger will be following new patterns, fulfilling new roles, working under new schedules, paying new bills.

One of the most drastic changes you will discover is that you will have to build new loyalties. I can remember that as a new bride I was tempted several times to call Dad and ask him what I should do about some little problem. I often wanted to run into his arms as I had done when a little girl and cried, "Daddy, pray!"

Now you know, of course, that your dad and I still seek Granddad's advice now and then, and I still appreciate the assurance that he is praying for me. But I must never, ever forget that the man I am married to is now my priest, my friend, my confidant. Above all other loyalties, I must be loyal to him. If that sounds like disloyalty to my own parents, let me remind you that they are the ones who taught me this truth from the Word of God, and so I teach you the same.

There will be times when you will think Roger's judgment in some matter is wrong, and it could very well be wrong occasionally. (Who could stand being married to a perfect man, anyway?) Your loyalty to him is what will make it possible for you to keep his wrong judgments to yourself. (Actually, you never did tattle or tear down other people when you were a little girl, and I doubt that you would now.) Loyalty in a wife is a quality so valuable that it can hardly be measured.

Then let this new loyalty for the man you have chosen to marry be something which grows and bears precious fruit in the years to come. You know that you will always be our little girl and our home and possessions will be no less yours than they have always been. Still, there should be a sense in which, for the rest of your lives together, home is where Roger is. As much as we love you, we realize that Roger must come first in every dream, every plan for the future, and in your time and attention. If you become a faithful, loyal wife, it will not diminish the relationship you have with your parents and brothers, but rather enhance every other relationship. Your dad and I will never lose in our relationship with you by encouraging your careful obedience to the Word of God in building and supporting your husband.

It would be a good idea to read, once in a while, the passage in Genesis 2:23,24: "And Adam said, This is now bone of my bones, and flesh of my flesh: she shall be called Woman because she was taken out of Man. Therefore shall a man leave his father and his mother, and shall cleave unto his wife: and they shall be one flesh."

Among all your precious "new" things, let your new "oneness" be the most important thing of all!

God bless you, Sweetheart!

Mom

For a lot of people, the prime requisite in marriage is having someone to talk to, and someone to listen.

Do you remember, Carol, the little poem you wrote when you were fifteen? . . .

LONELY

Where
are they
now that   you
need them.
Did they go?
Did they vanish
into thin air?
I talk—
but no one hears
I listen—
but no one speaks.
Was it just
yesterday
when we romped
and played in the sun?
Where
are they
now that   you
need them?

Dear Carol:

"Something borrowed . . ."

What will you borrow on your wedding day? Perhaps Grandmother Rice will let you borrow one of her beautiful old handkerchiefs. Or maybe you will want to carry that precious Testament given to her husband by the grandmother you never met, beautifully inscribed: To Arvid from Adina, Christmas 1923. Someone may want to loan you a penny to wear in your shoe. (Don't ask me why a penny is supposed to be significant—somebody's idea of a good-luck charm, I suppose. Fortunately, you've got something better than that to count on!)

Actually, lots of things get borrowed for weddings—punch bowls, lace tablecloths, aisle runners, candleabra, tuxedos. Most of these things involve paying a fee, of course, and once they have served their purpose they will be carted off in vans for someone else's special day.

I don't want to minimize the importance of "trappings"—borrowed or otherwise—for such a momentous event. I read statistics somewhere which indicated that the more planning and preparation involved in a wedding ceremony, the more likely the marriage is to last. That isn't surprising, when you think about it. The more public we go with our commitments, the more serious we are apt to be about them. (Remember my telling you about the woman who decided that since she and her boyfriend were going out to buy groceries anyway, they might as well stop by the Justice of the Peace and get married? "After all," she said, "when you've already been married twice before, there's no point in making a big deal of it!")

Well, you will undoubtedly have to borrow a number of things if this is to be the kind of "big deal" wedding you want it to be. Still, it is a good time for you to decide what your philosophy will be about borrowing as a regular practice. Your dad and I have learned by bitter experience that " . . . the borrower is servant to the lender" (Prov. 22:7). Of course you will want to establish credit, but the more you can avoid time contracts and charge cards, the freer you will be to move in any direction the Lord chooses to move you. How many

49

people who have started out to do the Lord's work have been sidetracked because of the accumulation of debts.

What is true of money is also true of other people's possessions. Take my word for it; it is always the borrowed object that gets lost, stolen, broken or otherwise damaged. Better to make do with second best of your own things, in most cases, than to borrow someone else's prized possessions!

If you are going to borrow anything at all, borrow brains! Get all the ideas you can for making your home and life successful. Don't be afraid to ask for advice from people whose lives God is using. Learn everything you can about cooking and homemaking, about keeping a schedule and rearing children, about serving the Lord and making people happy. Don't be sensitive about the suggestions your husband makes, and pay special attention to any help your mother-in-law gives. She knows more about your husband than anyone besides you, and she can give you clues to making him happy. Borrow all the wisdom you can get from others!

And if you come to one of those days when you feel you have been a failure, and you are convinced that you are the most stupid person in the world, then borrow all the resources God has made available to you in His Word. James 1:5 says: "If any of you lack wisdom, let him ask of God, that giveth to all men liberally, and upbraideth not; and it shall be given him." Add to that the wonderful promise in Hebrews 4:15,16: "For we have not an high priest which cannot be touched with the feeling of our infirmities; but was in all points tempted like as we are, yet without sin. Let us therefore come boldly unto the throne of grace, that we may obtain mercy, and find grace to help in time of need."

With fondest affection,
Mom

Reflections . . .

1. I would have more realistic expectations for myself.
2. I would learn to say, "This too shall pass."
3. I would make a point of enjoying every stage of life.
4. I would listen more carefully to the counsel of others.
5. I would cherish every friendship.
6. I would put less emphasis on material things.
7. I would refuse to take my own transient feelings so seriously.
8. I would worry less about failure.
9. I would spend less time wondering about other people's opinions of me.
10. I would talk less.
11. I would say, "I love you," more often.
12. I would fret less about the future.
13. I would smile more.
14. I would memorize more Scripture.
15. I would be more observant to the beauty God has put in the world around me.
16. I would work harder at understanding how other people feel and think.
17. I would be less critical of others.
18. I would learn to laugh at myself more easily.
19. I would be freer with my praise.
20. I would put a higher premium on integrity.
21. I would work for more consistency in practicing the Word of God.
22. I would make fewer excuses and take more responsibility for my own success and happiness.
23. I would put a higher value on every opportunity to learn and grow.
24. I would complain less.
25. I would tell the Lord more often how thankful I am that He chose me and that He loves me and that His plans for me are beyond my fondest dreams.

J.S.

Dear Carol:

" . . . something blue . . . "

I wonder why blue is considered important for the bride to wear? Perhaps it is because blue represents heavenly things. Blue was commanded to be put on the priests' ephods (Exod. 28:31) and it was an essential color in the design of both the Tabernacle and the Temple of Solomon.

There is a most unusual command given in Numbers 15:37-40:

"And the Lord spake unto Moses, saying, Speak unto the children of Israel, and bid them that they make them fringes in the borders of their garments throughout their generations, and that they put upon the fringe of the borders a ribband of blue: And it shall be unto you for a fringe, that ye may look upon it, and remember all the commandments of the Lord, and do them; and that ye seek not after your own heart and your own eyes, after which ye use to go a whoring: That ye may remember, and do all my commandments, and be holy unto your God."

When you walk down that aisle with "something blue," you may want to make it your own personal sign that you will indeed "remember all the commandments of the Lord, and do them; and that ye seek not after your own heart . . . . " It is, after all, your commitment to the Lord that will make your commitment to Roger work. I know this makes a wedding a tremendously solemn thing, and perhaps a little scary besides. (It's hard to imagine, isn't it, that anything which began so insignificantly with a smile, a pleasant conversation, and then a casual date, could grow into something so important that its consequences are eternal?)

It is that phrase "seek not after your own heart" that is so tough to practice! There used to be an old saying that "marriages are made in Heaven" but you will notice that people don't use it much anymore. Too many marriages we see now look like they were made anywhere else *but* Heaven!

I suspect there are many married people who, when the going gets rough, are tempted to ask themselves, *I wonder what would have happened if I had married so-and-so . . . ?* That is an indulgence you simply cannot permit in yourself even for a moment. Once you have committed yourself in marriage to one man, then you cannot fantasize about either the past or the future, except as it relates to the man you have married.

And that brings us to another important symbol in the color blue—faithfulness, remembrance, eternality. It is said of the virtuous woman of Proverbs 31: "She will do him good and not evil all the days of her life" (vs. 12). That's just about as faithful as a person can get, isn't it? It implies faithfulness to marriage vows, of course, but it also implies a patient, day-by-day fulfillment of whatever new demands marriage may make of us as circumstances and needs change. A lot of us are like the old woman in the divorce court who, when asked by the judge if she had not agreed to love her husband "for better or for worse," replied that she had not known how "worse" it was going to get!

Well—blue suggests happiness too. You know the old song that talks about "blue days," "blue skies," and "bluebirds of happiness." I hope you will remember, as you carry your blue "whatever" down the aisle, that you can be happy, that you *will* be happy whether days are gray or whether they are golden, because God will be with you to turn every experience into something good.

"Let your conversation be without covetousness; and be content with such things as ye have: for he hath said, I will never leave thee, nor forsake thee." —Hebrews 13:5.

With abiding love,
Mom

Love is not payment; it is a gift.

Love does not have a due date; it is eternal.

Love is not law; it is grace.

Love is not calculated; it is spontaneous.

Love is not a bookkeeper; it is a spendthrift.

Love is not measurable; it is infinite.

Dearest Carol:

When I think about the things I will miss after you leave home to get married, the first thing that comes to mind is your laughter. (Of course I will also miss seeing you hunched over a book with a glass of milk and two Oreo cookies in your hand, but I assume that is a pastime that will vanish with your other college activities, once you are married!)

I do hope you will never lose your ability to laugh heartily and often. I've talked about a lot of those deeply-serious qualities a girl needs to bring to marriage—commitment, faithfulness, patience, submission and more—and these are certainly essential to a good marriage. But they are all "heavy" qualities. You will discover pretty quickly that if earnestness and diligence and a sense of duty are not cushioned and lightened by a healthy sense of humor, life can become terribly austere, and sometimes downright unbearable.

Years ago a friend married a well-known Bible scholar and writer who was a number of years older than she. His associates were men of learning and fame. He spoke seven languages (and read several more besides)—a brilliant, gifted man.

As soon as they were married, my young friend began a campaign of self-improvement. She took college courses in history and archaeology. She set out to improve her vocabulary and broaden her reading.

One day this great man took his young wife in his arms and said to her, "Honey, I didn't marry you to discuss Bible archaeology or political events. I married you so that I could enjoy your sweet and beautiful face across from me at the breakfast table. I married you so I could enjoy the comfort of your arms, the sound of your laughter, the relaxation of your presence. I married you so I could be the father of your children and your companion in rest and pleasure. All I require of you is that you love me and enjoy being with me."

Some of us women—especially if we are conscientious and duty-oriented—have a tendency to make such a serious business of living that we neglect the delightful nonsense and laughter that eases the load and sweetens the hours for the men we marry.

Perhaps you will have had enough practice learning to accept the constant teasing of your brothers, that you won't have difficulty learning to laugh at yourself. I hope so. A bride who cannot learn to laugh at her first mistakes in the kitchen, her clumsiness in entertaining, or her awkwardness in her efforts to please her husband, is sure to have a tearful pathway along the journey of life!

Being a good wife and homemaker takes practice, just as surely as does any other great profession. A concert pianist, a secretary, a teacher, or an artist does not excel overnight. The road to success in anything is surely paved with "goofs." So, if there are going to be some failures and foolishness along the way, you might as well learn to laugh at yourself.

More important, don't be so sensitive that you burst into tears every time your husband laughs at one of your failures. (If you turn out to be the kind of scatterbrain I am—driving off with brownies on top of the car, putting salt in the refrigerator, etc., you will learn to tell the wild stories on yourself before someone else tells them. It's lots more comfortable that way!)

When your Roger becomes the great preacher and spiritual leader I believe he will become, he will especially need you to add sweetness and refreshing and lightness to his life. A man who is carrying heavy burdens and great responsibilities needs laughter and tenderness. That is what being a "helpmeet" is all about!

I'll miss you terribly, but give you happily to Roger.

Mom

Love laughs at itself but not at its beloved.

Love builds walls that protect

  and tears down walls that alienate.

Love does not ask, "What can you do for me?"

  but, "What can I do for you?"

Love sees beyond today.

Love is not conscious of itself, but of the beloved.

Dear Carol:

I suppose you knew, when we first started talking about your wedding, that sooner or later I would get around to talking about a wife's submission to her husband.

There have always been so many jokes made about it and the term "submission" is so often misused or misunderstood that most of us hesitate to get involved in much of a discussion about it.

Remember my telling you about that college friend who asked, "What do you believe about this submission business? I tried it for a while but it just didn't work!"?

Of course she was missing the whole point of God's commands. We do not have the option of deciding whether or not we will run experiments regarding God's Word. Once we are committed to obedience to God, we *make* it work!

One important principle we need to accept about submission is that it is first an attitude before it is an act. It comes out of a genuine desire to please another, and it does not demand its rights. It implies a quiet confidence that God will make a woman's submission to her own husband turn out right. This is what I Peter 3:4 means when it talks about how much God values a "meek and quiet spirit" in a woman.

Second, submission is something we give willingly, not only to our own husbands but to all other Christians: "Submitting yourselves one to another in the fear of God" (Eph. 5:21); " . . . in lowliness of mind let each esteem other better than themselves" (Phil. 2:3). Once we recognize the fact that a submissive heart, especially toward God, is the mark of a Christian, it is not so hard to accept the fact that God intends a wife to be in submission to her husband.

What does this mean, then, in practical day-by-day living?

Well, it means specifically that when you marry Roger you are really taking on the responsibility to be for Roger whatever his needs may require of you in the oneness of marriage. Certainly it would include meeting his physical needs, rearing his children, representing him well before others and upholding him before the throne of grace. If that really is a woman's motivation when she marries, there will not be a constant hassle over minor issues of "his rights and my rights."

It probably will even mean, if you are serious about this business of pleasing your husband and making him happy, that many of your tastes will, consciously or unconsciously, conform to his. I didn't start out liking brown bread or liver or black coffee, but through the years of living with your dad and eating with him, I have found that I want to enjoy what he enjoys.

It is also true, however, that in living with me, your dad learned to like lobster and cornbread dressing and quiche lorraine! That's the wonderful thing about working at learning to see the world through someone else's eyes and trying to think like another thinks. It makes possible a wonderful personal growth that broadens our thinking, enlarges our viewpoint and sweetens even the most mundane tasks of life.

Aside from peripheral benefits, genuine submission begets exactly the kind of love and honor every woman needs from her husband. You can count on the biblical principles to work. Obedience to God's Word has its own set of rewards not only in the hereafter but in the day-by-day experiences of life!

One last word: I don't want to suggest that submission is always easy. There will be times when you are absolutely positive your husband is wrong and you are right. God's Word applies even in these cases. The ultimate decision must be your husband's since God holds him, not you, responsible for the choices he makes. Let me remind you, however, that God does not demand of you a mindlessness in matters that pertain to your welfare. A woman who is discreet and gentle in her offering of advice, who lives daily according to the Word, and who reflects wisdom in other areas of her life, will often find that her husband listens carefully to what she has to say. It is possible for a wife to live in such a way that her husband develops absolute trust in her judgment.

Of course all this advice is useless if you do not see it work in my own life, and so I pray even as I write, "Let me be the best example to my beloved daughter in my attitude toward her father."

Fondest love,
Mom

As the bow unto the cord is,

So unto the man is woman.

Though she bends him, she obeys him;

Though she draws him, yet she follows.

Useless each without the other.

—Henry Wadsworth Longfellow.

Well, Carol . . .

We have talked about nearly all the wedding ceremony except that little part which reads:

> " . . . for better, for worse,
>   for richer, for poorer;
>   In sickness and in health . . ."

Those are awesome promises for any one individual to make to another person, when you think about it.

We do not know, before a crisis occurs in life, or more specifically in a marriage, how we will respond. Statistics indicate that crises—both good and bad—precipitate great physical and emotional stress and, therefore, can have a drastic effect on a marriage. The loss of a job, the birth of a child, a change in health, the death of a loved one, the receiving of an inheritance, a business promotion—all these experiences have the power to damage or to bless a marriage.

It will be important for you and Roger to decide now what principles you will use in dealing with changes when they come, because you can count on it, they will come.

Sickness, for instance. Most women say they would rather be sick themselves than to have a husband or a child sick. I suspect you will find this to be true, too. In the first place, God seems to have given women a higher pain threshold than men possess (perhaps in preparation for childbearing); so you may find yourself more tolerant of pain than your husband.

Oddly enough, some men feel that sickness is an attack on their masculinity and so they are impatient and frustrated when their physical capacities are temporarily impaired. You will need to ask the Lord to give you the coolness and compassion to be a cheerful and understanding nurse when the occasion arises.

Your dad, as you know, is the kind who generally turns his face to the wall when he is sick and wants to be left alone; but your husband may need a great deal of extra attention. This is where you will need your best women's intuition.

Now about your own health, let me make a few practical suggestions:

Learn to keep your mouth shut about minor discomforts and ailments. I wish I had learned this sooner. As a bride, I expected to fulfill all my responsibilities as a wife and mother (and I have rarely spent a whole day in bed, as you know) but I *did* want the whole world to know that I was sticking at the job at great cost!

One's family soon tires of listening to a daily recital of discomforts such as sinus headaches, sore throats, aching joints or whatever. It will be helpful to learn early to share even these burdens with the Lord alone. He will never get tired of hearing about your needs, and He is the One who can do something about them.

Take the responsibility for your own health. God intends for you to handle well any tool He has given you to use, and this includes your body. Since you will probably have to set the health patterns for the whole family, then don't be careless about regular visits to the doctor and the dentist. If some physical problem develops, don't ignore it and don't worry about it; get a reliable medical opinion, do what the doctor says, then leave it with the Lord.

You may remember hearing your granddad say that the best assurance of good health is not faddish health foods, not an extreme preoccupation with vitamins or exercise. He would say that the way to a healthy body is to (1) learn to rest in the Lord, (2) praise the Lord for all the good things He gives us to enjoy, (3) put as much variety in your life as possible of work and play, of food and people and learning, (4) be obedient to everything God gives you to do. That will take away the stresses and cares that create so many of our physical problems.

With fondest affection,
Mom

I Corinthians 13 — Revised

Though I send three-dollar valentine
cards and mail gift certificates and have
not love, my money is wasted.
Though I quote the marriage experts
and attend seminars and counsel others on
marital bliss and have not love, I know
nothing.
Though I make promises and pledge
undying love, yet fail to satisfy my husband's
needs, it profits me nothing.
Love laughs at old jokes,
ignores irritating habits,
and tenderly ministers to
a sore throat or a sore heart.
Love brags on the beloved
and seeks to make him look good.
Love always has time
to rub a tired back,
to iron a shirt,
to sit cheerfully through
the NBA Play-offs.
Love always believes the best;
Love is always encouraging;
Love never says, "What's the use?"
Age may alter the body;
Time may dissolve dreams;
Romantic aspirations may be submerged
in the realities of day-to-day living,
But faith and hope and love
last forever.
And the greatest of these is love.

J.S. 1985

Dear Carol:

Isn't it ironic that just about the time I started waxing eloquent to you about the importance of a wife's being cheerful and cool when her husband becomes ill, your dad got *really* sick? Since this is only the third time in twenty-five years of marriage he has ever had to miss more than a day away from his work, I had a chance to re-learn all the advice I gave to you! As you know, it wasn't easy.

Still, it proves the necessity of including in our wedding vows a promise to cherish "in sickness and in health . . . . "

But there is more: the wedding vows also include the line: " . . . in poverty and wealth."

When one is very young and very much in love, poverty can be, if not actually fun, at least challenging! When your dad and I were married, we expected to live sacrificially. We were serving the Lord and we already knew that people in full-time Christian work usually did not live by the economic standards that might be possible to those with the same amount of education who held secular positions. We had no car, but that didn't seem to be a problem—we loved to walk anyway. And since we were within a mile or so of most of the places we wanted to go, we rather enjoyed the exercise involved in "hoof-ing it." On very cold days or grocery-shopping days we often got a ride with another young couple who had a car.

We had to improvise a little in our furnishings with an old bor-rowed springs and mattress mounted on cement blocks, stools in-stead of chairs, and odd pieces of second-hand furniture, but we had a piano and a record player and so we felt we were living luxuriously.

But one day heartache came. Our longed-for first child was born and died within the hour. It was Christmastime; the baby had come earlier than expected, and suddenly there was not enough money to meet expenses. At that point poverty wasn't fun anymore; it wasn't even challenging. It was, plainly and simply, heartbreaking and frustrating.

For the first time, our funny little apartment looked cramped and shabby; having to share a bathroom with another apartment seemed unbearable; the lack of a car seemed unduly difficult. How gently the Lord led us through that experience and taught us (as He has sometimes had to teach us over again): "Let your conversation be without covetousness; and be content with such things as ye have: for he hath said, I will never leave thee, nor forsake thee" (Heb. 13:5).

In these years of serving the Lord poverty has never been too far away, as you know, but oh, how rich we are! I sometimes look at the things God has given us through the years—wonderful friends, great opportunities for service, the best education possible for our four fantastic children, the daily enjoyment of good books and music and art, a great church, opportunities for travel—and we shake our heads and say, as Grandma Sandberg used to say: "Too good for poor people!"

God's riches do not always show up on income-tax returns, but they will come just the same, when you are committed to serving Him and to serving each other "in poverty and in wealth."

When those days come, of wondering where you will get the money to meet the expenses, you may need to re-establish your priorities, to give God more, and then to ask Him to teach you whatever lessons He wants you to learn. Don't let any difficult experience be wasted: God means all of it—the hard and the easy—for good!

"But my God shall supply all your need according to his riches in glory by Christ Jesus."—Philippians 4:19.

Love from
Mom

Reflections . . .

I don't like to think of any of you going through "bad" times, and would even like to protect you from some of the heartaches your dad and I met along the way, but they *will* come, and you will discover, as we have, that God is sufficient . . .

Love is the measure of spiritual maturity.

Love makes poverty romantic, hard work a delight,
and dreams, reality.

Love is the passport that identifies a child of God
with his heavenly Home.

Love is the seal that marks an obedient Christian.

Love is not a penny valentine; it is a cross.

Dear Carol:

In these last few weeks before your wedding, you might want to listen again to the tape your dad and I had made of our wedding ceremony so many years ago.

Emotional as I am, I still get starry-eyed and a little weepy upon hearing again your granddad's sweet words spoken in that ceremony. You may remember my telling you that he said, in his last words of instruction: "A home may be a bare, rented room but it is a heavenly garden if love is there . . . . "

Once we have said everything there is to say about developing a biblical philosophy about submission, the use of money, the practical aspects of living together, the rearing of children, and so on— the one single, primary, overriding purpose of marriage is to build that "heavenly garden" your granddad referred to: a place where God's presence can be felt in the cool of the evening (or the heat of day), a place where love is expressed and lived out in actions, a place which is a sacred retreat from the evils and pressures of the outside world, a place where each member of the family is valued and respected, a place where prayer and laughter and shared confidences and comfort are common, a place where people are rested from labor and restored in mind and spirit.

In some sense this "heavenly garden" is a secret place, a sanctuary so sacred in character and so intimate that only God is welcome into its innermost recesses.

That does not mean that the partners in a marriage are in anywise restricted in this sanctuary. Perhaps there is no freedom in any relationship comparable to the freedom God gives a man and woman in marriage. First Corinthians 7:3,4 says: "Let the husband render unto the wife due benevolence: and likewise also the wife unto the husband. The wife hath not power of her own body, but the husband: and likewise also the husband hath not power of his own body, but the wife."

The reason I am saying all this is that you will be tempted to wonder what is "good" or what is "normal" within the bounds of your own secret garden. A great deal of what we read or see or hear through the media of the sexual "experts" would give the impression that there are standard needs and sexual responses. Remember that your home and your marriage is totally unique. The only restrictions God gives you in the enjoyment of your own private relationship is that it is totally exclusive of others; it is to be mutually satisfying, it is permanent, and it is to glorify God.

Of course the biblical behavior which applies in all human relationships is of primary importance in the intimacies of marriage: the command to "be of the same mind" (Phil. 2:2); to be kind and tenderhearted (Eph. 4:32); to avoid bitterness (Col. 3:19); to be enthusiastic (Col. 3:23); to be loving (Eph. 5:28, Titus 2:5); to esteem another better than oneself (Phil. 2:3); to be patient (Eph. 4:3). Isn't it amazing how practical the Scriptures are as they apply to every area of life?

Now that I have said all this, you may still want to read some good books by reliable authors which will be helpful in your marriage, and later in your counseling of others. Don't ever assume that you already know all there is to know. Determine you will never stop growing and learning ways to make your marriage better.

I love you!

Mom

I love you not only for what you are,

But for what I am when I am with you.

I love you, not only for what you have made of
yourself,

but for what you are making of me.

I love you for the part of me that you bring out.

I love you for putting your hand into my
heaped-up heart

and passing over all the foolish, weak things

that you can't help dimly seeing there,

and for drawing out into the light

all the beautiful belongings that no one else

had looked quite far enough to find.

I love you because you are helping me to make of
the lumber of my life

not a tavern but a temple:

out of the works of my every day,

not a reproach, but a song . . .

—Author Unknown.

70

Dear Carol:

The lines from an old wedding hymn keep running through my mind today:

"... Joy comes at last, crowning all the days of longing .... "

The thoughts of a bride going down the aisle on her wedding day are apt to be a strange mixture of solemn reflections, odd trivialities, sentiment, curiosity, amusement, and perhaps even a little anxiety:

"... I hope I don't trip going up those steps! ... How serious Roger looks. I wonder if he's scared? ... Oh, there's Uncle Ray! I'm so glad he came ... if only Mother won't cry! ... I hope everything goes well for the reception. ... Did I remember to pack everything for the honeymoon? ... I can't believe it—my wedding day is really here! ... How beautiful the church looks. ... Dear Lord, give us a happy home and make us a blessing today .... "

If those aren't your exact thoughts, I'll wager they will be close!

What is there more to be said? You have made just about all the preparations a girl can make spiritually and physically and emotionally, to be a good wife. You have had the Bible and other people's wisdom to help you in the days ahead; you have had the godly example of other great Christian marriages. And you have access to the very throne of God when questions come up for which you have no answers.

1. First, enjoy every minute of your wedding. Listen to every song; savor every word spoken; let every prayer and every vow be as sincere as if it were spoken in a closet to God and Roger alone. Relax and bask in the beauty of this special hour. Too many brides say regretfully, "I was so nervous I didn't know a thing that was going on."

2. Don't fret about details that may go wrong. Weddings are supposed to have some little funny mishap that you can laugh about and talk about to your grandchildren. The world will not come to an end if a candle is blown out by the air-conditioning, or if someone sits in the wrong pew. (In fact, it probably won't even come to an end if some attendant faints. I remember when a groomsman passed out at my best friend's wedding, the whole affair went right on just the same, minus one member of the wedding party!)

3. Ask the Lord to make your wedding a blessing to everyone who

comes. Everybody has some special need, even those people who come "just to be nice." What a wonderful opportunity to touch the lives of people who would not come to church for any other reason. If you can glorify and honor the Lord first of all on your wedding day, it will be a wonderful beginning to a lifetime of serving and praising Him.

God bless you, dear Carol, in these precious few days before the big event.

Your dad and I are proud of you, and we love you.

Mom

I have a true and noble lover;

    He is my sweetheart, all my own.

His like on earth who shall discover?

    His heart is mine and mine alone.

We pledged our troth each to the other,

    And for our happiness I pray.

Our lives belong to one another,

    Oh, happy, happy wedding day!

    Oh, happy, happy wedding day!

(Words to "My Hero" from *The Chocolate Soldier* by Stanislaus Stange, written 1908.)

My Dearest Carol:

This will be the last note I will have time to send you addressed to: Carol Joy Sandberg. That beautiful pearl-encrusted dress hangs, ready and waiting, for you to slip on. The invitations have been sent; the parties are over; the details are finished. Tomorrow you will step down that white aisle into the arms of one who loves you and who has chosen you above all others. If God wills, you will share together a long life of service to One who loves you both more than you could possibly love each other.

Of course I am crying as I write this (would you expect otherwise, knowing me as you do?), but I am not sad. Childhood is a precious time, and the rich experiences of your college years will never be forgotten. But it really is true that "the best is yet to be." And so, my darling Carol, your dad and I give you joyfully to Roger, and we give you again to the Lord, as we did so many years ago. We cannot anticipate your own particular set of joys and sorrows, but we have entrusted you to the One who has said, "I will never leave thee, nor forsake thee" (Heb. 13:5).

You have already seen this anonymously written "Christian Bride's Prayer" since your grandmother thoughtfully had it framed for you, but I would like to include it here for others to see:

"O Father, my heart is filled with a happiness so wonderful that I am almost afraid. This is my wedding day, and I pray Thee that the beautiful joy of this morning may never grow dim with years of regret for the step I am about to take. Rather, may its memories become more sweet and tender with each passing anniversary.

"Thou hast sent me one who seems all worthy of my deepest regard. Grant unto me the power to keep him ever true and to love him as now. May I prove indeed to be a helpmate, a sweetheart, a friend, a steadfast guiding star among all the temptations that beset the impulsive hearts of men. Give me the skill to make home the best loved place of all. Help me, Lord, to meet the little misunderstandings and cares of my new life bravely. Be with me as I start on my mission of womanhood and stay Thou my path from failure all the way. Walk Thou with us even to the end of our journey. O Father, bless my

74

wedding day, hallow my marriage night, sanctify my motherhood, if Thou seest fit to grant the privilege.

"And when my youthful charms are faded and the cares and lessons of life have left their touches, let physical fascination give way to the greater charm of companionship, and so may we walk hand in hand to the Valley of Final Shadow which we will then be able to lighten with the sunshine of good and happy lives where we have loved and trusted Thee, where we have been able to witness to others the message of Thy gift of salvation for those who believe on the blessed name of Jesus Christ.

"Thank you, Father, for all the many blessings You have granted to me from the day of my birth until now. Thank You for the gift of Your only Son who died for me and for the sins of the world so that in believing and trusting in Him, we might inherit His gift of eternal life. I pray this prayer in the name of Jesus. Amen."

. . . And so, dear Carol, we look forward with you to the days ahead. Although we will miss your daily presence in these familiar walls, there will never be a "No Vacancy" sign in either our house or in our hearts.

With love and prayers . . .
Mom

For my beloved I will not fear: Love knows to do

For him, for her, from year to year, as hitherto;

Whom my heart cherishes are dear

To Thy heart too.

—Amy Carmichael.

(From *In the Arena*, by Isabel S. Kuhn.)

When you got married, Carol, it wasn't hard for me to decide the things I ought to tell you in preparation for marriage. I could still remember all the things I wished someone had told me!

But when you got married a year later, Jim, it occurred to me that somebody ought to be telling young men (from a woman's point of view) how to treat a brand new wife.

And so here it is, Jim, just as I wrote it at the time—this packet of letters which I title: "Please Take Care of My Daughter-in-Law!"

Jim and Jennifer Sandberg

Dear Jim:

Gradually, I work at getting used to the fact that soon you will be leaving us to make a home of your own. Seeing yours and Jennifer's names on the newly arrived wedding announcements has reminded me of how close the wedding day really is.

Hard as it is to picture your empty space at the breakfast table, to lose your quick wit in verbal contests with your brothers, to be without the availability of your skills as our resident mechanic, plumber and typewriter repairman, these are the days for which we have planned and prayed and worked. The test of your dad's and my skills as parents (and the proof of God's grace and mercy when we *knew* we weren't smart enough to do the job right) has been your arrival at this particular point in your life—your graduation from college with highest honors, your ability to tackle a job and be successful at it, your unwavering commitment to the Lord and His will for your life, your patience in choosing a lovely, spiritually minded girl to love, and the willingness of both of you to wait until you finish college to marry. I don't really mean to say that your dad and I deserve the credit for what the Lord has done and is doing with your life, but people will give us the credit (or blame)—earned or not.

And that brings us to Jennifer: what a tremendous girl you have chosen! Traditionally, mothers are supposed to have a suspicious eye toward prospective daughters-in-law. After all, when a boy marries, a mother is never again "first lady" in her son's eyes.

Nor should she be! Although the Genesis passage commanding a man to "leave his father and mother" when he marries is a principle that ought to be practiced by both men and women when they marry, it may be true that mothers tend to cling to their sons more tenaciously than they do to their daughters.

Jennifer has the skill of making it easy for a mother to become a happy mother-in-law. She knows how to praise every dish she eats at our house and then eagerly asks, "Do you think that would be hard for me to learn how to cook?" even though *she* knows and *I* know that she has the right blend of adventure and skill and dedication to eventually make my cooking look rather ordinary!

Although Jennifer has the sensitivity to feel other people's hurts and embarrassments and burdens, she has learned to take with good grace the constant teasing she gets from your younger brothers. She will be a comfort and a blessing in your future ministry.

Some people say that a good criteria for judging what a woman will be like after she marries, is to look at her mother. If that is true, then Jennifer certainly comes with good credentials. I'm delighted that you think Jennifer's mother is great, but I am even more delighted that I thought so first, and that in God's providence you will marry the daughter of one of my dearest friends. How exciting it is to realize that after sharing so many other good things together, Marianne and I will be sharing our children too!

And so I want to say in writing what you have already heard me say in casual conversation, that we welcome Jennifer to our family with open arms and open hearts. Had I personally taken on the job single-handedly of making the choice, I could not have chosen a girl so ideally suited to your needs and your temperament, nor could I have found one whose spiritual dreams and dedication to duty so closely match your own.

Hooray for Jennifer!

From a proud Mom

80

Message to Roger, Jen and Kay . . .

It is hard for me to remember
    that just a few short years ago
I never knew you existed.
You were growing up—
    wearing braces
    skinning your knees,
    getting sunburned at summer camp,
    turning your nose up at broccoli,
    writing silly notes in church.
I never burped you,
    never saw you take that first step,
    never kissed your kindergarten face.
When I saw you first, there was no recognition
    of some familiar gesture, feature, walk—
" . . . his father's nose," "the way her mother laughs . . . ,"
    ". . . just like her brother . . . ."
You were—simply—you,
    not ordinary now, but special
    because my children loved you.
Now you are mine. As dear as though I named you,
    watched you grow.
As welcome to my heart and home as those I brought to birth.
Dear son-in-law;
    precious daughters-in-law,
    Completers of my own flesh-and-blood,
    Guardians of all that is dear to me.
Now you are mine. I share you joyfully
    with those who burped you . . .
    kissed your kindergarten face . . .
With awe I recognize familiar gestures,
    features, walk
reflected in my grandchild's face and form:
". . . his father's nose," "the way her mother laughs . . . ."

We both observe, and realize
the special union of those traits—
    yours and mine—
in the children we hold dear.
It is hard for me to remember
    that just a few short years ago
I never knew you existed.

J.R.S.

Dear Jim:

Having grown up in a predominantly female household, and now living in one which is predominantly male, I find myself constantly amazed at the differences between men and women. I've noticed that women do not view problems the same way men do, nor do they necessarily come up with the same solution. A man is sure to be puzzled by the kinds of things that make a woman cry, but a woman, on the other hand, may be shocked and frustrated by the things a man considers amusing.

Men do not think like women, nor do women think like men. Men and women do not respond emotionally to the same stimuli, and they do not necessarily reach the same conclusion, given the same facts. The simple truth of the matter is, women are drastically, irrevocably, amazingly different from men. Interests, thought patterns, physique, viewpoint, dreams—all are maddeningly, mysteriously, wonderfully different one from another.

Why, then, did God design that the closest of all human relationships should be between two such diverse creatures? Why did God not plan that Adam's "help meet" would be one who would more closely mirror his own image—mental, physical and spiritual?

It is precisely this fact—the differences between men and women—that provides the best proof of the rightness of God's plan in creating a man and woman to be "one flesh." Genesis 2:23,24 says: "And Adam said, This is now bone of my bones, and flesh of my flesh: she shall be called Woman, because she was taken out of Man. Therefore shall a man leave his father and his mother, and shall cleave unto his wife: and they shall be one flesh."

There is a sense in which a man without a woman is incomplete. There are pieces of the puzzle missing when a man does not have a good wife to add color and beauty and softness to his life; when there is no one to encourage his dreams, to modify his view of himself, or to expand his vision. We may grieve at the womanly susceptibility of Eve that made her the first victim of the tempter's influence in the Garden of Eden, but it was the same vulnerability, the same womanly instinct of wanting to know, to be led into knowledge of the truth, that made it possible for Mary of Bethany to understand

and accept the Lord Jesus' part in God's great redemptive plan, when the twelve disciples missed the point completely!

The fact is, a woman's vices are also her virtues. What makes a woman delightfully unpredictable and endlessly fascinating are the same qualities that can make her seemingly contradictory and infuriatingly changeable!

Instead of being frustrated at the differences between men and women, a Christian husband needs to be able to see his wife as an extension of himself, a completion of the person God intended him to be when the two become "one flesh."

Your choice of a bride has certainly proved that you like "girls to be girls." My prayer for you and Jennifer is that both of you will learn to take those attitudes and ideas which are so distinctly your own, and blend them into a precious instrument of righteousness and a source of personal joy and fulfillment that will influence and bless all those who touch the boundaries of both your lives.

Love,

Mom

"Whoso findeth a wife findeth a good thing, and obtaineth favour of the Lord." —Proverbs 18:22.

*   *   *

"House and riches are the inheritance of fathers; and a prudent wife is from the Lord." —Proverbs 19:14.

Dear Jim:

I had to smile at the dinner table the other night as I listened to you and Jennifer playfully tease each other about how you plan to spend money once you are married. I'm sure that both of you are beginning to realize that money decisions in a marriage are never quite so simple as they look at the beginning!

Take the value we place on such things as "adventure" or "security."

Now it is true that every human being requires a measure of both adventure (with its accompanying risks) and security (with its predictability). Still, it is probably true that women are nearly always prone to place a higher value on security, and men are quicker to give up total security for the sake of some adventure. The very fact that car insurance is higher for young men than for young women indicates that men—particularly youthful men—enjoy a certain amount of risk taking.

I personally believe, Jim, that a woman's sense of security ultimately depends more on people than it does on things, on relationships more than possessions. Now I know a woman tends to think of "home" in relationship to security, yet I have known women who made homes in very transient, unpredictable circumstances, and who made them comfortably and happily because they felt secure in the person who shared the home.

Think about Sarah, the lady who spent most of her life in a tent, perhaps not really understanding the call of God which brought her husband Abraham away from the comforts of a rich, sophisticated city to a life of endless wandering. Sarah's expression of faith spoken of so eloquently in Hebrews' "Hall of Faith" would never have been possible had she not been able to have confidence in Abraham and in Abraham's God.

Security does not necessarily come out of assets that can be handled or measured or evaluated in practical human terms; mainly it comes from the intangible qualities of character and commitment.

Let me suggest several things a man may possess, that will make his wife feel secure:

1. *Honesty*. A woman always needs to know that her husband has personal integrity—that his word may be trusted, that he will pay

honest debts, that he will fulfill his obligations to others. Now, of course these are qualities you have already taken for granted as a part of Christian maturity. Sometimes, however, a man may feel his business dealings are entirely his own affair, and he does not share with his wife the details of the way he is meeting his obligations. His silence may appear to be secretiveness and so she feels insecure and uncertain that the obligations *are* being met.

(Incidentally, a man who does not share with his wife information concerning insurance policies, wills, investments, and other financial dealings, does his wife no favor. I have talked to several widows who were left in serious financial confusion because of a husband who thought all money dealings were "his" business.)

2. *Repeated declarations of love.* Puzzling as it may seem, Jim, a woman's greatest security comes from hearing her husband tell her—in as frequent intervals as possible and in as many ways as possible—that he loves her. Sadly enough, the wear and tear of daily living, the pressures, disappointments and weariness of the road may erode a woman's confidence in herself as a worthy object of love, so she needs to be assured that she is, indeed, still lovable.

3. *A right relationship with God.* A woman who feels her husband will stay in the center of God's will is the most secure of all women. She rests not only in her husband's commitment to her, but also under the umbrella of God's protecting care. While there may sometimes be some personal inconvenience or lack of physical comforts in the will of God, there is always that beautiful assurance that God will not abandon those who are resting in Him, doing His perfect will.

Here again, it will not be enough for *you* to know you are in God's will, or for *you* to enjoy a private, personal relationship with the Lord. You will need to make the sweetness of this relationship such that it is reflected in every other relationship—expressed from the pulpit, as I know you intend to do, but also shared in every conversation, every conviction, every loving gesture. When a man's commitment to God is joyful, unshakable, uncomplaining, fulfilling, there is an aura of security absolutely nothing can destroy!

Well—forgive me for this rather heavy monologue. You'll do a great job, I know, in giving Jennifer the security every woman needs.

Your Mom

They say a wife and husband, bit by bit,
Can rear between their lives a mighty wall,
So thick they cannot talk with ease through it,
Nor can they see across . . . it is so tall!
Its nearness frightens them . . . but each alone
Is powerless to tear its bulk away . . .
And each dejected . . . wishes he had known
For such a wall . . . some magic thing to say.

So let us build with master art . . . my dear,
A bridge of faith between your life and mine,
A bridge of tenderness, and very near
A bridge of understanding . . . strong and fine,
Till we have formed so many lovely ties
There never will be room for walls to rise.

—Author Unknown.

Dear Jim:

This morning at breakfast, when you thanked me for the meal as you always do, I was reminded again of how important courtesy is in the home. I know you say "thank you" because you believe it is right to do (and because you are genuinely appreciative) and, lest you think I've taken your good habits for granted, I want to tell you again that your simple "thank you" always gets my day started right. A grateful child always puts plus points on the credit side of motherhood and homemaking!

I am glad you have developed the habit of that kind of courtesy as a single young man because I can promise you it will be one of the things Jennifer will value most in you when you two have been married for ten years or more.

Not long ago I noticed an article in the Sunday magazine that included an interview with a famous etiquette expert. When the lady was asked what breach of etiquette was committed most often, she replied that it was a failure to say "thank you."

Some failure to show good manners we may excuse as being due to a lack of experience or training, but saying "thank you" ought to be the automatic response from any grateful heart, no matter what the background. How sad that so many husbands and wives fail to make this simple courtesy an integral part of their relationship!

Have you noticed how frequently courtesy between two people is abandoned as soon as they get married? Husbands and wives sometimes use a tone of voice with each other they wouldn't dream of using outside the home; they indulge in sarcasm and bitterness and complaining as though that were a peculiar privilege in marriage. First Peter 3:7-9 talks specifically about this problem:

"Likewise, ye husbands, dwell with them according to knowledge, giving honour unto the wife, as unto the weaker vessel, and as being heirs together of the grace of life; that your prayers be not hindered. Finally, be ye all of one mind, having compassion one of another, love as brethren, be pitiful, be courteous: Not rendering evil for evil, or railing for railing: but contrariwise blessing; knowing that ye are thereunto called, that ye should inherit a blessing."

You have probably discovered already that even aside from these courtesies that have to do with good character and spiritual under-standing, there are a hundred other little gestures of courtesy that have to be learned and practiced simply because they are significant to a particular woman.

A lady does not need a car door opened for her because she is helpless but because she interprets the act to mean, "I care about you." As you and Jennifer live and work together in the years ahead, the common courtesies you practice now will have to be exercised with even more care. There is always a temptation to take for granted one's love for another, and to assume that courteous rituals are no longer necessary.

Oddly enough, the need for courtesy will become most apparent in the seemingly insignificant situations—when you are both trying to get dressed in the same bathroom at the same time, when one or the other of you tends to be a "dropper"—of clothes, shoes, newspapers, earrings, or whatever—when there are appointments to be met and deadlines to be reached, and both of you are running out of time. Courtesy in all these situations does not come naturally, even to very nice people. All of us who want to do right have to make thoughtfulness a daily matter of "dying to self."

You and Jennifer have already made a great start; I'll be eager to see how you make it work in your new home!

Mom

Love is not blind; it closes its eyes to the
faults of others.
Love collects the virtues and discards the
failures of others.
Love is the railing on a treacherous stairway;
the nightlight in a dark room.

Dear Jim:

Picturing you as a husband and father sure isn't easy! In my head, I know you are sensible and mature enough to be both, but my heart keeps dragging up memories of the fat toddler you were so many years ago and the teenager tinkering with motors so very, very few days ago . . . well . . . how about yesterday?

Will you be like your dad, I wonder? Have you been measuring the qualities of manhood by what you see in him? Although we have teased you about your oft-repeated question, "Is that true, Dad?" it is a point of pride and joy that as a child you felt you could measure truth by your father's word.

Let me tell you some things about your father that I think make him a great man. These are all qualities you already recognize in him, of course, but I want to emphasize how important they are to me as a woman, or more specifically, as a wife of twenty-six years. I can't believe these things wouldn't be important to any woman.

First, you already know how thoroughly your dad has already been involved in having a family. He has never been a man who thought his responsibility ended with bringing home a paycheck. How many men do you know who choose to shop for their kids' clothes, to invent family traditions (like Saturday morning chocolate eclairs and Saturday night popcorn), to plan exciting vacations, to buy lingerie for their wives for no reason at all, to watch *Buck Rogers* with their kids, and to run a vacuum sweeper occasionally?

And then, have you noticed that your dad has never felt he had to wear some "macho" image to prove he is a real man? You know how totally un-self-conscious he is, whether playing the piano, mowing the lawn, directing a choir, playing a game, cleaning a bathroom, or shopping in a dress shop. He loves to laugh, as you well know, but he has learned through the years to sometimes cry as well—a pretty important quality for a man whom God has called to be a burden-sharer.

Have you considered how predictable your dad is? Not predictable in the sense of being boring, but in the steadiness of his responses in every situation? You never have to worry about whether your dad has had a good day or a bad one, whether he will be cheerful or grouchy. He has so long lived by the scriptural principle, "This is the day that the Lord hath made; we will rejoice and be glad in it" (Ps. 118:24), that day by day his behavior stays steadily the same.

Have you ever seen a day when you had reason to wonder whether your father had lost his faith in the Word of God or had swerved from a day-by-day commitment to the will of God? Do you realize how rare it is for a man to measure his own behavior by the Word of God and to confess failure and ask forgiveness as your father does?

You probably aren't surprised to know that one of the qualities I value most in your dad is simply that he is so much fun to be around. His enthusiasm about everything from people to dogs, to gardening, to watching championship gymnastics on TV, to getting prayers answered, to directing a choir, to teaching college kids, to traveling abroad, to eating out, to playing games, to directing family devotions, to "fooling around" with his kids—makes every day a holiday!

Let me end with one more thing—a quality which we tend to minimize in this day and age. How faithfully your dad performs every duty and responsibility to the Lord and to his family without ever a complaint. You can always count on his being wherever he is supposed to be, on time and prepared for whatever job is at hand.

Wasn't I clever to pick out such a great model for my sons to follow?

Much love,
Mom

Reflections . . .

You know that I have always been an incurable list-maker. Whether I was writing out my "things to do" or my prayer requests, my grocery needs or simply "my favorite things"—the world always seemed more orderly and comfortable if the things that were important to me were recorded on a piece of paper.

So it happened that even my love notes to your dad ended up being lists . . .

Dear Sandy:

Thank you for all the things I already knew I was marrying you for:

Your love of life
Your spiritual concern
Your enjoyment of beauty
Your musical gifts
Your compassion for helpless creatures
Your interest in people

Thank you, too, for the things I didn't know about you when I married you:

The fact that you don't always have to be
    proving your manliness to the world—
Your interest in your home—
    offering to do the laundry,
    seeing about the garbage,
    cleaning the bathroom when company is due.
Your love of having people in the home,
Your interest in picking out my clothes.

Thank you:

For your patience with the foibles of women—
    especially the foibles of mine!
Patience with my interruption of your reading with,
    "Listen to this . . . "
For tramping through endless art galleries and
    museums.
For making popcorn in your own superb way.
For not falling apart when I cry for no obvious
    reason,
For bragging on me in front of others.
For never criticizing.
For hiding your frustration when the income never
    quite meets the outgo.
For liking my friends.

For keeping a steady and faithful relationship
    with the Lord,
For your cheerful consistency, no matter how you feel.
For being the kind of man I am proud to belong to
    and glad to be seen with.
For your youthfulness and your age.
For your clean and ordered ways.
For sharing with me music and beauty and laughter
    and tears and prayer and love.
For being YOU!—dearest and best—

                  I love you,
                  Jessie

Dear Jim:

Sometimes a man, in an attempt to describe sensibly and spiritually what love is, will argue that it is not silly sentimental songs, poetic words or pretty valentines with hearts and flowers. In fact, all of us are annoyed that advertisers use "love" to sell cosmetics, or cigarettes, or food. As believers in the Word of God, we insist that the real qualities of love are those expressed in I Corinthians 13.

Sometimes, however, in our efforts to keep our ideas about love spiritually oriented, we act as though love, as expressed in the Bible, has nothing to do with warm, romantic feelings.

The truth is, of course, that love is both emotional and intellectual, both deliberate and mysterious, both logical and intuitive.

As my dad reminded me so many years ago when being "in love" was a primary preoccupation in my life, we do not really "fall" in love—we "climb" in. Consciously or unconsciously, every person who loves someone else makes special choices about "who," "when," "where," and "why."

Long before you had decided that Jennifer was the girl for you, there was a type of girl to which you were attracted. You had already formed in your mind certain ideas of what makes a girl attractive (and don't assume that your own ideas of beauty are necessarily universal; every age and culture and individual man has a specific and particular taste) and you had spent all your early years, again—consciously or unconsciously—collecting information and "putting it into the computer" to determine the kind of girl you wanted to marry.

So far, so good. Your computer has done a great job of choosing a girl who genuinely loves the Lord and is spiritually minded, a girl who is beautiful and gifted, who loves people and is concerned about being a blessing to all those whose lives she touches. You have won the extra bonus of finding a girl who will add the enthusiasm and laughter and zest for living to this serious business of serving the Lord sacrificially and wholeheartedly.

Now that you have made good and right choices in your life concerning marriage and home, be sure you don't stop there. This is the point where the sentimental songs, the poetry, the hearts-and-flowers are so much in order.

A good marriage does involve important rational decisions day by day, but it is the abundance of romantic frills, the totally extravagant use of sweet words, the little love gifts for no reason at all, the tender kiss (administered while her hands are in dishwater as well as in the bedroom), the sentimental and faithful adherence to a multitude of private rituals that say, "I love you," and the daily awareness of the gentle touch that make an ordinary marriage good and a good marriage great. In fact, I would go so far as to say that there will be times in which the most spiritual exercise you can do will be to drop everything in order to assure Jennifer that she is more important to you than anything or anybody else in the world—save God Himself!

Take time for the romantic frills, and you will make it possible for God to make of your marriage something which will change the world!

Much love,
Mom

Reflections . . .

When the search for that right man or right woman is finally over and dreams have become realities, it will still be your reflections on those days when you first fell in love, the memories of all the good times together, the joys of sharing—that will bridge the dark and dreary days that are bound to come—when the baby is sick, the car breaks down, the breakfast burns, the bills say "past due," the sofa collapses, unexpected company arrives on the night you are serving macaroni and cheese, the roof leaks and it rains for nine days straight!

When you drop into bed exhausted, it is nice to reflect on the blessing of having someone who is working as hard to help carry the load as you are . . .

"Why should it please a man that he is wise if there is no one to hear his wisdom? Why should it please a man if he is brave when there is no one to protect and no one to praise his courage? And what would it matter to a woman if she could sing beautifully if there were no one who loved her to hear her sing?

"When two people walk together, if one stumbles, the other can hold him up. If one be discouraged, the other can encourage him. If one be hurt, the other can help him.

"Two people can sleep together warmer than if one sleeps alone. Two hearts together can be more cheerful and happy than either of them alone.

"You see, man or woman necessarily needs fellowship. At very best it is lonely enough in this world. At very best there are many of the secrets of the heart, the longings, the aspirations, the memories, the burnings of conscience that one cannot tell anybody. Oh, how each of us needs someone dear and sweet and near, loving and forgiving and understanding and believing, to share with us!"

—John R. Rice
(From *Home: Courtship, Marriage & Children*.
Sword of the Lord Publishers. Used by permission.)

"Two are better than one; because they have a good reward for their labour. For if they fall, the one will lift up his fellow: but woe to him that is alone when he falleth; for he hath not another to help him up. Again, if two lie together, then they have heat: but how can one be warm alone." —Ecclesiastes 4:9-11.

Dear Jim:

I have noticed, in talking to young women who were unhappy about their marriages, that the problems often spring from the differences in which men and women perceive their own role in the partnership, as well as the role of their mates.

What is the "right" response for a wife, according to one man's viewpoint, may not be the "right" response for another man. All of us come to marriage with pretty definite ideas about what husbands and wives are "supposed" to do. Because I came from a family made up of girls, my whole concept of how men were supposed to behave was based on my knowledge of my dad. I didn't know which parts of Dad's ideas or interests or actions were made up of background or personality and which parts came from specific beliefs and practices based on his study of the Word of God. I would have said, probably, "All good Christian men like . . ." or, "A good husband always . . ." entirely in relationship to my knowledge of my own father.

Now, after twenty-six years of marriage and having the additional insight of living with three grown sons, I have learned that the qualities of Christian manhood may differ greatly from man to man and still be consistent with what the Word of God teaches. We are, each of us—whether male or female—distinctively unique.

You have already noticed, I am sure, the great differences between "good" pastors' wives. One woman may be busily and happily involved in many areas of her husband's work (with his blessing), while another takes an exclusively supportive role in her husband's ministry. What is "right" for each of these women is related to her own innate gifts and her husband's wishes in the matter.

I still remember a particular young man engaged to a gifted and popular girl on campus. She was active in the church bus program, involved in many speech and music events and enjoyed a host of friends. He couldn't understand when she was shocked and hurt at being informed by him that after they were married, he did not want her to take any responsibility outside the home, either professionally or in the church. He had fallen in love with a girl while she was involved in many activities, and then presumed that she could become an entirely different sort of person once she was married!

Now I do think there are cases when a woman does indeed need to change her idea of what her role should be. (You already know that my own personal, selfish preference for my life involves more time spent in crafts and homemaking projects, and I do the extra "outside" things I do because your dad wants me to teach and to minister to women. He also knows that I tend to feel "guilty" and restless if I do not have some positive outreach of influence and blessing.)

Whatever demands the circumstances may make upon a woman's life, we must never forget that God does give particular gifts and interests to every woman. And a man would be foolish to try to change his wife into another kind of woman once he is married to her.

I suppose it is possible for a man to be afraid of being overshadowed by his wife's gifts or personality, but a good partnership allows for the differences and uses them for assets in the ministry rather than a source for competition and jealousy. If there is a strong commitment to each other, and a pride in the qualities God has given each partner, any couple can use these diverse gifts to enhance and promote the ministry of each other.

Every young Christian couple needs to learn to pray, "O Lord, give us a ministry together that will bring the greatest blessing to the greatest number possible. Bless all the work of our hands to Your honor and glory."

For a family with small children, that ministry will certainly include lots of cooking and scrubbing and caring for the needs of the family, but in God's plan and wisdom, there may be more God wants a woman to do. I'll be praying that God will give you both wisdom as you find His perfect will for you.

"And whatsoever ye do in word or deed, do all in the name of the Lord Jesus, giving thanks to God and the Father by him."— Colossians 3:17.

Love from
Mom

102

Love does not scatter; it gathers.

Love judges by the heart as well as the head.

Love expands in the heat of pressure.

Love makes excuses for others and takes
responsibility for itself.

Love never gives up.

Dear Jim:

Do you get a little bored by all this discussion on the subject of love? It is probably true that love gets talked about more at your stage of life (just before marriage) than at any other time, before or afterward. (And that's pretty sad, in a way, because the Bible has a great deal to say about love at *every* stage and in every circumstance of life. First John ought to be read frequently, not in some detached "spiritual" way but as a practical application to the problems of adjusting in marriage and getting along with people in every relationship.)

The problem with loving is that we sometimes have difficulty knowing how to say, "I love you," to the person who is dearest to us.

Of course there are the traditional ways of saying, "I love you"— and don't forget that just because they *are* traditional and old-fashioned and cliched, doesn't mean they aren't necessary.

First, a woman always needs to be *told* she is loved, over and over again, in as many ways as possible. (And while you are at it, you will also want to tell Jennifer some of the reasons why you love her. Some of the reasons may be trite: "Because you have a cute nose!" Some may be frankly, outrageously flattering: "Because you are absolutely the most fantastic, the most perfect girl in the world!" But somewhere along the line the reasons should be serious: "Because you are so kind and compassionate when other people are in trouble.") A woman never gets tired of being told she is loved.

Second, a woman wants *other people* to know she is loved. You can say whatever you want to say about the fact that women worry too much about what other people think; it is still true that a woman tends to measure a man's love by his willingness to let others know. That's really why women like corsages, and having doors opened for them, and having husbands who brag on them in public. It says to the world: "Somebody thinks I am important"—something all of us need to believe.

Third, a woman always needs a tender touch to be assured that she is loved. Sometimes a man gets the idea that any caress or touch outside the bedroom is unnecessary and, as one man said, "a bad influence on the children," but this just isn't true. A quick hug, a tender pat on the cheek, a squeeze of the hand, and kisses when leaving or arriving are always appropriate. This example may actually be the best preparation for marriage your kids ever get. Children need to see affectionate touch between their parents for their own security.

Last of all, a woman needs to see love in action. That precious, intimate love expressed between two people is effective only as it is lived out in godly and kind behavior day by day. You know, better than I, what particular actions are going to say "love" to Jennifer, but you will constantly need to work at learning more fully what will nurture and enhance this tremendous love God has given you. We never really "arrive" in this matter of meeting the needs of others and so we must make the task of learning "how" to love in marriage as significant a spiritual concern as we do winning others to the Lord Jesus or learning how to pray.

Much love,
Mom

Your grandfather was such a romantic person! Even when he had to spend most of his waking hours working on the financial needs of THE SWORD OF THE LORD and answering countless letters, he would often stop what he was doing to pick out the melody of "Whispering Hope" on the piano or to quote a few lines of Tennyson's poetry.

I just found this little poem written in his own hand to a sweetheart on January 24, 1917. He was twenty-two years of age at the time . . .

> Spoiler of hearts,—
> Thinks it a lark;
>   Dear little heart of gold.
> Blue of your eyes
> Comes from the skies,
>   Half hidden lights of the soul.
>
> Sweeter than honey
> Worth more than money
>   Sweet-odoured flowerlet true;
> Mystery enthralled—
> Innocent of all—
>   Dearest to me: that's you.
>
>   J.R.R.

Dear Jim:

Well . . . this is it. For several weeks now I've been telling you how to make Jennifer happy. In spite of all this maternal advice you've been getting, I already know—down deep inside—that the qualities you need in order to make a happy home had to have been there long before I started writing these letters. Ultimately, the things that make it possible for us to have good relationships with other people are not so much what we *do*, but what we *are*—not so much "activity" as "attitude." And so, whatever wishes and dreams I have for your spiritual, mental, physical and material prosperity, they are really dreams for Jennifer's happiness, too.

First, Jim, my prayer for you is that you will be a great man of God, not necessarily, however, in terms of fame or position or honor. I want to see God do something with your life that will make a difference in your generation. If you are God's man, doing God's work, in God's way, then you will not be so easily distracted by the temptations that go with self-centered pursuits. A man who knows he is in the center of God's will, will be happy with himself, and a man who is happy with himself is an easier person to live with, generally.

I say this cautiously, because commitment to the will of God sometimes means great sacrifice, and whatever sacrifices you choose, or God chooses for you, will, of course, be shared with Jennifer. It will be your responsibility to convince her (by your own glowing faith, mixed with a whole lot of common sense!) that your choices are right.

Second, my prayer for you is that you will discover that serving the Lord together is twice as exciting as serving the Lord alone. I pray that you will both learn to remember the things that should be remembered (each others' virtues, birthdays and favorite things), and that you will learn to forget the things that should be forgotten (each others' failings, irritating pettinesses and both your disappointments with each other). And when the day comes that you and Jennifer keep remembering the bad things and keep forgetting the good things about each other, I pray that you will be tolerant and patient, realizing that "this too shall pass." Don't ever take yourselves or your problems so seriously that you lose your cheerful perspective.

Your dad and I don't have any great monetary inheritance to pass on to you, the eldest son, on the day of your wedding. Nevertheless, you have a great legacy in your name—your upbringing and your grounding in the Word of God. It is all we have, but it ought to be enough.

God bless you, dear, dear Jim,
Mom

I once jokingly said that I had all my children close together so that they could help rear each other. Actually, that is exactly what happens in a family of children close in age, when there is a pattern of loving and caring for one another already established in the home.

There were other advantages, too, of having four children growing up closely together. It was much easier to adapt our daily routines to a house full of babies first, then to a house full of young children, and later to a house full of teenagers. Whatever was required, at any given time, of childrearing paraphernalia, we had lots of it! We certainly got our money's worth out of the cribs, the sports equipment, the musical instruments, the icemaker and the Encyclopedia Brittanica, with four children who at various stages used them constantly!

The only problem is that children who arrive in a home in just a few short years also tend to leave the home nest in just a span of a few years.

And so it was that you, Jim, had no sooner begun your new life with Jennifer, than Don began to fall in love with Kay, and soon we knew there would be another wedding in the family . . .

A Question of Terminology

How absurd a heart can be!

When it's bound, it feels most free.

When it's free, it wanders 'round

Seeking, so it can be bound.

All this simply means to me

Words do not say as they sound;

Freedom's not till love is found.

—Robert Zacks.

(From *Ted Malone's Adventures in Poetry,* William Morrow Company, 1946.)

Dear Don:

I know you've heard me tell the story of the mother who was asked, "Which of your children do you love best?" Her reply was, "The one who is sick, or away from home, or in trouble."

Since I'm sitting in your hospital room waiting for you to return from surgery, I don't have to remind you of how dear you are to me at this moment (or for that matter, at any moment)!

Now I know, technically, that having one's wisdom teeth cut out hardly ranks with major surgery, but that doesn't keep me from wishing I could bear the discomfort for you. Part of me is proud of you because you have always wanted to minimize any kind of pain and because you have carefully instructed me not to make a "big deal" out of this particular experience. The other part of me wants to gather your six-foot-one frame in my arms just as I did when you were little and hurting.

My reactions to your needs are stronger than usual, I suppose, because this experience is just one more reminder that our major investment in your life (in terms of money, time and influence) is almost over.

In just a few short weeks you will graduate from college, and not many weeks after that, you will marry "our" precious Kay. (You'll notice I call her "our Kay" because, whether you realize it or not, I chose her too!) Of course your dad's and my role in your life has been constantly changing from the day you were born, but we are getting closer to seeing more of the major parental cords clipped in the next few weeks.

Soon it will be *your* medical insurance that pays your hospital bills; it will be *your* lawn that you cut, *your* garbage that you remove, and *your* home that you will gladden with your jokes, your cheery laughter and your quick hugs.

Although a mother never really lets go of her children easily, I have been gaining practice at retiring gracefully from professional motherhood. Seeing what a wonderful job your older sister and brother have both done in their own homes and in their work for the Lord has given me confidence that God can be trusted to complete

Don and Kay Sandberg

His work in all your lives without too much managerial assistance from me!

* * *

Now the doctor has called to say you are in recovery and doing fine. "Those were tough teeth to remove," he said, "but everything went just as planned."

I am reminded of the other "tough" things and easy things that life will include for you and Kay—a whole wide spectrum of experiences, of great joys and perhaps of great sorrows, of brilliant highlights and routine drudgery, of breathtaking success and disappointing failure.

I am glad that God has reminded us that the "tough" things are perfectly normal for a Christian. I am glad, too, that in your reaching adulthood you have learned not to make a "big deal" out of any difficulty God has given you to face.

God bless you, Don, and make you a great servant of Jesus Christ,

Much, much love from
Mom

"Life is impossible to understand apart from a personal relationship with Jesus Christ. Even as Christians, there is much we cannot understand. We spoil our children when we communicate to them that life is a bowl of cherries, nothing bad happens to Christians, or that our children should be able to understand all that comes into their lives. Their confidence must never be in us. It must never be in their ability to understand. It must only be in the character of God and His unfailing commitment to them."

—Walter A. Henrichsen.

(From the book, *How to Disciple Your Children,* Victor Books.)

Dear Don and Kay:

Such an exciting stage of life this is for you! You are finishing up sixteen years of education and getting ready to begin the work you've dreamed about for so many years. It is true that you are both already talking about graduate school, but there is a sense in which *this* particular graduation will have more emotional overtones for you than anything which comes afterward.

You will barely get your graduation from college behind you before "the wedding" takes over as a prime priority in your life, and fast on the heels of that big event will come the beginning of your work in Christian education—so many major changes in your lives to absorb in one short year!

In just a few days, Kay, you will have your first wedding shower. You are not a thing-oriented person, I know, but you will find special delight in each object people give you, partly because the gifts are symbols of people's love for you, and partly because "things" very quickly define the style of your way of living. In a way, the objects with which we surround ourselves tell as much about us and our values as the things we say or the way we dress.

You will soon discover that "things" can be either a bane or a blessing. Possessions add color, beauty and convenience to life, but they also deteriorate or break or wear out; and so it is true that the more things we possess, the more involved we are with getting things repaired, or gotten rid of, or replaced.

Some of the things that fill up our lives and our homes are the objects we *acquire* in relationship to some particular need or want. You two have already been acquiring certain things which you have felt were important to your work—a car, a piano, a set of mechanic's tools, a library of books related to your teaching.

Very soon you will begin to *collect* certain items which you will consider to be important to your own lifestyle—pretty dishes, no doubt, miscellaneous furnishings and various other household items which up to this point (as college students) you barely noticed in other people's homes.

Along with the objects you are acquiring and collecting, you will discover to your dismay that you are also *accumulating* certain things which you did not specifically choose to own, but which still have to be handled and dealt with—bills, yesterday's newspapers, garbage, old boxes, junk mail, out-of-date clothes. Ecclesiastes 3:1,6,7 says: "To every thing there is a season, and a time to every purpose under the heaven . . . A time to get, and a time to lose; a time to keep, and a time to cast away; A time to rend, and a time to sew . . . ."

Because you have both been reared in families that know and serve the Lord, you have already learned that God loves to give good things to those who put Him first. (First Timothy 6:17 says that God "giveth us richly all things to enjoy.") You have also learned that the Christian must learn to "possess his possessions without being possessed by them."

In the same passage where we are given permission to richly enjoy all things, the Apostle Paul warns: "But godliness with contentment is great gain. For we brought nothing into this world, and it is certain we can carry nothing out. And having food and raiment let us be therewith content" (I Tim. 6:6-8). It is a wonderful thing to discover that your happiness and fulfillment in the days ahead will have less and less to do with what you own, and more and more to do with who you are.

Of course we, as your parents, would love to furnish you with all those things that make life convenient and comfortable, but (perhaps fortunately) we cannot.

We do give you our love, our prayers, our influence, our support and encouragement and we are available when the emergencies come.

Much love,
Mom

Reflections . . .

Lord:

I do not need
these mirrored walls
or cushioned chairs
or growing things
    with all their bright allure.

Not deeds or documents,
nest egg, insurance forms,
inheritance or windfall—
    I know that these will not endure.

My power to work—
to earn my way
with tongue or pen,
to teach or paint or sing—
    I dare not lean on these.

The love of those
    whom I hold dear—
my lifelong friends,
my children and their children,
Indeed, my "other self" —
They cannot meet my needs.

Ah, my Alpha and Omega,
    my Changeless One
Who knew me, planned me,
from the beginning of the world,
Who sees the glory of my destiny
    and sings with joy.
In Thee and Thee alone
    I rest secure.

                    J.R.S.

"The Lord thy God in the midst of thee is mighty; he will save, he will rejoice over thee with joy; he will rest in his love, he will joy over thee with singing." —Zeph. 3:17.

Dear Don and Kay:

Have you ever thought about how much of life is divided between our "want to's" and our "ought to's"? Of course the nicest experiences in life are those which combine the "wants" and the "oughts." Unfortunately, many of the necessary responsibilities of life we begin with enjoyment and enthusiasm, then discover that duty does not always stay delightful. The promises we make to the Lord or to other people we keep simply because we've hopefully developed enough character to motivate us after the pleasure has gone.

Marriage is a strange combination of "wants" and "oughts." A young man who falls in love may actually enjoy waiting on (and for) his beloved. He is quick to open every door, to carry her parcels and help her with her coat. (Need I say, Don, how impressed I was when your dad actually knelt to help me on with my boots when we got ready to walk in the snow on one of our first dates?

A girl who is in love will make sure she is as beautiful as care and attention can make her. She will keep her voice low, soft and sweet, and she will listen with rapt attention to the minutest details of her beloved's conversation. She would not hesitate to spend hours preparing her beloved's favorite meal.

These are the occasions when "wants" and "oughts" are the same thing.

Eventually, a man who still genuinely loves the woman he marries may have to deliberately and patiently go through the rituals which, in the pressure of multiplied responsibilities seem tedious, simply because those gestures express caring. By the same token, a woman who wants to please her husband and make him happy will need to be as attentive to those details that won his heart in the first place—now as she did then.

Love can be expressed in many ways, of course, but if we do not advertise the product in a language or in symbols that are understood by the person for whom the message is intended, we should not be surprised when we fail to "make a sale."

Love may be expressed in sweet words, a romantic card, flowers, candy, a fresh cake from the oven, clean shirts, a diamond ring, a meal served on time, a lingering kiss, a wink, candles on the table, dinner in a nice restaurant, or a thousand other ways. None of these will be convincing, however, unless they are accompanied by practical habits of thoughtfulness and by an attitude of genuine concern for the needs and desires of the loved one.

First Corinthians 13 tells us that love is never impatient or unkind; it is not envious or self-seeking; it is careful about both behavior and thoughts, and it is always optimistic.

When you offer your "love gifts" to one another from time to time (and I hope they will be often), don't forget to offer the gifts of the heart!

Love,
Mom Sandberg

P. S. Remember that story about Dad and the boots? I don't wear snow boots anymore, but yesterday when I went to retrieve my "garden shoes" from the basement door I found that your dad had cleaned the mud off them. Now that's what I call love!

Reflections . . .

How sad it is when partners in a marriage start keeping score! Like this love poem written by one who learned too late . . .

LOVE SONNET

Why did I weigh each word and pray that I
Had given not one jot more love than you?
Now, if our vanished ties I might renew,
To give more lavishly would satisfy
Passion that long outgrew all measurement.
How petty to give only as you gave!
Perhaps this cautious giving made the grave
In which my hopes are sealed. If I had spent
Myself in reckless prodigality,
Content to give and asking less of you,
I should be rich in warming memories
And you, perhaps, would still remember me
As not possessive but as one who knew
Unstinted giving leaves the heart at ease.

—Barbara Palmer.

(From *Ted Malone's Adventures in Poetry,* William Morrow & Company, 1946.)

Love is not cautious;

it is extravagant.

Love forgets slights;

it remembers favors.

Love is not a casual feeling;

it is a deliberate choice.

Dear Don and Kay:

Your dad and I have just gotten home from a vacation we had been looking forward to for a long time. You already know the kinds of things we did—walked on the beach for an hour early every morning, ate out, read, sat in the sun, and your dad played tennis while I worked on five paintings. The frosting on the cake was that we got to enjoy the fellowship of family and special friends while we did all these activities.

As much as we enjoyed that delightful week, we came home ready and anxious to plunge into all the work waiting for us at home—the college summer school teaching schedule, the church responsibilities, the yard work, the writing, the delayed spring cleaning, and the dozen other projects one always optimistically believes can be accomplished in just a few short summer months.

Isn't it interesting that God knew we needed contrasts and varieties in our lives to function well? That's why the preacher of Ecclesiastes 3 reminds us:

"To every thing there is a season, and a time to every purpose under the heaven: A time to be born, and a time to die; a time to plant, and a time to pluck up that which is planted; A time to kill, and a time to heal; a time to break down, and a time to build up; A time to weep, and a time to laugh; a time to mourn, and a time to dance; A time to cast away stones, and a time to gather stones together; A time to embrace, and a time to refrain from embracing; A time to get, and a time to lose; a time to keep, and a time to cast away; A time to rend, and a time to sew; a time to keep silence, and a time to speak; A time to love, and a time to hate; a time of war, and a time of peace." —Vss. 1-8.

In marriage, especially, there is need for contrasts. I can remember when your dad and I got married I thought, "Now I don't ever have to be separated from him again." But of course I was wrong. Not only did the circumstances of our lives require that we sometimes be separated; our emotional needs required a certain amount of privacy and "aloneness" as well. It was our experiences apart that added richness and excitement to our times together.

In the providence of God, your lives together will be full of contrasts. Perhaps there will be times of financial stress and times of financial prosperity. There will possibly be times of illness and times of abundant good health. Hopefully there will be a great deal of important work for you to do. But there will be times when the most spiritual activity you can engage in will be to play. There will be exhilarating experiences of travel and celebration and discovery, and there will be hours of tedium or frustration or failure.

One of the most important keys to success in marriage is a joyful acceptance of the highs and lows in life, the dark colors on the canvas as well as the light colors. The good qualities which you love in each other have their dark sides as well. These difficult traits which you will discover in each other are only the alloy which makes the gold stronger. You will have to learn to love the whole person.

I hope you will be able to say with the Apostle Paul: "I know both how to be abased, and I know how to abound; every where and in all things I am instructed both to be full and to be hungry, both to abound and to suffer need. I can do all things through Christ which strengtheneth me" (Phil. 4:12,13).

Much, much love,
Mom

Love listens.

Love assumes the best possible motive.

Love is, according to a great poet,
    "kindness set to music."

Love is the best medicine for
    a sick world.

Dear Don and Kay:

Day after tomorrow you will meet at the end of a church aisle decorated with flowers and candles, to say your wedding vows to each other, just as millions of other couples before you have done. In spite of the fact that the rituals are as old as time itself, your wedding will be absolutely unique, and it will mark one of the most important milestones of your life.

In a way, Don, your dad and I feel we have already cut the last major parental cord that has tied you to our house and schedule. Watching you (and helping where you would let us help) load up the trailer that would carry your possessions to Augusta and your new work and home was a painful but necessary step in learning to let you go. The "Dr. J." posters are gone from your closet door; the books, the shark jaws and cougar brain (which I never learned to live with comfortably!) and plastic skull and transparent man have all been packed away in boxes for the transference to your new classroom where they will hopefully amuse and educate the young people who will sit under your teaching. Your closet is hauntingly empty except for an old sports trophy, a pair of "dead" tennis shoes, an old sweater and a leftover toy or two from your childhood.

I can imagine, Kay, that your mother is going through the same painful process of mentally trying to fill up the holes you will leave in your own home, not only those holes created by your physical absence, but all the other special qualities and contributions you added to make your family and your family's lifestyle what it was. Your family will miss the piano you have taken away, and no doubt they have already worked to rearrange the furniture where it stood; but more important, they will miss the music you made in your own special way.

Whatever we do to fill in the empty places you have left, we still rejoice in the prospect of your lives together. We are so very proud of you both and are excited about what we know the Lord has planned for your lives together.

May you have lots of laughter along with the tears, great successes along with a few failures, wonderful answers to prayer along with the hard work, and great opportunities for bringing glory and honor to

125

the One who saved you and sent you out to do His work.

We, along with your parents, Kay, thank the Lord for every single contribution you have both made to our happiness. Let me remind you again that we have already cashed in a million times on every investment we have ever made in your lives. You were well worth every single penny we ever spent, every tear we ever shed over you, every moment of time, every ounce of energy, every prayer and every pain that was ever expended on your account.

Now your own commitment to the Lord's service in Christian education and soul winning and in rearing children of your own for the Lord gives us the assurance that we haven't finished clipping our coupons yet.

> God bless you both, our dear, dear children,
> Mom Sandberg

"Be ye therefore followers of God, as dear children; And walk in love, as Christ also hath loved us, and hath given himself for us an offering and a sacrifice to God for a sweetsmelling savour."—Ephesians 5:1,2.

Reflections . . .

. . . But what if "falling in love" and marriage and building a family of one's own do not come in a predictable scheme of things following school days?

God does not produce His children on the assembly line, as we quickly learned from our own maturing family. Your graduation from college, Mark, was another reminder that God's plan for each of you children would be unique . . .

Mark Sandberg

Our dear Mark:

At last the day has come. Today you will march down the aisle to the old familiar "Pomp and Circumstance" and receive the diploma for which you've worked so hard. You've been elected to "Who's Who in American Colleges and Universities" (an honor which is "no big deal" to the kids who receive it, but which really impresses their parents!) You are graduating with highest honors—and that *is* a big deal!

There is a sense in which today marks the end of an era for your dad and me. For so many years our major and most fulfilling role has been the rearing of four precious children. We have been actively involved with clothing, feeding, loving, disciplining and educating each of you and have watched with joy as you grew in the Lord and in your relationships with others.

I think you already know how proud we are of you. We like to tease you about your early comment ("We can't *all* be perfect, you know!") because, as a matter of fact, you really were about as easy a child to rear as it is possible for a set of parents to have.

Your steadiness to a cause you believe in, your loyalty to the family, your wide interests and abilities in so many different areas, your quiet common sense, your faithfulness to the Lord, your good mind (and good *use* of a good mind!)—all add up to the great person you are.

Not once have we heard you complain about the difficulties of this year, the loneliness of being the only child left at home, the inconvenience of having no money when the job was slow in coming through, the pressures of school and church and home responsibilities. The truth is, I wish you *had* complained to me a little bit. I needed you to need me (but I guess that is typical of a mother losing her last child).

In some ways I sense an evidence of the Lord's special leading in the plans for your life. Back when you were a little boy and told us that you felt God had called you to be a missionary to Sweden, we were pleased that you *wanted* to serve the Lord, but I will acknowledge that we were a little surprised that such a determination would never fade in all the years of training and maturing.

Because Sweden will require you to have a "profession," there will still be some years of education ahead for you as you work toward graduate degrees in English and Bible, and perhaps you will wonder if you are *ever* going to get out into the work. I can assure you that your present service in church visitation, Awana, and Camp Joy will be as important to the Lord as what you ultimately do on the field. Don't be discouraged at the delay!

I believe God is going to use you in some remarkable way, and perhaps that is why you have always seemed so much your own person. It is as though the Lord were reminding me that you are more His than mine. While I crave that intimacy and dependence on me (at least emotionally) that is often the relationship of a "last" child to his mother, I have told the Lord that what I want most is that He will be glorified in your life and work and future. I know that is going to be true.

And so, you are the final crown to your dad's and my work. We have watched Carol and Jim and Don leave our home to serve the Lord faithfully and well, and we look with confidence to what you are going to do as well.

God bless you, our dearest, dearest Mark!

Much love,
Mom

Reflections . . .

God gave you some special lessons in loving and in being loved, Mark, and there was pain in the process, but your dad and I could see how God was using heartache as a tool to prepare you and refine you for some great work ahead . . .

Dearest Mark:

I've been meaning to write you for several days but can't quite get my act together enough to settle down and do it. We are about to get our new house in order, but the details are keeping me pre-occupied.

Almost every hour I think of you and wish I could be there to make things easier for you. It's one thing for kids to go away to school and know that they have a dear familiar place to come home to. You are in the position of having your folks move out and leave you in a nearly empty house that is so full of memories and so terribly quiet.

I know that this is especially difficult for you, too, because your relationship with Sonia doesn't seem to be working out. You tend to invest everything you have with people who are important to you, and so that means that you will always be vulnerable to the hurts that come when love is not returned.

I don't know if I ever shared with you the letter my dad wrote to me when I got my own heart broken in college; I guess I've read it to fifty other young people who needed it as I've counseled through the years, but it seems especially appropriate for you now. Let me just quote part of it, leaving out the things that applied to me particularly as a girl:

"If God wanted you to be . . . ordinary . . . of small vision and small usefulness, it would not take much heart preparation. But if God wants you to be . . . some mighty man of God, then it would be well for you to have whatever training the blessed Saviour knows you need, to ripen your heart and make it humble, and make it appreciative and make your vision large and your charity and sympathy great. For I tell you now, there is no way to learn to know about other people's hurts and to help carry their burdens, like having your own heart broken. . . . Bruises and hurts are sad for the moment, but like all chastisement from the hand of God, they afterward work 'the peaceable fruit of righteousness.' God is too good ever to allow a pain that does not mean blessing."

What I want to say is sort of personal and hard to talk about but I think it has everything to do with what God is doing in your life right now. I believe I can say that my whole life long I never wanted to be ordinary, and from the time I have been old enough to make responsible decisions I have told the Lord I was His—"lock, stock, and barrel," as my dad would have said—and that He has a right to do with me whatever He wants to do.

There were many ways in which I did not feel I was like my sisters; I was always the "sensitive" one and thought I felt things more deeply; therefore, I was more subject to pain. Now I understand more clearly that God uses the tools that work best on the "stuff" of which we are made. What hurts us most is also what shapes us best into what God wants us to be.

You already know the painful tools God used in my life to mold me—the frequent illnesses I had as a child, the loss of our first baby, some of the humiliation that came when my dad took a stand on issues that were not popular, the attack of the man who tried to rape me, and then the things which happened later . . .

Now, in some ways, you are having to go through things your sister and brothers didn't have to handle. It may be that in some ways your dreams have been a little higher and so God is requiring more of you to make your commitment deeper. You have always been unusually self-reliant, and it may be that the Lord is teaching you to need people more. You have always been orderly in your mind and schedule; now other people and their plans have disrupted your life in a number of ways. You have not particularly needed a great deal of free communication with other people, but it could well be that the Lord wants you to feel enough pain and insecurity and frustration that you are forced to relate some of your feelings to others.

Actually, I have no business even trying to pretend I know what God is doing with you and for you, but I do know, out of my own experience, that God is to be trusted. While I would not have chosen the particular heartaches God allowed in my life, I do see how He has been using them to change me and conform me to His image, and I would not, for anything in the world, go back to being what I was! If God is using me now in my writing and speaking and counseling and teaching—and I believe He is—it is directly in relationship to the prayers, tears and hunger for the Word of God that have come out of things I thought I might not survive.

Thank you for all you are doing to take care of the house until it is sold. Call us collect if there is anything we can do—or call us if you just need to talk. We are so proud of you and know you are going to come through this tough time shining like gold!

Much, much love,
Mom

Reflections . . .

Now you are all gone, busily finding God's will for your own lives, and there is nothing more for your dad and me to do but to pray . . . and love . . . and give advice where it is asked (and to keep our mouths shut when it is not asked)!

There is one last tribute due, one last love note to be written, one last explanation for the sum of all you children turned out to be, all the joy you have given.

Here is a salute . . .

To the Father of My Children:

When a girl marries a man, she pictures him in all sorts of future situations, and on those future dreams she stakes all she has and hopes for.

After almost twenty-five years of living with you, I have found that reality has been far beyond my greatest expectations.

I have loved:

Eating breakfast with you at Gulas . . .

Sharing choice tidbits from our bedtime reading . . .

Planning a Christmas smorgasbord . . .

Buying groceries together . . .

Planting the garden together . . .

Praying together over a problem . . .

Trying to keep out of each other's way in the bathroom . . .

Sharing cheese and crackers in a romantic Paris hotel
  bed at 3:00 in the morning . . .

But somehow, I never pictured what a spectacular father you would be.

Carrying our first newborn in your arms,
  talking "love talk" . . .

Saving treats in your lunchbox for toddlers . . .

Playing "piggy back" . . .

Teaching boys how to do the laundry . . .

Shopping for dresses with Carol . . .

  Giving baths . . .

   reading stories . . .

Laughing with teenagers across
   the Generation Gap . . .

Inspiring the pride and admiration of your children

So that they talk like you
  and about you . . .

They choose your company . . .
  and they have chosen your Saviour.

Thank you for being that kind of husband and father!

I love you,
Jessie

"That our sons may be as plants grown up in their youth; that our daughters may be as corner stones, polished after the similitude of a palace: That our garners may be full, affording all manner of store: that our sheep may bring forth thousands and ten thousands in our streets: That our oxen may be strong to labour; that there be no breaking in, nor going out; that there be no complaining in our streets. Happy is that people, that is in such a case: yea, happy is that people, whose God is the Lord." —Psalm 144:12-15.

For a complete list of books available from the Sword of the Lord, write to Sword of the Lord Publishers, P. O. Box 1099, Murfreesboro, Tennessee 37133.